THE ARCHBISHOP

Books by Clay Blair, Jr.

Novels:
The Board Room
The Archbishop

Nonfiction:
The Atomic Submarine and Admiral Rickover
Beyond Courage
Diving for Pleasure and Treasure
The Strange Case of James Earl Ray

Collaborations:
The Hydrogen Bomb, with James R. Shepley
Nautilus 90 North, with Commander William R. Anderson, U.S.N.
Always Another Dawn, with A. Scott Crossfield

THE

Clay Blair, Jr.

ARCHBISHOP

The World Publishing Company New York and Cleveland

Published by The World Publishing Company
2231 West 110th Street, Cleveland, Ohio 44102
Published simultaneously in Canada by
Nelson, Foster & Scott Ltd.
First Printing—1970
Published by arrangement with Bantam Books, Inc.
Library of Congress Catalog Card Number: 70-124276
Printed in the United States of America

WORLD PUBLISHING
TIMES MIRROR

for Marc Jaffe

We have been born in an important age full of kaleidoscopic experiments, adventures and clashes, not only between the virtues and the vices as formerly, but rather—and this is the most tragic of all—between the virtues themselves.

NIKOS KAZANTZAKIS
Report to Greco

AUTHOR'S NOTE

On July 29, 1968, Pope Paul VI issued his now famous encyclical, *Humanae Vitae,* reaffirming the Catholic Church's traditional ban against artificial contraception. Notre Dame theologian, the Reverend John A. O'Brien, wrote: "This document produced a painful crisis of conscience for many churchmen—and a crisis in the Church itself more serious than any since the mighty religious upheaval of the sixteenth century, which split Christendom into fragments."

Among the millions of Catholics who were dismayed by the encyclical were a group of fifty-five priests in Washington, D.C. When their bishop, Patrick Cardinal O'Boyle, insisted they enforce *Humanae Vitae* to the letter, the priests "revolted." A public controversy ensued. That "revolt" inspired certain portions of this novel. However, I wish to make it clear that none of the Washington clergy involved is known to me personally, and the clergy in this work, except for a few allusions to well-known public figures, are purely fictional—imagined by me. If there is any resemblance to any Washington clergy, living or deceased, it is pure coincidence. I have also taken pains to fictionalize the geography and command structure of Washington Catholicdom. It purposely bears only slight resemblance to fact.

C.B., JR.

BOOK ONE

MARCH, 1968

I

Jean Favrot's small world, a castle of toothpicks, collapsed quite suddenly on a Saturday afternoon. It happened at the intersection of Old Chain Bridge Road and Old Dominion Drive at the traffic light in the heart of McLean, Virginia, a suburb of Washington, D.C. It was five ten. The sun had set in a cold, clear, late March sky. The Ford Galaxie wagon was loaded with grocery bags and children—five grocery bags and seven of Jean's nine children. She had waited through three lights, inching her way up the left-turn lane, smoking, pushing at her hair, which should have been set, oblivious to the din in the rear of the wagon, the blast of the Jefferson Airplane on the hard rock station, WEAM, thinking of her husband, Bob, worried that he would have one vodka too many after golf and might still be loaded when they arrived for dinner that night at Senator Root's. The senator, for whom Bob worked as administrative assistant, was not noted for his sobriety. Even so, in Jean's eyes, Bob had made a fool of himself too many times at his home.

When Jean was certain she could make a left turn during the next cycle of the long light, she turned on the flasher. At that moment, the motor sputtered and died. Jean put the gear shift in neutral and turned the key. The starter turned over but not the motor. Jean's eye scanned the fuel gauge. The lifeless needle hung below E.

The left-turn arrow glowed. The driver behind Jean waited only three seconds before lightly tapping his horn. The younger children shouted: "Go!" Jean pumped the gas pedal, turning the starter motor until the battery seemed to be draining ominously. Now, behind her, other motorists were blowing horns. Jean smashed her filter cigarette into the overflowing ashtray. She lunged at the door handle, shoved the door open, climbed from the car. She stood in the middle of the intersection, hands on hips, glaring at the long line of cars behind

3

her, a portrait of pure rage. Her angry dark eyes fixed on the third driver back, a teen-age girl with long blond hair in a Mustang.

"Shut up!" Jean shouted, her voice, normally cool, verging on hysteria.

Then she buried her face in her arms on the roof of the Galaxie and cried.

She had been in the wagon most of the time since ten thirty that morning. First she had driven Paul to a birthday party. En route, she had stopped at People's Drug Store to pick up a present. At the checkout counter, she realized she had forgotten her purse. Sheepishly she set aside the gift, dashed home for the purse, returned, paid, then dropped Paul. Afterward she swung by the Boys' Club to pick up Bob and Joe, who had reported for the preliminary organizational meeting of the baseball teams. She then took them to the Sports Shoppe for new mitts and cleated shoes. After that she dropped Chris's bike off for a new tire. Returning to McLean she picked up Nancy at the beauty parlor and drove her to a CYO luncheon. Then she stopped at Dart Drug to pick up a prescription for Carol, who was in bed with flu. Then she took Mike to the dentist for his semiannual checkup, leaving him there alone, while she swung back to the house to pick up Bill and Joe to take them to the movie in Fairfax, one of the rare movies approved in its entirety by the Legion of Decency. After that she picked up the vacuum cleaner at the repair shop. Then she stopped in the Virginia ABC store for two fifths of vodka, then to the Super Giant for groceries, bringing Chris along, cashing her weekly household check, large enough to pay for the groceries and the maid, Emma, who was taking care of the baby, John. After that she had begun rounding up the children—Nancy, Bob, Joe, Mike, Paul, and Bill—to drop them at All Saints' for weekly confession, while she unloaded the groceries at home.

There had been no room in her tight Saturday schedule for running out of gas. Usually, she was good about that, always filling the tank in time, having the oil and water checked. But she had been preoccupied that day, first by the dream of the night before, a ghastly nightmare in which her youngest, John, had suffocated in his crib, and then by something Helen Hanrahan, the Catholic spiritualist, had written in her column that morning, a prediction—artfully disguised as usual—that some clergyman, whom Jean took to be Pope Paul, would be assassinated.

Those two things, and then the letter. The letter had come that morning. Jean had read snatches of it while waiting at stoplights. It was from a girl—she was a woman of forty like Jean but Jean still thought of her as a girl—Jean had known in New Orleans, when they were both students at Sophie Newcomb College, aeons ago. The girl—woman—had been a college confidante, a sorority sister—Tri Delt—an anthropology major, who had gone on for her doctorate, and who had lived much of her life in Yucatan, unmarried, digging in the Mayan ruins of Chichen-Itza, writing learned papers for obscure anthropological journals. Jean had not heard from the girl in ten years. As she read snatches of the letter, Jean recalled her own college dreams, of traveling, of becoming an expert in something—foreign languages maybe, leading perhaps to a glamorous job as a translator at the United Nations. This reminiscing led, in turn, to disturbing thoughts of all the possibilities in life that had been open to her and rejected. Infinite possibilities! Writing. Acting. Politics. Teaching. She had consoled herself—momentarily—that her job, homemaker and mother, was *the* most important in life. That dicta had been drilled into her from early childhood by the Sacred Heart nuns. It had not even been faintly shaken by the jabs of liberalism she experienced in college. Somewhat smugly, she had looked between the lines of the letter for hints of despair and tragedy in what must have been—for all its seeming glamour—an arid, loveless life. But she could find none. This annoyed her.

Jean was busy—frantically busy most of the time—and she seldom permitted herself the luxury of introspection or self-evaluation. In fact, that activity frightened her and she consciously avoided it. But the letter led now—as she had pulled out of the Boys' Club, almost colliding with a VW going too fast—to a sudden, agonizing vision of her husband, cavorting—that was the way she thought of it—on the fairways at Congressional Country Club. She saw him, bald, florid-faced, a potbelly hanging over his ridiculous ochre golfing slacks, the ubiquitous stinking cigar between his yellow teeth.

Bob had, for many of his youthful years, been "promising." He was a one-time student council president at Tulane, editor of the bar review, a state legislator at age twenty-five, would-be governor of Louisiana at age thirty—would-be, except for an untimely shift in the party power that had left Bob, at age forty, an aging boy wonder, a $28,000-a-year lush, a political hack buried on the Hill, little more than a glorified bellboy for Louisiana's senior senator, LeRoy Root. Bob Favrot (she thought, grinding her teeth) was a failure who refused to accept that fact himself, a weak father-figure for his children, an arrogant, selfish, pompous toad, a satyr in bed, who expected the household—with seven boys!!—to run with all the efficiency of Robert Kennedy's home, Hickory Hill.

That stark, harsh vision had caused her to drive faster and more aggressively than usual. Moreover, the comingling of unsettling notes in her mind that morning had touched off curious thoughts and fantasies. Fantasies of herself as Ethel Kennedy skiing at Sun Valley, Jackie splurging tens of thousands at Norell's, Grace Kelly reigning at a state ball. She even saw herself the wife of an astronaut, wringing her hands before the TV, then later, after a safe splashdown, modestly facing TV cameras in front of her home, arms around the children. Her hair would be luxuriously radiant, her skin tawny, tanned, and wrinkle-free, her body trim and supple like the models on TV. If only she had time to attend to herself.

The fantasies gave way to thoughts of the Pope, his impending assassination, if Helen Hanrahan was right. She felt little pity or compassion. She did not like Pope Paul. His face was cold and lifeless —too bony. She had much admired Pope John, without knowing quite why. He was *human,* she thought, jolly and rotund. In some mystical way, John exactly understood *her* problems. Especially birth control. He had called the Vatican Council, asked for fresh winds. To Jean, all that pomp and ceremony in St. Peter's boiled down to a single imperative issue: pill or no pill. For a while it seemed to her the Vatican was going her way, toward approval. Then John died and Paul came, closing the windows, retreating, going all the way back to Pope Pius, to his encyclical, *Casti Connubii,* which, stripped of its elegant theology, said it was murder. And why (she thought with mounting frustration) did 46 million American Catholics listen to yet another wop in the Vatican? Where was the American representation?

Thus preoccupied that day, she forgot to stop for gas. As Jean later rationalized it, long after the typhoon of emotion that arose in the following weeks and months had swept on, if she had not forgotten to stop for gas, if she had not been humiliated to tears at the intersection, if the frozen food had not defrosted in the car, if the screeching of the children had not driven her right around the bend, she surely would never have blurted what she did in the All Saints' confessional.

II

Father Daniel Joseph Daugherty lifted his black cassock from its peg in the All Saints' sacristy. He was wearing tennis whites—flannel shorts, polo shirt, tennis shoes, fuzzy white athletic socks. Earlier, he had played three brisk sets with Marvin Klein, managing editor of the *Tribune,* a worthy opponent, whom Daugherty had met in the course of his work with runaway children. Daugherty had been, since age ten, an excellent tennis player. He might well have been Davis Cup or a pro. He kept it up in the seminary and later, on a catch-as-catch-can basis in the Navy. He resumed a regular routine when he reported to All Saints', playing not less than three days a week. The All Saints' pastor, Monsignor Ryan, did not like it. They were short-handed, like all suburban parishes in Washington, and Ryan resented the time it took. Besides that, Daugherty sensed, Ryan thought his assistant pastor looked undignified in tennis togs, a bit frivolous, a bit too much like the rich playboy. Ryan was strictly old-school. He had been taught, and believed, that a priest should hold himself aloof from temporal activities, sports, movies, cocktail parties, never be seen out of uniform, nor upset the popular conception of priestly character as popularized by Barry Fitzgerald, Bing Crosby, and Spencer Tracy. The people, the flock, *wanted* the stylized conception, Ryan argued. An aloof and dignified priest was more credible. He helped support their faith, the mystical loyalty and obedience to the Eternal Church. Let them see no chink in the armor. Never let them sense that a priest might have human failings—fear, anxiety, money worries, sex problems. Nor should a priest ever project an image of having *fun.*

To Daugherty, tennis was not precisely *fun.* It was many things. It was a way of keeping in shape physically, which he believed to be important to his general well-being. It was a way of escaping, at least momentarily, the Niagara of trouble that deluged him seven days a week, in the confessional, the rectory, in the hospitals, homes for invalids and aged, the juvenile courts, psychologists' offices, retreat houses, schoolrooms. The steady procession of ill-advised marriages, illnesses, physical and mental, unwanted children, alcoholic parents, wayward teen-agers, unwanted aged, and finally (blessedly!), the funerals and the anguish—some real, some phony. On a good, hard clay court, Dan Daugherty put all that aside, restored his mental equilibrium. Then too (he knew well), tennis was his one way of forcefully expressing his manhood. Facing an opponent like Marvin Klein, Father Daugherty's primitive instincts—aggression and hostility, the territorial imperative—took charge of his being. He played with savage, killing fury. He played to win, usually did, and this gave him intense satisfaction. He would not give it up, no matter how bad it was for his image. Not that he bought a single line of Ryan's argument anyway.

He slipped the cassock over his head. It was fresh from the cleaners yet still smelled faintly of stale perspiration. It was tight in the bodice, with a flaring skirt, like a well-tailored dress. Daugherty did not like the uniform. For one thing, it was feminine, like much of Mother Church. He felt that, in a real sense, it did much to deny the manhood he fought for on the courts.

He snapped on his fresh white collar, walked nimbly from the sacristy to the altar. It was getting dark. The altar was appropriately dark and somber. The red tabernacle light was burning, dramatically signifying the presence of God. Father Daugherty had never understood the need for this showmanship. The first words of the Baltimore Catechism taught that God was everywhere. He did not need a light to call attention to His being.

Father Daugherty genuflected before the altar, hoping his tennis shoes and bare legs would not be noticed. Then he walked down the aisle in the dimness toward the confessional.

All Saints' was a new parish. The church was new, built at huge expense. Daugherty thought of it as "suburban contemporary," the worst possible taste. The shake-shingle roof was pitched steeply, like an Alpine ski chalet, beneath which, inside, were thick wooden beams. The wall-to-wall carpeted floor sloped down toward the altar, like a theater. The walls were fieldstone, rough on the exterior, polished on the interior. The modern stained glass windows were thin triangles. The church was "fully" air-conditioned. The PA system was stereo, all speakers "scientifically positioned." The altar was stark, the crucifix above it a hideous creation of gleaming bronze, canted rakishly forward, toward the congregation, like the figurehead of a clipper ship.

The macadam parking lot outside had a capacity for four hundred cars. Every detail of the layout had been executed in exact accordance with the Chancery's board of facilities, the members of which had recently established new criteria for "contemporary worship," a misguided effort to create the impression the Roman Catholic Church —the Washington diocese at least—was "keeping pace" with "changing living habits."

Yet—as Father Daugherty saw it—nothing of substance had changed. The facade was different. They had a ski lodge in place of a baroque, miniature copy of some foreign cathedral. But, inside, the atmosphere was much the same. It was cold, forbidding, silent, reverential, solemn. The parishioners still tiptoed when they entered, still spoke in whispers. Too much of the time, the place was empty and dark, like a mausoleum.

It is not likely that any church, however ingenious, would have pleased Father Daugherty. His views on churches were radical. He was fundamentally opposed to the very concept of a church, that is, a specific structure where people gathered to worship God at a stated time each week in a formalized ceremony, the Mass. All that was obsolete. He believed in what he called a "living religion"; that people should love God, communicate with God all day long, wherever they might be. To Daugherty, churchgoing was a sign of weakness. Weakness on the part of the flock for feeling the need to be congregated specifically to communicate with God; weakness on the part of the Church for fostering that feeling of need, demanding that one attend or face eternal damnation.

Daugherty, going on thirty-one, had been a priest for nine years. He was the youngest of ten children of wealthy Main Line parents —devout Catholics. As a young boy, he was shy, and not an especially bright student. He attended a private Catholic school—St. Joe's, a Jesuit prep school on City Line Avenue. There he fell under the spell of a persuasive teacher. He entered Philadelphia's Immaculata Seminary at eighteen, was ordained at twenty-two by the Bishop of Philadelphia. He served two years as a curate at the cathedral in Chestnut Hill, where he was bored and frustrated by his piddling chores and slow progress. He requested military service and served a four-year hitch in the Navy, with the Sixth Fleet in the Mediterranean, where his horizons were broadened. Two years ago he had turned aside yet another Philadelphia assignment, and wound up at All Saints', as assistant pastor.

His first job had been overseeing the construction of the new church. In this capacity, his first brash move was to propose that the church itself be abandoned, not built. In a letter to the Chancery, he pointed out that a new Episcopal church was about to be erected across the street; that it would be a "simple matter," perhaps, to "join forces" with the Episcopal clergy, that is, to share a single facility, each congregation splitting the cost. He showed, by means of an intricate chart, how both congregations could utilize the structure, with time to worship "staggered" to accommodate the needs of each. His proposal was not unprecedented, he took pains to point out. In the Navy, where he had served as a chaplain, the fantail of the same ship was used, alternately, for Catholic, Jewish, and Protestant services, with "no apparent loss of souls." (The impertinence of this comment escaped him.) He concluded by suggesting that the money saved on the new All Saints' Church could be invested in a mutual fund, and the non-taxable dividend yield on the stock distributed to worthy projects in the ghetto and other deprived areas. He attached a clipping from the *Tribune,* written by Marvin Klein, which shrilly pointed out the desperate need for a teen-age neighborhood recreation center in the heart of the ghetto. The Chancery had not replied to this fantastic suggestion; the new church soon loomed high on a hill between Oak Vale and Stonehenge Manor subdivisions.

There were now, in the rear pew of the church, a dozen parishioners, kneeling in prayer, preparing their confession. Father Daugherty passed them silently, head bowed, properly aloof, yet longing—feeling an almost uncontrollable compulsion—to reach out and touch them, to prove he was human, sympathetic, compassionate. He wanted to hear noise, to shout, bring the dead building alive, make the big beams overhead reverberate with joy and happiness, wanted *everyone* to rejoice, to celebrate that God had given them life, a being, and then to send them away, to help the less fortunate, to experience the warm glow of giving, to understand, as Christ had said, that there was no greater reward. He wanted to banish them from the ski lodge, so to speak. But if he did, they would surely put him down as a nut. Like Christ, in his time.

He pulled back the heavy green drape and entered the confessional. It was a duty—a chore—he detested. He would remain there on the hard oak seat two hours, sliding open one little door and then the next. He would hear, for the most part, a routine, mechanistic litany of sins from the young, for which he was required, like a judge in court, to dole out routine, mechanistic penance. He would hear of mortal and venial sins—felonies and misdemeanors—and all the while, he would feel monumentally superfluous. After all, no man needed a priest to serve as a go-between to God. God was Man. Man was God. God was everything. Everything was God. One had only to say, sincerely, *mea culpa*. The confessional was obsolete too. Group therapy was an infinitely more effective cathartic.

They came in endless procession. It was not yet a large parish. He recognized them through the screen, knew the shapes of their ears and noses, the smell of their bodies and breaths. The little Burroughs boy. Used the name of the Lord in vain five times. Say five Our Fathers and five Hail Marys and a Perfect Act of Contrition. Pretty Nancy Favrot, leader in the CYO, faltering, twisting her handkerchief, whispering almost inaudibly: she had had evil thoughts seven times. Dear Nancy, he thought, and longed to say, it is the natural human condition. Instead: Did you touch yourself? No, Father—aghast. Say ten Our Fathers and ten Hail Marys and ask God to keep your thoughts pure. Caught in this piddling, false routine, while the greater sin, the dishonesty and hypocrisy of the Church, went unpunished, the crisis went unheeded. He asked the next confessor, the Rogers woman— poor arthritic vegetable—to give him spiritual strength, remember him in her prayers.

He could use a little help. Or perhaps a great deal. For some time now, he did not know precisely how long, he had suffered a crisis of faith. It had begun with his doubts about Church policy on celibacy.

As a young seminarian, it had been easy for Daugherty, approaching the subdiaconate phase of his Major Orders, to sign that solemn Latin document. As a teen-ager, his sex drive had not been strong. He seldom dated, preferring a good book to a silly girl. For him, an erection, a nocturnal emission, had been a rarity. He believed then that celibacy was a gift from God, an extraordinary state of being that lifted him above the common man and brought him into a mystical union with Christ—an "objectively superior state of life," as it had been declared by the Council of Trent. He did not believe in marriage for priests. He accepted the view that Scripture forbade it. He believed that a married priest would inevitably face a crippling conflict of interest—be torn between his obligation to God and his duty to wife and family. Celibacy was, as Pope Paul defined it, a "crowning jewel."

Daugherty had held to that view, more or less adamantly, until the

Second Vatican Council. During those years, when it had been fashionable in private conversation among priests to examine almost everything they held dear, Daugherty explored the question in depth. He read much Church history—by non-Catholic historians. He explored the new theological books by liberal Catholics. Until this thorough survey, he had not realized—or rather, had not allowed himself to realize—that there was serious doubt about the controlling Scripture; that in all probability, ten of the twelve Apostles had been married, including Peter, that both Paul and Augustine—chief sources for the Church's arguments for celibacy—were probably neurotic in their views on women and sex, that until the First Lateran Council of 1123, married clergy—including popes—were the rule rather than the exception. He began to feel that his own views on the question were extreme, that perhaps he was the victim of some childhood sex hangup. Seeking the truth about his own sexuality, he took graduate courses in Freud and his disciples at George Washington University, in the evenings. This intellectual plunge left him profoundly disturbed.

He was influenced, too, by the swelling underground opposition among the younger priests. Many of his seminary classmates, who held stronger opinions about celibacy, had deserted the priesthood, joining what seemed to Daugherty the growing throng already outside. How many exactly, he had no way of knowing. Two, at least, or three, and probably four thousand U.S. priests were leaving every year —perhaps as many as one in six. Many of them liberals and intellectuals, the cream of the seminary classes. They had left quietly. Most had married. Outside, they were living exemplary lives, raising children, doing good work, finding fulfillment, many even making handsome salaries in colleges, welfare programs, government agencies. It was no longer a humiliating disgrace to be a defrocked priest, no longer necessary to cringe and hide, like a common criminal, or beg for food.

The study and thought, together with the plunge into Freudian self-analysis, had brought on the crisis of faith. From celibacy, Daugherty's doubt spread to Church views on other matters—divorce and contraception, for example. From what he had seen in parish work— the misery and despair—Church policy seemed stupid, cold, unmerciful, almost un-Christian. Rome ruled dictatorially, like a divine monarchy. It seemed to have lost all feeling and compassion. It was obsessed with the Three P's (as Daugherty thought of it)—pageantry, pomp, and property. What had happened to the human element? In time, his doubts ranged across the whole body of his religion: Scripture, liturgy, doctrine, dogma, canon law.

Several times, he thought he must leave. He *must* be a fraud. There had been some colossal mistake. Those solemn words of the ordination, "I live now, not I, but Christ lives in me," did not apply to him. Earlier that year, in a moment of deep despair and frustration, Daugherty felt compelled to get away from the parish, to make a retreat, to think. There—in the quiet of the Appalachian foothills— Daugherty had met an extraordinary man who became his confessor.

His name was Andre LeGuiese. He was a Dominican from Belgium, a visiting professor of theology at Catholic University, a theologian of incredible erudition and urbanity. Physically he was a wisp of a man, not more than 120 pounds of flesh, soaking wet. But his face and voice were unforgettable. His eyes were greenish and deeply set, like Bishop Sheen's, with a powerful, hypnotic quality. Meeting him, Daugherty found it almost impossible not to stare. His voice was high-pitched—squeaky—yet curiously commanding. He spoke with a French accent. He wore rakish sideburns and a well-trimmed Van Dyke beard, all snow-white.

Daugherty met LeGuiese on the tennis courts. It was a bitterly cold day. LeGuiese was there, in long white flannels, seeking an opponent. They played three sets of singles, a grueling workout for LeGuiese, who was older than he appeared, probably sixty-five. He was a good player—not spectacularly strong, but steady, sure, unflappable. Daugherty felt lucky to have carried the contest 6–3, 6–4, 6–2. Afterward they went to Daugherty's room to crack a bottle of Scotch, to talk long and intimately about the Church, Daugherty's doubts.

LeGuiese, as Daugherty learned that evening, identified himself with the liberal intellectual wing of the Church. Under various pseudonyms, he contributed radical theological articles to the radical weekly, the *National Catholic Reporter*. He had been a key organizer of the faculty-student revolt at Catholic University the year before—protesting the lack of academic freedom on the campus. He had been a friend of the late Father John Courtney Murray, whose views on religious liberty had so profoundly influenced the Vatican Council. Years before, he had been a disciple and friend of the late Tielhard de Chardin, the radical Jesuit. He was a devout man, overflowing with love of God and the Church.

He did not think Daugherty should leave. He argued that too many young, able, right-thinking priests had already left, that if the exodus continued at the same rate, in a very short time the Church would be handed over to the conservative element—left in the hands of the blind, stupid, marginal people. If that happened, there would be no hope for Roman Catholicism. It would be even more oppressive, inflexible, dictatorial. People like Daugherty should remain and "tunnel from within."

LeGuiese was certain that within a very short time, Pope Paul would take drastic steps to liberalize the Church. Public pressure was mounting against the Vatican, the obstinate, Italian-dominated Curia. It could not be ignored. The dissent and unhappiness in the Church was widespread. It must be taken into account. Accommodations must be made. With the world population now doubling every thirty-seven years, the Pope could no longer oppose birth control. It was suicidal. Common sense would prevail. The bishops, and laity, ostensibly granted more power at the Council, would see to it eventually, and probably quite soon.

LeGuiese dwelled at some length on the Dutch Catholics, his neighbors, about whom he was well informed. In the last ten years, the Dutch Catholics had performed a complete about-face, changing from an obsequious, groveling bunch, to a militantly independent, liberal body, forcing through reforms at all levels. The Dutch primate, Cardinal Alfrink, who brought out the New Dutch Catechism, had drawn the line against Rome. Dutch Catholics practiced birth control; Dutch priests approved it. An overwhelming percentage of the Dutch priests opposed celibacy. The Dutch priests had all but done away with private confession; they had abandoned the pomp and pageantry of the Mass. They wore simple, dignified clothing. Mass attendance had soared. The Dutch were leading a reform—setting an example—for the whole Church to follow. It would, in time.

When?

LeGuiese thought the climate was only a matter of days, weeks, months, at most. The hope lay in the Pope's special commission on contraception, called after the Council to advise the Pope on this thorny subject. LeGuiese had a close friend on the commission. He knew from him that the commission had voted 70-14 in *favor* of authorizing contraception. The report had been passed along to the Pope. It seemed unlikely that Paul would overrule the commission. In a little while, he must hand down an encyclical, following the recommendation of the commission. In short, reversing the centuries-old ban against artificial contraception. Then, LeGuiese felt, other reforms would follow quickly. In view of this, LeGuiese said, it seemed wise to wait—tunnel from within.

Father Daugherty was waiting. Like tens of millions of Catholics everywhere.

As he opened the window now on the familiar silhouette of Jean Favrot, Daugherty was conscious of a curious force in the air. As though the mere act of sliding back the little board had somehow released pent-up forces that had long been gathering. The sight of her pretty face through the screen, the smell of her perfume, the recollection of her good work for the parish in spite of the burden of all those children—six tumultuous boys and a baby, plus two girls—and the knowledge of the chaos she endured moved him, profoundly, to pity. In the desperate brown eyes that peered toward him through the screen, he saw, summed up, his own personal crisis. He had an urge to tear away the screen, to see her face to face, without artificial barriers, without ceremonial trappings. Somehow, he sensed that if he could penetrate her spirit, he would find his own strength, that his own problem was inextricably interwoven with hers. It was as though she had appeared as a holy vision, an apparition. A sign?

Jean Favrot had, literally, fallen on her knees in the confessional. The contact with the hard wood hurt. Beyond that, her mind was utter confusion. She had meant to drop the children, rush the groceries home, then return for her own confession. Instead, she had parked and run headlong into the church, leaving the children to straggle inside. She had knelt before a statue of the Blessed Virgin, lit a candle, and waited for the familiar, comforting release. This time, it had not come. Rather, the anxiety, the peculiar feeling that she was separating from herself, floating away helplessly, overpowered her. She did not know how long she had knelt, staring unseeingly at the votive candles. Nor was she aware of Nancy's guiding her to the confessional whispering, "Hurry up. The food's defrosting."

Now she saw, in the dimness of the box (as she always thought of it), the handsome, virile features of Father Daugherty, his dark hair, good clean nose, the jutting chin, the long sideburns sweeping rakishly forward on his cheek, the youthful face turned down and away. She smelled his sweat—athletic sweat. She heard him sigh, too, a deep, tremulous sigh for so young a man. She did not bless herself.

Waiting for her to begin the stylized ritual of the confessional—"Bless me, Father, for I have sinned . . ."—Daugherty turned his head toward her slightly. He saw the tips of her fingers pressing tightly against the outside molding of the window. Then, looking closely, he saw a mask of anguish, a woman desperately reaching to—or beyond—her depth.

"Go on," he said gently.

At last Jean found her voice.

"I've had it," she said through the screen. "Right up to here."

She raised one hand, flat and level, to her eyebrows. Her voice was cool.

Father Daugherty leaned forward, ear close to the screen.

"Go on."

Jean Favrot put her mouth against the screen. Her voice came like the hiss of broken steam pipes: "I've absolutely reached the end of my rope. I can't go on like this. Not a day longer. What kind of God is this anyway? My husband, a damned lush, out playing golf, leaving me with nine children and all their endless errands and the car's broken down half the time and *he* goes on trips and what do I have to show for what I've done? Look at me, worn out, bedraggled, my hair a mess, no clothes, a damned maid, a slave, and believe me, there is plenty in life I *could* do . . ."

She went on, almost incoherently, damning her lot, her family. Father Daugherty sat back, sighed, tapped his right tennis shoe against the carpet. He listened, yet he did not. He heard snatches. All too familiar snatches. Let her blow off steam. The unhappiness of the world knew no boundaries. It was all wrong. Then he heard her voice, sharp, clear, forceful:

"I *hate* God."

The eyes were gone now, buried in her hands. He could see that she was trembling, sobbing. He coughed gently. She looked up, tears streaking down her cheeks.

"I *have* to have peace of mind," she said. "He doesn't give me any."

The clichés and platitudes on the Sacred Sacrament of Holy Matrimony that Father Daugherty had amassed over the years to haul up for such occasions now crowded his mind, lifeless, absurd. We were brought on this earth to suffer, to atone for Christ's suffering, for all the sins since Adam and Eve. Suffering makes us stronger. It leads to the eternal reward, the sight of God, a seat at His feet. Suffering builds character. Suffering reaffirms the Faith. If we do not suffer, then how can we recognize pleasure when it comes? God is punishing you, my dear, in his mysterious way.

"I want to get away," she hissed. "I *hate* my children. My life. I want to take the pill. I want to commit sin. I think about it all the time. The commission . . . they will approve the pill, won't they? Why can't I begin now? I want to live—not just exist. I . . . I want to *enjoy* sex, but I don't want any more children. Can't you tell me *something?*"

He let her run on, knowing now his premonition had been correct. A strange, indefinable alliance had been joined this day, in this confessional. They were alike in their doubts, yet Jean had faith. That she was here now—however desperate—was proof. He had to help her. In Jean Favrot's spiritual strength perhaps he might find his own. No soul, no family in the parish was in graver danger. She did not need confession. Jean Favrot needed release—urgent release—from the stupid, stifling bonds of the Roman Catholic Church. She must be saved, whatever the price.

"Jean," he said softly, but firmly. "In matters of sex, let your conscience be your guide. Try to make it with Bob, if you can. If your conscience tells you to use the pill, use it. I can't officially condone it. You know that. But if you want my opinion, you've done enough —brought enough life on earth."

He saw in her face a ray of hope, then anger.

"Bob won't buy it. I'd have to do it secretly."

"You can't deceive him. You have to work it out together."

"Why am I in this incredible position? That I have to go groveling to him after I've given him nine children. Answer that."

Father Daugherty sighed again, pausing to gather his thoughts.

"Jean, I can't help you. You know the rules. I can't say, here or elsewhere, use the pill. When I say let your conscience be your guide, you know what I mean. You've been reading the theological arguments. By advising you to follow your conscience, I'm guilty of . . . of heresy, because you know what my meaning implies. I could be fired tonight if this got out. I never told anyone that before . . ."

"I need *help!* This church isn't giving it to me."

"Could . . . could you and Bob come to the rectory later?"

"He'll be stoned. We're going to his boss's for dinner. Anyway, it would be pointless."

What was a religion then, Daugherty thought, that could fail a woman at a time like this? His mind searched feverishly for some answer, a word of hope. Then he thought of Dr. Cantor, the psychologist at the McLean Guidance Center. They had first met at city hall on a juvenile delinquency panel discussion. Cantor was young, brilliant, practical, a non-Freudian who believed strongly in the new theories of group therapy—had in fact developed some techniques of his own. Daugherty had never sent a parishioner from the confessional to the clinic. Yet . . . He turned to the face in the window.

"The best advice I can give you, Jean, from my heart, is go over to the McLean Guidance Center and talk to a psychologist named Dr. Cantor. Join a group therapy session. It may do you a world of good. If I had the time, or the competence, the professional competence, I would gladly give it. But you can get it there, better, I know."

"Bob wouldn't permit it," she said.

"Don't tell him."

"And the pill?"

"I told you. That's for you to decide. Your conscience, and Bob's. That's all I'm going to say."

"But . . ."

"Go in peace," Father Daugherty said, closing the window. And to himself: "Pray for me."

III

The See of the Washington archdiocese was located on Massachusetts Avenue, near the Naval Observatory, in an elegant tree-shaded neighborhood known as Embassy Row. The Chancery was a mansion, a copy of the Petit Trianon, with a sweeping circular driveway, ornate fountains, meticulously manicured gardens of English boxwood and Japanese cherry trees. Acquired by the Church for a pittance at the turn of the century, the mansion had once been the French embassy. Through the years it had been modernized with elevator, air-conditioning, and other comforts to ease the burden of the reigning Catholic luminary, who lived, in considerable luxury, in a private apartment on the second floor.

The reigning luminary was the Archbishop of Washington. His Excellency Lawrence O'Fallon McInnerney. He awoke in his giant, ornate mahogany bed shortly after six thirty, rested, fit, eager to face what would surely be an anxious, yet momentous day. He lay for a while, eyes closed, praying. Then, as every morning, he thanked God for bringing him safely through the night and then prayed for the repose of the dearly departed—his mother, father, three brothers, two sisters, Popes Pius and John, President Kennedy, who had been a special friend, and a long list of clergy, professional associates, and classmates at the seminary, who had passed on. He reserved his longest prayer and meditation for the repose of the soul of His Eminence, Francis Cardinal Spellman, gone only a few months. For forty-five of McInnerney's seventy-two years, Spellman had been the single most important mortal in his life, a living saint, inspiration, counselor, teacher, confessor. Few in the Church had suffered more deeply from this recent loss. McInnerney could not yet really believe he was dead. The Cardinal's face, his memory, his spirit, were still vivid and real, much the same as they had been on McInnerney's last visit to the New York Chancery, when Spellman, very near the end, had given McInnerney his final instructions and told him, among other things, that he was now on the list for the College of Cardinals.

This last was belated recognition for a thankless job well done. The Washington archdiocese had never been an easy or sought-after post. Washington was not a Catholic town. It had no large Irish or Italian populations, like Boston, New York, Philadelphia, Baltimore. It was, in fact, overshadowed by Baltimore, the Catholic population of Maryland, the first Catholic colony. The government, the military, the antheap of bureaucrats, were traditionally WASP. The Congress was dominated by southern Protestants. Washington society—the cliff-dwellers—worshipped in the great Episcopal Washington National Cathedral. True, there were great Catholic institutions in Washington, namely, Georgetown University and Catholic University. But Georgetown was Jesuit, answerable to the Black Pope in Rome. Catholic University was—for years—second- or third-rate, an administrative headache, since, in theory, it was the Pope's personal institution, answerable to the Vatican, yet supervised by the Washington Chancery. It held title to vast property in northeast Washington. But the property was nonrevenue-producing; the students at CU were historically and notoriously niggardly at collection-plate time. Other Church property in center-city Washington had been first surrounded and then overrun by the massive northward migration of the blacks, largely non-Catholic, who drove out the white Catholics and drastically depressed property values. In sum, the Washington archdiocese did not enjoy the prestige normally bestowed on the archdioceses of large American cities; it was in a perpetual financial crisis, made acute by the need to provide churches and parochial schools for the displaced whites, who fled to the Maryland and Virginia suburbs.

Sixteen years before—in 1952—Spellman had handpicked McInnerney for the job of "fixing" that troublesome archdiocese. He was then only fifty-six, one of the truly bright comers in Spellman's New York brain trust, a monsignor, elevated to bishop over many of his contemporaries because of his unswerving loyalty to his cardinal and the splendid results he achieved in "integrating" Puerto Rican immigrants into the Catholic structure of the archdiocese of New York. Inside the Chancery he was known as a "minority specialist," yet there was nothing about him, or his methods, to suggest a liberal viewpoint usually associated with such titles. He was, like his mentor, conservative, traditional, reactionary in all matters, ecclesiastical and secular. He enjoyed Spellman's absolute confidence. He brought cohesion and efficiency to the Washington Chancery, together with an "enlightened" (yet careful) approach to the burgeoning black community and the mushrooming white suburbs. All Saints' parish in McLean was a "model" example of the latter.

More "political" than his predecessors, McInnerney enlarged the Chancery's intercourse with the federal government, at times serving as Spellman's personal lobbyist on the Hill for certain legislation, especially federal aid to parochial schools, a delicate issue. When Kennedy came to power, McInnerney built a bridge between the Chancery and the White House and was thereafter a fixture at New Frontier social and political gatherings. His elevation to archbishop in 1962, with Cardinal Spellman presiding, was an impressive ecumenical pageant at which both the President and the First Lady received Communion. Truly Spellman could not have asked more from McInnerney.

It had been Spellman's desire to cement this church-state relationship (within the traditional limits of separatism), and to transform the Washington diocese into a glittering citadel of affluence and influence, visually as well as spiritually impressive. That line of thinking had led, by a circuitous route, to the creation of the Shrine of the Blessed Sacrament, the largest religious structure in the Western world. Towering over the CU campus, the shrine was awesome in dimension, the quintessent expression of Spellman's brick-and-mortar concept. A similar line of thought had inspired Spellman's dream for a theological center, to bear his name, and to rise in the shadow of the shrine, a structure of marble that would surpass in majesty and grandeur all the government buildings in Washington. It was Spellman's hope, expressed in private to a few trusted souls, including McInnerney, that the center would attract the most brilliant Catholic thinkers in the world. These thinkers, under his guidance, would counter the heretical trend in Catholic theology. They would lead, with articulate pens, the counterreformation which Spellman believed must follow the hurricane of fresh winds sweeping the Church. Death had overtaken the Cardinal before he could launch the center. His final instructions to McInnerney were to see the center to completion, "at any cost," meaning, of course, not merely financial, but also spiritual. Pope Paul, Spellman said, had given more than his blessing. He had told Spellman in the final months that the center was "essential."

So the dream had passed on to McInnerney's hands. It was his project now, urgent and imperative. Not a single day could be wasted. The sooner it became operational, the sooner it would attract those it was intended to house, and the sooner it would become the bastion from which the salvation of the modern Church could be launched. Its completion, McInnerney knew, would guarantee his election to the College of Cardinals, and then, perhaps, to the unofficial post of spiritual leader of all America's Catholics, as Spellman had been. And from there . . . who knew?

Today, this day, the decision to proceed with the center would be ratified in the Chancery, first by McInnerney's own staff, then by the financial council, a group of lay businessmen of taste, business acumen, and discretion, who met monthly to "advise" the Archbishop on archdiocesan financial problems. There would be objections on all levels, some shrill. These, McInnerney must overcome. The center would never become a reality unless he had the total support of every Catholic in the archdiocese.

He leaped from the great mahogany bed. For a man of his age, McInnerney was in uncommonly good health and spirits. It was said, by those who knew him well, that he was a "stranger to depression." That was for the most part true. He was naturally buoyant, the eternal optimist, a "can-do" man who believed that hard work and dedication would overcome almost any shortcoming of talent. He was a spare man, thin-boned, taut-skinned with small hands and feet, a flat stomach, thin, straight gray hair. As a young boy he had been a rebel, waterfront Boston Irish to the core. But after countless years as a Shepherd of Christ, he had curbed youthful impulses, willing himself to be gentle, unabrasive. Rocking on the balls of his feet, he now proceeded with his morning exercises, toe-touching, knee bends, squat thrusts, push-ups, sit-ups, leg raises, ten vigorous minutes of temporal concern, never overlooked because he believed, as Spellman had, that a sound body made for a sound mind.

If there was an outward weakness of character, it was his insatiable longing for cigarettes. He was a compulsive smoker. In truth, he enjoyed only one a day, the first, in the morning before Mass, before coffee. But he smoked on and on—two and sometimes three packs a day. Except now. He had foresworn them for Lent, the supreme sacrifice, a claim that was disputed by no one who knew him, especially those who lived in the Chancery.

Exercise finished, the Archbishop went to the bathroom to shave and dress in somber purple Lenten vestments. He left the apartment and walked with energetic steps down the corridor to his private chapel. The Chancery staff, the half dozen monsignors and younger priests, the dozen servants, were already in their pews. The Archbishop's second in command, the Vicar General Ignatius Prial was waiting on the altar to serve the Mass. It was a brief, almost Spartan ceremony, entirely in Latin, devoid of the innovations approved by the Vatican Council. The Archbishop had not agreed with the decision to bring English to the Mass, or to turn the altar around. He had voted against these innovations, and others, at the Council. The Mass, like many others in the Chancery chapel for the last few months, was offered up for the repose of the soul of Cardinal Spellman.

McInnerney distributed Communion. As he placed the Host on the outstretched tongues of the maids, the houseboys, the chauffeur, gave them the Body of Christ, he felt not patronizing, but humble, as though, symbolically, he were washing their feet.

After Mass, he returned to his apartment. He changed from vestments to his "working uniform," black suit, rabat, Roman collar. One of the Irish maids brought his breakfast on a heavy silver tray: carrot juice, coffee, dry toast. While he ate, and read the morning papers— the *Washington Post, New York Times, Wall Street Journal*—the housekeeper came to make his bed, tidy the room, and carry away the dirty laundry. By eight the Archbishop had moved to the massive oak desk in the living room. For an hour, he occupied himself with incoming and outgoing mail that required his signature. Promptly at nine, Vicar General Prial rapped on the door for the morning conference.

The Vicar General entered, carrying an armload of papers and financial reports. There was a larger than usual stack today because of the financial council meeting and the plans and specifications for the theological center which would be presented to the council. Prial carried these without strain. He was a chunky, muscular man, tall and dark, with hamlike hands and a thick neck. Although he had turned fifty, his hair was still jet-black. He wore it close-cropped, well trimmed, like a military man. Usually he arrived in a cloud of cigar smoke. Today, he chomped on a cigar, but it was dead. It would not be lighted until Lent had passed. He had also given up all spirits, a larger sacrifice than the cigars. He drew a chair to the desk and spread the papers and reports in a systematic row before him. He was, in all matters, obsessively neat and orderly.

The Vicar General was, among other things, a financial specialist. Not by choice. The role had been forced on him, years before, when he was a young priest, a member of Cardinal Spellman's staff in the New York Chancery. He had been assigned to work with Monsignor James Francis McIntyre, an amazing financial wizard, a former Wall Street broker, who made a fortune, renounced it, became a priest. He became Spellman's chief financial adviser, founded an archdiocese bank (to help finance new construction), oversaw the vast finances of the Chancery until 1948, when Spellman sent him to rule in Los Angeles. Prial had learned much from McIntyre. In his position he had, of necessity, cultivated New York businessmen, picked their brains, and, later, at McIntyre's suggestion, attended the Harvard Graduate School of Business. His financial specialty—rare in the Catholic hierarchy—had brought him rapid advancement and power. Like Spellman, McInnerney knew little of high finance. He had handpicked Prial six years ago to manage that area. He relied completely on Prial for fiscal judgment. Beyond that, as second in command of the Chancery, Prial had gradually assumed larger responsibilities in the field of personnel and education. He also served as sounding board, confidant, and intelligence-gatherer for his superior.

McInnerney peered at the reports through his thin, gold-rimmed spectacles, frowning. He picked them up gingerly, as though they were contaminated by the Devil himself. A sea of prayer over the years had not cleansed them.

"By the way," the Vicar General said. "Before we get into this, Helen Hanrahan telephoned this morning. She was quite upset and insisted that she see you before noon. A matter, she said, of urgency.

I tried to put her off, but she was quite emotional. So I set the appointment for eleven."

A telephone call from the mystic Helen Hanrahan was not lightly treated at the Chancery. Her column circulated to 850 newspapers, more than Drew Pearson. Her following was, in a word, enormous; her influence, incalculable. She had been a special friend of Cardinal Spellman, who believed, with fervor, that her visions were divinely inspired. McInnerney, who had known her well for years, held the woman in highest regard, perhaps with a touch of awe. She was profoundly devout, a daily communicant, a tireless benefactress of the poor, the feeble, the infirm. Perhaps a saint. He too was convinced that her visions were authentic. The history of the Catholic Church was replete with cases of people who had the gift of prophecy. Much of Catholicism turned around visions. His own mother had had premonitions that proved to be uncannily accurate.

"Delighted to see her, as always," McInnerney said, without exaggeration.

They returned now to the business at hand.

"When the Good Lord founded His Church," McInnerney said, "he forgot about prime interest rates and mortgages."

It was his stock comment when presented the financial reports for the council. Prial had heard it so often he did not feel a riposte was called for. He was then marshaling his argument against the theological center, a subject often discussed between them of late. He had stayed up until three o'clock going over the figures, looking for some feasible way to finance it, looking until his mind was drugged with figures, so sleepy finally that he collapsed on the Spartan bed in his third-floor cell in his clothes. He attacked the Archbishop obliquely.

"I wish we had a better balance sheet to show the council," he said glumly.

Working as a team, McInnerney and Prial had done much in the past to improve the archdiocese financial picture. But beginning in 1965, it had begun to go downhill again. The Chancery was caught in a classic squeeze: rising costs, declining revenue. School expense (a one-line item on the balance sheet) was the fastest swelling figure, outrunning even the darkest forecasts. There seemed no end of demand for new classrooms. There was a critical shortage of teachers. Too many nuns were resigning their orders—a staggering 9,000 a year. Not nearly enough were coming into the other end of the pipeline, as

Prial was fond of expressing it. Total enrollment, down 6,000. As a result, the parochial schools had to hire expensive lay teachers—the total number up forty percent in five years. Now these were demanding a cost-of-living raise.

Prial now came directly to the point.

"I feel obliged, Your Excellency, to go on record, for the last time, and with as much force as I can, as saying I do not believe it is financially feasible to begin the theological center at this time."

He sat back, removed the cigar from his mouth, stared morosely at the unlit end. He did not ordinarily address McInnerney in formal terms. But here, he had been speaking for the record, so to speak. He added, almost as an afterthought:

"Maybe next year."

McInnerney was aware that Prial, by his language, had transformed a casual morning meeting into a historic occasion, a moment of formal decision for which he did not want to be held responsible. He was not surprised. It was Prial's job to tell him when he was going off half-cocked. This time, however, McInnerney was determined to override his adviser. Paul had declared the center "essential."

"The time never seems ripe," he said. "I don't want to be reckless. But it seems to me that, historically speaking, if man always waited until he had the money in hand, nothing would ever have been accomplished. There probably would have been no Acropolis, no pyramids, no St. Peter's, no Notre Dame, and, for that matter, no Empire State Building. If Zeckendorf can do it with mirrors, why can't we?"

"Because he builds income-producing properties," Prial said, "and we build churches and schools and seminaries and homes for old priests, which have marginal resale value. He qualifies for big mortgages. We don't. Not now, at least, not anymore. Not with these income figures spiraling down. It's that simple."

There was, in truth, only one way to raise the bulk of the money. That was to launch an archdiocesan fund drive, a massive campaign. Prial had argued against that, too. For one thing, there were already local fund-raising campaigns in most of the parishes to help finance school construction. The last archdiocesan fund campaign—goal 15 million—had been a dismal flop. The projects tied to it—a home for retired priests and a retreat lodge in the Blue Ridge Mountains—had been deferred or canceled, the little money raised diverted to operating expenses, legerdemain that was not revealed outside the Chancery.

The laity, like the clergy, was beset by rising costs. It simply did not have money to contribute. It would resent a "nebulous thing" (as Prial had irreverently termed it) like a theological center at CU, especially when Catholic children were now crowded forty pupils to a classroom. The climate was not right. McInnerney had countered with this simple statement: "When did you ever know the climate to be exactly right for a fund drive?"

Then, in the midst of these prolonged discussions, something had happened that, to McInnerney, brought the center within the range of practicality. That this event was heaven-sent he did not doubt in the slightest. The good Cardinal up there, pushing all the right buttons. What happened was this: a quasi-governmental agency, the Institute for Defense Analysis (IDA), which was looking for a building site for a new headquarters building deep in the ghetto so that the agency might qualify for Health, Education, and Welfare Title B Financing (under Job Opportunity and Urban Renewal auspices), telephoned the Vicar General asking if the archdiocese might like to sell off St. Luke's Cathedral. St. Luke's had once been a Byzantine marvel, next to St. Matthew's the showplace of the archdiocese. Now it was a shabby wreck, with leaking roof, crumbling walls. The surrounding neighborhood was a black slum of the most offensive kind. The few indifferent black parishioners contributed almost nothing to the upkeep of the church, such as it was. The adjoining school building had been condemned by the city.

Priding himself as a shrewd businessman, Prial had replied with casual indifference. He doubted if it was for sale. But privately, he rejoiced. It was a miracle! There was good land there, a full city block. If he played the deal right, it might bring $5 million. Five million! With that kind of money, he could meet the gap in operational expense, even have money left to meet soaring construction costs for new facilities in the suburbs. Almost breathlessly, he conveyed the substance of the telephone call to McInnerney.

That was when McInnerney felt Spellman had been pushing all the right buttons. The $5 million could be the down payment for the theological center, a hefty underpinning for the fund drive, should the donations flag.

In a twinkling, Prial's dream of a solvent archdiocese evaporated. It was useless to argue, he knew. Yet he tried. He began: What would they do to provide the black parishioners with a place to worship? McInnerney responded: What had they done so far to provide for themselves? Nothing. There were not enough souls there to count anyway. One, two hundred, the attendance falling off every week, the collection plates returned bare. The cathedral had not been built by blacks; white money put it there. What about the political impact? The Church selling out to a defense agency? (Presented without enthusiasm; Prial wanted to unload that white elephant as much, or more than McInnerney.) The agency would provide good jobs in a deprived area, the Archbishop responded. Several hundred, perhaps. The blacks would be foolish to protest—bite the hand feeding them. Handled right, the Church might be applauded for making those jobs possible. The black women—the mothers and wives—would muzzle the men, if they were inclined to stage a protest. Anyway, that was mostly IDA's problem. They faced similar problems every day. They must know what they're doing. Finally: What if our own white liberals learned that we had sold off a black church to fund a (they would say) reactionary theological center. Response: The Chancery would never link the two moves publicly. There was no public accounting of Chancery finances, no right to know.

So the decision was reached. The money realized from the sale of St. Luke's would back-stop the fund drive, at the very least provide the down payment. The Vicar General would set aside all other work and concentrate on closing that deal on the most favorable terms for the Chancery.

The Archbishop now reflected lovingly on that property. He had offered up an ocean of prayer that the deal might go through.

"Is there anything new we can add on Luke's for the council?" he said.

"Nothing new."

"You are still perfectly confident?"

"Yes. I think we can tell them it's solid. I have a signed letter of intent, with all the contingencies. Legally, it's not worth the paper it's written on. But, morally, it amounts to something."

"Put the best possible face on it," McInnerney said.

The financial council was without real power. It could not veto Chancery business. It could merely propose to advise. Yet McInnerney always approached it with kid gloves, like a corporation president facing his board of directors. The men were the most influential Catholic businessmen in the archdiocese. It was important, from many standpoints, to have them believe the Chancery was fiscally sound—and properly conservative. Never irresponsible. The council's approval, professionally and spiritually, was crucial to the success of the fund drive.

The members could make or break it, merely by word of mouth. Prial did not need to be reminded of this fact. He would put a good face on it.

"I'll have that," he said, chewing on the dead cigar, "and the preliminary architectural renderings."

"Good."

The Vicar General gathered up the financial reports. He had done his duty, as he saw it. His advice, carefully arrived at, had been ignored. But he understood, better than most, the Archbishop's commitment to the center. He would support his decision with all his prayers and strength.

Alone at his desk, the Archbishop, longing for a cigarette, and consuming Lifesavers to help ward off the longing, worked over the accumulation of papers, letters, documents, dictating into a machine. Occasionally he paused to pray, to ask the Holy Family, once again, to guide his hand, to give him eloquence to persuade the financial council.

At eleven, Helen Hanrahan arrived for her appointment, escorted to the Archbishop's apartment by a young priest, detailed to convoy VIP's, and make pleasantries along the way. She was a white-haired woman, in her late sixties, with pale blue eyes and a soft, silky air about her, as though she were adrift on some distant cloud. She wore expensive clothing; her hair was beautifully coiffured, every strand in place. The Archbishop, who stood at least a foot shorter than the woman, met her at the door, smiling, genial. She knelt and kissed his ring. Then he led her to the couch. A maid served tea.

"I can't stay but a minute," Helen Hanrahan said, suddenly somewhat agitated.

"I'm sorry to hear that," the Archbishop said sincerely. "I was hoping we might have a good, long chat."

"Some other time, please. I'm scheduled for a luncheon talk at the Women's Press Club. I've been so upset, I haven't got my thoughts in order. I don't know *what* I'll say."

She seemed depressed.

"You'll think of something pithy," the Archbishop said cheerily. "The Holy Ghost will provide."

McInnerney could not bring himself to say "Holy Spirit," as Rome had decreed.

"I must tell you straight away," Helen Hanrahan said. "Last night I had the most painful vision. I awoke with a vision of a cathedral, amid a mosaic of violence. Blood. Fire. It was simply ghastly. I . . . I was wracked with pain."

"There is violence everywhere," the Archbishop said gently.

"Yes. But this is different."

"Is it related to your prophecy of a clergy assassination?" the Archbishop asked, changing his tone to a somber pitch. "I saw your column on that last Saturday."

"I'm not sure," she said. "It wasn't clear. But, now, twice, I've seen the Church and violence. I felt a tremor, just now, when I came in the room. Something tells me you're about to do something you shouldn't. I . . . I . . . see the university . . . CU . . . books. Scholars."

The Archbishop leaped to his feet, astonished. He knew full well he should not have been. She did this all the time. Yet it was unnerving.

He sat down again. He told her about the theological center, the pressing need for it, how Spellman had given him deathbed orders to see it through. He asked her support. It was a worthy, even essential project.

"I don't know . . . I just don't know," she said vaguely.

The Archbishop pressed.

"Let me think," she said. "Give me time."

"You see the course of the Church," he said gravely. "The center could counter . . . could bring a modicum of sanity . . . of responsibility . . ."

"Perhaps," Helen said. "Perhaps not. It may be too late."

"Don't be defeatist," the Archbishop said sternly. "It's not like you. Not like you at all."

She fixed her eyes on his. That powerful, electric gaze disturbed him. It was as though he were looking into the eyes of the Holy Mother Herself. There was clear warning there, an ominous current against which he felt powerless. He turned his eyes to the floor.

"Pray for me," he said, voice trailing off.

"And you for me," she said. "But, Your Excellency, let me say it again. I have seldom felt such strong vibrations. Not since Jack Kennedy."

With a stab, McInnerney recalled those painful days. Helen had had a vision. Something violent would befall the President in Texas. She had come to McInnerney first to discuss it. Then, in the days that followed, the frantic effort to warn the President, the skepticism and indifference, even ridicule from the Secret Service, White House aides, and, finally, a good-natured laugh from Kennedy himself. Ever since, McInnerney had felt guilty. Had he been more forceful, he might have convinced the President.

"What can I say?" the Archbishop said, lifting his arms, a gesture of helplessness. "I'm committed."

"I'll do what I can, or feel I can," she said. "Now I must be running along."

"Keep in touch," the Archbishop said.

When she had gone, leaving behind the odor of strong perfume, the Archbishop walked to the French windows overlooking the garden in the rear of the Chancery. He stood at the window a long time, praying for guidance. He believed Helen Hanrahan, yet he did not. This time, he did not *want* to believe. But he could not dismiss her, even though common sense argued that the vision must be wrong, a fluke, a spurious signal. He was still standing there, lost in conflicting thought, when Prial came to announce that the financial council had gathered in the first-floor library. The Archbishop descended in the elevator, resolved now that there should be no doubt, no hesitation. He was, as he had said, committed.

IV

The custodian of All Saints' Church, John Joseph Scafidi, worked in utter solitude, running the vacuum cleaner nozzle along the rug between the pews. The church was dark because Scafidi preferred to work that way, late in the evening, after the last parishioner had departed, while the pastor and assistant pastor were dining in the rectory. He disliked the church as much as Father Daugherty, although for very different reasons. To Scafidi, raised in a Philadelphia slum, accustomed to Spartan churches with hard stone floors and harder oak kneeling benches, All Saints' was almost blasphemous in its luxury.

He worked bent over, dragging his deformed right leg from pew to pew, humming to himself (Italian folk songs, learned from his

mother), his feverish mind held in the grip of an idea that had occurred to him, as though a divine inspiration, earlier in the day.
Scafidi had been for some years now obsessed by UFO's—flying
saucers, or formally, Unidentified Flying Objects. When the first for-
mation appeared over the state of Washington in 1947, he became a
believer. There and then, he began a scrapbook into which he pasted
newspaper clippings about UFO's. The first was soon used up. So were
the second, third, fourth, fifth. He now had almost one hundred in his
rooms, filed, like a library, by date, country, or shape, all indexed and
cross-referenced. He also had dozens of UFO magazines, books, pamphlets, reports. He was beyond question an expert in this curious
field. Skeptical statements, disavowals, emanating over the years from
the Air Force, federal government, or independent scientific investi-
gating agencies had not dissuaded him. These had, in fact, reinforced
his belief. He knew the government, the CIA, the FBI, were covering
up, fearful that an official acknowledgment of what was perfectly obvious to experts such as himself would touch off a nationwide or
perhaps worldwide panic.

Where were they from? This question had gnawed relentlessly at
Scafidi for many years. At first he believed they were military vehicles, U.S. or Russian. Then he believed they were from the moon.
Then Mars. But he soon became aware that the men who flew these
machines, and the machines themselves, could not be explained by the
ordinary physical laws of the universe, at least not by the limited mind
of man. He had puzzled over this for months and years, growing more
baffled as the "official sightings" increased in frequency and authen-
ticity, each exhaustively investigated by independent UFO experts (be-
lievers), and detailed in written reports in the society bulletins. But
that day Scafidi, in a stroke, had solved the riddle, at least to his
own satisfaction. UFO's, he knew with unflinching certainty, were the
work of God, divine chariots based in Heaven. This galvanizing idea
drove him instantly to the Scriptures. Yes. It was full of references to
UFO's, even back then. In *Samuel* 22:11: "And he rode upon a
cherub, and did fly: and he was seen upon the wings of the wind."
And *Deuteronomy* 31:15: "And the Lord appeared in the tabernacle
in a pillar of a cloud: and the pillar of the cloud stood over the door
of the tabernacle." And so on.

Scafidi was not unaware that his was a radical idea. He knew that
he must unveil it with caution. The UFO society was, at heart, a
conservative outfit. It fearlessly exposed fake reports, phony theories,

spurious accounts of conversations with the humanoid pilots. When his time came, Scafidi's case would be rock-solid. He would comb the entire Bible, extract every conceivable reference to clouds, fire, cherubs, flying objects, to back his theory. It must be thorough, exacting, meticulous. It would galvanize the society, the covering-up government, the world.

He dragged the vacuum cleaner to the last pew, planting his infirm right foot in a steady position. Soon the work was finished. He stored the vacuum cleaner, locked the closet, hobbled across the parking lot toward the rectory, toward the bright lights of the kitchen, where the housekeeper, Mrs. Munally, would have his good, warm supper.

It was a clear night and cold. He looked skyward, at the stars, the incredible universe receding from below. He saw it with sharper eyes, greater comprehension, now that the mystery was solved. For now, the incredible secret was his alone. He savored it, nourished it, reveled in its infinite dimensions. Then he put it away.

The thrice-weekly supper with Mrs. Munally in the rectory kitchen was, so to speak, Scafidi's primary contact with the real world. For the most part he lived in total solitude in his rooms, lost in dreams, memories, or the UFO literature. He avoided people. People avoided him. He was only dimly aware of the momentous events that swirled around him in Washington, the changes of government, the military crises, the riots, protests, and civil strife that daily jarred the nation. These matters were, in truth, too mundane to require other than a fleeting glance. Most of that trouble he attributed to this or that conspiracy, minor intrigue in a major conspiracy, evoked by the self-destructive, consuming greed and the evil of mankind, especially what he thought of as the Wall Street crowd.

He knew them well. For a time, his mother had worked for one of them, as a maid in a vast, rich Main Line mansion. Scafidi had, in fact, been born there, in the servants' quarters over the garage. They had not found his father, a ne'er-do-well gardener, who fled to parts unknown when the scandal erupted. He had no memory of the place at all. His mother was fired, denied references, cast out, banished to the downtown Italian quarter, the unspeakable slum, where she slaved as a charwoman in the Curtis Building to provide for herself and John Joseph, the cripple. He had no memory of the place, but his mother told him all about the people. They were amoral, vicious, depraved, devils in disguise. He did not doubt it.

Against unthinkable odds, his mother had decided early that John Joseph would be a priest. She was candid about her reasons. It was an

article of Italian faith in those old days that the mother of a priest
would automatically be saved. Never mind the physical handicap.
That could be repaired later, at Lourdes. Never mind the social
stigmas, the lack of money, connections, and other factors necessary
to gain the priesthood. Never mind the prejudice against Italians on
the part of the Irish who controlled the seminaries, churches, schools.
A "good mind" and "firm faith" could overcome these shortcomings.
So during that ghastly, lonely, fearful childhood, he had worked hard
at his books and prayers, determined that his mother should gain
salvation. It was never to be. She had overreached by a stupefying
distance. The news—the rejection—had killed her. She died of a
broken heart. Left alone at eighteen, John Joseph had drifted, a
handyman, janitor, dishwasher, ridiculed, spat upon, trampled, eking
out a bare living, along the forty-two year road from Philadelphia to
Washington. The journey had left him bitter yet still—miraculously—
unbeaten. A profound, ingrained faith had sustained him.

He rapped on the back door of the rectory, feeling the stab of the
March wind through his thin coat and cotton shirt, both threadbare.
The door swung open, pushed against the wind by the buxom body of
the housekeeper.

"Come out of the cold," she gushed cheerily, stepping back into
the blaze of the lights in the kitchen.

Scafidi hobbled up the steps, pulling himself on the icy handrail.

The housekeeper, Bridget Munally, waited, hands on hips while the
struggle ensued. She was a pious, good-hearted woman who had found
her place in the world and worked diligently to keep it. She was a
cousin of the pastor, Monsignor Ryan. Their mothers had been sisters,
living in South Boston. At age sixteen Bridget had entered a convent.
She stayed only seven weeks. The confinement, the silence, the silken
oppression had almost destroyed her. She fled before it was too late.
She married a grocer, a good man, who had been killed in World War
II. Childless, lonely, devout, she went to help Ryan in a Boston parish,
then moved to Washington with him. She was a good cook, a bossy,
gregarious housekeeper who kept the rectory running like clockwork.

To Mrs. Munally, Scafidi was a cipher. He had appeared out of
nowhere to answer the ad, two years back. He lived in the shabby,
block-long "slum" of the parish, a no-man's-land of junk cars and
shanties, in a ravine between two subdivisions. (The land there had
not been worth acquiring because of the fill dirt required; it had
fallen between the stools of both builders.) Mrs. Munally had felt
sorry for him (in spite of the fact he was obviously Italian)—a cripple,

a Catholic, a member of the new parish. The Monsignor, who could
not conceal his contempt for Italians, had said that was her one failing,
always feeling sorry for people. She had responded, rather tartly, if
that was her one failing, it was a good one to have. He had good
references—from a long line of parishes. So they had hired him to
clean, without knowing much about him. Since he deflected questions
about his past, Mrs. Munally, for all her diligence, did not know, after
two years, very much more. But she wondered.

Scafidi removed his coat, hung it on a peg.

"We need two new furnace filters," he said, dragging himself to
the chair at the kitchen table.

Mrs. Munally immediately noted that on her Things To Do list,
clipped to the kitchen bulletin board, which was filled with reminders,
efficiently arranged, and a copy of Sunday's bulletin, which listed all
the parish activities, handy reference for the endless, scatterbrained
parishioners who called for that information. The new filters would
not be overlooked. They would save pennies on the gas bill. But,
over the years, pennies mounted up.

The fare that night was thin. Fish. Monsignor Ryan had decreed
that, during Lent, the rectory would observe the old custom of ab-
staining—a slim piece of meat once a day. He himself was fasting.
Father Daugherty, with his prodigious appetite, had objected. Rome
had long since abolished these archaic rules. He wanted three square
meals a day. He did not get them, not in the rectory dining room.
But, as Mrs. Munally knew all too well, he raided the refrigerator for
cold cuts and cheese and pie and cake, a sacrilegious act of piracy
that left her torn. She liked to bake. She liked to see men eat her
food. Even if it broke the local rule.

She apologized to Scafidi for the fish.

"It's Lent," he said. The change in the rules had not reached him, or
if it had, he had seen fit to ignore it. He spooned the fish hungrily,
head bent low, a pathetic portrait to Mrs. Munally. She sat on the
chair opposite, somewhat repelled by his table manners.

"I have some fresh pie," she said. "Peach."

"Where do you get peaches this time of year?"

"They're canned."

She spoke it as though admitting a mortal sin.

He ate the remainder of the food in silence, wiping his lips with the
back of his hand. Mrs. Munally fetched the pie, serving him a huge
piece.

"I can't eat all that. Take some back."

"Take it home with you."

"All right."

She cut the piece on his plate in half. While he ate, she put half in a paper bag. She wondered what he ate at home. She sat again.

"Oh, I almost forgot," she said, jumping up, rushing to the front hall. She returned with a topcoat slung over her arm. It was black wool.

"Father Daugherty said to give you this," she said. "He got a new one."

Scafidi felt the material. He did not know Father Daugherty at all. He had seen him, from time to time, crossing the parking lot, dressed in richly tailored sports clothes. He did not seem like a priest. He was too young. He lacked dignity. Scafidi looked at the topcoat label. It was from a well-known Philadelphia store.

"Is he from Philadelphia?" Scafidi asked.

"Yes."

"One of those rich kids?"

"He must have been well-to-do," Mrs. Munally said. "His family sends him things."

"Main Line?"

"I don't know. Bryn Mawr, I think."

"That's Main Line. The heart of it. Everybody there is a millionaire."

She wondered how he knew, or if it might be true. Yet she hesitated to ask. He would change the subject. Instead she sighed:

"It must be nice."

"He's a modern, isn't he?" Scafidi said, not concealing the contempt.

"He has some *different* concepts," Mrs. Munally said, rushing to caution. Daugherty was, in her view, a dangerous radical. She had so spoken her mind to Monsignor Ryan on many occasions. But Ryan was generous, unflappable. They *all* are these days, he had said, reminding her, again, that they were still shorthanded, that they must make do with what they could get. The Chancery had not yet sent the third priest they were entitled to. There was no sign it ever would.

"Tell him thanks anyway," Scafidi said, spurning the coat. "Spring's coming. I don't need it."

Unspoken was his true reason. He would not accept a handout from a spoiled Main Line playboy, posing as a priest. He might be, for all they knew, a devil.

Sensing this, Mrs. Munally did not press. She felt sorry for him, wondering what episode in the past had warped his mind to this foolish degree. She regretted that she had said it was from Daugherty.

"Give my best to the Monsignor," Scafidi said, getting up from the chair.

Monsignor Ryan fulfilled Scafidi's concept of the proper priest. Scafidi had chosen him for confession. He attended his Mass—sitting alone on a folding chair in the little alcove near the baptismal font. Ryan knew Scafidi's innermost secrets, his damnable, incurable sin of the flesh. For this reason, and others, Scafidi avoided a face-to-face encounter in the rectory or anywhere else. So did the Monsignor.

"I will," she said, knowing well she wouldn't, that the sudden affability was Scafidi's way of saying thanks and good-bye. He had never yet thanked her for a meal, or for his weekly pay envelope, or for any other favors. She forgave him this rudeness, wondering what she might be like if she were a cripple.

Scafidi pulled on his thin coat, descended the steps, and loped to his car in the parking lot. It was a wreck, an ancient Ford with smashed fenders, wheezing motor. But it was enough to take him back and forth the short distance to his rooms. He drove slowly, winding through the subdivisions, turning down the dirt road, threading his way through the potholes and ruts to his driveway. He turned off, eased into the ditch, then up again to his yard. He parked in the lee of the small frame shanty. He covered the hood of the Ford with a tattered Army blanket kept on the front seat for that purpose.

The house was freezing. He lit the kerosene heater and stood over it, briskly rubbing his hands, eager now to attack his Bible. The glow from the heater cast a dim light over the room, the stacks and stacks of UFO books and reports, the scrapbooks filed systematically in a wall of shelves made of grapefruit crates. He had seriously considered giving up his study for Lent. He was glad now that he hadn't. Otherwise the idea might not have struck.

When the room was warm, he took off his coat and sat at his "desk," an old door resting on several cinder blocks. The top of the desk was crowded with unfiled, unindexed UFO literature. He pushed these aside to make room for his work on the Bible.

He began with *Genesis,* reading slowly, silently mouthing the words, pausing occasionally to print an excerpt on cheap tablet paper, a laborious process in which he took unfathomable pride. He worked for two hours, much pleased by his progress. The allusions he discovered far exceeded his expectations. He closed the book with a gratifying sense of fatigue.

Now he faced the ordeal of going to bed. He felt, as always, the terrifying stab, the curious, unmanageable compulsion that overcame him nightly at this time. He heard the voice dictating, and felt his limbs moving, as though by command. It was the Devil's voice, against which he was utterly powerless. It led him to the adjoining room, a low-ceilinged shed attachment to the other room. In the corner of the space, in a niche, he saw the small statue of the Blessed Virgin. With trembling fingers, he struck a match, lit a votive candle which cast eerie shadows on the statue. He fell to his knees, crossing himself, murmuring prayers in Italian, words from his own mother's lips. He implored the Blessed Virgin for help. A fruitless pleading. She would not be here. She would not hear. The Devil was in command.

He groped for the bed. He collapsed on top of the ragged covers, trembling, tearing off his clothes and shoes, suffering the tormenting cold, hoping to freeze out the desire, the voice, the Devil, the compulsion, knowing full well this too was futile, that he would sin, *must* sin. His hand probed beneath the mattress. His fingers felt the object he sought, then tugged. It was a thin, dog-eared magazine, *Gents*. He opened the pages, turning so the dim glow of the votive candle gave light. He turned to the picture of the naked female with the head snipped away. He felt the rush of blood and heat in his groin. The pain was excruciating. It erupted in one intense, blinding microsecond of pleasure. He lurched and turned on his side, gasping and shaking. The magazine slipped from his hand to the floor.

V

Sister Mary Frances Murray, Religious of the Sacred Heart, parked her red VW against the curb, immediately in front of the old St. Luke's parochial school, ignoring the rusty "No Parking—Entrance" sign, carefully avoiding the glass and other debris in the gutter. The surrounding neighborhood was black, sullen, dangerous to a white woman. But here, in the heart of the ghetto, she felt safe. Here she was well known, admired for the volunteer work she did in her special school for crippled black children.

She alighted from the bug, carrying a large brown attaché case, jammed with papers related to the school. There was nothing about her appearance to suggest her calling. She did not wear the traditional black habit of her order, rather a habit of her own design: gray wool, knee-length dress, black pumps, a gray modified nurse's cap. Her long, glistening, well-combed hair fell to her shoulders. She wore pale, almost invisible makeup. There was no meek or humble cast to her bearing. She was businesslike, brisk, confident, a woman of the world, going not by the name of her patron saint—Cecelia—but her own.

Sister Mary was a graduate student at Catholic University, working toward a doctorate in philosophy. She carried her thesis, "The Application of the Montessori Method to Ghetto Deprived," in her attaché case. It was almost finished. In a few weeks she would sit for her orals. By late May, she would be finished with her schooling; then she must decide how she would apply it. As part of her thesis, she had established this ghetto school, a "working model" of her theories. She came here five mornings a week. As a "detached student," she was not required to observe the traditional, severe routine of her order. She lived alone, dressed as she pleased, and went about on the streets feeling no need for the traditional "prudent companion." She had lived this way in the "outside world" for two years, her modest living expenses paid by the order, her tuition waived by the Washington Chancery in accordance with a plan conceived some years back by Archbishop McInnerney, reacting to criticism that too many teaching nuns lacked higher degrees.

She mounted the worn wooden steps of the building. The steps reminded her, again, that the building had been condemned. It was structurally unsafe; the plumbing was deplorable. The danger of the building had been made clear to her on any number of occasions when the city engineers paid their monthly visit. They always threatened to padlock the door. She had, on each occasion, pleaded: she was not Rockefeller, she was a single, penniless person in the world, with only the most meager resources at her command. What little help she was able to provide the retarded and crippled children of the black community was better than none. Month by month, the engineers had compromised. First they boarded the stairway to the second floor. Then they shut down all but one bathroom. They permitted a butane stove for heat. But it could not go on forever like this. It was truly unsafe.

She walked down the dingy corridor to the "classroom," a large area that had once been the cafeteria. Her spirits were high today, for no special reason. That was her style—high-spirited, indomitable, a big Irish smile on her lips, a fetching young woman of twenty-nine, who, in another place, might well have been a magazine cover-girl. She thought of herself as a very different, a very useful person.

Mary Murray had been the third of six energetic, handsome children, daughter of a devout "black Irish" mother and a moderately successful New York stockbroker. They lived modestly in Greenwich, Connecticut, amidst the captains of industry, celebrities of the entertainment world, publishing, and Madison Avenue. Mary was a bright child, eager, curious, athletic. She won a high school scholarship to the Sacred Heart Convent at Kings Street, nearby. Then to the Sacred Heart College, Manhattanville, in neighboring Rye, New York. She was popular with boys, congenial with girls, and very serious about her academic work, a straight A student. Her home life was pleasant and warm, decent, religious. In this lush town of transient rich homes broken by alcohol and divorce, the Murrays were known at the bank and elsewhere as "solid." Middle class, not flashy, not rich, but sturdy and dependable.

There had never been push from the home for Mary to enter the convent. It was all her own idea, conceived and nurtured at Manhattanville. Conceivably it arose from a deep and close relationship with one of the younger Sacred Heart nuns, a woman Mary admired boundlessly, and to whom she still wrote once a week. She had been, among other things, the athletic directoress. Mary had been captain of the hockey team. Beyond doubt, Mary was also influenced by her general distaste for suburban housewifely life as she had observed it in Greenwich. Women, chained to schedules and station wagons, escaping in alcohol, living beyond their means, compelled to claw up the social ladder, pushing their children, taking occasional infidelity for granted, otherwise flailing around on what Mary thought of as "the hollow-laugh circuit." She had seen that in abundance and wanted none of it. Her life, her only life on this earth, must count for more than that.

Unlike her contemporaries, she did not attach herself early in life to one boy. She did not feel that dependence. She played the field, until her junior year at Manhattanville. Then she met a boy with something to him. He was a law student at Fordham, a brilliant, handsome, articulate boy with a limitless future. Mary fell in love with him at once, a dizzy hurricane of delight. The affair ended in a ski chalet in Stratton, Vermont, on a house party. She awoke early—before dawn—feeling gloomy and depressed, for her a rare sensation. Beneath heavy quilts, now fearful, she had clung to his hard, virile body. The evening before, she had not hesitated to bed with him. But now she felt a curious revulsion on top of other dark emotions. She got up quietly, dressed, and left the cabin. They never saw each other again.

That summer, as though doing penance, she joined her nun friend, and others, on a special project in Harlem, teaching little black children to read. It was an experimental project, a forerunner of Head Start and other aid to the deprived. It was not very well organized. They might have done much better. But Mary had never been so happy. Her life now overflowed with meaning and purpose. She knew that she had found her calling. She was a teacher, instinctive, good, inspiring to her students even though she was young, inexperienced, and white. This realization coincided with her growing love of the order, the way of life, the opportunity to be a "wife" of the church. Upon graduation, she entered the convent, suffered its humiliations, took her major vows.

Her first assignment was routine drudgery: right back to Kings Street as a nursery school teacher. Her heart was not in this—not in bringing along the spoiled little children of the affluent of Greenwich and Rye. Nor did she like the atmosphere behind the walls, the pettiness, even childishness of the older nuns, the insistence on pious silence, inward-reeling meditation, the unreality of the monastic little cell where she slept. She fretted. She was bored—until she received permission to attend night classes in Fordham (in company with a prudent companion, another young nun) to work toward a master's degree in philosophy.

The encounter at Fordham drastically altered her life, her outlook. The department of philosophy there, energized by the Vatican Council, was then swerving wildly from traditional theology. She sat in her seat awestruck by what she heard. Almost every line of Scripture, dogma, liturgy came under attack by brilliant, iconoclastic scholars who believed themselves to be "liberated" after years, some for decades, of silence. Tielhard de Chardin (on the Index of Forbidden Books until Pope Paul VI abolished the controversial list) was all the rage. The *National Catholic Reporter*, muckraking in the Chanceries, was the unofficial "Bible." She met "spoiled" priests and "fallen" nuns. Among others, she met a group of cocky young men and women, some former seminarians, all free-thinkers and a trifle rebellious. They were hell-bent to revive the Montessori method of teaching, with the ambitious goal of forcing it upon the parochial school system. They had launched an experimental Montessori school in Greenwich— Whitby—which had been sponsored by a half dozen millionaires. It had become a celebrated experiment. Mary visited there on many occasions. Like others, she became a believer. The conversion led Mary to higher goals, to CU, to her ghetto experiment.

The black children were already present when she entered the classroom. To an outsider, they might have seemed a pathetic lot with their crutches, braces, and harnesses. But Sister Mary no longer saw these outer bindings. What she saw was their spirit: the agonizingly slow progress toward a time when these derelicts could stand independently in the world, able to cope in spite of the physical handicaps. And there *had* been progress. Of that there was not the slightest doubt. It was demonstrated five mornings a week to her, in a hundred different ways: a sudden smile on wrinkled, tortured lips, or a whoop of joy for a small task accomplished, or the sudden, unexpected tug on her skirt from a proud little black hand.

It had not been an easy thing to start the school. Mary had no money, no real reputation as an educator, no facility. But her will found a way. Boldly, she applied to The Office of Economic Opportunity (OEO) for a Head Start grant, stretching her meager experience to the point of fib on the application form. She was lucky. OEO was then beating the bushes for worthy projects. They gave her $15,000. She combed the ghetto looking for a place to put her school. Again, luck. The Chancery, Vicar General Prial, was then on the lookout for a project that would bring credit to the archdiocese for work in the ghetto. Although Mary's operation would be small, Prial was impressed by the OEO grant and the (Mary sensed) potential for publicity that the crippled children offered. It would not cost the Chancery a dime. Mary's school had opened its doors in the fall of the previous year.

There were two mothers in the classroom, supervising the work of the children. They were not trained in Montessori, but were voluntary helpers who collected and delivered the children and gave them milk and cookies during the morning recess. One of these was now supervising one of the children, a spastic, who was sponging a tabletop. The other was standing over two children who were lying on the floor, piecing together a puzzle map of South America. Sister Mary smiled and waved. The mothers returned the greetings; the children, absorbed with this or that apparatus, did not look up from their work.

Sister Mary placed her attaché case on a table near the rear of the room. This was her "office," as she laughingly described it to the many professional educators who came to the school to "observe." She sat at the desk, put on horn-rimmed glasses, opened the attaché case, and removed the papers. They were very important papers, requiring her immediate attention. Her OEO program year was coming to a close. She was submitting an application for a supplementary grant renewal, a very complicated government form, to be filled out in quadruplicate. She had stayed up late the night before, preparing a rough draft of the application on foolscap; now it must be typed on the battered "office" typewriter.

She bent to this task at once, glancing up occasionally to see that the children were being properly cared for. She felt guilty, stealing this hour from them, but the grant renewal was crucial. Without it, there could be no more school. She pecked slowly on the keyboard, now so absorbed that she did not hear the city engineer enter the room. He walked to the rear of the room, hesitating to interrupt, and coughed discreetly.

"Sister Mary?" he said.

She turned in her chair, taking off her glasses.

"Oh, hello, Mr. Knight. Won't you sit down?"

He sat down in a spare chair. He was a black man with enormous hands, belly. He had a gold inlay in a front tooth that glistened.

"You not gonna like what I have to say, Sister Mary," the engineer said.

"Don't tell me," Sister Mary said, hand going to her mouth.

"Yassum. The boss laid into me like all git out this morning. He comes in there, running and screaming, shaking those reports over his head like a tomahawk. He said to me, he says: '*Mr.* Knight, can you see the headlines if that firetrap burned down with all those crippled kids?' I tried to cool him, Sister Mary, but he warn't in a cooling mood. He said this is final. I got to padlock this place, much as I hate to. Today."

"May I talk to him?"

"You can talk to him. But I can tell you it won't do no good. He's made up his mind. And that's that. You couldn't even *pray* him out of it, that's for sure. I know."

Sister Mary could not hold back the trickle of tears. She turned away, flustered, angry. Why was it so difficult to do anything constructive?

"He know the good you doing," the engineer said. "That ain't the point no mo'. He's just plain scared. I'm scared too. We just got to find a new place."

Sister Mary dabbed her eyes with a handkerchief.

"You see these forms I'm filling out?" she said. "This is for an OEO grant renewal for the next program year. I *have* to show them we have adequate housing for the school. Otherwise . . ."

"I know, Sister Mary, you know I can't help it. I got my neck out to here already . . . If I don't put a lock on this place today, it'll get chopped off. That's for sure."

"Give me one week. Just a week more."

The engineer fixed his eyes on the ceiling. Then he looked at the children, with compassion in his dark eyes. He crossed and recrossed his huge legs. Then he looked at his shoe.

"A week you say?"

"One week."

"And you be out for sho?"

"For sure."

"All right. But if anything happens . . ."

"Nothing will happen, Mr. Knight. The Lord will look after us. He'll provide."

"I sure hope so."

"I think we can count on it. Thank you, Mr. Knight. And thanks to your boss for me."

"No, ma'am. I ain't saying nothing to him. Far's he know, it padlocked. Don't you go cross me up, now."

Mr. Knight raised his vast bulk from the chair and said good-bye. He walked toward the main door, eyes fixed on the children, his head nodding affirmatively, as if he were reassuring himself on his decision. Going through the door, Mary observed, he almost collided with Charles Seymour Jones, who seemed to be in a great hurry.

Jones, a young man wearing a dashiki and Afro hairstyle, was a neighbor and a ghetto celebrity of sorts. He directed another OEO youth project, the neighborhood center, next door in the old St. Luke's gym. The gym was not yet condemned. It was stronger, newer than the school building itself. Jones was a student at Howard University who intended, after graduation, to spend his life working with deprived youth. He was a Catholic, a clean-cut boy, up from Mississippi. By some miracle, he had survived a shattering childhood in the Delta, finished high school, and captured an honors scholarship to college.

The local newspapers had seized on him as a good example of what a dedicated nonviolent black could do to help his community. He had led Project Clean, a massive attack on the uncollected garbage and trash in the ghetto streets. Then an equally massive attack on the rats infesting the tenements. OEO considered him a good risk and happily funded the center. His head had not been turned by the publicity, unlike some of his more militant brothers. He had helped keep the uneasy peace in the Washington ghetto, where, thus far, there had been no burning, no riots, no looting, no snipers.

He came through the room toward Mary's desk, a bundle of energy. The impromptu visit would be important, Mary knew. Jones did not ordinarily interrupt her during school hours. After hours, they had had many long, intriguing discussions about Catholicism, black power, the Establishment, discontented youth, campus revolt, the Movement. Jones did not reveal his innermost thoughts, nor did Mary. For all she knew, he might hate her as another do-gooding white liberal, salving a conscience. It did not matter, really. What could she do? She found him interesting and useful. She was learning from him—and what she learned had influenced the direction of her thesis. He was the only black she felt she really knew well.

Midway through the room, Jones stopped. He watched as one of the children poured a beaker of pink-colored water into a small glass, an exercise in dexterity. Then he turned and resumed his rapid pace toward the "office." In his right hand, he carried a sheaf of papers. He saw the look of dismay that still hung on Sister Mary's face.

"The ax?" Jones said, his voice low, cool.

"The ax," Sister Mary said, sighing. "One week from today."

"Uh-uh," Jones grunted. "That's too bad. I hope they don't come round my way."

"You're not a school," Sister Mary said. "You don't fall under these stupid city regulations."

"More black kids die of rat bite than school fires," Jones scowled. "But it don't get the publicity like a school fire. So they don't do anything about the rats. It's politically safe. But a school fire . . ."

"I know, but I've *got* to find a new place. You have any ideas?"

Charles Seymour Jones stood in deep thought, stroking his thin, wispy beard. His dark eyes lit up, white teeth gleamed.

"You could bus 'em out to the white suburbs!"

He exploded with laughter.

"Come on now, Seymour, I'm serious. It's got to be near here. The children can't travel far. No one can afford a taxi."

"Let me think on it, Sister. I'll put it to my boys. Maybe they can come up with something. You need this much space, I suppose? For all that equipment?"

"Yes."

"That's gonna be tough. All this, and for free."

"Yes.

"Maybe we can put the heat on one of those Jew furniture-dealers over on Fourteenth Street. They got these big warehouses."

"No coercion, Seymour. I don't want any rockets landing on the Chancery. I have to finesse them, as it is."

Jones smiled knowingly. He had had his problem with the Chancery, with Prial, who had been reluctant, at first, to let Jones use the gym.

"I know . . . I know . . . all right, I'll get on it," he said. "Now you help me. You know how to con those studs in OEO headquarters. Last month, they say I filled out these CAP 15 forms all wrong. And the month before that. The problem is, those idiots in Grant Accounting keep changing the method of reporting. Now they want reports every month. Look here, they want me to be a CPA or something. Can you make sense of this?"

He laid the governmental forms on the desk. Sister Mary abandoned her own forms to help him fill out his CAP 15. His work was as important as hers. And there was no sense filling out her own forms now, until she found a new home for the school.

It was noon when they finished. The children were ready to go home. Mary and Seymour helped the volunteer mothers lift the children down the steps to the cars. A few of Seymour's "boys" drifted over from the gym to help. Amid the jumble of braces, deformed limbs, casts, leather straps, Mary saw the faces of the children: smiling, grateful, loving. She said to Seymour:

"I *can't* let them down."

Touched, as always, by the sight of the children leaving, Jones said:

"We won't."

Mary returned to her desk, the empty classroom. It was empty but orderly. All the apparatus was properly stored, the little chairs neatly lined at the worktables. Children were born with an innate sense of order. Disorder and mess confused them. This was apparent, even with these children. She took out her thesis, spread it on the desk. She would work for an hour or two in solitude.

The telephone rang. It was an old, heavy black phone. Mary answered.

"Mary? This is Dan."

Her heart skipped and she felt a stab in her stomach. The sensations annoyed her. She fought them away instantly, with a little prayer devised for that purpose. It happened every time he called, which was more and more frequently. It was a dangerous signal, she knew. Except when he called, she would not let herself think about it, or *him*.

She had met Father Daugherty several months before at a small gathering of students and faculty at Monsignor LeGuiese's apartment near CU. Daugherty had come in mufti, a rather elegant sport coat and gray flannel slacks, and she had no idea, at first, that he was a priest. She had felt the ominous sensations first, that day when she met him. She was not blind to the signs. She had felt them before, at Manhattanville, with the law student. She knew from hushed talks with her young nun friend that they were not uncommon. After all, beneath the habits, they were still women, with "all the equipment," as her friend put it. From her, and others, Mary had learned the tricks to overcome these emotions. The quick prayer, the cold shower if the sensation persisted, the deep meditation, the race to the confessor. Mainly, it was willpower. This had to be cultivated in most people, including Mary.

That first day, she had been doubly appalled by her momentary slip when she learned that Daugherty was a priest doing a job in the suburbs that, he revealed immediately by his attitude and words, he hated. A priest and a first-class tennis player (as he informed her, she sensed, to prove he was not a "flit"). Overcompensating for the slip, Mary was determined not to give the impression of being a priest-teaser, in her mind the most odious of women. In fact, she left abruptly after they had exchanged a few words. Later they met there again. This time Mary was better composed. They talked formally and somewhat awkwardly, confining the conversation mainly to the wonders of Professor LeGuiese's mind.

These little meetings of the "cell" (as LeGuiese jokingly termed them) brought them into close contact. Mary learned in some detail about Daugherty's inner conflict, his growing doubts. It was nothing new—or shocking—to her. She had heard it all from other young priests, fellow students, both at Fordham and CU. It was a search for a solution to *his* problem that led Mary to conceive yet another helping-hand project. She proposed that "to help work off steam" and "do something you can feel," he establish (unofficially) a sort of "halfway house" down in the hippie district, a home for wayward teen-age runaways. He could run it in his spare time. He would find it extremely rewarding and meaningful. There was much to be learned from the young. They had got onto something that was truly Christian. For a slipping faith, it was a powerful antidote. She might find time to help him.

So had begun the place with the unimaginative name of "Halfway House." It had gone along very well, very smoothly, for the first six weeks, with Father Daugherty and Sister Mary pitching in on nights and weekends, between other duties. They had scrounged up money to sustain it—five dollars here, five there—on an austere shoestring basis. No one was the wiser until, out of the blue, Marvin Klein of the *Tribune* appeared on the doorstep, notebook in hand. He had given it impressive space under the cliché headline: "Shepherd to the Hippies." The publicity brought more funds, a shower of gold. But it also brought a rocket from the Chancery and a stern lecture from Monsignor Ryan, who disapproved angrily, especially at the photograph of Daugherty in sweater and slacks. Fortunately, Klein had not published a photograph of Mary, who was also wearing slacks. Now Daugherty telephoned every day or so to discuss some detail of the home.

"Dan," Mary said, grateful for someone to share her most pressing problem. "I've been axed. The engineer was here again. This time it's final. We're getting thrown out. In one week. I'm just *sick.*"

"Don't feel down," Daugherty said cheerily. "You were there on borrowed time anyway."

"What am I going to *do?*" she persisted.

"We'll find something. Don't worry about it. As Ryan says, the Lord will provide."

"I think maybe I'll go see the Great Prial. They've gotten enough mileage out of this. Maybe they want me to keep it going."

"Rots of ruck."

"Be serious. This is a . . . a *catastrophe.*"

"I know. I'm thinking . . . maybe Seymour has some ideas."

"I checked him. No vibes."

"Did you ask him about Sunday?"

"Yes. Yesterday. He's working up something from Boyd's book."

"Good. I want this first one to go well."

"Are you sure you're not dragging in a black face just to be . . . so we have our resident black?"

There was a pause, as though Daugherty were seriously weighing the jibe. In fact he was. He had worried about that several times privately. He wanted to be certain of his own feeling, to be brutally honest with himself, because he did not want to be dishonest with Seymour Jones.

"No. He has a good head. I like him. The kids will like him. He plays better than any of them. That will be good for him and for them too. You've got to have that bridge between them, as we said before. Otherwise neither one will ever get anyplace."

"A noble sentiment, and maybe correct. But when I see some of those really *mean* ones, I wonder . . ."

"Anyway. Enough of this. The reason I called, I can't get down tonight. The old Muir gal finally died. She's laid out at Humphrey's. I've got to go stand watch. Do the rosary thing. Big dough involved. Ryan's hoping for a chunk from the will. Thinks it's there. Been working on her personally for a year. But tonight he's got a conflict of interest. Knights of the Holy Eucharist dinner. Maybe *really* big dough. So, will you take care of things?"

She felt a twinge of disappointment. She wanted very much to talk to him face to face, impress him with the urgency of finding new quarters for the school. . . . But why was she becoming so dependent? Why must her problems become his? This was truly dangerous. Anger welled up. She turned it away.

"We don't need you. We'll manage."

"Mary, are you bitter?"

"I'm bitter about my school. That's all."

"I don't blame you. But . . ."

"I'm sorry, Dan. I'm upset. Don't . . . I didn't mean to be owly."

"Say an Act of Love."

"Hope, you mean."

"I've got to run. So long, we'll see you. Sunday?"

"Sunday."

She hung up. Alone in the room, she felt a sudden longing for company, voices, people. She gathered up her papers, stuffed them hurriedly in the attaché case, and drove her car back to CU, back to her dormitory, where she found much comforting feminine company, noise, laughter, and silliness.

VI

Marvin Klein awoke in his bed and reached for a cigarette. He knew better than to smoke before breakfast. But it was the one cigarette of the day that brought him genuine pleasure. He believed it cleared his mind of cobwebs, somehow energized his blood.

His wife, Serena, was a late, deep sleeper. Her back was turned to him, shoulder bare. He leaned over and kissed it. She stirred slightly, pulling the blanket up, as if to keep his lips away. Klein was offended. He thought—fleetingly—that he should wake her and have a candid talk. Of late, it seemed, Serena had been neglecting him, withdrawing into some distant cave. The night before, at a dinner party for the steering committee of the Kennedy Center for the Performing Arts, of which Serena was a tireless member, she had scarcely noticed him. She had been cornered all evening with a famous conductor. Afterward, at' home, she had gone to bed without kissing him good night, falling asleep instantly. Klein, an insomniac, had read late into the night—*The New York Times,* the *New York Review of Books, Ramparts,* and Norman Mailer's latest work, *Armies of the Night,* published almost in its entirety in *Harper's.* These papers and magazines lay scattered on the floor by his bed.

Klein had tried every conceivable aid for sleep. For two years he had taken Seconal, but his system had built up a tolerance to it. When he finally quit, he was taking three pills before going to bed, and two Miltowns on arising, to calm jittery nerves, the Seconal hangover. At the end, he felt as though he were living his waking hours in a haze. He was bombed on two or three shots of Scotch. He was turning into a paranoid. So he gave up Seconal. Better to go sleepless than be poisoned.

Klein was a journalist, like many, by chance. Son of a New York banker, he had attended good private schools (Dalton, Lawrenceville), then Harvard, with the vague intention of going on to medicine. He was a brilliant but unsure student until he met Serena, who, at Radcliffe, had cultivated an interest in writing—American literature. She kindled a like interest in Klein. He won a job as a reporter for the *Harvard Crimson,* became an overnight campus sensation, and, in his senior year, an angry columnist. After graduation, his father financed a year abroad—a year of drifting around to no special purpose— after which, he married Serena. A heart murmur—undetected until then—kept him from military service. He went to Washington, landed a job as a local reporter on the *Washington Post* where, for seven years, he distinguished himself by his solid, perceptive reporting on black problems. Then he moved to the *Tribune*—to larger responsibility and more money.

Klein crawled from his bed and went to the kitchen to make coffee. While waiting for the percolator to rumble, he fetched the *Washington Post* from the doorstep. He read the paper swiftly and with professional admiration. In an era of big-city newspaper failures, the *Washington Post,* like *The New York Times,* had prospered incredibly. Klein attributed that to good reporting, good editing. Management was not miserly with the editorial budget. The *Post* attracted good people, the best young journalists coming out of the good schools. Klein remembered his days as a *Post* reporter fondly. He had learned a good deal there. The city editor had honed his ideas, prodded his social conscience.

He gulped his coffee, shaved and dressed. He did not kiss Serena good-bye. She was still sleeping. She would sleep until noon. Then she would tidy up the house—a townhouse in the new section of southwest Washington, very modern, very stylish. The neighborhood had once been a dingy ghetto. But under an Urban Renewal program, the tenements had been razed, replaced by contemporary "clusters" of townhouses, elegant garden apartments, and twelve-story high-rises. The blacks could not, of course, afford to live in the new dwellings. Displaced, they had moved northward, crowding the already crowded ghetto. Families such as the Kleins, who considered it chic—and convenient—to live in the new section, replaced them.

There were some inconveniences, to be sure. Being so close to the ghetto, it was not safe to go out at night. Many of the homes and apartments had been burglarized so often that all had elaborate electronic security devices. Roving gangs of young black boys had ripped off the padlocked rear gate of the Kleins' patio and slashed the tires on a visitor's car parked out front. Serena had suggested that they buy a gun for self-protection. But to Klein, who had crusaded shrilly for the gun-control law and bitterly resented the watered-down version voted out by the Congress, it was unthinkable that he would now buy a gun and keep it in his house.

Klein drove a Jaguar. It was pasted with McCarthy stickers and had an artificial red carnation (Serena's touch) wired to the radio antenna. It was also equipped with stereo tape. The car was a luxury, an indulgence, like the Calder mobile in the living room. They had bought both when Klein got his new job with the *Tribune,* and the raise to twenty thousand.

Driving up through the ghetto, the filthy streets, toward the Tribune Building, Klein thought again about the dinner party the night before. It had been an elegant affair in a Watergate penthouse with a stunning view of the steel-cold Potomac. The people had been mostly the phony hangers-on from the days of the New Frontier, the super-rich with no power, little hope of regaining power unless Bobby made it, clinging to the Kennedy Center as though there were nothing else in life. There had been much anti-Johnson, anti-McCarthy, anti-Wallace, anti-Nixon talk—a few funny jokes well told—but no *positive* talk. They were people without a clear-cut purpose, a vapid, unhappy group, like exiled royalty in a foreign capital. Time and circumstances were passing them by. Or so thought Klein.

He came to the Tribune Building, an old brick structure, with a modern façade, on upper Thirteenth Street, the edge of the ghetto. He swung into the lot, parked in the space reserved for *Tribune* editorial. He waved good morning to the armed guard—on duty to prevent addicts from breaking into the cars—and hurried to the building, the elevator, the city room, his desk. It was not yet seven o'clock when he reached it. But the city room was already coming to life. Klein hung up his coat, sat at his desk, scanned the wire service overnights, his mind now firmly fixed on a vision of the front page. In a few hours it would be reality. It would be on the newsstands, in the homes, on important Washington desks. There was a deadly sameness in the overnights: small-scale action in the war; an update on the trial of the draft-card burners in Baltimore; another student riot at Berkeley; a Coast Guard rescue; the ponderous pontifical backgrounders from foreign capitals; a few lifeless, inconsequential crime pieces; routine reports from the campaigners. Nothing yet to provide a good lead; a bold, eight-column banner headline that would move papers off the stands. If it did not come by deadline, Klein would resort to ingenuity. He was famous for that; pulling the eleventh-hour rabbit out of his hat—an armed robbery or a shooting or some other act of violence. Around the city room, it was known as "Klein luck."

The *Washington Tribune* was an afternoon paper. In times past, it had been rich, powerful, conservative in outlook, a family enterprise. In the 1950s the *Tribune,* like many big-city afternoon papers, faltered. Circulation fell, advertising revenues declined, while the cost of labor, newsprint, and distribution climbed steadily. In 1967, when the paper was awash in red ink, the family sold controlling interest to a New York syndicate. The syndicate brought in seed money, editorial talent, and a fresh, liberal point of view, a cheaper tabloid format. Klein was a key figure in the transfusion. Hired away to be the *Tribune's* new managing editor—top editorial boss—Klein had angled the paper toward the black community. The *Tribune* became, in a sense, the voice and conscience of the ghetto, the deprived. It had profited somewhat from this change in editorial policy. Circulation rose, the drop in advertising linage decreased. The paper had been saved from certain death. Klein was justifiably proud of the role he had played in the rescue. It had brought him power and independence in the management group.

That day there was a note impaled on the spindle of Klein's desk:

LUNCH: VICAR GENERAL PRIAL, CHANCERY. 1:00 P.M.

The Vicar General had telephoned the week before, gracious, unctuous. He had told Klein that he wanted to talk about a subject of "great interest" to the paper, a "good story." Klein did not usually go out for lunch. He ate a roast beef sandwich on poppyseed roll at his desk, washing it down with a bottle of Heineken's. But, in this instance, he had made an exception. His nose for news had long since turned toward the Catholic Church. The dissident winds stirring there appealed to his crusading spirit. If a Catholic revolution swept Washington, he wanted to be on top of it, the *Tribune* first to break the story. He read assiduously. He followed the proceedings of the Vatican Council. He went out of his way to cultivate brilliant, young, outspoken priests, such as Father Daniel Daugherty of All Saints', with whom he regularly played tennis. He publicized Catholic-sponsored projects, such as Sister Mary's Montessori school, Daugherty's Halfway House for hippies.

After the paper was bedded down and assignments were made for the day, Klein left the city room, took a cab to the Chancery. There, a maid promptly escorted him to the library, where Vicar General Prial and two assistants, both young priests, specialists in personnel and finance, were waiting. The younger priests sipped martinis. The Vicar General was friendly, congenial. He offered Klein a martini. A maid served hors d'oeuvres on a silver tray.

It was Klein's first visit to the Chancery. Until now, it had been a distant, mysterious place, a seat of power, a bastion of tradition from which emanated incredibly dull press handouts for the Saturday religion page. One surprise came atop the next. First, Prial. On the telephone, Klein had formed an image of a fat, dull, white-haired Irishman. Now here was Prial, looking more like a pro football-player than a priest. Very trim, big-shouldered, ham-handed, congenial. Klein had not expected to have company, the younger priests, who seemed, in spite of the formality of the room, easygoing and unimpressed by rank. Then the drinking. Klein had simply assumed alcohol was off limits in the Chancery, as it was on naval vessels.

The Vicar General may have appeared congenial, but inwardly he was edgy. For one thing, he did not like Klein, or any Jew. In the new spirit of ecumenism, he made a fawning pretense of cordiality when, because of his position, he encountered a Jew. But for all the new pretense, Prial was basically shanty Irish, a product of the streets of Brooklyn. He could not erase from his mind what had been pounded into it in the old days by the nuns at his parochial school, by his mother and father, and by Spellman and the others at 452 Madison Avenue. The Jews crucified Christ. He knew nothing of Klein's religious beliefs, if he had any. To Prial, Jews were Jews. Their interminable, often incomprehensible religious schisms and squabbles had, over the years, baffled him, when he bothered to take note. Jews were not Christians, so it was all irrelevant—a tempest in a teapot—anyway. Basically, Prial felt, to court a Jew was tantamount to courting the Devil. Also, Prial was disconcerted by Klein's appearance. He seemed much too young for so large a job. He was small of stature, mousy, and his posture was poor.

He swallowed his pride in the name of Archbishop McInnerney and the Church. The luncheon had been carefully staged and then rehearsed under direction of the impending fund drive PR consultant, a Catholic adman who said he could "get to" Klein. If there was to be opposition, the Vicar General knew, it would most likely originate, at least solidify, in the editorial rooms of the *Tribune.* The *Washington Post* and *Evening Star,* and their television and radio affiliates, would cooperate with the Chancery, as they always had over the years, he was sure. But the *Tribune* was unpredictable, a strident upstart which could, if so motivated, seriously impair the fund drive. To curry favor with the paper and Klein, to lure both into the fold, the PR man had proposed that the Vicar General "break" the story of the center and the fund drive in the *Tribune*—give Klein an exclusive. There was a calculated risk involved. The *Post* and *Star* might be miffed. But the PR man reasoned that the larger papers were also larger in spirit, that they would soon forgive and forget and provide support in spite of being "scooped."

The stage had been carefully set. Not merely the props—the graceful renderings—but the actors and their lines. The Vicar General had picked the two priests for the lunch because they projected an image of youth, vitality, and change. Even the anti-Catholic joke the one priest told had been suggested by the PR man. Now, as the four men sat at the table, the Vicar General took the floor and moved straight to his set-piece.

"Mr. Klein," he began, smiling, cupping his hands apart, as he had in the old days in a pulpit, "the archdiocese—Archbishop McInnerney —has for some time had under study a proposal to build, on the campus of Catholic University, not far from the Shrine of the Immaculate Conception, a new theological center, which, when finished, will probably constitute the most up-to-date center of theological study in the world. As you are well aware, Washington is the geopolitical center of the Western world, in some respects the financial center, certainly the sociological and scientific center, and the military center. The Archbishop thought that it should be the theological center as well. It will bring to the community, this intellectual, political community, a new level of religious sophistication, and of course, income . . ."

The purpose of the lunch, not even hinted at heretofore, was now clear. Klein's reportorial instinct put him on guard. If the Chancery were unveiling a thing of this scope, where were the other reporters and editors? Why had Klein been singled out for this lavish personal pitch? What lay beneath this carefully staged occasion, the Chancery's obvious need to get him in their corner? He felt immediately that he was being conned, that somewhere, deep in the Chancery, there was more to it, much more. And for some reason, he felt himself leaping to a negative position about the center. Was that his "automatic response," going against anything proposed by the Establishment, about which Serena nagged him relentlessly? He wished now that he had not accepted the invitation. He felt that his presence in the lair of the Establishment was somehow a betrayal to his readers. But he *must* keep an open mind. . . .

"Income how?" Klein broke in. He was tempted to add: "Through the sale of indulgences?" but thought better of it.

The Vicar General, not expecting interruption, struggled to conceal his annoyance.

"Staff salaries and so on," he said.

"How big a staff?" Klein said.

"I was coming to that," the Vicar General said. "Perhaps fifty to seventy on the teaching staff, another fifty or hundred research assistants, secretaries, clerks, librarians and so on . . . a major installation."

"How much will it cost?" Klein forked a piece of thick rare beef offered by a maid.

"Twenty million," the Vicar General said, now abandoning his carefully structured set-piece. The young priests looked on.

"Where will you get that kind of money?" Klein asked.

"A special fund drive," the Vicar General replied. "For which we would like your support. Your paper's support."

Klein ate rapidly, although he was not hungry. The ceremony of the luncheon or dinner table bored him. Food was merely a means of acquiring energy, recharging his batteries. He reached now, back into his memory, the memory of a good journalist, a good editor.

"Whatever hapened to that drive in 1964?" he said. "For the—what was it?"

"A retirement home for aged priests," the Vicar General said. "It—the goal—was not reached. Primarily, I think, because we were babes in the wood in the areas of promotion and publicity. This time we hope to do better. Frankly, that's why we invited you here."

"The old priests' home was never built?" Klein said.

"It was deferred."

"What happened to the money you raised?"

The Vicar General felt the blood rising in his temples. He held his fork firmly.

"It was diverted to other useful works," he said. "Charity. We have no end of work to be done."

"If this drive fails, then what will become of the money?" Klein asked.

"It won't fail," the Vicar General said unhesitatingly. "Because I won't let it fail. A home for aged priests is one thing. The center is another. We consider it—Cardinal Spellman considered it—the most important single new Catholic institution in America."

"I see," Klein said. "But I wonder if it's . . . proper to raise money for one purpose and divert it to another?"

The Vicar General laid his fork on his plate, fighting to control his anger.

"It couldn't be helped," he said. "That last project has only been deferred anyway. This time, too, we're better organized. There is a reserve, a contingency fund available to see the center through."

"How much?"

"I'm not at liberty to say at this time."

"Why not? Off the record?"

"The archdiocesan fund—all funds—by tradition are not made public."

"I don't agree with that policy," Klein said. "If you solicit funds from the public, employing public media, then there ought to be public disclosure."

The Vicar General pushed his plate aside, wiped his mouth with a large, pure-white linen napkin. He was immensely put out that the talk had strayed so far from *his* point. He had not meant to get into a policy discussion of the See's most sensitive secrets.

"We are not, after all, a fly-by-night outfit," he said icily.

"I didn't imply that you were." Klein said. "But it seems to me—the more I think about it—you have a public responsibility, a fiscal responsibility."

"You are not equating us with the state?" the Vicar General smiled acidly. "Judging by your editorials on aid to parochial schools, I'd have guessed you stood quite firmly for separation of church and state."

"You're lapsing into sophistry," Klein smiled back. "If I didn't know otherwise, I might take you for a Jesuit."

The two younger priests chuckled nervously.

"A compliment, I assure you," the Vicar General said. "But, to get back to the center, let me tell you more about the philosophical goals . . ."

The Vicar General now resumed his set-piece, painting a picture of the center as an intellectual breeding ground, like Princeton's Institute for Advanced Study, with renowned theologians and philosophers in residence, the Catholic intellectual elite of the nation, drawn there by their peers to study and contemplate. He stressed the ecumenical

design; the fact that Jews, Protestants, Hindus—anybody qualified intellectually—would be welcome to work side by side with the Catholics.
The briefing for Klein differed from the briefing for the financial council in only one important detail. The Vicar General did not say, or
even hint, that the center might become a bastion of conservatism, the
theological ramparts from which the counterreformation would be
launched. Nor did he tell Klein that the sale of St. Luke's Cathedral to
IDA would back-stop the drive. When he finished his briefing, Klein
was silent. He wolfed down his baked Alaska, sipped hot coffee. Then
he said:

"I suppose a project of this magnitude would drain all other archdiocesan projects of funding?"

"Oh no," the Vicar General said. "On the contrary. It will be business as usual. More schools, more hospitals, more seminaries. Especially
schools. We'll keep pace with the requirements that have been projected. This is over and above our normal construction activity. The
way we've laid it on, we definitely will not rob Peter to pay Paul, so
to speak."

"Including ghetto projects?"

"Yes. *Least* of all ghetto projects."

"How many ongoing ghetto projects do you have?" Klein said.

The Vicar General offered a cigar to Klein, who refused. The Vicar
General pressed.

"Cuban," he said. "Very hard to come by."

"Thanks, no," Klein said. "How many . . . ?"

"I don't save the figures offhand, the inventory of projects."

Klein lit a cigarette. The figures, he knew, were slim, insignificant.
The major archdiocesan effort was directed away from the city, the
ghetto, toward the suburbs.

"What about projects like Father Daugherty's and Sister Murray's?"
Klein said. "Will they continue to receive support?"

The Vicar General shifted in his chair.

"Neither of those are official archdiocesan programs," he said. "And
are not apt to be. They are OEO and privately funded, as you probably know. If they remain so, then so much the better. The more we
can do in the private sector, the better."

"Both excellent," Klein said. "And deserving of support. That's the
kind of missionary work we need in the ghetto. Shirt-sleeve stuff
. . . not lofty pronouncements."

"They get enough publicity," the Vicar General said, his meaning clear. Much of the publicity had originated in the *Tribune,* and spread from there to other newspapers, other media.

"They deserve all they can get," Klein said. "It's a realistic type of thing."

"Yes," the Vicar General said, without conviction. In truth, he thought of the two projects strictly in terms of publicity. He knew Father Daugherty and Sister Mary only casually. They were both young and, in his opinion, publicity hounds. It annoyed him that Klein had broached the two projects. The Catholic Church, the archdiocese, was more—far more—than Father Daugherty and Sister Mary. He directed the talk back to the center.

"I'll have somebody look into it," Klein said. "But I can't promise anything. I'll let my reporter call his shots the way he sees them."

"All we ask is an objective approach," the Vicar General said, regretting his words instantly.

"What is objectivity?" Klein said, smiling.

"All right," the Vicar General said. "A break. Frankly, we need your support."

"But you won't make public disclosures of the archdiocesan financial picture?" Klein said.

"I'll speak to the Archbishop," the Vicar General said. "But I can't make any promises."

"Neither can I," Klein said.

The Vicar General escorted Klein to the front door of the Chancery. There he called for the Chancery limousine, a new black Cadillac. But Klein declined politely. He returned to his office in a cab, carrying a manila envelope full of fact sheets, architectural renderings, and a press release about the center. He gave these to a young reporter and returned to his desk. He picked up the telephone and said to the operator:

"Get me Father Daugherty at All Saints'."

VII

Father Daugherty hurried from the rectory to the church, cutting between cars on the parking lot, jammed for eleven o'clock Mass. This
was the Pastor's Mass, the ceremonial high-point of the week at All
Saints'. Everything must be just so. The service would begin precisely
on the dot. Ryan had a thing about punctuality, one of his many
eccentricities. The front doors of the church were to be locked (violating fire regulations) at precisely the instant Ryan walked from the
sacristy; the congregation then rose for the beginning of the service. It
was Daugherty's job, one of many small, supporting chores during
the service, to slam home the bolt, to bar the late-comers, whatever
their excuse.

He took up his post just inside the foyer, trembling from the cold,
eye on the sacristy door. Now it was time. His hand went to the bolt.
Through the small stained-glass window in the door, he saw a family
rushing up the steps—the Donovans, substantial parishioners, never
late before. Daugherty's hand paused on the bolt. To lock or not to
lock? The usual tardy teen-agers, perhaps. But he could not shut out
the Donovans, even though he knew it meant a stern rebuke later. He
stepped aside. The Donovans bustled through, glancing guiltily at
Daugherty, thanking him with their eyes. Down the aisle, at the altar,
suitably austere for Lent, Monsignor Ryan, wearing plain purple vestments, observed this infraction, leaving Daugherty with a sinking sensation in his stomach.

The organ thundered. The Mass was on. Daugherty walked down a
side aisle, toward the sacristy. Along the way, he passed the custodian,
Scafidi, withdrawn into the baptismal alcove, sitting on a folding chair,
black eyes avoiding Daugherty, fixed fiercely on Ryan. Daugherty
nodded perfunctorily, observing the man's clothes. He was not wearing
Daugherty's old coat, but the same old, thin, olive-drab one. Had Mrs.
Munally passed his coat along? Queer man. Some kind of nut, a recluse.

He continued on, head held reverently down. He saw the Favrots in the second-row pew, Bob and Jean and seven of the children, including the baby. All the boys had close-cut hair, including Paul and Bob, who were on the altar, serving. The psychologist, Alan Cantor, a good man, had telephoned. He had enrolled Jean in a group therapy session, a good first step. There were many frustrated housewives in the parish, like her, Father Daugherty thought. And this thought brought a pang of guilt. But, other than murky double talk from the confessional, what could he do for them?

Jean seemed composed now, holding the baby, following Ryan with her eyes. Bob Favrot thumbed his missal. He looked as though he had a hangover.

Daugherty sat on a wooden bench along a wall in the sacristy. He watched Ryan through the sacristy door leading to the altar. The altar faced the congregation. Ryan had been opposed to that. What a tempest in a teapot! That and the Mass in English! He had bucked it straight up to the Chancery. But Prial had overruled him. All Saints' must be, outwardly at least, right up to date.

Ryan was never in a rush on the altar. He recited his prayers with deliberate cadence. He read every item in the bulletin, even though the bulletins were distributed to one and all and, Daugherty was sure, all in this parish could read. His sermons, laboriously drafted during Saturday, were insufferably dull, an insult to the unusually high intelligence level of the congregation, strictly old school homilies, delivered (despite the stereo) in a mumbling, numbing voice which invariably put Bob Favrot and other male parishioners sound asleep. Communion, too, was agonizingly slow. His prayers after Mass droned on and on.

Archbishop McInnerney had appointed Monsignor Ryan to his post at All Saints' for two reasons. First, All Saints' was new—a plum. The men were old friends, contemporaries, one-time classmates in a Boston parochial school, later in the seminary. Beyond that, Monsignor Ryan had, over the years, earned a reputation as a canny fund-raiser. By any yardstick, All Saints' had been a costly venture. The mortgage —in the Archbishop's name—was not an insignificant debit on the archdiocese balance sheet. The Chancery could depend on Monsignor Ryan to meet the mortgage payments, to tithe his parishioners without a troubled conscience, to contribute handsomely to the Chancery, to Rome, to the central Catholic high school, the athletic fund, Catholic charities, and numerous other worthy projects. In the words of the

Vicar General, All Saints' must be a "profit center," an affluent parish, to help subsidize the less profitable parishes.

Monsignor Ryan, in spite of his age, had thus far given the Chancery no reason to doubt its choice. He kept meticulous books. His checks left the rectory promptly. His parish census was a continuing wonder, a card-file system that would make the FBI envious. His weekly bulletin was studded with slogans and copybook maxims ("A penny saved is a penny earned"—"waste not, want not") designed to stimulate the flow of cash and envelopes to the collection plate. His weekly Sunday sermons were, at bottom, frank appeals for money, usually launched on a lugubrious note, like a television commercial. He discouraged visiting missionaries, with their hypnotic snake-and-lion stories, their cunning ways of siphoning off the parish cash flow.

After the sermon, Daugherty left the sacristy to oversee the collection, another of his small chores. As the ushers came forward with their baskets, Daugherty walked to the rear of the church, to stand beside the sexton. He felt awkward here, as though he were a bank guard or a gimlet-eyed examiner. Every Sunday, they followed the same routine. The ushers came up the aisle, dumped the returns in a white canvas bag held by the sexton. The sexton snugged up the drawstrings of the bag, gravely handed it to Daugherty. Father Daugherty carried the bag down the side aisle to the sacristy. There, he closed the door leading to the side aisle. Then he put the bag in a wall safe, hidden behind a portrait of Jesus. The safe had been Ryan's idea, a way to thwart the robbery he was certain would come.

After that, Father Daugherty helped with Communion. He distributed on the left side of the rail, Ryan on the right. The lines were long, as they usually were during Lent. Bob Favrot and the children came to Daugherty's side, turned out in Sunday best. Jean remained in her pew, perhaps to hold the baby. When Daugherty saw the inside of Bob's mouth, smelled his stale breath, he was sure he had a hangover, an epic one. Although Scafidi was sitting on Daugherty's side of the church, he took the longer route, down the side aisle to Ryan's side of the rail. The housekeeper, Mrs. Munally who, like Scafidi, never failed to appear at eleven o'clock Mass, also went to Ryan.

After Mass, Father Daugherty collected money from the poor boxes and the coin receptacles under the book and magazine rack in the foyer and beneath the banks of offertory candles. This, too, he placed in the safe, in a separate bag. Later in the afternoon, Monsignor Ryan would return to slide home the pick-resistant locks on the doors, and spend the rest of the day and evening counting and sorting the money, placing the coins by denomination in brown rolls, and the bills in stacks of one hundred dollars, held snug by a rubber band. He would log the donations in the envelopes, by name or number, in a ledger which was also kept in the safe. Any donor who fell short of his tithe would receive a handwritten note from Monsignor Ryan no later than Wednesday. The whole thing was a marvel of efficiency.

There was little communication between Father Daugherty and his pastor. They had lived in comfortable circumstance in the new parish rectory for two years. But they rarely spoke, other than to exchange perfunctory greetings. Father Daugherty's duties had been spelled out in writing by Monsignor Ryan. They were the simple routine of a curate. At All Saints', Daugherty felt he was not a priest but a glorified messenger, or a junior bank teller, a lowly cog in a vast financial machine.

A visiting priest (not a missionary) said the twelve-thirty "Drunkard's Mass," with Daugherty assisting. After that, Daugherty returned to the rectory to snatch a bite to eat. Then back to the church, the baptismal font, to baptize four babies. From the young fathers, Daugherty received four envelopes, each containing a ten-dollar bill. In any other parish, these donations would be Daugherty's, along with his hundred dollars a month salary. But at All Saints', baptismal donations went directly into the safe. When the young people were gone, the church was empty, Daugherty put the envelopes in the safe.

Now came the awkward moment, the time to run from this fleecing machine, as he thought of it, for a few hours. Go to the one place where he felt spiritually at home, and needed, Halfway House, his home for wayward hippies. Monsignor Ryan objected to his work there more than to his tennis. He was needed at the parish, Ryan said, God knows, shorthanded as they were. Ryan simply did not understand that, to Daugherty, Halfway House was vital, absolutely *essential* to his spiritual life, as tennis was to his physical life.

Fearing Ryan might call upon him for additional chores, Daugherty did not return to the rectory to change clothes. Still wearing his cassock, he went directly from the church to his car, a battered black MG—his own property!—parked behind the church, away from the rectory. He climbed in, feeling the cold of the leather seat through his trousers.

The battery was low. Father Daugherty turned the ignition key, biting his lip, hoping there was spark enough to turn the motor. Then it caught—a throaty rumble. The muffler was shot. He put the car in gear, backed swiftly, then turned and sped out to the driveway, fast. He felt, then, the release; once again he had escaped. He raised his eyes toward a heaven beyond the rotting canvas roof, and spoke aloud:

"God have mercy on his miserly soul. Forgive me, Lord. I don't understand. Open my eyes. Please give me *strength*."

He drove fast, skillfully, down Massachusetts Avenue, south, toward New Hampshire, angling off DuPont Circle. Then he was there, parked between two derelict cars across from the house. It was an old brownstone, once elegant, now shabby, like the neighborhood.

Daugherty took off his Roman collar, his cassock, and pulled on a maroon turtleneck. Discarding the clerical garb gave a sudden lift to his spirit. He felt natural, a man in the world, with high purpose, a true calling. He strolled casually up the sidewalk, joy flooding his soul. A blue and white police car cruised slowly by. Father Daugherty waved. The policemen returning his greeting.

He bounded up the steps into the foyer, the living room. It was crowded with young people in strange clothing: Mexican serapes, camouflaged ponchos, Mexican blankets, an odd assortment of boots, sandals, huaraches, tight trousers, bell-bottoms, strange blouses, pendants, beads, leather belts, pouches, knapsacks. The boys wore beards and grannie glasses, the girls, saucerlike tinted sunglasses. They all had long hair. They were arranged about the room as though attending a quiet party. Some were standing, talking. Others were relaxed in the seedy overstuffed chairs and couches. Some were watching the television set in the bay window in the rear. There was a gentle air about them. Father Daugherty thought of them as innocent lambs. His job, his calling, was to prevent their psychic slaughter. Or to heal the wounds of those he had not caught in time.

Some of them lived in the half-dozen bedrooms on the two upper floors; others came from sleazy flophouses along the street. Many of the boys and girls shared the same bed, like husband and wife. When Sister Mary had first conceived the idea of Halfway House, and Father Daugherty had rounded up his first dozen recruits, he had been shocked by their life-style, their habits, their philosophy, the deep-seated bitterness toward society, their parents, and religion. But now he took all these in his stride. He had reached—or was reaching—their souls and that was what mattered to him most.

One of the young girls turned, saw him standing alone, near the doorway. She beamed and cried:

"The guru!"

The boys and girls in the room turned to greet him. Those on the floor stood up, pressed forward. They reached to touch him, communicating in the touch warmth and love, a strange gentleness. Father Daugherty laughed, feeling exhilaration from the touch.

"God bless all," he said, remembering Christ's words: The meek shall inherit the earth. And he saw the faces before him, his lambs, in that incongruous role: the great hope for the world, for society, a fresh wind of sincerity, of dedication to the ideals of humility and love. Truly, he thought, they had been born in the spirit of the Saviour.

One of the girls came up to Father Daugherty, leading a stranger by the hand. The stranger was a young girl, perhaps sixteen or seventeen, with long blond hair, a turned-up nose, very pretty and winsome. But her brown eyes were hollow with despair. Her name was Sharon. She had arrived, out of the blue, the day before, a displaced soul, a runaway. Father Daugherty led her from the room to the "office," a cubbyhole off the main hall. He closed the door.

"Things can't be that bad," he said cheerily, offering her the chair opposite his. "Cigarette?"

She accepted, smoking with a pretense of sophistication, yet self-consciously. She wore a miniskirted, low-belted dress, loafers—all expensive.

"It's pretty bad," she said. Her voice was hollow like her eyes.

"Tell me about it."

"I don't want to talk about it."

"Well, there's no need," Daugherty said. "Have they fixed you up? Do you have a place to sleep?"

The girl broke into tears. She crushed the cigarette in the ashtray and buried her face in her hands. Daugherty got up, put his hand on her shoulder.

"It would be better if you thought you could talk to me."

"I'm *pregnant!*" she blurted between sobs.

"Well now," Daugherty said thoughtfully. "That's a start, anyway, Sharon. How do you know?"

The girl looked up in amazement, tears streaming down her cheeks.

"How far along, I mean?" Daugherty hastened.

"Three months."

Daugherty sat down again.

"My mother threw me out," Sharon said.

The story now gushed forth between gasping sobs, the too-familiar tale of the paradisiacal suburbs. Sharon's father was a builder—$50,000 subdivisions. He drank heavily, seldom came home, was probably having an affair with his secretary. Her mother, a nut about horses, also drank heavily and was probably having an affair with a friend of her father's. The house in Potomac, a horsey suburb, was chaotic. Mother and father fighting, throwing things, Sharon the helpless target of much of the rage. Desperately seeking escape, love, and affection, someone to share the burden, Sharon had taken up with a boy, Peter, a public high-school senior. They had made love—in her own bed-room, her bed. She loved him. No, she had not taken precautions. Three nights before, her mother had come home unexpectedly early. She found them in the bedroom.

"She blew her mind," Sharon said simply.

"Yes," Daugherty said.

"She was juiced," Sharon rushed on, voice edging on despair. "She went screaming downstairs, out of her mind, and into the Caddy and tore down the drive—zow!—straight into the ditch, across the road, into the other ditch, up through the white rail fence. Totaled the car. We don't know where she was going. I don't think she did either. She came back to the house all bloody and we drove her to Suburban Hos-pital. Broken nose."

"Go on."

"After she sobered up, she said I had disgraced her and the family and ruined my own reputation and my life, that I was a slut and all that. Then Dad came home and they talked in the library and he was . . . he got juiced and then she got juiced again and they had a tremendous fight, both accusing each other . . . it was awful and un-believable . . . and then he blamed her for what I did and so on and called *her* a slut. He staggered out and said—screamed at me—'you've destroyed all of us,' and went off. I haven't seen him since. When Mother sobered up the next day, she asked me if I had . . . if I had . . . you know, missed my period, and when I said yes, she passed out. Cold. When I saw her again she was like out of her mind, you know, and telephoning people to find somebody to abort me and finally she said I was going to Sweden—right then. I told her I *wasn't* going to Sweden and I wanted to have Peter's baby. So . . . she . . . she slapped me and screamed, saying: 'Get out! Get out!' She said I was crazy. So I left. Peter drove me here."

She stopped talking then. Her eyes were dry. She was composed.

"Well, Sharon," Daugherty said, choosing his words. "You're not crazy. What you did was . . . well, I wouldn't recommend it, so to speak, but you did it because you were driven to it. You understand that? Now, the sin is not yours. Not all of it. I don't want you to feel any guilt whatsoever. We all . . . God knows . . . we all have our moments . . . our lapses. You understand that?"

"Yes."

"No guilt what-so-ever?"

"Father, I'm really not sorry I made love to Peter."

"Don't call me Father. Just Dan. OK?"

She nodded.

"Are you a Catholic?"

"I was. I stopped . . . gave it up when we . . . I mean, I couldn't go to confession. I *couldn't.*"

"Of course. But you understand now, that if you choose to call it that, you've just been to confession?"

"I *have?* But . . . I'm not *sorry.* About Peter . . ."

"Do you love God?"

"Yes."

"That's all that counts, Sharon. You love Him. He loves you. Now, we don't give penance here, in the usual sense. All we ask is that you make a real effort to straighten up and fly right. I don't mean you have to be sanctimonious or any of that. We just ask that you make a *real* effort to become a useful person. Is that clear?"

"Yes. I *want* to try."

"Not try, Sharon. We need more than that."

"Yes. I *will* do something."

"That's the spirit. Now, you know, legally they can't throw you out of your own home. You . . ."

"I don't care! I don't *want* to go back. Not ever. I *hate* her!"

"Of course. But, Sharon, you shouldn't hate . . . later, perhaps you'll see it differently. We must all learn to forgive our parents. You may not understand that now. I don't expect you to. But you'll see. Where do you—did—you go to school?"

"Sacred Heart—Stone Ridge."

"Did you get good grades?"

"Up to midterm. Then everything went to . . . I let it go. I didn't care."

"Sports?"

"Basketball."

"Do you use drugs?"

"No."

"Ever?"

"I tried grass. You know. I didn't like it. It made me sick."

"Does Peter?"

"Yes."

"Which?"

"Grass. He's tried . . . mescaline . . . speed."

"Did they tell you the rule here?"

"Yes. No drugs on the premises."

"And for you, no wine. No alcohol. Not until you're eighteen. We can't afford to get busted."

"I understand. I don't want grass. It might hurt the baby."

"Now, Sharon," Daugherty nodded. He said. "You understand I'll have to call your parents. That's our policy. We have to do it to keep peace with the fuzz. Don't worry about it. I know what to say. You won't have to go back if you don't want to. You just make yourself at home. Have you met Mary Murray?"

"Yes."

"Did she give you an assignment?"

"Yes, the kitchen."

"You don't feel down now, do you?"

"Not now. Not anymore."

"And you're going to . . . ?"

"Make a useful person of myself."

"Some day next week, I'd like to meet Peter. Some evening when I'm down here. Can you arrange that?"

"Sure."

"How old is he?"

"Eighteen."

"Will he graduate?"

"Yes."

"All right, Sharon. You strike me as a very sensible, mature girl. I like you. I think you're going to be a real asset around here."

"Thank you." She smiled. Her brown eyes glistened, a film of tears, but not tears of sorrow.

"How *about* that?" Daugherty said, smiling back. "What do you think of *that* lecture?"

"Groovy!" she exclaimed. "Beautiful."

"Good. Now let's go see what everybody's up to. We're going to have a little . . . an unorthodox-type Mass around here. Maybe you can lend a hand."

"Good. I'd like to, if I can."

"You can."

Daugherty walked down the hall to the kitchen. Sharon came behind, head high, spirits climbing. Daugherty was not worried about Sharon's future. Her self-esteem was not shattered. It had been temporarily bent. But with a little gentle massaging, with small achievements, with love, it would snap back. In a few weeks or months, she would be good as new. He would have to do something about the baby. That would be difficult, but not impossible. Later he would call her parents. They would be tough, perhaps intractable, certainly hostile. By now Daugherty had faced angry parents many times. He could be tough, too.

Mary Murray was in the kitchen. She wore white corduroy slacks, a green velveteen turtleneck, ballet slippers, pale makeup, silky black hair held by a band on her forehead. She looked not much older, or wiser, than the girls in the living room. She was standing at the sink, washing coffee cups, humming to herself, absorbed in her work. Daugherty observed the small, delicate curve of her back, the pale, exquisite nape of her neck, with a sudden, alarming stab of desire. It was a fleeting, almost microscopic sensation, yet the impact rocked him. He clenched his fists, bit the tip of his tongue hard. In Latin, he said silently: "Jesus, Mary, Joseph, pray for me."

Sensing his presence, Mary turned.

"Dan! Hi, Sharon."

She had turned in time to see the look in his eyes. Across the gap between them, unspoken, a communication made its way, uncertain, tentative, irresolute.

"Hi, Mary," Dan said, forcing cheer. "You know our latest volunteer, Sharon?"

"Oh yes," Mary said, drying her hands on a paper towel.

"We had a little chat," Daugherty said. "She's a very fine person. She's going to be very good for everybody."

"I know," Mary said smiling at Sharon. "And she can start right now. Here, love, will you finish these cups?"

Sharon came to the sink eagerly. Dan and Mary sat on battered chairs at the kitchen table.

"Did you bring Seymour?" Dan said.

"He's in the living room."

"Good."

He jabbed his finger toward Sharon surrepetitiously.

"No sweat."

"*Very* sweet," Mary said, lowering her voice to a confidential tone.

"Oh, I forgot. Did you find a place for the school?"

Mary's eyes clouded. The problem had been set aside momentarily.

"No, damnit."

"Did you go to the Chancery?"

"Not yet. I have an appointment for tomorrow."

"You may be right," Dan said. "They might want to keep it going for the PR value. I haven't had a single idea. You could always go to see Marv Klein."

"Court of last resort," she said. "I don't want to use him unless I really have to. He's already been so nice . . ."

"He's always looking for a story."

"That's true," she said. "But let's see what Prial comes up with."

"Speaking of Klein," Daugherty said, snapping his fingers. "I almost forgot. He called the other day. *He'd* been to the Chancery. Seems there's another fund drive being cranked up. Chancery deal. For a pretty nebulous thing. Some kind of theological center at CU. Have you heard about that?"

"Not a word. A *theological* center?"

"Some idea Spellman had, Klein said."

"Spellman!"

"Before he died. It's to be . . . I suppose it will be another monument. Part of the canonization effort."

"Dan! Don't be sacrilegious."

"If you don't think that Irish Mafia in the New York Chancery isn't going to try . . ."

"Did you mention this to LeGuiese?" Mary said. "Maybe he knows."

"I haven't talked to him. Besides, Klein said it was confidential. They gave him an exclusive. Don't say anything, just keep your ear to the ground."

"The Chancery is bribing him to get his support."

"He knows that. He wanted my reaction. Provided, of course, it was antagonistic."

"Not for quotation, I hope?"

"No."

Mary was lost in thought, puzzling the news. Her eyes narrowed.

"Maybe it was like a trial balloon, or whatever they call it."

"No. He has drawings and everything."

"How much will it cost?"

"A fortune. Maybe twenty million."

"Zow!"

They sat in silence for a moment, avoiding eyes. The constraint was starting, building up between them. Mary came to it first. She lowered her voice.

"Can we talk privately sometime? Not here. Someplace?"

His look of utter consternation cut off her words.

"I know what you mean. Later . . ."

They both stood, feeling awkward. Daugherty glanced at his wrist-watch. He said:

"It's time for Mass."

They went to the living room, to join the crowd. Daugherty found Seymour Jones sitting on the floor in a corner, plucking chords on his guitar, as though composing a melody. He looked up, flashed a grin.

"Guru! Great White Father!"

They shook hands warmly.

"Where you been, man?" Seymour said. "You ain't been making the scene."

Daugherty laughed.

"Been working my tail off out there."

He pointed his finger in the air. Jones nodded slowly, like a judge weighing testimony.

"Mary says you've been working up something?"

"I hope so," Jones said.

"Well, let's get it on," Dan said.

They had not yet staged a Mass at Halfway House. By order of the Chancery, "experimental" Masses were forbidden in the archdiocese. But for some little time now, both Daugherty and Mary had been aching to bring some form of collective religious demonstration to the boys and girls. Dan had read accounts of Folk Masses and had seen portions of one on television. The kids had urged it. Now, as he raised his arms to them, Daugherty felt a surge of doubt. He was not sure what he would do after Seymour, after certain specific prearranged assignments. He spoke in a loud voice:

"Let us begin. Let us meditate on Jesus."

He turned to Seymour and nodded. Seymour stood with his guitar, face cast in a pose of loneliness and despair.

"Now all you heads gather round," Seymour said, voice low, almost a chant.

The boys and girls pressed toward Seymour Jones.

"Listen to me, God," Jones shouted.

From the kitchen, Mary brought Daugherty's chalice, brimming with wine. Behind her, Sharon carried a small loaf of French bread. They set these on a table, then joined the crowd.

"This is Malcolm Boyd, set to music," Jones went on talking, strumming the guitar, shifting to a blues chord.

"Are you running with me, Jesus?" he shouted.

"Yes, I'm running," the boys and girls chanted.

"Then lissen," Jones said. "I'm carrying and shouting inside tonight, Lord, and I'm feeling completely alone. Lord, I hear you. I know you. I feel your presence in this awful moment, and I thank you. Help me onto my feet. Help me to get up."

He stopped as suddenly as he had begun, head bowed low. It had not been much, yet not the words, but the effect had been electrifying. Daugherty could feel the current crackling in the room. He raised his arms again and spoke conversationally.

"In olden days, most of the priests, from the Apostles on down, were part-time priests, worker-priests, who held jobs. They worked and preached on the side. They had no churches, no seminaries, no monasteries, no theological centers, no universities. They went from house to house to inform gatherings like this one, spreading the Word of Christ and His Grace. There was no quote approved unquote form of liturgy—way of saying the Mass—then, and everybody did pretty much what he wanted. Now, we want to revive the old way. I want you to be relaxed, casual, and do everything you can to project yourselves into the proceedings. The idea is to . . . to *relate*. Like an audience-participation TV show. You see?

"Now it's all legitimate. That is, it may not be officially approved, but I can say with all sincerity that this Mass we have is as good as any other and counts the same. Now, everyone who can, sit down and take it easy. We're just going to start right in here, anyplace. Mary, would you like to begin? Read us something, please?"

Mary stepped forward. In her hand she held a dog-eared pocketbook, *Invisible Man,* by Ralph Ellison. She read brief excerpts, Ellison's fantasy of a black boy's adventures in a plant which manufactured white paint. In the background, Seymour Jones strummed a soul rhythm on his guitar. As Mary read, and Seymour played, the boys and girls began to hold hands. When Mary finished her reading, Daugherty, with mounting enthusiasm, exclaimed:

"Good. Good."

"Cool," Seymour smiled. "Do your thing, Guru."

Father Daugherty explained the symbolism in the passage Mary had read. Then he went beyond, praising Ellison as a black who had overcome his environment, had assumed dignity, had become a great artist. Concluding, he held his arms outthrust, and said with rising voice: "Celebrate, let us celebrate every upset, every confusion, imprudence, foolishness, joy. Celebrate Jesus the light, life, the gadfly. He Who is always annoyance, wisdom, power, meaning, absurdity, confusion, harmony. Who is alive wherever there are people."

Then he turned to Mary. She handed him the chalice of wine and the bread. He prayed for his lambs, looking directly into Sharon's face, asking God's help, thanking Him for having provided the home, this warm shelter, from which he drew spiritual strength. He then passed the chalice and bread—the Body and Blood of Christ—to Mary, who ate and drank, and passed them on to eager, outstretched hands.

Sister Mary closed her eyes. She felt the presence of Christ in her soul, the infinite euphoria of Communion. She thanked God for the miracle of life, for her school, and she asked that He find new quarters. Then she opened her eyes and saw the black face of Seymour Jones, swaying as though in slow motion. His music thundered into the room, bringing with it a kind of ecclesiastical majesty, as though Heaven itself had erupted over them. Sister Mary felt warm, transfixed, holy, pious, needed—a rushing of emotions that left her giddy and lightheaded. Then she saw the face of Dan Daugherty, frozen in reverence, eyes uplifted, in perfect communion with God. The sight brought tears to her eyes. Then her heart went out to him with a rush so sudden it frightened her, and caused her to say aloud: "Dear God, help us."

VIII

Jean Favrot glanced at herself in her vanity mirror. She was a mess! She had meant to wash and set her hair, but there had been no time. Emma had phoned in sick this morning, of all days! Emma thought she might have Carol's flu, or maybe, worse, Hong Kong flu. It was going around. Everybody had had it—except the Favrots—and they said it was dreadful.

It was Jean's group night, her second session. It would begin in fifteen minutes.

In her one office session with Dr. Cantor she had not learned much. He had not asked her to lie on a couch; had not asked her about her mother, father, her childhood—as she had expected from the accounts in the women's magazines. They had not even touched remotely on sex. He had asked questions like a personnel recruiter: name, age, birth place, number of children, husband's job, income, telephone numbers, religion. He made a point of emphasizing that his treatment was not covered by Blue Cross or Blue Shield, or any other medical plan. The group would cost her $70 a month. Could she afford that? She could, if she bootlegged it from the household money. He asked if he should send the bill to her home. She said no, she would pay in cash, once a month. That done, he assigned her to a brand-new group. She was not to reveal her last name to the group. Under no circumstances was she to have outside contact with any member of the group. She should dress informally.

She rushed to the kitchen. Nancy had finished rinsing and stacking the dishes in the washer. Jean swept a damp cloth over the tabletop. Then she went to check the baby. He was sleeping soundly. Then Carol. She was asleep—wheezing. She would be all right. The boys were making a pretense of hard study. Nancy, who "had no homework," was already on the telephone. Bob was in the den, slouched in a chair, watching TV, a vodka-tonic in his right hand. Jean paused at the door.

"I'm leaving," she said.

"What?" he said, reaching to turn down the volume. It was a great effort. His belly sagged beneath him like a sack of meal.

Bob tore his eye from the tube with evident difficulty.

"I'm leaving," Jean said crossly.

"Where you going?"

"To sewing class. Remember?"

She did not like the lying. In seventeen years of marriage she had never lied to Bob about anything important. This was important— important to her. Important to her sanity. Anyway, she had dispensation, sort of. Daugherty had told her it was all right to conceal the group from Bob, if necessary.

"Oh yeah," Bob said, eyes returning to the TV. He sipped his drink. "I don't think you ought to go out with Carol sick."

"I just checked on her. She's all right now."

"Still . . ." Bob muttered.

"Oh hell!" Jean said angrily.

She left the house. The cold air struck her cheeks and she hurried to the car. Her anger gave way to guilt, the feeling she was deserting her family, her husband, her sick child. She did not plan to go on lying. Someday soon she would confront him with the group, argue him down.

She drove into the night. Her feelings of guilt ebbed, replaced by an exhilarating sense of adventure. She had been leery of group at first. Ten total strangers, informally dressed, known only by their first names, sitting in lounge chairs in a conference room, smoking, drinking coffee, talking. Her first thought was she had been suckered into a con game. She was suspicious and guarded. She sat in a chair off to one side, watching, waiting for some incredible revelation, a galvanizing insight. The other people, too, sat in silence, as though *afraid* to speak.

They sat like this, like people in an airport waiting room, for ten minutes. Then Dr. Cantor spoke from his chair behind them.

"Well, let's get the ball rolling. Suppose we go around the circle. Each of you give your name, tell a little something about why you're here. Describe your problem. Tell what you hope to get out of group. All right? Why don't you kick it off, Margo?"

Margo, a pretty woman with short hair, groaned, slumped in her chair, like an unprepared schoolgirl called on to recite.

"I'm Margo," she said. "I'm here . . . I'm here because Dr. Cantor *told* me to come."

The group tittered.

"What is my problem?" she said, searching the ceiling. "I have so many . . . it's hard to settle on *the* problem. I . . . I guess the main thing is I want to find out who I am. My identity. I want to stop being all things to all people."

She sat up now, pleased with herself. The man on her right now spoke, somewhat defiantly.

"Dr. Cantor told me to join this thing. I don't really have a problem. There's nothing wrong with me. It's the other people in my family who have problems."

He fell silent, staring at the floor. The girl to his right opened her mouth to speak. But she dissolved in tears. As she wept, Jean felt terribly embarrassed for her. The girl on her right picked it up.

"I'm Joan," she said. "I'm here because I think I am going out of my mind. I mean . . . *sometimes* I feel that way. I have this inferiority complex. I get the shakes and feel I can't go on in the morning without a drink . . ."

So it had gone, around the circle, to Jean, who was last. It was all very vague, uncertain, embarrassing. When her turn came, Jean didn't know what she would say. Her mind was reeling, almost feverish. She really didn't know why she was here, or what she hoped to gain from it. She gave her name, afraid that someone in the group would recognize her, at least know her by reputation. She folded her hands in her lap.

"If I knew why I was here, maybe I wouldn't be here," she said. The group tittered again. "It all began one day when I ran out of gas in the left-turn lane in McLean . . ." She stopped. *That* didn't make sense. It would take hours to unravel all that detail. "I guess I'm like Joan," she resumed. "I think I'm losing my mind."

That done, the group breathed easier, smoked in silence. A long uneasy silence. Dr. Cantor spoke again from his chair.

"I want you to join hands with the person next to you. Pair off. Hold hands."

The person in the next chair to Jean that night was a man named Kenneth. The thought of holding hands with him was repellent. She had not really held hands with another man since she had married Bob. It seemed childish. Besides that, she felt Kenneth to be rather unattractive. He was fat, like Bob, and he needed a shave. She did not like the pattern in his cheap plaid sports jacket.

Kenneth had not reached for her hand. It seemed he had a phobia about touching other people. Jean was relieved to discover that. Then she became curious. She asked Kenneth why he feared touching other people. Kenneth did not even attempt to answer her question. He was, she discovered, almost inarticulate. Jean could see that he was deeply troubled, in far more dangerous psychic waters than she. She felt that, given the right opportunity, she could help him.

She drove fast toward the clinic, looking forward to this second session. The group had become to her "another world," another family, which she found totally absorbing. She thought about the people, off and on, all week, wondering who they might be, where they lived, what they did for a living, especially one man, Mike, whom she found attractive.

She parked in the clinic lot. She looked at the other cars, hoping they might reveal some concrete fact about the other members. She tried, in her mind, to fit each car to a particular person. She was certain in one or two cases. Surely that was Mike's Porsche. But by and large, the cars revealed nothing. She felt guilty about doing even that. It seemed a violation of the rule against outside contact. Dr. Cantor would disapprove. Jean felt the need for his approval. She scarcely knew him, yet . . .

She went directly to the little room at the end of the hall and made a cup of instant coffee at the little hot plate. She carried it to the conference room, the last to arrive, one minute before eight fifteen. Dr. Cantor insisted on promptness, like a schoolteacher. Jean nodded to the others and took her chair. Her eyes roamed to Mike. Yes, he was as handsome as she had remembered. Well dressed, too. Clean-shaven. Dr. Cantor sat in the shadows, with a yellow legal pad in his lap, aloof from the proceedings, yet there all the same, the peculiar guiding force.

They sat in total silence, for eight or nine minutes. Jean smoked and sipped her coffee with a mounting sense of frustration. When they did not talk, she felt a sense of waste, as though a taxi meter were ticking away and the vehicle was not moving toward the destination. Waste not, want not, the nuns had said.

"Somebody *say* something," she said aloud.

"Why?" Mike said. It pleased Jean that he had noticed.

"Because I came here to get something out of this," she said levelly. "We're just killing time."

Dr. Cantor spoke.

"Go on, Jean. Why don't you elaborate on what you told us last week. You said you thought you were going out of your mind. I'm sure we'd all like to know why."

Why *me?* Jean thought, feeling panicky. She was sorry now she had opened her big mouth. That was one thing she could work on. Keeping her mouth shut at strategic moments.

"Go on, Jean," Dr. Cantor said. "Tell it like it is."

Jean lit another cigarette, gathering thoughts. If they were going to accomplish anything at all in the room, she thought, they might as well get down to brass tacks. She glanced at Mike. He was leaning back in his chair, waiting. His expression seemed to say he was genuinely interested.

"I'm absolutely miserable," Jean said, inhaling, blowing the smoke toward the ceiling. "I've been married seventeen years and I . . . we . . . my husband and I (she almost revealed his name) have . . . seem to have nothing in common. He's . . . he doesn't have any ambition anymore. He expects me to . . . he takes me for granted. My opinion is worth nothing. Everything I do is wrong. I feel *crushed* around him. He treats me as though I'm not even there. Like a child. A . . . a nonperson. He complains about the money. Constantly. He doesn't seem to realize prices are going up and up. He expects me to run the household like we did in 1955, or something. He lies around like some potentate . . . drinking all the time . . . looking at television. We don't even *talk* anymore."

She stopped, eyes fixed on Mike. Did he understand? His eyes said nothing. He looked away. Jean felt compelled to go on. Her case seemed weak, full of self-pity. Typical female bitchery.

"The main thing," she said, "is I don't want any more children. He doesn't understand that."

"How many children do you have?" Margo said.

Jean felt the panic rising again. If she told them exactly, they would surely know her identity. Or soon find out.

"A lot," she said.

"Four, five?" Margo pressed.

Now she felt stupid. She did not want to tell them.

"More," she said softly.

"My God," Mike whistled.

Always before, Jean had been proud to ring out the number. She was a good, decent Catholic mother, doing the right thing. Now she felt like some illiterate peasant, an animal.

"Tell them, Jean," Dr. Cantor prompted. Then to the group: "She's afraid of revealing herself."

"Oh hell!" Mike said impatiently. "We don't care who you are, Jean. Does anybody care?"

"No," Kenneth said. "What difference does it make anyway?"

"I have nine," Jean said, looking at the floor.

"Holy God!" Margo burst out. "How old?"

"Sixteen on down . . . a baby."

"You know what causes it, I hope?" Mike said.

"Don't be funny," Jean said, glaring. She felt suddenly depressed. Confidence oozing away.

"I assume you're Catholic?" Joan said.

"Yes," Jean replied, feeling a little ashamed.

"I thought the Pope said the pill was OK," Margo said.

"No, he didn't," Mike said. He looked at Jean. "Isn't that right?"

"Yes," she said, glumly.

"But the Vatican Council . . ." Margo insisted.

"They just named a commission to study it," Jean said. "That's all. Paul is a hard-liner, I think."

She stopped to regroup her thoughts. Non-Catholics had no idea about the Pope, the pill. Mike might be a Catholic, she thought. Mike? Michael what?

"What kind of religion is this?" Kenneth said. "You have nine children, you can't get some kind of waiver? It's ridiculous. How are you going to educate all those kids? My God. It's costing me four grand for my daughter per year of college. Sixteen grand to graduate. You . . . my God . . . sixteen times nine, a hundred and forty-four thousand dollars to put those kids through college . . . not to mention . . ."

Jean felt despondent. She had done that arithmetic more than once. Once she had even drawn up a graph, showing the relative ages of the children, how many would be in college at the same time, what it might cost in cash outlay per year. It was a staggering, even stupefying exercise. Bob would not even look at it. They'd find a way, he said.

"What do you do?" Margo broke in. "Do you have sex? I mean go right on, willy-nilly?"

Jean blushed. She lit another cigarette, fingers trembling. Damned if she was going to discuss the secrets of her bedroom with all these strangers. She did not answer.

"Do you play Vatican roulette?" Margo pressed. "The thermometer bit?"

Jean had not used the thermometer since the first year of her marriage. As all good Catholics know, the rhythm system didn't work. A few drinks, a good party, who then felt like consulting charts and temperatures? You just fell into bed, if you wanted to, and did it. In the old days.

"Sometimes," Jean lied.

"Tell us about it," Margo went on. "I never really knew a Catholic. I'm dying to know . . ."

"Somebody else talk," Jean said.

"I just want to know one thing," Margo said. "What do you do about sex?"

"I don't *have* any sex!" Jean said angrily. "Now what else do you want to know?"

Margo lapsed into silence. She seemed in a mild state of shock.

"But you have all those children," Mike said gently.

Jean felt this called for an explanation.

"My husband gets loaded sometimes," she said. "I'm his wife. I seem to get pregnant if he hangs his pants on the bedpost."

The group fell silent, as if contemplating this mysterious phenomenon.

"God!" Joan said, voice verging on real despair. Tears came to her eyes.

"I thought a lot of Catholics used the pill," Kenneth said. "I read these polls here and there."

"That's true," Jean said. "But I think they're mostly younger people. The middle-aged ones—at least the ones I know—just stop. Abstain."

"That's cruel," Joan said. "Really cruel."

"If they do approve the pill, that will make a difference won't it?" Mike said.

"Yes. I suppose so. To many people, anyway."

"And you?"

"I don't know. I . . ."

She did not want to go further. She did not want to tell them the revulsion she felt for Bob, his touch.

"You don't love him, do you?" Margo said.

"I don't know," Jean said, voice trailing away.

"Have you ever loved anybody else?" Mike said. "I mean, what if someone else came along?"

"There has *never* been anyone else," Jean said icily as though her honor had been questioned. "There will *never* be anyone else. I don't believe in that or approve of people who do."

"I'm sorry," Mike said. "I didn't mean to imply . . . it just seems like a natural thing. I mean, if you . . . oh hell. Forget it."

"You've never had an affair?" Margo said. "Not even a mild flirtation?"

"Certainly not," Jean said, voice tinged with anger. "Have *you?*"

"Of course," Margo chuckled. "I'm having one right now, with two different men."

Her words fell on the group like a grenade. Jean reeled back in shock.

"Are . . . you . . . are you married?" she stammered.

"Yes. Very happily married. I have a very satisfactory sex life at home."

The group pondered this.

"And three normal children," Margo added. "Doesn't everybody have affairs?"

"I do," Joan said. "One man at a time, though."

"Why . . . Why?" Jean gasped, feeling the panic again, convinced that Dr. Cantor had locked her up with a group of sex fiends. Nymphomaniacs.

"Because," Joan said, "it makes me feel good. There's this tremendous excitement. A surge of euphoria. The discovery . . . telling each other all the little things . . . making plans that you know will never be, but making them anyway . . . a kind of fantastic *intensity* I can't even begin to describe . . . the haunting feeling of wanting to be with him all the time . . . desperate for him to telephone . . . and then the conspiratorial part . . . sneaking here and there to the motels . . . and for me anyway, the sex is just out of this world."

Jean stared at her in amazement. She seemed so plain, so withdrawn, demure. What was locked up inside her?

"Then the breakup," Joan went on dreamily. "It always ends the same way. You know from the beginning it's coming . . . inevitable. Such *delicious* agony."

The tears came again to her eyes. Jean thought: a weepy nut.

"Try two at a time," Margo laughed. "*That'll* drive you straight up a wall."

Jean shifted her stare to Margo. Incredible! It was a *game* with her. How could she . . . *do* it, night after night, and then with her husband too? They were all crazy. She tried hard to imagine the world they inhabited. Running from motel to motel, man to man. She couldn't.

"Honey," Margo said, looking at Jean. "The affair is a part of the language . . . everybody does it. Where've you been? This isn't the Dark Ages. What do you say, group?"

She cast merry eyes at the others. Most of them nodded agreement.

"You mean . . . you . . ." Jean stammered, "*all* of you have affairs?"

"Sure," Mike said.

"And you . . . you . . . you don't think it's *wrong?*"

"It's fun," Margo said. "It's renewal, in spades! I mean, like, it's just great!"

Jean fell silent. Later she would talk privately with Dr. Cantor and tell him a few straight facts. He had obviously misplaced her. She didn't belong in this fast company. This was some kind of poor-man's jet set. She would ask for an all-Catholic group. People like herself who still had some sense of propriety, values, respect for the family, for the vows of marriage. My God!

"Well," Dr. Cantor spoke, "it's about that time. See you next week."

Jean's eyes leaped to her wristwatch. It was ten o'clock. Impossible! The time had flown. She had talked the whole time, almost. She wanted to shout an apology to the group. Next time, next week, damnit, she would shut up and listen. God, in a way, it was fascinating. She wanted to know more about Margo and Joan and . . . and Mike. He hadn't said a thing about himself. She avoided his eyes as she picked up her coat and left the room, the building.

The night was cold, clear. It would be a cold Easter. She paused for a moment, by her car, looking into the heavens, letting her mind soar skyward, to the moon and beyond. She felt good. That Margo was impossible! Yet she was . . . seemed to be . . . a good person, somebody you would want to know. And the others. Pioneers on the plains of self-discovery. Maybe she wouldn't call Dr. Cantor. Maybe she ought to stick with this bunch for a while. Another week or two.

She drove home in a good mood. She was not troubled, now, that she had run out on Bob, or Carol. The sex. Boy, how she could burn their ears if she told them everything! The thought made her shudder. She parked the car in the garage.

Nancy was still on the telephone. Bob was asleep in his chair in front of the television, one leg draped over the arm, mouth open,

snoring. She shut off the TV and went to the bathroom, peeled off
her clothes. She stood, naked, looking in the full-length mirror on
the back of the door. She was shocked by the way she had let herself
go. Her face was plump, colorless. There were wrinkles, crow's-feet in
the corners of her eyes. Turning, looking critically at her waist, she
seemed to see, for the first time, the tire, the tummy-hump below her
waist. Her hair was a mess, too long to be stylish, no body, no shape.
She looked in her closet. All her shoes and dresses were drab. The
hemlines hung well below her matronly knees.

She must make an immediate appointment with David to have her
hair cut and set. She would go on a crash diet—hard-boiled eggs, lean
meat, and water. She would buy some new clothes. She would telephone her Beauty Counselor representative, whom she had not seen
for months, order lotions and creams. She would take her dresses to
a seamstress to raise the hems one inch above the knee. She would
dig out the dusty Bonnie Prudden exercise record and strain through
the leg raises, jumping jacks, sit-ups, and deep knee bends. She would
go over to All Saints' rectory and volunteer for whatever work she was
qualified. Anything to get out of the house . . . to do something useful.

IX

Sister Mary pushed the doorbell of the Chancery firmly with her forefinger. For this official call, she had shifted to her regulation Sacred
Heart habit. Her long hair was pulled back severely and pinned up,
her face scrubbed of all makeup, for she was well aware that McInnerney had publicly fought any innovation in dress for the nuns in his
archdiocese. On this day, she did not want to raise unnecessary issues.
Outwardly, she was, in every sense of the word, conventional—as approved by the Vatican, her Mother General.

A maid answered the door. Sister Mary smiled softly and asked for
Vicar General Prial. Yes, she did have an appointment. While the
maid clicked away down the polished Italian marble corridor, Sister

Mary remained standing, gazing at a color photograph of Pope Paul, framed on the wall. The photograph, she thought, made him seem hard. He was not smiling. His burden seemed grave. She said a brief prayer for him, asking God to ease the weight of his Holy Office.

The maid returned shortly. The Vicar General was with the Archbishop now. Would Sister Mary mind waiting? She invited Sister Mary to sit in a Queen Ann wing chair in the foyer. Mary sat down, folded her hands, and waited, unawed by the splendor of the mansion or its costly furnishings. As a Sacred Heart nun, she had grown accustomed to such homes converted to religious purposes.

Her "case" had been thoughtfully and carefully prepared. She was confident that it was sound, persuasive, that Prial would find what she needed. There was no need to go over it again. Her mind wandered to Dan Daugherty.

They had not had time for further talk. After the Folk Mass, the singing, Mary had been busy. All those people to feed! Sharon had helped—willingly—in the kitchen as Mary prepared the giant pots of spaghetti and the meat sauce, her specialty, the Sunday ritual. After that, Dan had been on the telephone for two hours, tracking down Sharon's parents, convincing them that—temporarily—Sharon was better off at Halfway House than home, that she could repeat a semester of school, that this burst of "independence" was essential, that Sharon must have the baby, that the father, Peter, would be called to account, but that a shotgun wedding was not the solution. Dan had a marvelous way with the parents, with the kids.

Then one thing and another until it was time to return to the dorm. She had left the house with an empty feeling, that she was leaving behind that which was most important: It was strange how that attitude had set in. Not long ago, she could think of nothing but her school. Now, it seemed, the school was inching into the background, Halfway House was moving—leaping—forward. Perhaps it was because she had finished her thesis. The school was no longer so important. Halfway House gave her a larger sense of fulfillment, as a woman. She was almost like a mother to those kids. And how that poor Sharon had edged into her heart! The baby would be beautiful! And Dan was there, at Halfway House. Making the truly important decisions, and even the small ones about money and discipline. His strong voice filled out the empty corners of the rooms.

Damnit! She tore her mind from Dan Daugherty. She did not want to think about him now. Not here. Not this morning. She had come in

behalf of her school, her *other* children. She must focus on them. They
were there, in the classroom, where she had left them, happy and content, making progress. Only Mary stood between them and a cold, encircling world that, given the opportunity, would remand them to dark,
indifferent institutions, destroy hope, enter them on the muster of the
defeated, leave them broken, crushed, useless wards of society. God
did not mean that for little children.

Upstairs, in the Archbishop's apartment, the Vicar General and
McInnerney were reaching several important decisions. The Vicar
General, having given honest counsel and been overruled, was now
pledged completely to the theological center and the fund drive to
build it. All the previous week, he had been dealing with the most
urgent phase of that plan, the sale of St. Luke's to IDA, nursing the
agency from letter of intent to hard contract. It was a bewildering,
mind-boggling deal (the draft contract was 210 pages of fine print),
with endless meetings of lawyers. It was not easy for Prial to keep the
prime goal—$5 million in cash—firmly fixed in his mind. If he let go,
momentarily, it sank beneath the morass of details. There were times
when he sincerely wished they had never become involved. He resolved
never again to do business with a government agency, or even a quasi-
government agency.

One problem was the need for speed, hurrying the deal along without
revealing his hand. McInnerney had decided that the fund drive should
be announced in the week following Easter. The deal should be "set"
by then. That was only two weeks away, seemingly an impossible
deadline. It went against Prial's grain to rush. He knew from experience that in matters of high finance, haste made waste. The Archbishop
seemed oblivious to the many details, the legal footnotes. Each morning,
he asked "How much longer," gently and unnecessarily needling.

These matters they now discussed.

"I had an inspiration this morning," the Archbishop said, beaming.
"I've decided to bring Ryan into the Chancery, on temporary assignment, to oversee the mechanics of the drive. He's damned good at that,
you know."

Prial could not conceal his displeasure. Bringing Ryan to the
Chancery was, in a sense, a slight. Chancery finance was Prial's prime
responsibility. He objected at once.

"We need Ryan at All Saints'," he said. "The parish is supposed to set
the example for the drive, provide leadership . . . a carrot. Besides
that, who will you send to All Saints'?"

"Nobody. Ryan will be here just temporarily. To get things organized and rolling. A few weeks. In his absence, that young fellow Daugherty can hold the fort."

"They're already shorthanded."

"Ryan can keep an eye on it."

"But Daugherty won't have time to run the parish *and* mount a really strong drive. Good Lord . . ."

"He can if he puts his mind—and time—to it. If he gave up that hippie drug project . . ."

"Halfway House," Prial said, with irritation.

"Exactly," the Archbishop said. "We'll name him acting pastor for the time being. He'll be so busy he won't have time for that place. You —discreetly—drop the word to the proper authorities to keep a sharp eye out down there. It makes me nervous. If anything happened, it would hurt us—the Chancery. Give the Church a bad name. During this drive, we can't afford to take a single chance. The people in the archdiocese who cough up money don't like hippies. So we kill two birds with one stone."

"Which brings up a related problem," Prial said, not yet convinced. "Last week the IDA people raised the problem of the neighborhood center in the St. Luke's gym. They took the position Seymour Jones was a squatter, legally, and saw potential trouble. They don't want to be in the position of evicting Jones—a black. It could blow up into a PR problem for them. They'll have all that they can deal with as it is. We presented our agreement with Jones—we have full right of repossession with fourteen weeks notice—but they wouldn't buy it. *We* have to do that piece of dirty work. They want a letter of eviction to Jones incorporated into the contract."

"Give it to them," the Archbishop said.

"It may cause trouble," Prial said. "That damned Klein made Jones a hero. He pressured us on the gym. Now, if Jones is evicted, he may raise hell."

The Archbishop felt no concern about this decision. His public record on civil rights was sound. He was proud of that—his foresight. In New York, he had pioneered in the Puerto Rican integration. In Washington, years before the Supreme Court decision, he had desegregated archdiocesan schools. In those days, the press had championed him— favorable profiles and manufactured "news" stories. That record still stood if anybody wanted to look it up. St. Luke's had served the black community well. For many years, with little return to the Chancery. They had no right to make a big thing over Jones. It was clearly understood when Jones took possession that it would not be forever. Klein knew that. The Chancery could certainly weather a minor storm over Jones if Klein chose to cause one. They could show Klein the record. It spoke for itself.

"Can we find him another place?" the Archbishop said, weighing alternatives.

"There isn't any place. Right now, I've got Sister Murray on my doorstep. The city is evicting her because the building is unsafe. This is just a damned coincidence, but it couldn't have come at a worse time. It's as though the Devil were conspiring . . ."

"Her problem is not our problem."

"She and Jones are friendly neighbors. I'd hate to see them *both* running to Klein. The last thing we want to do is call attention right now to St. Luke's. Sister Mary, the little crippled kids, have strong public appeal."

"It seems to me we're mixing apples with oranges. Jones is a small matter. We don't owe him anything. If Klein wants to crusade for Sister Mary, that's the city's problem, not ours. If he wants to jump on the mayor, let him jump. How long will we have this Sister Mary in the archdiocese? Isn't she due to leave? Have somebody look into her status."

"I did. She gets her degree this year."

"Then send her back to the convent where she belongs."

"I'll write the Provincial."

"That should solve that," the Archbishop sighed.

"I'll go ahead with the notice to Jones," Prial said. "I'd rather defer this. But I don't see how we can get around it. Meanwhile, I'll stall Sister Mary until I hear about her future status."

"Nate," the Archbishop said softly. "Your nose is not really out of joint about Ryan, is it?"

It was a rare, intimate gesture for McInnerney to call the Vicar General by his seminary nickname. To Prial it was reassuring. It lifted his spirits. He smiled sheepishly.

"Ryan is an old man like me," McInnerney went on. "He's serving out his time. He has this genius for organizing nickels and dimes. It's the kind of knack for detail you shouldn't even concern yourself with. You'll be happy to have him take that load. You'll see, Nate. Don't think I'd let anything come between us. You know where you stand with me. I'm grooming you for the utmost responsibility. The very top of the heap."

Prial chewed throughtfully on his dead cigar.

"I'm getting punchy," he said. "As a matter of fact, I was thinking about just who I might saddle with collecting all those nickels and
dimes. I'd have never thought of Ryan. I don't like to leave All Saints'
unguarded. But, frankly, I couldn't have thought of a better man.
That's why you're where you are and I'm where I am."

"I've been around longer, that's all," the Archbishop said. "When
I was your age, a thing like this would have been a lead-pipe cinch.
That was back in the good old days. When we had so much money we
didn't know what to do with it. We could hardly give it away fast
enough. Those days—sadly—are gone forever. We *need* people like
Ryan. He knows how to steal pennies. But he could never have put this
IDA deal together. People like you have come into your own now. Not
a minute too soon, Lord knows. OK?"

"OK," Prial said. "I'm learning."

"So are we all."

"I better go deal with Sister Mary."

He left the room, almost charging down the enormous red-carpeted
stairway. He glanced at his wristwatch. He winced. Sister Mary had
been waiting an hour. Coming to the first floor, he saw her sitting in the
chair in the hallway. Very pretty, he thought. And probably mad as a
wet hen. He hurried to her, holding out both hands.

"I'm very sorry," he said. "You caught me at a bad time. Please come
in. Will you have something to drink? Coffee? Tea? Lemonade?"

Sister Mary rose from the chair, impressed, as always, by the imposing
physique of the Vicar General. Beside him, she felt tiny and insignificant.

"Thank you," she said. "I'd love some tea."

The Vicar General spoke to the maid. Then he led Sister Mary into his
office. It was a small room, with a modern steel desk, filing cabinets,
three or four pull-up chairs. Sister Mary sat in one of the chairs, facing
the desk. The Vicar General eased his bulk into his swivel chair, behind
the desk.

"Now then, my dear," he said. "What can we do for you?"

The maid served tea. Sister Mary waited until she had withdrawn.
Prial politely offered sugar and lemon. Sister Mary declined both.

"I've come to ask for a bit of charity," she said, fixing her dark eyes
directly on him, sipping her tea daintily. She was, in spite of the habit, a
woman. She had not forgotten how to use her eyes, her voice, her charm
for something she wanted very badly.

"Specifically?" the Vicar General said, leaning forward in his chair,
his eyes already saying no.

Sister Mary set her cup aside. Then, very succinctly, very eloquently, she told the Vicar General that she must find a new home for her ghetto school and how important it was.

"I thought perhaps you could suggest some building," she concluded, "that you plan to vacate shortly, or that might otherwise be available."

The Vicar General got up from his chair and walked to a filing cabinet. He opened the drawer and withdrew a manila folder. He sat down and opened the folder, running his eye down an inventory of archdiocesan property in or near the ghetto. He knew there was nothing that had not already been condemned or was being used for some other purpose. Yet he did not want to tell her so directly. Not now.

"There is one possible place I scouted out," Sister Mary said helpfully.

"What's that?" the Vicar General said, looking up from the folder.

"The basement of St. Luke's," she said. "It was used, at one time, for Sunday school. I understand from the pastor that it is not being used now, except for storage."

Oh, my God! the Vicar General gasped inwardly. Jesus, Mary, and Joseph. When would these people stop meddling? He looked at Sister Mary coldly.

"That, I'm afraid, is out of the question."

"Why?" she said, made curious by the quick, emphatic tone.

Prial laid the folder aside, leaned back in his chair, clasped his hands behind his head. He chose his words with care, wishing to avoid, at all costs, further inquiry.

"That space is set aside as part of a long-range plan we have," he said. "I wouldn't want to see you move in, get all settled, and then have to move again. It's much too complicated to go into."

"Oh?" Sister Mary said, thinking: What long-range plan? The pastor at St. Luke's (who, she knew, saw PR advantage in having the school in his basement) had not mentioned it. Perhaps he did not know.

"Will you give me a few days to think on it?" the Vicar General said.

"Of course," Sister Mary said. "But we don't have too much time. I'm being evicted by the city engineering department at the end of this week. The building has been condemned."

"Yes. I know."

"It is a very worthy project," Sister Mary said. "As you know, I have OEO funding—a Head Start grant—but unless I can show adequate housing, I don't think I can get a grant renewal."

"I understand," the Vicar General said. "Yes. It has been a worthy project."

The Chancery had been pleased by the publicity. But the Archbishop had taken sharp exception to Sister Mary's role. When he saw her picture in the *Tribune,* and later, her face on television, McInnerney became angry. He did not approve of nuns going about the world, the ghettos, doing good works and getting publicity. He saw this—and the relaxation of discipline in the religious orders—as a dangerous trend. He believed a nun's place was strictly in the cloister, or the schoolroom, where discipline was absolute, the faith held strong and secure. His views had been made clear in directives to the orders stationed in the archdiocese. Prial had thought McInnerney's reaction a trifle strong, too reactionary, and had so counseled him. But now he saw clearly that McInnerney had a point. If Sister Mary was back where she belonged, she would not be sitting here complicating an already complicated deal.

"It's a worthy project," he repeated. "But in the long run, the overall effort, it may not be worth the time and money."

"I have forty-six crippled children," she said coldly. "They are worth my time and effort, and your time, the Church's time, at least the ten minutes I have imposed on you, after waiting an hour."

Prial set his elbows on the desk sternly.

"Suppose every nun in the archdiocese decided to embark on some project of this kind?" the Vicar General said, more harshly than he had intended. "What then of my time? The Church's time? The Chancery's time? The Church, Sister Mary, must remain a cohesive totality, a system of closely locked, interrelated activities, mutually supporting, and administered from a central authority which in turn is answerable to—and totally loyal to—the Holy Father in Rome. You people don't seem to understand that. The Miracle of Existence—two thousand years on earth, due, in part, to its monolithic character. We can't have this Church fragmenting. We can't have people like you—independent agents—running wild in the archdiocese, reporting to no authority, and financially unaccountable."

Sister Mary clasped her hands in her lap tightly.

"I would hardly describe my work as 'running wild,' " she said calmly.

"I'm sorry," the Vicar General said. "My language was harsh. But I hope you grasped my point."

"Your point is that you don't want to help me."

"Your project is not officially approved by the Chancery," the Vicar

General said. "All we know about it, really, is what we read in the paper. There has been much of that. Perhaps too much. You know very well how the Chancery feels about your picture being in the newspaper, and on television."

"When I left for the convent, and later, when I took my vows, my picture was quite prominently displayed in the *Catholic Standard*," Sister Mary said. "Mainly, I suppose for propaganda purposes, to encourage other girls to join. I fail to see the difference betwen that type of propaganda and favorable publicity, which glorifies God, the Chancery, the Church, my order, and which, indirectly, was beneficial in my receiving funding from OEO."

"We've strayed from the central point," the Vicar General said. "The central point is one of obedience. Discipline. Central control. Do not think, for a moment, we are without problems here, Sister . . ."

"I'm sure you have many problems," she said, "that I am detaining you from now. I'm sorry. I didn't come here for a lecture. I came here for charity."

She stood now beside the desk, her dark Irish eyes defiant. She left the room quickly.

The Vicar General rose from his swivel chair, disconcerted. He was damned sick and tired of the continual need to explain everything to everybody. He picked up a pencil, then flung it on his desk. He buzzed for his assistant, a young priest who specialized in personnel and facilities. When the priest entered the room, the Vicar General snapped:

"Go ahead with the eviction letter to Jones."

When the priest had gone, Prial turned to his dictating machine. He spoke slowly into the mouthpiece. "Letter to the Provincial, New York Province, Society of the Sacred Heart, Dear Mother, His Excellency, blah blah sends his greetings and best wishes. He asked me to inquire into the future status of Sister Mary Frances Murray who has been attending CU for the last two years comma tuition expense waived by this Chancery comma and who comma His Excellency feels comma may be now well qualified to render a valuable teaching career at the convent period As you know the number of tuitions we waive is limited . . ."

X

Father Daugherty knelt on the linoleum-covered floor beside the bed, praying. The old lady in the bed, poor Mrs. Zanowski, was wheezing. Three weeks ago, her doctor proclaimed she would not last another two days. The cancer had eaten away her insides. But she had clung to life. Father Daugherty saw her, now, every other night. He was gentle, compassionate, and had become, almost against his will, swept up in her final struggle. He had told her that she was lucky. She had led a pure, holy life, devoted to Christ. She had not been flung into eternity by a sudden, violent accident. God was taking her slowly. Her soul was pure. She had confessed. Father Daugherty had administered absolution. Now she had but to close her eyes, wait, and soon she would see the Kingdom of Heaven.

When Father Daugherty finished his prayer, he looked up at the woman. Her wizened head was propped on a bank of pillows. Her eyes were closed. He stood up, bent over, placed his ear near her mouth. She was breathing lightly. She was not dead. She was sleeping. Her right arm, thin, emaciated, lay on top of the sheet, a rosary intertwined in her bony fingers. She was—God knows—safe. Father Daugherty left the room.

The old lady lived in a tiny, sagging frame house on a dirt road, in the derelict neighborhood, next door to the custodian, John Joseph Scafidi. The Catholic population of this neighborhood amounted to six souls, not counting Scafidi. When Monsignor Ryan spoke of contributions for the "poor" of the parish, he evidently had these souls in mind. But, as far as Daugherty knew, none had ever received a penny. Spiritual care of these poor souls fell to Daugherty.

Mrs. Zanowski was being looked after by her daughter, who had left her husband and six children, temporarily, in New Jersey. Father Daugherty met the daughter in the adjoining room, decorated as a living room–dining room, with a few tattered chairs, wobbly tables. The daughter stood in the middle of the room, a desperate look in her eyes.

"It won't be long now," Daugherty said.

"Thank God," the woman said. "Father, I know it sounds awful, but this has been a nightmare."

He looked about the room. It smelled of boiled cabbage. The old woman should have been put in a home or hospital.

"It's always a nightmare," he said.

He was sick of death. He saw it all week long, in hospitals, funeral homes, on the streets in twisted automobiles, everywhere it seemed. He had watched many people die. Good Catholics. They didn't die any better, any braver than anyone else. They died in fear and pain, most still unsure of their faith after a lifetime of prayer and devotion. They seemed to wait until the very end to spill all the venom. It came in a vast, stinking cascade to his ear. Hate. Bitterness. Ghastly sins and secrets whispered out. If he had time to keep notes, he could write a book about death all by itself. Expose the stupid saccharine deaths on the film screens and television. Tell it like it really was. That would blow some minds. It would surely make some people think twice. And he thought: Why, dear God, why this final, ghastly, obscene ending after a lifetime of suffering . . . of hell? Why, why, why?

"My kids are running wild," the woman said.

"I'm sure," Daugherty said, standing awkwardly. He wanted to get away from death, the smell of cabbage.

"The phone bill is fantastic," she said. "I have to call up there two or three times a day. That idiot who calls herself a maid—at sixty dollars a week live-in—doesn't know the time of day."

"It can't go on much longer," he consoled.

"Why doesn't the Church have a place for these people to die?" the woman said.

"I don't know," Daugherty said. Thinking: The Church was organized toward death, the life hereafter, the eternal reward, yet it was true, there was no facility for the transition. The facilities were designed for the living. Except the old homes for priests. They had plenty of those. The priests looked after their own.

"I can't tell you the money this is costing. All those drugs! Wasted. Why do we keep them alive?"

She was tired and bitter.

"Have you made the arrangements? The funeral home?"

"God yes. Ten times over. Never mind what *that* cost."

"I suppose so."

Daugherty knew that scene, too. The unctuous, repulsive morticians, with their black suits and "Specials" and "Package Plans," and the kickbacks—substantial revenue over the year—to the rectory, to Ryan, for the referrals. It was logged in the ledgers as "business" contributions. Daugherty was proud that he had never become a part of that slimy racket.

"Here's something for the kitty," the woman said, offering Daugherty an envelope. He refused it politely.

"Put it against the phone bill," he said smiling.

She did not press. She laid the envelope on the table.

"You ought to have somebody here," Daugherty said. He had thought that on previous visits, but had said nothing. There was nobody available. Her husband, a steamfitter, worked seventy hours a week—one regular job plus moonlighting—to pay the mounting bills. "Are there any neighbors?"

She shuddered. "Everybody on this street is crazy. Especially the guy next door. Scafidi. Your janitor."

"That's right!" Daugherty said, snapping his fingers. "I forgot he lived over here."

"Nutty as a fruitcake," the woman said, rolling her eyes. "I went over there last night to borrow some coffee. Have you been in there? The whole place is jammed with books on flying saucers! Hundreds and hundreds of books, a regular library."

"Flying saucers? I didn't know . . ."

"You know what he told me? He said flying saucers come from . . . well, he says they're manned by humanoids—whatever they are—and come from Heaven or Hell. Brother! I got out of there as quick as I could."

"Hmmmmm," Daugherty said.

"I'll make out," the woman said. "Can I get you some coffee?"

"No thanks. I've got to run. Several more calls. Look, I think you better call the doctor or the funeral home or somebody. Alert them. She can't last the night."

"I've heard that before. No, I'll wait. They're all alerted. My God, what do you think I do around here all day? Thanks for coming by."

"Anytime," Daugherty said.

He pulled on his coat and went to the car, the rectory Chevvy, all black, no chrome, no radio, mechanical shift. He backed down into the drainage ditch, onto the dirt road. He drove slowly past Scafidi's house, seeing the dim light in the room, a figure bent over. Flying saucers with humanoids!

He had no further calls. He had told her that to be polite. He drove back to the rectory, circling through the rows of California ranch houses, Williamsburg colonials. They looked warm and comfortable. He parked in the rectory lot and went inside.

The rectory was the architect's idea of contemporary styling, designed to be "compatible" with the ski-chalet church. It was furnished with Danish modern and wall-to-wall carpet. Like the church, it was cold, somber, silent. Mrs. Munally lived in a comfortable room at the back of the house with a separate entrance. Father Daugherty and Monsignor Ryan lived on the second floor in separate bedrooms. There were two unused bedrooms, space for "expansion," when, or if, other priests to be assigned to the parish ever came, or for visiting clergy. These rooms were sparsely furnished: single bed, crucifix on the wall overhead, bureau, chair, mirror.

Father Daugherty went up the stairs to his room. It was, by any rectory standards, snug and comfortable. In addition to the regulation furnishings, he had added personal touches: a small, portable TV set, a gift from his aunt, a huge bookcase filled with paperbacks, mostly philosophy, psychology, but quite a few good novels, including all of Dostoyevsky, Camus, Sartre and others, plus books by contemporary blacks—LeRoi Jones, James Baldwin, Eldridge Cleaver. His closet included, in addition to his vestments and black suits, several stylish sports jackets, gray flannel slacks, his tennis whites. The closet floor was awash with used tennis balls, and four or five old and new tennis racquets. Everywhere in the room were pictures, of his mother and father, his brothers and sisters, classmates from the seminary, Pope John, and, on the bureau, a gift from LeGuiese, one of the late Jesuit, Teilhard de Chardin.

It was not yet eight thirty. Father Daugherty changed into slacks. He went back downstairs and got a tray of ice from the refrigerator. Ryan's room was dark, silent. He could hear the TV in Mrs. Munally's room. She would emerge when she heard him. He waited to exchange the ritualized words.

"Oh, Father, it's you!" she said, peeping from her door. "I heard a noise."

He stood waiting, holding the ice tray. It was freezing. She came from her room, still dressed.

"Are you hungry?" she said.

"Thirsty," he replied, hefting the ice tray.

She did not approve his taking ice to his room, or what he put the ice in. At first he had felt guilty about it. Now he was merely annoyed.

"It's not trouble to fix you some bouillon," she said, smiling, eager.

"Not hungry," he said. "By the way. I meant to ask you. Did you give Scafidi that coat?"

Her eyes turned away. Sheepishly she said:

"I tried to. He . . . he said thanks anyway. I gave it to the Catholic charities. He's very proud, I guess, though God knows why. It's pitiful . . ."

"Has he told you about his flying saucers?"

"Saucers?" her eyes widened.

"UFO's. He told Mrs. Zanowski's daughter they come from Heaven, or someplace. Do you really know anything about Scafidi?"

"Not really."

"He looks creepy to me."

"Poor thing. I think his heart is good."

"Where did he come from?"

"I don't know. His references were good—he's always worked for the Church. Originally, I think, he comes from Philadelphia."

"I guess he's all right then," Daugherty joked. Actually he felt no loyalty to his hometown, Philadelphia. The Main Line was now only a hazy memory, something that may or may not have happened to him.

"He's all right, poor thing," Mrs. Munally persisted. "I admire him for holding down a job. He's *dependable*. That's more than you can say for most of them these days, especially the niggers."

The word offended Daugherty.

"They call themselves blacks nowadays, Mrs. Munally."

"Niggers. Colored. Negroes. Blacks. I called them all that. But I'm too old to keep up with all the changes. I've gone back to niggers. The way they carry on down here, they don't deserve to be called anything but niggers. I tell you, Father, most women I know are afraid to walk on the streets of Washington. It's a disgrace."

"It's better than Harlem and Newark and Detroit. At least they haven't burned us down. Well, I better get upstairs. Where's the good Monsignor?"

"He got a call from the Chancery," she said, lowering her voice to a confidential tone. "He's down there. The Archbishop himself called."

Daugherty was curious but he knew better than to question. She would tell him nothing.

"Good night, now."

"Good night."

Going up the stairs again, he wondered why Ryan was downtown. It was a strange time to go calling at the Chancery. Father Daugherty closed his door. He took down a bottle of Scotch from the shelf in his closet, went to the bathroom, cracked the ice from the tray, and poured a drink on the rocks. Then he sat down in his lounge chair, snapped on the reading lamp, and stared at the literature stacked on the table: the *National Catholic Reporter,* the Brooklyn *Tablet, Commonweal, America,* the *St. Louis Review, Cross Currents,* all containing important articles he should read—controversial, complicated stuff on the problems of the Church, the dissent, the division, the revolution.

He sipped his drink, feeling no desire to tackle any more journalistic theology. Instead, his mind returned to Mrs. Zanowski, her daughter's question: Why did they keep them alive? There was, nowadays, a whole new population to care for, the senior citizens, kept alive by superior medical care, flocking in greater numbers than ever to the parish churches. One more burden on the hopelessly overworked clergy. Another insoluble problem.

This thought led Daugherty to remember the new paperback book LeGuiese had given him last week, a prepublication review copy that had come to LeGuiese. He had passed it on to Daugherty, remarking that it was the most important book he had read in ten years, that every thinking Catholic should see it, that every priest should tout it in the pulpit. It was entitled *The Population Bomb.* It was written by an eminent scholar, Dr. Paul R. Erlich, Professor of Biology, Stanford University.

Daugherty went to his bookcase, searching for the book. He found it, beneath the Kerner Report, another book he must soon tackle. He returned to his chair, read slowly, thoughtfully, and with growing astonishment and alarm.

Dr. Erlich argued, convincingly, that if man did not stop having so many children—stop multiplying at the present, fantastic rate—there would soon be no room for him on earth, and no possible way to feed him, or to preserve an environment in which he could survive. His indisputable statistical argument was contained in a brief paragraph on what he called "doubling time"—the time necessary for the world population to double in size. Daugherty read it three times, committing the figures to memory:

It has been estimated that the human population of 6000 B.C. was about five million people, taking perhaps one million years to get there from two and a half million. The population did not reach 500 million until almost 8,000 years later—about 1650 A.D. This means it doubled roughly once every thousand years or so. It reached a billion people around 1850, doubling in some 200 years. It took only 80 years or so for the next doubling, as the population reached two billion around 1930. We have not completed the next doubling to four billion yet, but we now have well over three billion people. The doubling time at present seems to be about 37 years. Quite a reduction in doubling times: 1,000,000 years, 1,000 years, 200 years, 80 years, 37 years . . .

Until now, Daugherty had been bored with alarmist tracts about the population explosion. It had always been inconceivable to him that man was running out of land, water, food, air. The statistics were dull, boring. There was plenty of land out West—vast stretches, unpopulated, untilled. Daugherty had seen them from airplane windows. Science would find a way to make that land useful, to supply food and water. Yet he now read with close attention, perhaps because LeGuiese had found the book so important. Dr. Erlich made his case with few statistics, no hysterics. It had now been proven beyond doubt, he wrote, that because of the "doubling time," man, perhaps by the year 2000, would be hard pressed to survive. Already three and a half million children were dying each year from hunger and malnutrition. Some biologists were forecasting a worldwide famine by 1975! The Catholic Church, with its frenzied, willy-nilly multiplication rate, was the worst offender. It must be stopped.

The Pope would certainly stop it, soon, Daugherty thought.

He visualized the problem in his own back yard, thinking of the Favrots. Two parents, nine children. He reached for a pencil and paper. If each of the Favrot's nine children, in turn, had nine children then—let's see—that would be 81 grandchildren. If each of the grandchildren, in turn, had nine children, that would be—he multiplied—729 great-grandchildren. If each of the great grandchildren had nine children, that would be 6,571 great, great-grandchildren. . . . He threw the pencil away in despair, mind swimming with numbers.

Surely, the Pope understood this simple arithmetic, he thought. Certainly his commission understood it.

He rattled the ice in his glass thoughtfully. The whole population thing was more than he could comprehend tonight. And then he thought of Sister Mary.

She had wanted to talk yesterday. There had been no time. Too many people. Besides that, Daugherty did not want to talk. Not yet. It was too big a thing to deal with. Dealing with it honestly led directly to very big alternatives, decisions. Before they had their talk, he must sort out, completely, how he truly felt about everything, his life, his vocation, the Church. He must see LeGuiese again this week. This waiting, waiting for the Pope's decision, was foolish. There was so much more to it than birth control.

Down there, at Halfway House, they were almost like man and wife. Supervising their children. It would be fun to stay there, all the time. All day and night. Not coming back here or to the dorm at CU. Lying together in bed, warm, affectionate. Legally man and wife, their lives and bodies intertwined, one.

He sipped the dregs of his drink, feeling a sudden, intense loneliness. His eye swept the pictures in the room—the miracle of life, mother, father, brothers, sisters—and he felt the denial strongly. He was missing out on a vast slice of life, perhaps the most rewarding slice, the intimate pleasure, the love one human being could provide another, the comfort, even the distraction, the noise. Yes, it would be good to have noise in the room, the rustle of another human being going about, performing some piddling task. He turned on the television. It was a Western. In a while, the Johnny Carson Show would come on. Then Father Daugherty would have companionship, a lighthearted moment of fun, projected from a sterile screen.

He watched the Western, his mind elsewhere, tuned now to Sister Mary—Mary Murray. At this moment she would be alone, too, in her little cubicle in the dormitory at Catholic University. His mind leaped the distance. He saw her, lying on her small bed, reading; or perhaps watching the same Western on television, or perhaps washing out her stockings. Did she, in fact, wear stockings? He tried to remember. He could not remember stockings. Then he saw her, sitting in the tub, full-breasted, reaching for the slippery soap.

The vision brought on an erection, a sweet, powerful sensation. He let it linger. Then he set his drink aside and went to the shower. He ran the water cold, down his trembling chest. He shut off the shower, rubbed briskly with a towel. He returned to his room, towel wrapped around his waist. He put on his silk pajamas, made another drink.

There was a knock at the door. He walked quickly over, swung it open. It was Monsignor Ryan, still wearing his black topcoat and hat. He had the air of a man who had just returned from a funeral.

"May I come in?"

"Of course."

Father Daugherty stepped aside. He felt very light-headed, almost tight. Monsignor Ryan removed his hat and coat and tossed them on the bed. His stony old eyes roved the room.

"Will you have a drink?" Father Daugherty said.

"I don't mind if I do. I could use one."

"I have some Scotch."

"Fine."

Monsignor Ryan sat down on the Spartan chair. Father Daugherty went to the bathroom and made the drink. Ryan was a "social drinker." He drank only in company of important, hard-drinking parishioners. He did not keep a bottle in his room. Drinking was an expensive habit, he had told Mrs. Munally, who had relayed this rather pointedly one day to Father Daugherty. He had never had a drink—alone—with Daugherty. They raised their glasses.

"How's Mrs. Zanowski?" Ryan said.

"Going fast," Daugherty said.

"Too bad," Ryan sighed morosely. "Will the funeral be here?"

"No. Up there."

"It's been a long siege."

"She really hung on," Daugherty said, nodding.

He sipped his drink slowly, waiting for Ryan to reveal the purpose of this informal visit. As he waited, Daugherty was overcome by a sudden presentiment of doom. He remembered Scafidi.

"By the way, is this fellow Scafidi OK?"

Ryan's brow furrowed.

"OK? What do you mean? He does his work."

"Everytime I see him, I wonder about him. People like that, withdrawn, recluses, bottle up a lot of rage. Sometimes they explode. Trunk murders. Sex crimes."

Ryan laughed.

"Mrs. Munally really doesn't know beans about him," Daugherty went on. "Did anybody actually check his references?"

Ryan frowned again. "I don't remember. But don't worry, he seems OK to me. Nothing untoward in two years. Nothing missing. Mrs. Munally keeps a sharp eye on him."

"I mention it only because . . . well, I wouldn't want anything to happen. No scandal."

"Of course," Ryan said, sipping his drink thoughtfully. The idea had not occurred to him before. "Well, keep an eye on him yourself if you're worried," he added. "Check him out. Meanwhile I have some important—and highly confidential news."

Father Daugherty sat on the arm of the lounge chair, waiting. He sipped his drink. The feeling of looming catastrophe heightened.

"I've been down to the Chancery this evening," the Monsignor went on, affecting a grave and solemn manner. "Big things are afoot. They're organizing a new fund drive and they want me to come down there, on a temporary basis, to help work on some of the details. A personal request from McInnerney."

"I see," Father Daugherty said. He remembered the call from Klein. The theological center at CU. It must be the same deal. Klein had not yet published anything about it. It was a very well-kept secret.

"I have this would-be talent for setting up a systematic method," the Monsignor said, with false modesty.

"Yes. It *is* a talent."

"Now, I don't like to leave the parish, especially right before Easter. But His Excellency feels this is an extremely vital and urgent undertaking for the archdiocese. A matter of top priority. Everybody has got to get behind it. An all-out effort. Personal considerations must be placed second. So we discussed what should be done here. I must tell you in all candor that I did not recommend you to him as acting pastor, primarily because of your, what I would call, indifference to the critical financial situation here in our own parish. I can understand your attitude in part. Anybody who was born and raised with as much as you had probably does not understand money. The need for it. People like myself and the Archbishop, who came from humble circumstances, have a more realistic approach. This is only natural."

"I suppose so," Father Daugherty said, hand tightening on his glass, anger rising at the reference to his heritage, over which he had had no control and which, by his vow of poverty, he had renounced.

"Now, with the drive about to be launched, the finances of this parish are even more important. Not only must we accommodate our own requirements, not inconsiderable, we must also lead the archdiocese in the drive. Set an example. The Archbishop wants this parish to provide the drive leadership. For that reason, I did not think it wise to leave it in your hands."

"Well, thank the Lord . . ."

"Let me finish, please," Ryan said. "I recommended pulling in someone else, specifically Monsignor Devlin, on a temporary basis. He has a good track record. But he's sick, I'm told. Dying. So, to make a long story short, McInnerney made the decision to name you acting pastor in my absence, which shan't be long, two, three, maybe four months, perhaps more, depending."

"Do I have a choice?" Daugherty said.

"Technically, yes. I mean, legally. Morally, no."

"I don't want it," Daugherty said emphatically.

"But you'll take it, of course."

Father Daugherty thought for a moment.

"Will I have the same authority as though I were pastor?"

"Authority *and* responsibility."

"And will I be expected to devote much of my time to the drive?"

"As much as possible. With direction and guidance from the Chancery, and as much personal attention as I can give this parish, from a distance. Luckily we have a good lay organization in the parish, to help. Bob Favrot is as good a fund-raiser as I ever knew."

"*I'm* not a good fund-raiser," Daugherty said, looking in his glass.

"I know that. None of you new people are."

Ryan waved his hands toward the bookshelf.

"The emphasis in the seminaries these days is misguided. You could throw all that out and substitute a course in accounting and finance. More emphasis on pastoral theology. Business administration. This is not a corner drugstore. We deal in big money. People like Prial get the breaks these days."

"I don't set the curriculum at the seminary," Father Daugherty said archly. "And, as a matter of fact, while we're being candid, you have more or less shut me out of the financial picture here. I haven't the faintest clue about our financial situation."

"I'll spend a few days briefing you," Ryan said. "Now, besides that, you realize, of course, you'll have to curtail your extracurricular activities? McInnerney was emphatic about that. He spoke specifically of your hippie house. He is of the opinion that such activity fragments the general forward, integrated thrust of the archdiocese, and that an incident down there would be harmful. Damaging. He wants total teamwork, a vast pulling together in this thing, toward one goal. A consolidation . . ."

The presentiment was now fact. Catastrophe.

"I *can't* give up the home," Father Daugherty said. "There are kids down there who need . . ."

"There are other agencies to care for them," Monsignor Ryan said curtly. "Or you could send them back to their homes. McInnerney is adamant about this. During this drive, especially, he does not want the impression abroad that our efforts or funds are being diverted to projects of that kind. Particularly hippies. You know how the average parishioner feels about drugs and hippies . . ."

Father Daugherty stood angrily.

"No drugs are permitted there," he said. "Besides, I have never received one red cent from the Chancery for this project."

"I know that. But the laity does not. Anyway, the matter is final. Settled by the Chancery."

"If you make me abandon my home . . ." Daugherty said, voice trailing away. He did not finish. He was sick, sick, sick. Keep your mouth shut until you see Mary, talk to LeGuiese.

Ryan was now fatherly in tone. "You'll learn," he said, "as we all have, that there are times when we must bow to authority . . . swallow pride. God knows, I learned that a long time ago. You can't fight city hall. Or Rome. Thank you for the drink. I'll talk to you tomorrow. We'll go over the books."

He picked up his hat and coat as though the issue were settled. He closed the door going out. Then, in a moment, he returned.

"I forgot to emphasize," he said, "that all this is very confidential. At least for now."

"You said that," Father Daugherty said curtly. "You needn't have said it twice. By the way, you didn't say what the fund drive was for."

"It's for a new theological center at CU, a brainchild of Cardinal Spellman's. It's going to cost about twenty million. A real doozer."

Ryan left again.

Father Daugherty stood in the middle of the room, smashing his fist into his palm. His whole world seemed to be collapsing before his eyes. Halfway House, the kids . . . his lambs . . . Sharon, Mary. She couldn't carry on by herself. She had her orals coming up, she had to find a place for her school, the OEO grant renewal, a million things. A fund drive for a theological center! Another damned intellectual mausoleum! A place for old men to huddle and tish-tish about the halls, writing their interminable books that no one could read, no one wanted to publish, no one would buy. It was crazy. And now, because of it, he was beached, confined to All Saints', to collecting money, time-serving as Ryan's substitute. Halfway House going to hell . . .

He poured another drink. *By God, he would not take this lying down.* He chug-a-lugged the drink. *He would talk to LeGuiese tomorrow. This was too much.* He poured another drink. *This was all a mistake.* That was clear now. *He was certainly not cut out for this.* He sipped the drink. Mind reeling, legs unsteady, he fell on the bed and slept.

XI

Charles Seymour Jones, young scholar with high purpose, lived in a light-housekeeping room, not far from the Howard University campus. The house was an old brownstone in a neighborhood once occupied by middle-class whites who had moved on to the suburbs. It was owned now by a decent family, a government worker. It was clean, convenient, quiet, a good place to study.

Jones sat at his small desk, sipping instant coffee brewed on a hot plate, studying for his classes that day. His (he thought) was not a brilliant mind. He was a plodder, a detail man, a tortoise. What he learned, he learned thoroughly and did not forget. He won scholarships because he was thorough, dependable, well rounded, and ambitious. He had noted with satisfaction, recently, a magazine article which stated that most of the famous generals of West Point came from the middle of the class—Eisenhower, Bradley, Patton, Ridgeway, others. With the exception of Robert E. Lee, who stood number one, most of the brilliant West Pointers had disappeared into the Corps of Engineers and were never heard from again. At Howard, Jones stood about the middle of his class.

He finished his coffee and set off for the campus, walking at a brisk pace, books and notes packed in a worn attaché case. His first class, an "innovative" course in black history, met in makeshift quarters, a corner of the Union basement. He descended the stairway, peeled off his topcoat, took his seat in an arm-desk. The professor was an anthropologist, very old, slow, a graduate of Tuskegee, who, until now, had been an administrator, not a teacher. The class, twelve handpicked students, was a "pilot project" to help the university devise a hard curriculum in black history for itself, and for white universities around the nation. The project was supported, in part, by a Ford Foundation grant. Seymour's class, one of a half dozen on campus, met twice weekly. For most of the year they had been exploring slavery in America. For the last two weeks, this exploration had focused on a new book, *The Confessions of Nat Turner,* by William Styron, the story of the "first" slave revolt in America in 1835. The class had dissected the book, page by page, not without controversy.

Of the dozen students in the class, seven, by Seymour's count, were "militant," hot-headed advocates of the Movement. They had, more than once, ridiculed Seymour as "too passive," an "Uncle Tom," and worse, "a tool of Martin Luther King," whom they despised. They raged at everything white, including the white author of Nat Turner's revolt. Styron was Establishment, Literary Establishment, a propaganda branch of the Central Establishment. Styron, they hissed, was a Virginian. A racist. His book was bigoted. It was a slur on the black race. Styron had depicted Nat Turner as an idiot (a "house nigger"), indecisive, stupid, Bible-quoting (aping a white Christ), perverted, an abysmal leader. Not only that, one student pronounced triumphantly this day, Turner's was not the "first" revolt in America at all. In 1795, fifty black slaves in Pointe Coupee Parish, a settlement downstream from New Orleans, rose up against their masters. Twenty-five fell bravely in the battle. Twenty-three had been captured. The latter were manacled, shoved on a flatboat, and floated down the Mississippi River. At each little settlement, one of the blacks was led ashore and hanged from a tree in front of the parish church, the local priest officiating.

The last fact jarred Seymour. He was not unaware that the Catholics had fostered slavery in America. Catholic Portugal had introduced black slaves to the Iberian Peninsula. Catholic Spain had enslaved Indians in the New World. When these 20 million souls (according to Bishop Las Casas) had been wiped out by white man's disease, they had imported blacks from Africa, the beginning of the vast, sick traffic in human lives. These black slaves supported Spain's colonies for decades, centuries, making possible the rape of the New World, the flow of precious metal to the Old World, which financed the religious wars against Protestant heresy, the whole brutal sweep of sixteenth- and seventeenth-century European history.

The class had studied all that in detail. It was big, impressive, impersonal, at times hard to comprehend. But the picture of a Catholic priest stringing up a black man on the banks of the Mississippi was vivid and real, almost personal, reminding Seymour of the brutality he had witnessed in his childhood. He left the class in a dejected mood.

Going out into the morning air, he wondered why he was a Catholic. It was strange. Black Catholics were rare—a tiny minority within a minority. Probably only about a million all told—one forty-sixth of the U.S. Catholic population, one two-hundredth of the whole population. There were (he had read) only 165 black priests out of a total of about 60,000 in the U.S. One black priest for every 6,000 black Catholics— a discriminating ratio if there ever was one. There were only nine-hundred black nuns—out of 167,000. The numbers alone proved the Church was racist, or patronizing, or both.

He was a Catholic because his mother had been a Catholic. His mother had been Catholic because *her* mother, a slave, had been Catholic, like her mistress and master. So it had passed down like that, accepted uncritically, like their name, his name, Seymour. The most important things about him, his name and religion, were a white man's legacy. Surely that did not make sense. Martin Luther King was a Protestant. Seymour was a disciple of Dr. King, a believer in his method. So why did he go on being a Catholic? It was habit. He must puzzle this through someday, along with five thousand other questions.

His next class met in the afternoon. He would pass the time at the neighborhood center. It was not a long walk. Seymour headed that way, lost in thought. The OEO forms had been submitted to the regional office in quadruplicate. Next month, he supposed, they would change the reporting method again. He had in mind writing them a strong letter, pointing out that almost half his available time for the center was now spent filling out forms. It would help if they standardized the reporting method.

The ghetto streets were filthy again, littered with glass, trash, stripped and abandoned automobiles. The people were inside their homes, huddled against the March cold. Soon it would be warm. They would sit on their rotting porches and front stoops, in sullen, angry clusters, some lazy, many drunk on wine or stoned on grass. The long, hot summer, it was called. Maybe this time, real trouble. The militants demanded it.

H. Rap Brown was all over the ghetto, making inflammatory speeches. Stokely Carmichael too. Get off your knees, they cried. Better to die on your feet than live on your knees. Someday there would be real help for his people. Bobby Kennedy might help. He would try. But Seymour knew his own people must help themselves too. Anybody with a will could help himself. He, Seymour Jones, was living proof of that.

Reaching the gym he felt a surge of pride. He could hear the steady thump-thump of the basketball on the floor, the shouting, the angry insults. This was his creation. He had conceived it, organized it, found money, volunteers. Now it was a place where many dropout kids found something. Not much—not yet—but more than they found at home. Seeds were being planted. . . .

Inside, the gym was warm, noisy. It smelled of sweat—black sweat. Seymour crossed the floor, waving to his boys. One of them, he was certain, would be another Wilt Chamberlain. The other kids already worshipped him. H. Rap Brown would not understand that. Nor would the guys in his black history class. They would say Chamberlain was a tool of the Establishment, like Jackie Robinson, Rosey Grier, James Brown, and Bobby Mitchell. How they hated!

Off the gym in the rear, Jones had transformed the old coach's office to his own. It was decorated with posters of great athletes, all black, a battered old desk, swivel chair, a few broken steel lockers in which Seymour stored government forms and other papers related to the center. This morning his desk was littered with mail—brought in by one of the kids. As always, Seymour pawed through the pile, looking for mail bearing the OEO regional office return address. Anything from there was handled with dispatch, going into the return mail, if possible. Seymour would let nothing interfere with that.

There was nothing from OEO. There were two or three newsletters and broadsides from the Movement, appeals for money to help the Biafrans, an announcement from a book publisher offering the "genuine" (not the authorized) version of Che Guevara's diaries. There was also a letter from the Chancery of the Archdiocese of Washington. Jones opened this immediately. He read:

Dear Mr. Jones,
This is to inform you that, much as this office regrets the fact, you and your organization must vacate the gymnasium on the property of St. Luke's Cathedral within fourteen weeks. This is official notice, pursuant to the Letter of Occupation Agreement of

February 16, 1967. The building will be utilized by His Excellency, Lawrence O'Fallon McInnerney, Archbishop of Washington, in furtherance of a larger project that will be of great benefit to the black community as a whole.

Yours in Christ,

Monsignor Ignatius Prial
Vicar General
Archdiocese of Washington

Jones read the letter twice, scarcely able to believe the words. Then disbelief turned to anger. He crumpled up the letter and threw it with all his might against the wall. He sat down, breathing hard, mind racing. Just like that. No explanation. Hard, cold. Fourteen weeks notice. Fourteen weeks? Early July, when the kids were out of school, pouring into the streets. The gym, a perfect place, vital to the OEO grant. Without it, probably no money. Like Sister Mary.

Sister Mary!

He ran from the office, across the gym floor, down the worn stone steps, across the macadam play yard, around the corner of the school, up the sagging steps. Her VW was parked out front. Good.

He raced to the classroom. She was there, alone, talking on the telephone. Seymour stopped. The letter! She would want to see it. He turned, ran fast back to his office, picked up the letter, unballed it, running back to Mary's classroom. She was off the phone now, looking depressed, dejected. Seymour thrust the wrinkled letter beneath her nose. She read it through horn-rimmed glasses.

"Oh, no!" she sighed.

Seymour sat down. He tapped his forefinger on her desk. Sister Mary read the letter again, puzzling. Here was the second reference from the Chancery to a "project" for St. Luke's. The first had been Prial's words to her, mysterious, indefinite. Now Seymour evicted! She glanced at the date, Prial's signature. Yesterday. He must have known then, while she was at the Chancery. Must have been preparing the letter. Why hadn't he told her?

"I guess we're both in the same boat," Sister Mary said.

"What's going on?" Seymour said.

"I haven't any idea," she said. "Not a clue."

"They can't do this," he said. "All my kids . . . summer coming. My grant . . ."

"I know. I know. I don't understand it."

"Can you help me, Sister?" Seymour said.

Sister Mary thought. The pressure to padlock her school could have been brought by the Chancery. The Chancery was evicting Seymour from the gym. She had been denied the basement of the cathedral. Not even the pastor knew why. All very mysterious. Too mysterious.

"They're throwing us *all* out of here for some reason," she said. "Maybe they're going to demolish the church."

"St. Luke's? How can they demolish a cathedral?"

"They can do anything they want."

"But where would people go to Mass?"

"I don't know," she said, still thinking. "The land *can't* be that valuable. Or could it? A full city block. Yet . . ."

She reached for the telephone. She dialed All Saints', hoping Daugherty would answer, not the nosy Mrs. Munally. She held her breath. The ringing stopped. A pause. It was Mrs. Munally.

"Is Father Daugherty there?" Mary said.

"Father Daugherty is out now. May I take a message?"

"This is Sister Mary Murray. I have an urgent message for him. When do you expect him back?"

"He didn't say. Can you leave your number where he can reach . . . ?"

"Do you know where he is? How I might reach him?"

Mrs. Munally was silent for a moment.

"If it's important," she said, "try him at 445-1769."

"At 445-1769? Thank you very much."

"Not at all."

Mary hung up. She recognized the number. It was Monsignor Le-Guiese. She dialed it without hesitation. A strange voice answered. She asked for Daugherty.

"Dan? This is Mary. I'm sorry to bother you. The most awful thing just happened."

"What is it?" Daugherty asked in a low voice.

"Seymour got a letter today from the Chancery. A notice of eviction."

"You're kidding!" Daugherty said.

"No."

"What does it say?"

"Nothing. No reason, except that he must move to make way for some larger project of benefit to the black community. They want him out in fourteen weeks."

"I'll be damned. What larger project? Do they have a legal . . . ?"

"I don't know. Yes. Yes. They have a legal right, a signed paper."

Jones butted in: "I *had* to sign it."

"He had to sign it," Mary said to Daugherty.

"Hmmmmmmmmm," Daugherty said.

"Something odd is going on," Mary said. "I think now Prial probably brought pressure on the city to close *me* down. They wouldn't let me move into the basement over there because of some long-range project. Prial said he wouldn't want me to get all settled and then have to move. See?"

"See? See what?"

"Don't be dense."

"You sound paranoid."

"It's not *imagined* persecution," Mary said indignantly. "It's real. I think they're going to demolish everything and maybe build something new."

"Why don't you call Prial and ask him?"

"I don't think he would tell me. *You* call him."

"Mary, listen. Can I call you back? I'm in conference here. Very important. I'll tell you about it later. I know . . . Why don't you get Jones to call Marv Klein and have *him* call Prial? He swings a lot of weight. This is right up his alley. Maybe he already knows about it. I'll call you in an hour. As soon as I can get to a phone booth. I can't talk here. Not now. Please understand."

"I do," she said. "Call me at Halfway House."

They hung up. She stared at the telephone. Why was he with LeGuiese? What was so important? A good idea, calling Klein. She passed it to Seymour Jones, but he hesitated.

"He'll make a big story out of it," Jones said. "Maybe we don't want publicity. It might be some routine error. Maybe I ought to run out to the Chancery. I'd hate to bring Klein in when we might settle it quietly without him. He always inflames everybody down here. Besides, I don't want OEO to know yet. Not until I can find someplace else, or something. They'd cut off my money tomorrow, maybe."

"You have a point. Yes, I think you're right. Go to the Chancery. Talk to Prial. That's sensible."

"Damn!" Jones said, standing up, holding the letter between thumb and forefinger, as though it were infected with the plague. He looked at his watch.

"I'll drive you," Mary said. "Come on."

They drove northwest on Massachusetts Avenue, out of the black community, then to the white section, the rows of apartments around DuPont Circle, then out Embassy Row, passing the mosque, the enormous British embassy, the elegant mansions going up the hill toward the Naval Observatory.

"You know what I found out today in history?" Jones said.

"What?"

"Nat Turner's was not the first slave revolt."

"No?"

"There was one in Louisiana in 1795."

"Oh," she said, thinking. "Maybe they mean *American* revolt. Louisiana was . . . let's see . . . 1795 . . . French, I think. Or Spanish. It changed hands a couple of times right in there. We didn't get it until 1803. Louisiana Purchase."

"About fifty slaves formed an army," Seymour went on. "Half were killed in battle, the other half captured. The parish priests hanged one each in front of the churches as a warning. I don't see how a priest could do a thing like that, do you?"

Mary frowned.

"Some of them did worse than that," she said. "Much worse."

"Such as?"

"Oh, you know. The Popes . . . the Borgias . . . the Inquisition . . . the standard chamber of horrors. There's no denying it."

"No," Jones said. "I'll have to read about that."

"Plenty has been written," she said, whipping the VW out of traffic, into the circular driveway of the Chancery.

"I'll pull around the corner and wait," she said. "No sense in giving the impression we're a cabal."

"A *what*?"

"A conspiracy. Get in there. Give 'em hell."

She pulled away quickly, onto the avenue, around the corner. Seymour pushed the doorbell. He asked the maid for the Vicar General. She looked disapprovingly at his clothes, his face, asked him to wait, and closed the door, leaving him on the doorstep. A few minutes later she returned and led him down the hall to Prial's office. The Vicar General came to the door, smiling genially. He had been expecting Jones but not so quickly.

"You didn't waste any time, did you?" Prial said. "Come on in. Coffee?"

"No . . . no, thanks," Jones said. He had not been in the Chancery before. He was awed by the splendor, the gleaming brass, the crystal chandelier in the hallway, the polished marble floors, slippery underfoot. Inside the office, Jones took a chair in front of Prial's desk.

"I'm sorry we have to move you," Prial said. "If you've come to appeal, I'm afraid the decision is final. Naturally we weighed this with utmost understanding, knowing your situation, what a splendid job you've done. Really, you're a credit to your race."

Jones was crushed. There could be no appeal. That was clear not only from the words but also the tone, the look in Prial's eyes.

"It's tough on the kids," Jones said. "Twelve weeks from now school will be out. They don't have a place to go."

"Yes, I know," Prial said. "It's a tough break. But—you remember— we said last year it would not be a permanent deal? You've been there a full year. Actually that was longer than we thought it might be available. You remember that conversation?"

Jones did not. Nothing had been said to him either during the preliminaries or when he signed the paper for the newsmen, and later, again, for the television cameras, with the Archbishop decked out in full regalia. No time limit had been set.

"The Chancery does everything it can for the ghetto," Prial said. "The poor. You realize, probably, that the Archbishop desegregated the schools down there before the Supreme Court order? There are—today— some six thousand black children enrolled in our 19 predominantly black parochial schools. These are good schools, heavily subsidized by this office, as I'm sure you know. That's a heck of a lot more than any other church has seen fit to do. The Archbishop received the annual award of the N-double-A-C-P for that work."

Prial reeled off further statistics. These had been prepared by the staff yesterday afternoon, drawn up into a "fact sheet." Prial had studied it last night, committing the essential points to memory.

"There's nothing I can do?" Jones said, now feeling that his effort, the neighborhood center, as seen from the lofty perspective of the Chancery, was nothing. Piddling. He rose to leave.

"I'm afraid not," Prial said. "We're very, very sorry. If we can be of further service, please call."

Jones retreated to the front door. Going down the hall, he wondered: What untold riches were managed here? Hundreds of millions, maybe billions, he thought. Half the real estate in Washington. Ownership passing down, generation after generation. Much of it, originally, made possible by slave labor. Blacks. He left the building, seething. That patronizing son of a bitch! I'm a credit to my race!

He found Mary parked on a side street. He climbed in the car. They moved away.

"A waste of time," Jones said sullenly.

"Did you ask him what was going on?"

"No. He was waiting for me. Snowed me with statistics, how much the Church is doing in the ghetto."

"The party line," Mary said, cutting sharply back onto the avenue.

"Drop me at the *Tribune,*" Jones said curtly, then added: "Please."

"OK."

They drove on in silence. Mary was thinking now of Dan Daugherty. Why was he with LeGuiese? His voice had sounded troubled. Something *very important.* But what?

Seymour got out at the Tribune Building, thanking Sister Mary for her help. He found Marv Klein on the editorial floor, talking on the telephone. He hung up when he saw Jones.

"Hello, Seymour," Klein said. "What's new?"

"I got trouble," Jones said.

"What now?"

"We're going to be evicted from the gymnasium."

"*Evicted*—why? Who says?"

"The Archbishop—the Chancery."

"What the hell *for?*"

"You asking me? I can't read the man's mind. He says get out in fourteen weeks."

"No reason given? Nothing at all?"

"He says he's got some larger purpose for the gym."

"Larger purpose? What larger purpose?"

"Like I tell you, man. I don't know. That's why I'm here. Maybe you can help me. Sister Mary's been evicted too. She's got to move her Montessori school. They won't let her move into St. Luke's basement."

"What the hell's going on?"

"I don't know, something big."

He gave Klein Prial's letter. Klein read it, chewing on the end of his copy pencil. His brow furrowed. News ticker piled up on his desk.

"I went to the Chancery to see Prial," Jones said. "No good."

Klein laid the letter aside. He looked at Jones, his creation. Men like Jones were indispensable to the black cause. He might be, in time, another Martin Luther King, leading his people to nonviolent legal victory, the bridge between the revolutionaries and the Establishment on which compromise must be built. The mention of Prial's name reminded Klein again that he did not trust the man. He was an Irish con artist, peddling his boondoggle at CU. Not a word about Jones being evicted, either. Klein was glad now he had killed the piece on the theological center.

"You have no idea what this is all about?" Klein said.

"No," Jones said.

"Have you talked to the pastor at St. Luke's?"

"He's out of it, man. I deal directly with the Chancery. They keep him in the dark."

"Let me call Prial," Klein said.

He picked up the phone, gave instructions to the operator. The Vicar General answered cheerily.

"We've been waiting to see something on the theological center," he said. "When is it coming?"

"We're still working on that," Klein said, evading.

"Keep us informed," Prial said.

"Say," Klein said, "I've got Seymour Jones in my office. He says he's being evicted from the St. Luke's gym. Is there any way you can be persuaded to change your mind?"

There was a pause.

"I'm afraid not," Prial said. "We let him stay over a year. We'd like it to be permanent, but we made it clear that it would not be. We need it back now."

"Why?"

"Oh . . . for good reasons, believe me."

Prial followed this with a brief version of the fact sheet, an ocean of statistics. Klein began jotting notes on newsprint. Then he gave up, cutting in.

"OK, OK," he said impatiently. "But what about Sister Mary? She's being evicted too."

"The city's doing that," Prial said. "The building was condemned months ago."

"Where will she relocate?" Klein said.

"You have to ask her that. The school is not an authorized project. It's strictly informal."

"I see," Klein said. "What about the cathedral?"

"What about it?" Prial said, voice lowering. Then: "Look, Marv.

Can I help you further on the gym thing? You caught me at a busy time. Up to my neck . . ."

"No. That's all right. Thanks a lot."

"Let us know on the center. Remember, we're holding it for your exclusive."

"OK. So long."

Klein hung up, weighing Prial's words. Klein had not missed the sudden evasion when he mentioned St. Luke's. His journalist's instinct told him he had struck a sensitive nerve. Yes. There was more to the Jones deal than Prial admitted. He turned to Jones.

"Seymour, let me handle this. Give me a few days. OK? I might be able to muscle him around."

"Anything you can do, Marv," Jones said. "This is as much your thing as it is mine."

"I know," Klein said.

"By the way, I heard something today that might interest you," Jones said.

"What's that?"

"I found out Nat Turner's revolt was *not* the first in the United States."

"Really?"

Jones now told his story again. Klein had liked *Nat Turner*. The book was still newsworthy—the subject of much controversy. This tidbit from Jones—if it checked out—would make a good feature. He jotted brief, shorthand notes. He buzzed for a copyboy. He sent a note to a reporter saying: *See me about Nat Turner feature.*

"Thanks for that, Seymour," Klein laughed. "I ought to hire you as my resident historian. Keep in touch. I'll let you know what I hear from the Chancery."

"OK. Thanks a lot, man."

Seymour left. Klein got up, stretched, walked through the city room to the desk of a reporter, a young black, George Emerson. He was Klein's protégé, a specialist in investigative reporting, a quiet, bespectacled Harvard man, a one-time *Crimson* reporter, very thorough. When he saw Klein, he stood.

"Seymour Jones was here just now," Klein said. "The Chancery is forcing him out of the gym at St. Luke's. Sister Mary's got to move her Montessori school too. The claim is, she's being forced out by the city because the building is condemned. But the two things may be related. The Chancery has plenty of drag down at the District Building.

I talked to Prial, but he wouldn't give. Here's his letter to Jones. I have a feeling they're doing something big—maybe involving the cathedral itself. Why don't you poke around the neighborhood? Go see the pastor at St. Luke's. Jones says he doesn't know anything, but he might. Dig in, and then make a run on the Chancery. Talk to Prial. See if you can get to McInnerney. If something doesn't fit, I know you'll smell it out."

"Very odd," George Emerson said, polishing his glasses. "I heard a rumor last week that a lot of land was being bought up all around St. Luke's. I tried to get a line on it by phone but didn't have time. I don't have anything solid, just rumor. I wonder . . ."

"I don't know," Klein said. "Find out. Give it all your time. Let it run. Even if nothing turns up, the Jones eviction, plus the Sister Mary eviction, is a good, hard news story. Worth the front page."

"OK," Emerson said. "I'll see what I can do."

The investigation, Klein knew, was in good hands. He returned to his desk, put on his coat, and left for home.

XII

After she got the children off to school, Jean Favrot returned to her bedroom to dress. She had carried out the deadly chores of breakfast with her usual brisk efficiency, but her mind had been elsewhere. It was fixed, almost continuously, on her group. On Margo, Joan . . . Mike. Especially Mike. She had decided that he must be a lawyer. She was certain that he had a sailboat and two teen-age children, that his wife had been put away in a home for alcoholics.

Sitting before her makeup mirror, ringed with small bulbs, Jean rubbed lotion on her face and hummed "Hello, Dolly." The diet was already working. Her face had lost the puffy, bloated look. Her skin was clear and clean—not as many wrinkles as she had first suspected. Her hair was trimmed stylishly short, and—so it seemed to Jean—it had a new luster, new body. There was life in the old girl yet, she thought. Plenty of life.

She left the house feeling very good. She was doing something important—helping with a new parish census. She wore new underwear, her new paisley, new low-heeled pumps. In her hand, she held a piece of paper with the list of unfamiliar names, the new people who had moved to McLean recently, All Saints' parish. These names had come to Monsignor Ryan through his ingenious grapevine which included tipsters at moving companies, the dairies, the telephone company, the Welcome Wagon ladies, and the paper boys. Jean, and other volunteers, called on the new people to welcome them to the parish.

Her list was comprised mostly of people who had moved into a new garden apartment. The grounds were yet a sea of frozen mud. She followed the new sidewalks from building to building, still a trifle light-headed from the diet, yet feeling pulses of the old energy. It required forced boldness on her part to confront total strangers, pry delicately into their lives. Yet it was interesting—better than housework, and she knew Dr. Cantor, the group, would approve.

She pressed the doorbell of apartment 6B, noting the elegant calling card, Scotch-taped to the door below the peephole. WILLIAM M. CLARK. It matched the name on her list. She heard chimes, very soft. She held her list in a prominent position, so the Clarks would know immediately that she was not a door-to-door saleswoman. The door opened. To her surprise, Jean found herself looking not on a housewife, but a man, tall, slim, suntanned, athletic-looking, casually dressed in cashmere sweater, gray flannel slacks, brown suede shoes. He was about forty-five.

"Good morning," she said, recovering. "My name is Jean Favrot. I'm a volunteer worker for All Saints' parish. I'm helping conduct a parish census. Your name is on my list. I . . . May I talk to you and your wife?"

He smiled pleasantly. His teeth were straight, white, sound. His eyes, deep blue, wide set beneath bushy brows, sparkled merrily, as though he were amused.

"I'm Bill Clark. Won't you please come in? I'm afraid there's only me."

He held the door open, standing aside with charm and poise. Entering the apartment, alone with a strange man, Jean felt uneasy. The room smelled of pipe tobacco—masculine. Where was Mrs. Clark? Why was *he* home—not in his office? The furniture was expensive, Californian, contemporary, tasteful. It suited the room, also contemporary, with much Thermopane, overlooking the pool. There were many books on shelves.

"I was just making some coffee," Bill Clark said. "May I get you some? I'm afraid it's only instant."

His voice stirred her. It was deep and firm. The accent was, what, Midwest?

"Thank you just the same . . . I can't stay but a minute."

"It's no trouble. Will you have sugar or cream?"

She was cold, slightly hungry. The coffee would be warm, invigorating, and it would kill her hunger pangs.

"No," she said, "just black. You're sure it's no trouble?"

"Absolutely. Have a seat. I won't be a second."

He disappeared into the kitchen. Jean sat on the couch, sinking deep into down cushions. She thought of her own couch, her furniture, battered by successive waves of bouncing boys, pillow fights, dirty sneakers. One day soon, she would have it reupholstered. Or maybe she would simply sell the AT&T—her inheritance—and buy a whole new living room set. This time, contemporary.

Bill Clark came from the kitchen with the coffee. He carried it across the foyer into the living room with a very steady hand, without spilling a drop. The cup was very good china. He gave it to Jean, sat on a leather hassock.

"How in the world did you come by *my* name?" he said.

Jean blushed. It was a question often asked.

"They come from lists of new people." she said. "Movers and so on."

"But the movers don't know I'm Catholic," he said.

Jean was now quite uneasy. Perhaps there had been a mistake.

"Are . . . *are* you Catholic?" she stammered.

"Sort of," he said, eyes going to his cup. "That is . . . I *was* a Catholic. I'm divorced."

"Oh . . . ," Jean said, quickly adding: "I'm sorry."

Bill Clark furrowed his brow. He thought: How extraordinary! Here he was, not one month in the apartment, and this woman coming from the Church. Incredible efficiency. But how did they get his name? Had they traced him back to Palo Alto? Back to St. Anthony's? Were they computerized? Impossible. He looked at Jean: good Catholic mother on earnest business for the Church. Stunned to find a lonely divorced man on her list! Very pretty, well-bred, intelligent wide-set eyes. Like Angela, in a way. But softer, friendlier. A new dress, too. Then he remembered. On the apartment application form, he had printed "Catholic" in the question marked: "Religious Preference." He had thought of putting "Ex-Catholic" but that seemed flippant. But how had *they* managed to find out?

"Your pastor must have a hell of a grapevine," Bill said, laughing.

"He's very thorough." She held the list aloft, as though in proof. She did not know what to do or say. Divorced! It was the first time in her census-taking she had hit a situation like this. She was relieved that he seemed understanding. He might have been bitter, resentful. Slammed the door in her face. She wondered why he was divorced. Probably another woman. Jilted? Left behind in California? She set the empty cup on the coffee table.

"Well, thanks for the coffee. I guess we really goofed this one."

"Not at all," he said. He found the situation amusing. He chuckled. "I'm still wondering where they got my name."

"Me, too," Jean said. "I feel ridiculous."

"No. No. Don't. It may have been a goof—back in California. Maybe my old pastor—or somebody in the rectory—sent my name along when I moved, forgetting that Angela and the kids were staying out there. That must be it! Either that . . . either that or somebody who hates my guts did it for a joke."

"Some joke," Jean said, wondering about his life there. About Angela, the kids, his pastor.

"The pastor was pretty old," Clark said. "Maybe senile. He might have done it by mistake. Anyway . . . I wish I could be of service. And I must congratulate *your* pastor. He certainly picks charming census-takers."

Jean blushed. No one had called her charming in aeons.

"Well, anyway," she said, getting to her feet, "welcome to McLean. If you . . . if you need some spiritual counsel, we have a great priest . . . very understanding . . . named Father Daugherty. I'm sure he'd be glad to meet you. Even if . . . I mean . . ."

She stopped in confusion What *did* divorced Catholics do? Give up completely? Go to Mass anyway? She had known one or two Catholic families that broke up. But the people had all moved away, scattered in the wind. She didn't know what they did afterward about religion.

"Thank you very much," Bill said. "But if I want to go on with it— and I'm not sure what I want to do—I better find one of these underground priests, don't you think? I mean, I've read your Archbishop

McInnerney is as old-fashioned as they come. A Spellman man. Last I heard, they hadn't bought divorce."

He smiled.

"Not that, I suppose," Jean said. "But, really, we're quite modern at All Saints'. Not the pastor, Monsignor Ryan. But Daugherty seems to be."

Why did she feel this compulsion to rescue Bill Clark's spiritual life? She had never seen the man before. She had known him ten minutes. Yet here she was . . . feeling inside that she should persuade him to see Father Daugherty. She felt sorry for the man. Alone now, in this apartment, his children—how many?—three thousand miles away. When would he ever see them? What led to the divorce? He seemed so gentle, so lacking in guile. He could *not* have been the guilty party. Yet . . . *she* had the children. He must be guilty. She burned with curiosity.

"You're very nice to mention him," Clark said. "Everybody has been very nice. I like your town. It's very friendly. Very clean and pretty."

"It used to be very quiet," she said, remembering. "Virginia countryside with a few sleepy roads, farms, a few big houses, like Hickory Hill. Now, it's a rat race. Growing like mad. Have you seen the traffic on Dolly Madison at five o'clock?"

"Yes. I work over there. At the new electronics lab. On my days in the office, I get caught in it."

"What do you do?"

She knew she should be leaving. She was prying where she shouldn't. His life, his work, his family, his religion were no concern of hers.

"I'm sort of a mathematician," he said. "I worked in a think tank on the Coast, an Air Force kind of thing. Now I work for Data Inc., a subsidiary of IDA, which, if you don't know, is an outfit that analyzes Pentagon war plans and weapons. I've only just started. Our computer is not on the line yet. It'll take another month or two to de-bug it. Meanwhile, I just run over every other day and check in . . . punch my time card, so to speak . . . then I hurry back here and work on my first love, a history of mathematics that I'm writing."

He did not know why he ran on and on with this woman. She could not possibly be interested in his problems, his life. She probably had a hundred names on the list to check out, a half dozen kids at home to supervise after school. Yet she seemed in no hurry. He was happy for the company. Outside of the office, and one or two dinner invitations from the brass, he had not yet talked to a soul from McLean, other than the apartment manager, the shopkeepers, the milkman. It was good to have company. She was a little shapeless in the middle, but she had very fine legs and a strange, enticing voice.

"Don't rush off. Please sit down," he said, smiling, thrusting a hand toward the couch behind her. "Let me get you some more coffee."

"I shouldn't . . . really."

"Oh come on. You must be . . . your feet are probably tired. Give them a rest."

She said all right, just a half. While he went to the kitchen, she examined the books on the shelves, row after row of famous novels and biography and history. Reminding her, that among other things, she must get back to reading. Her mind was rusty. As a child she had been an omnivorous reader. Since she married Bob, a nonreader, she had scarcely opened a book. *The Caine Mutiny. By Love Possessed. The Man in the Gray Flannel Suit. Dr. Zhivago.* What else? Her eyes darted from the books to his desk. There was a portable typewriter, a stack of manuscript, heavily edited in a neat, precise hand, a pipe stand with a dozen well-chewed pipes. Feeling as though she were a Peeping Tom, she turned back to the couch and sat down.

Bill boiled the water on the electric range, spooned out the coffee into the cups. The jar was low. He made a note on his shopping list. He was becoming a list-keeper these days. She was very sweet, that Jean. With that curious accent. Not accent, really, but musical note to her voice. It was fascinating. Strange, too, having a woman in the place. When he moved in, he had enjoyed many erotic fantasies. But no woman had yet crossed the threshold except Jean Favrot. He had turned into a lonely recluse. He had channeled that pent-up energy into the book, having read that Papa never humped when he was writing. He did not think of himself as a budding Hemingway, but welcomed all helpful-writing-hints from the masters. It was much harder work than he ever imagined. He carried the cups to the living room.

"Where do you come from?" Jean said, accepting the cup. "Are you a native Californian?"

"No. Indiana. Are you a native Washingtonian?"

"No. Bob . . . my husband . . . and I are from Louisiana."

"Ah . . . *that's* it. Your accent. Favrot. Are you Creole?"

"No," Jean laughed. "We're Cajun."

"Evangeline and . . . and . . . what's-his-face?"

"Gabriel. Arceneaux."

"Yes. Fascinating."

"We're from Breaux Bridge, the crawfish capital of the world. Isn't *that* fascinating?"

"I've always wanted to see that part of the country. I've been to New Orleans, the French Quarter. That was fabulous. The food . . ."

"It's a good place to eat and drink. But I hate New Orleans. It's so dirty, dingy . . . a backwater now . . . losing shipping to Texas and Mississippi. Or so I've heard, anyway. I don't get down there much anymore."

"What does your husband do?"

"He's an AA—administrative assistant—on the Hill for Senator Root of Louisiana."

"Must be interesting," he said.

Not in many years had Jean thought of Bob's job as interesting. Nor had it occurred to her that anyone else might think it so. He was being polite, she thought. A very well-mannered man.

"We meet a lot of interesting people."

"I'll bet you do."

The political world was foreign to Bill Clark. A mysterious jungle about which he knew nothing solid, except for the turgid novels of Allen Drury. He did not think of himself as "political." In California, he had been a registered Democrat, voting, somewhat desultorily, against Ronald Reagan. Since the divorce—his clean separation from the Church—he had become more sympathetic to liberal causes.

"Your work sounds interesting, too," she said. "Are you one of those mathematical geniuses?"

"Of course!" he laughed. "A mad genius."

"I can't keep my checkbook straight," Jean said.

"Neither can I," Bill said. "I'm lousy at arithmetic. My forte is mathematical theory. If you stay in theory, nobody can disprove you."

"That's nice. My bank disproves me every month."

"How many children do you have?"

"Nine," Jean said, feeling again what she had felt at group, the shame, that she was a peasant, an animal.

"Wow!" he said. "I thought six was a bunch."

"You have . . . had . . . *six?*"

"Yes," he said, the pain in the chest coming now, the onset of the aching and depression that came when he talked, or remembered them.

"How old?" Jean said, seeing the dark shadow in his eyes, determined to steer off the subject as soon as he answered this mandatory question.

"Ah . . . let's see. Sixteen through four. Girl-boy, boy-boy, girl-boy. How old are yours?"

"Sixteen through . . . we have a ten-months-old baby."

She had thought to omit the last. It seemed ridiculous at her age.

"Do any of them ski?"

"Gosh no!" she said. "It's too expensive!"

She had once looked into the cost of outfitting the older ones with ski gear. The sport was all the rage now, with the new slopes in Maryland and southern Pennsylvania. Outfitting them would have cost a small fortune. Bob had said no.

"My kids are great skiers," Bill said. "We lived on the slopes, practically. Especially after Angela and I broke up. It's a great way to spend the day with your kids. You'd probably make a good skier. You have the build. The legs."

The reference to her body brought color to Jean's cheeks, a sudden racing of her heartbeat. For an instant, she pictured herself on a slope with Bill Clark, wearing stretch pants, stylish parka, a knitted cap, sunglasses. Like the Kennedys and McNamaras. Afterward, in the ski lodge, drinking Campari and soda, lounging by the fire, then doing the Monkey and the Frug, a genuine jet-setter, carefree, irresponsible, fun-loving. Still later, in the chalet, tender affections, whispered promises, the feel of his firm, masculine hand on her breast, the wild, desperate embrace. She blinked her eyes to wipe away the vision.

"I'm sure I'd break my ankle. Bob would love that!"

"Maybe I can get you some more coffee?"

"Oh, no thank you. Absolutely not. Look at the time! I must be running."

"Say," he said, sitting forward in his chair. "Maybe you can help me. I need a good typist, preferably some gal in the neighborhood, maybe a housewife who can spend two or three hours a day on it. Do you by any chance know of someone?"

"Typist?" Jean said, again feeling her heartbeat quicken. She had, at one time, been a fair typist. Not fair, excellent. She had typed Bob's campaign speeches, all his correspondence in the old days. Over the years, she had let it go, but she had a portable with script typeface on which she typed letters. But no! What was she thinking?

"Let me think," she said, resting her forehead on her fist. "Typist. Typist. Who can type? I can't think of anybody offhand. But I will certainly look around and give you a ring if I find someone."

She rose to leave.

"That would be very nice of you," he said, standing. "I tried the employment agencies. They turned up a few gals who thought they might be able to handle it. Hopeless dreamers and romanticists—carried away by the thought of typing a writer's manuscript. None of them could pass the agency typing test. I'll tell you, these days a typist is worth her weight in gold. If I could find a good one, I'd marry her. Here, let me write down my number in case you get an inspiration."

He wrote it on the top sheet of the telephone pad, tore it off. Jean put it in her purse. She was suddenly awash with feelings of conspiracy, as though the number were a stolen secret document.

"Very nice meeting you," she said, extending her hand. "Please forgive this stupid intrusion."

"It was my pleasure. I enjoyed it, believe me."

His hand was firm, not large, but firm. Exploring the sensation, she let her own hand remain in his longer than she might have. She withdrew it, awkwardly. It was a small thing, but surely he noticed. She should not have done it. He might have got the wrong idea about her.

He opened the door.

"Good-bye now," she said.

"So long."

She descended the stairs, determined not to look back. Going down, she hoped she would hear his door close. She did not. She looked up and back, through the rail. He was leaning on the door jamb, watching. She smiled sheepishly and waved. He returned the wave. She hurried off down the sidewalk to the next name and address.

She worked the rest of the morning, finishing the list in a haze of confusion. She could not get her mind off Bill Clark. She could think of no typist other than herself. Now, driving home, she thought. It would be good for her to take on a *real* outside project. Something more than this stupid census. It would clear the cobwebs in her mind, give her something to think about besides the children. It would be fascinating, too. After all these years, she would have her own personal income. She could blow it—*all* of it—on new clothes? Join the Book-of-the-Month! Dr. Cantor and the group would really be impressed.

She turned into the driveway slowly, thinking. What would Bob say? Her working in close relationship to a divorced man who lived alone? What would his neighbors think? Her going in and out of the apartment at all hours? Bob would say they didn't need the money, that it embarrassed him to have her working. It would complicate his income tax return.

She parked in the driveway. The house was quiet. The children were not yet home from school. She went immediately to her bedroom, sat down on the bed, fished the number from her purse. With trembling fingers and butterflies in her stomach, she dialed his number. He answered on the second ring.

"Mr. Clark?" she said.

"Yes, this is Bill Clark."

"Hi. This is Jean Favrot. I was just in your—"

"Of course, Jean. Did you finish your list?"

"Yes."

"Turn up any more lemons?"

She laughed. Then she turned serious, businesslike:

"I've been thinking. I'm a pretty fair typist. Do you think I might qualify to type your book?"

There was a pause. Jean's heart sank. This was stupid. Really wild. She had never acted so impulsively.

"Could you spare the time?" Bill Clark said.

"Oh yes," she said. "I have a full-time maid. I . . . I've been looking for something. To take my mind off the children and the housework."

"From my point of view, it would be just fine if you have the speed and accuracy. I need someone right away. I'm already pretty far down the road—a hundred and fifty pages or so."

"A hundred and fifty pages! How long will it be altogether?"

"I don't know, maybe twice that—at least. You're sure you can type?"

"Oh yes. One, two, three days, I'll be right up to snuff."

"All right then. If you're sure, shall we talk money? I pay the going rate—sixty cents a page for original and two carbons. You supply paper and all that, plus a pica-face typewriter. If you don't have one, you could rent an electric. I'll pay the rental."

Jean mentally calculated: One-fifty times sixty cents—almost a hundred dollars. Twice that—two hundred. Enough for three or four dresses, if she were careful.

"That sounds fine by me. I'll begin tomorrow."

"Wonderful."

"I'll come by tomorrow and pick up some copy."

"Fine. See you then."

" 'Bye."

Jean hung up slowly, overcome by an eerie feeling. Was she losing her mind? Bob would be furious. She didn't care. To hell with him! She would snatch a tiny bit of her own life for herself. Live it as she pleased. It was no sin. God! Speaking of sin, look at the girls in group! Margo, Joan. They were leading double, triple lives. So what was a little part-time job like this? They would really be surprised when they heard.

She tore the telephone number into tiny shreds and flushed them down the toilet.

XIII

Helen Hanrahan's day was, as usual, a long, busy one. After Mass and Communion, she had stopped by the home of her gardener, who had been stricken with a fatal illness, to bring him carrot juice and words of encouragement. Returning to her luxurious home on Foxhall Road, she spent the rest of the morning typing out her column, a spiritually uplifting daily message for her millions of readers, working with her secretary, sorting through the mail, hundreds of letters a day from people the world over, asking for help, both financial and spiritual. To most of these, she returned an inspirational prayer card. To a few of the most pathetic cases, she sent a personal letter, suggesting they place their faith and hope in God, Who would answer their prayers.

She spent two hours on money matters, not an inconsequential detail. Her late husband, an industrialist, had left her and her married children millions, a vast portfolio in several private trusts. She watched these investments with a hawk eye and regularly forwarded the trustees in New York her own uncanny predictions on the stock market. Her columns, books, lectures, and television appearances brought hundreds of thousands of dollars annually. She supported a large research and clerical staff. Then, too, she was involved, lately, in a large and demanding work of charity: fund-raising for a crippled children's hospital, for which she already had pledges amounting to $50 million.

She lunched at the Sulgrave Club with a magazine writer who was doing a profile on her, which would include a detailed account of her premonition that John F. Kennedy would be assassinated, and the futile moves she had taken to try to prevent the tragedy. In the afternoon, she went to St. Elizabeth's, a hospital for the mentally disturbed. She visited with many of the less violent patients, bringing the Word of Christ. By mid-afternoon, she was home again, feeling fatigued. She lay down for a nap.

The fatigue soon vanished. She felt lofted on a distant cloud, held there by the strange euphoria that usually signaled the coming of an important vision. She had been expecting it. Three days before, at a bridge luncheon with the wife of the French ambassador, she had felt the first signs. A sudden sense of unreality, a detachment from her surroundings, the almost indescribable feeling of oneness with God. That night she had awakened to see a bright shaft of light cutting through her winow. The light reappeared the second and third nights. And all this day, as she went about her works of charity, the rapturous vibrations inside her had mounted in intensity, like music played by a cosmic symphony orchestra. She slept.

She awoke an hour later. She felt as though the air had changed. Her heart surged with love, the curious euphoria. She glanced at the clock: four one. Added sideways, the numerals totaled five. Since childhood five had been her guiding number. Her good days were always fives. The time, she was certain, had come.

Her gentle eyes went to the window. Almost at once, she saw a blinding shaft of light, then heard the heavenly music. She rose from her bed. Her step was light, as though her feet were not touching the floor. As she approached the window, the shaft of light suddenly broadened. The room, the yard, the sky, were bathed in a fantastic reddish-yellowish glow. She stood at the window, spirit consumed by the light, the music. Everywhere she felt warmth, love, the infinite goodness of God, as though nothing of the world could touch her.

As she peered lovingly into the light, she now saw a strange sight. Before her, to infinity, stretched a placid vermilion sea. Coming over the horizon toward her, she saw what at first appeared to be a golden ship under full sail. As it came closer, she realized it was not a ship, but a chair, a golden throne. Seated upon this throne, she saw what appeared to be the figure of Pope Paul, his gaunt face a mask of agony, his thin hands turned white, so firmly did he grasp the arms of the throne. Then, before her eyes, the throne was suddenly sucked into a vast whirlpool. It spun round and round the walls of the whirlpool, sinking deeper with each revolution, until she could no longer see the Pope's head. The whirlpool closed as quickly as it opened. The surface of the sea, now calm, was filled with flotsam and jetsam. Amid this rubble, Helen saw the throne, overturned, bobbing gently. And then she saw a hand rise above the water, a white, bony hand, clutching frantically at the air. She heard—distinctly—a cry of death. Then she saw the hand no more.

There was a great stillness on the water now. It was calm, like a millpond, reflecting a dazzling rainbow of color. Now, over the same horizon, Helen saw tiny figures moving toward her. Mere specks at first. As they came closer, she saw that the specks were little children. She believed she knew at once who they were: Lucia dos Santos and her cousins, Jacinta and Francisco Marto. The children of Fatima. Each of the children was tugging a golden rope garlanded with roses that wrapped over their shoulders and fell behind them for a vast distance toward the horizon. The children crossed her field of vision and passed on. The rope went on and on and on, until at last Helen saw that it was attached to a strange vessel which now appeared on the horizon. It came forward, majestically, solemnly, bathed in a vast halo of light. Angels swooped, like seagulls, across the bow, some sounding trumpets. There were others in the water, like porpoises, playfully bobbing ahead and to the side.

As it drew nearer, Helen saw, standing in the bow, a man, dark-skinned, kindly, almost Oriental in aspect. He was naked from the waist up. His eyes were dazzlingly black. He raised his right arm and with that gesture, the sea disappeared. In its place, there appeared a verdant valley filled with plumed birds, sheep grazing on hillsides. A gentle wisp of smoke curled skyward from a distant hillside. It was peaceful and quiet. The man stood on the crest of a small hill overlooking the valley. Behind him, seemingly growing from the ground, she saw a small cross. Then in the valley, she saw thousands of upturned faces, black, white, yellow, all wreathed in smiles.

Entranced, Helen could feel herself, her spirit, moving from the room, the house, the yard, floating into the scene before her eyes. She felt the warmth of the people, the power and love of the man on the hillside. She felt like a tiny seed that had sprouted, that was growing, burgeoning into a colossal flower. And she thought: Here is the beginning of wisdom. The man on the hillside raised his arms toward her and her flight was suddenly arrested, as though she were held in the grip of a powerful magnetic force. The man looked toward her with liquid eyes and spoke: "Go, ye, and tell all men what you have seen. And they shall come hither in great multitudes and then there will be peace on earth. For I come again to this vale of tears, this valley of the shadow of death, to plant my seed."

Then it was gone. Helen found herself staring into the commonplace of her side yard, the walnut grove, dark and somber in the growing dusk. She returned to her bed, weak, light-headed. But the meaning of the vision was perfectly clear to her. The appearance of the Fatima children told her that her vision was related to their last secret prophecy, the one that lay yet unopened in a vault in the Vatican. Like her own vision, she was sure, the last unopened Fatima prophecy foretold Apocalypse. Fire. Blood. Violence. A vast upheaval of mankind, followed by the end of papal authority, the end of the Popes, the Catholic Church. And, in place of that, a new Church. A new, universal religion, embracing all mankind in a peaceful, nonviolent world, watched over benignly by the strange man on the hillside, the new saviour who would descend to the earth.

When her mind was clear, Helen felt compelled to telephone Archbishop McInnerney, to relay the news of the vision. She dialed his private, unlisted number. He answered at once.

"Your Excellency, this is Helen."

"Good evening, Helen. What can I do for you?"

His tone was unrushed, friendly, solicitous.

"I must talk to you at once."

"What is it? What's the matter?"

"I've had a vision. It was wonderful . . . wonderful and frightening. I must tell you about it."

"All right. Why don't you come over tomorrow morning?"

"Not tomorrow. Tonight! This is urgent."

"Tonight? Well, to tell the truth, Helen, I was just on my way out. I'm going to stop briefly at Tom Bennett's party. I don't make a practice of gadding about during Lent, but well, as you know, Bennett is Bennett. I'm just putting in a brief appearance."

Thomas Bennett was a renowned Washington political columnist, television commentator, backstage friend of Presidents. An invitation to his Georgetown home was considered by most in Washington officialdom a command performance. He was a Catholic convert, dedi-

cated anti-Communist, and like many pundits, an unflagging megalo-
maniac. Helen had regretted the invitation. The small Georgetown
house, jammed with guests, gave her claustrophobia. There was always a parking problem.

"Oh yes," she said. "I hadn't planned to go."

"Well, why don't you come anyway? We can find a quiet corner,
if that's possible, and you can tell me all about it. I'm really very
anxious to hear."

Helen hesitated. She did not really feel up to it. Yet she felt there
was not a moment to lose.

"All right," she said. "I'll see you there."

She hung up and dressed, selecting a silk dress from her massive
wardrobe closet. She did her face, brushed her hair, put on her jewelry. For a woman of sixty-eight, she was uncommonly beautiful,
youthful-looking. She rang for her chauffeur and soon they were fighting the narrow, traffic-filled streets of Georgetown, inching toward
Bennett's house, one in a long row of black Cadillac limousines. Impatient, Helen alighted from the car and walked the last two blocks
to the house, shivering inside her mink coat.

There was a receiving line just inside the foyer. The guests going
through it were backed down the stoop, the wives elegantly turned
out, but cold. Two or three Secret Service men stood to one side,
hatless, coatless, briskly rubbing hands, eyeing the line of guests.
Helen took her place in the line behind a small, dark man with
hunched shoulders, who seemed vaguely familiar. He turned and
smiled wanly.

"Hello, Helen," he said.

"Hello . . . ?" Helen groped for his name.

"Marvin Klein . . . *Tribune.*"

"Oh yes, of course."

It was an awkward confrontation. Until Klein took charge at the
Tribune, Helen Hanrahan's column had been a regular feature. But
Klein judged Helen Hanrahan (and *all* so-called spiritualists and
prophets) a fraud, the treacle she pumped out silly and (for some
readers) dangerous. He killed the column, settled her contract with
her lawyers. A massive backlash had followed. Frantic letters of protest poured in. The advertising department went into shock. The ad
salesman pleaded with Klein to restore the column. He held his ground,
positive he had done the right thing. Helen shifted her column to the
Washington Post.

The decision had a personal backlash, too. Until the column was dropped, Klein had not known, had not even suspected that his wife, Serena, was an avid Helen Hanrahan fan. A true believer. The cancellation had led to an epic family quarrel. Klein denounced Serena for being stupid and unrealistic, for believing in fairy tales. Serena denounced her husband for being intellectually arrogant and myopic, a troublemaker. The fight went on for days as each party dragged up—and hurled—larger and larger rounds of ammunition, all the repressed hostility of seven years of marriage.

Serena, cold, shivering beneath her wool coat, turned to see to whom her husband had spoken. She recognized Helen Hanrahan at once. She had seen her on television many times. She jabbed him in the ribs with her elbow.

"Oh, Helen," he said, "I'd like you to meet my wife, Serena. Serena, this is Helen Hanrahan."

Helen smiled and held out her gloved hand. Serena shook it warmly.

"I'm *so* pleased," Serena gushed. "I read you every day. Do *tell* me something."

Klein winced inwardly, fearful that this fresh contact with the fake seer would renew the family row. They moved up one step. Soon they would be inside.

"I'm afraid your husband might find it frivolous," Helen said, smiling icily.

"Never mind *him*," Serena sneered.

"All right," Helen said. "Hold your hands over mine."

Serena did as instructed, holding her hands flat, palm down, immediately over Helen's upturned palms. Instantly Helen drew back, as though stabbed, her face a sudden blank mask, like death. Serena was startled, frightened.

"What is it?" she said.

"I don't know . . ." Helen said vaguely. She turned to Klein, raised his hands. Klein drew them back. He was not going to be drawn into fake vaudeville.

"Please," Helen insisted.

"Go on, Marv," Serena said.

"Never mind," Helen said. "Never mind. I felt it."

"Felt *what?*" Serena said, eyes like saucers.

Helen did not know exactly. After a vision, her perception, usually keen, was murky and confused. Yet she had felt something hard and dangerous. It came to her in a flash.

"Mr. Klein," she said, "let the Church solve its own problems. Those things that interest you most—social problems—are better solved, if possible, by those whose responsibility it is. The Church is not concerned with making a Heaven here—but rather in the life beyond. The Archbishop has much trouble, much, much trouble to deal with. It is not right that you should cause him more. There is going to be terrible violence. A great chastisement. Fire, blood, and death. Armageddon. The clergy will be in peril. As a journalist, you should do everything in your power to minimize the trouble. Do not inflame."

"When will all this happen?" Klein said, not concealing his skepticism.

"It is imminent," Helen Hanrahan said.

"Do you have a date?"

"No. But soon."

"That's what the Fatima child—Lucy?—kept saying," Klein said. "And it never came to pass."

"Never came to pass?" Helen said incredulously. "Don't you read? Hasn't the world gone exactly the way she predicted? Didn't we have World Wars One and Two? Wasn't Spain destroyed in civil war? Hasn't Russian Communism dominated the globe?"

"Yes, but . . ."

"Haven't sixty million people been killed so far by war in this century?"

"Yes. I think that's the total figure, if you count all the Russians."

"Then how can you possibly say her predictions never came to pass? And, young man, hear this. The warning of Our Lady of Fatima has not been discredited but ignored. Where is the veneration to the rosary? The Scapular? Where are the prayers? She said only by immense prayer would the world be saved . . . the Communists held at bay. She was ignored. Now there will be a great chastisement. An Apocalypse. Don't fan the fire!"

Klein was now thoroughly convinced that Helen Hanrahan was a nut, a kook. Most thinking people had long since discredited the Fatima predictions. Anyone who read the *Tribune* these days with Hanrahan's conservative bias might well come up with the same advice. Her predictions! Anyone who followed the news could make predictions with, probably, eighty percent accuracy. Drew Pearson did it. For that matter, so did Klein, every hour of the day, in his choice of "news" for the front page, his journalistic foresight, his assignment of reporters.

"I've warned him," Serena confided to Helen Hanrahan. "He won't listen to me."

"Or me," Helen said sadly.

Klein was rankled. Serena had called him a troublemaker, now she was making a fool of him in public. He was sorry he had let Serena push him into coming to Bennett's. He did not care for Bennett or his views, especially on the war. Klein considered him an apologist for the Administration. Now Helen Hanrahan, of all people!

They moved up the stoop to the warmth of the foyer. A check girl took Helen's coat. She shook hands with the rotund host, Thomas Bennett, who stood, drink in left hand, beside his wife.

Helen paid her respects to host and hostess, then moved beyond the reception line, searching for Archbishop McInnerney. A crush of fawning dignitaries impeded her. The Vice-President, genial but insecure since the President announced his decision not to seek reelection, drew her aside. From his standpoint, the polls, the pundits, the private forecasts by the experts, were uniformly gloomy.

"Don't despair," Helen said. "Your party will come very close in November. So close, I can't predict."

That news pleased him. It was the first encouraging word he had heard. But he was not entirely satisfied.

"But who will head the ticket?" he said.

"You will," she said without hesitation.

The Vice-President beamed. He (like most politicians) set great store by her predictions. She had rarely missed.

"But . . . what about Bobby? McCarthy?"

"They will fall by the wayside. But . . . be careful of Nixon. He's going to run a strong race. It will be very, very close. I can't call it. Not yet. It's too early."

Near one of the tables of hors d'oeuvres, Helen saw Archbishop McInnerney and Vicar General Prial. She felt suddenly fatigued, depressed. She experienced a heavy presence—like death—smothering her. It was the same suffocating sensation she had had the morning her late husband took the plane to New York. She had pleaded with him to delay his trip. But he had gone anyway—to a fiery death. Seven years ago.

Helen pushed politely and graciously through her admirers to the Archbishop.

"When I saw you just now," she said without preliminaries, "I had a feeling of death. It came over me quite suddenly, quite positively.

Only . . . somehow . . . I do not see death for *you*. It is a larger death . . . I can't explain it. Let me touch your fingers."

The Archbishop placed his fingers lightly on Helen's outstretched palms. The Vicar General listened closely. Helen closed her eyes, probing for a psychic connection. She felt it now, very positive, unmistakable, ominous. She opened her eyes and sighed.

"There's no doubt. It's not you. Some larger death. Death all around us. Somehow related to you. I'm very upset. When I was on my way in tonight, I saw Mr. Klein—the *Tribune* editor. We stood together and I . . . I felt something around him too."

Vicar General Prial turned to let his eyes sweep the room, searching for Klein. A fortunate coincidence that he was here, he thought. It would be a good, informal time to mend fences, find out when Klein was going to publish the exclusive on the theological center. The deadline was closing in. According to the PR man, the groundswell should build, gradually, over a week or two, toward the official launching of the fund. Prial pushed off into the crowd toward the bar, leaving Helen and the Archbishop huddled in the corner.

"You seem truly distraught," the Archbishop said to her.

"I'm *frantic*," she hissed. "Let me tell you about the vision."

She told him the vision in complete detail, all that she could remember. Her voice was low—but emotion-charged. The Archbishop listened pensively—straining to catch every word—twisting the glass of ginger ale on his palm. His face assumed an expression of profound gravity. Her words troubled him. This, he thought, was no ordinary vision. The meaning of it was yet unclear—violence, death, Apocalypse, the Pope drowning. When she finished, he sighed in a melancholy way and asked:

"What do you make of it?"

"I think it is the last Fatima prediction coming to be. I have been told to warn that it is coming."

"God have mercy on us," the Archbishop said, inwardly asking Him for strength. "But I don't see how it pertains to me."

"Your Excellency," she said earnestly, "cancel the big plans you have for the spring. The fund drive. The theological center. The time is absolutely wrong. Put it off until next year."

The Archbishop felt a chill in his heart. She had been right . . . often. Too often. She might be right again. But he could not put it off. St. Luke's . . . the plans . . . the PR . . . Monsignor Ryan and his machinery . . . everything was set. To cancel it now, merely on the strength of Helen's vibrations, would be folly. He would be ridiculed. How would he explain it to Prial? The financial council? The men would think him completely irresponsible—silly. He turned to look deep in Helen's eyes.

"St. Thomas Aquinas wrote that a vision is inflexible," he said somberly. "Unchangeable. It represents the absolute will of God. The coming event is immutable. You—some of you with the gift—can see it coming, but it cannot be prevented. So there is no need to worry. No need for me to change plans. Let us put our faith—and hope—in God's mercy."

There was a sudden and great stir at the far end of the room. All eyes turned that way. Then a babel of alarmed voices. spreading outward like ripples in a pond. Everywhere there were expressions of disbelief or horror, cries of "Oh, no!" Then the host, Bennett, standing unsteadily on a chair, raised his hands for silence. A hush fell over the room.

"Ladies and gentlemen," he shouted in his famed squeaky voice. "Your attention, please. The Vice-President has informed me that he has just heard from his office that Dr. Martin Luther King has been shot in Memphis, Tennessee. Apparently it is very serious. Perhaps fatal. I'm sorry to interrupt with this . . . there is a television in the den. We will try to get something solid from Memphis for you."

The party froze in shock. Helen Hanrahan felt a constriction in her throat, an overpowering sensation of terror and anxiety. The Archbishop, crossing himself, fell into deep and intense prayer for Dr. King. Vicar General Prial, leaving the Kleins, pushed his way toward his bishop, already composing the statement the Chancery must issue tonight in the Archbishop's name. His eyes met Helen's.

"That was your premonition," he said. "Dr. King! The larger death! Related to the Archbishop. Both are prominent clergy. Don't you see?"

Helen Hanrahan did not see. No, that was not it. She was certain of that. She had not thought of Martin Luther King for days. Not since she heard his sermon at the Washington National Cathedral last week. No, it was not so simple as that. It was more—much more.

BOOK TWO

JULY, 1968

I

By eight o'clock, Archbishop McInnerney's desk ashtray, a metallic gondola, souvenir of Venice, was overflowing with half-smoked, mangled cigarette butts. He was going through the mail, waiting for the morning conference to begin. Presently there was a light rap on the door.

"Come in!" he called cheerily.

Vicar General Prial swept into the room like a fullback, cigar clenched firmly between his front teeth, a portrait of energy and strength. Behind him came Monsignor Ryan, shoulders bent, eyes downcast, black shoes scuffing the carpet.

Monsignor Ryan had, at Archbishop McInnerney's suggestion, become a temporary member of the morning conference. Prial had welcomed him sincerely. The Monsignor had taken over all the nagging details of the fund drive. The interminable meetings with the fund-raising consultants. The preparation of the letters of exhortation. The special calls on the Washington businessmen. The publicity. Coordination with the pastors. A thousand other things, including the daily reports to the Archbishop. Prial was especially grateful for the latter. He did not like carrying bad news to the Archbishop. Each day, it seemed, the news on the fund drive was worse.

As Prial had said often, by way of softening the blow, they could not have picked a more inopportune time. The city, the nation, was torn by dissent, by revolution, chaos, anger, and frustration. After Dr. King was shot in Memphis, the blacks burned the Washington ghetto, looted, ran wild. For days the city was an armed camp, ruled by martial law. Soldiers and National Guardsmen patrolled the streets, emplaced machine guns on the Capitol parapets, the White House lawn. A curfew kept people indoors. The energies of the suburban congregations had focused on collecting food, clothing, and money for those left homeless in the ghetto, black refugees cast up by the violence of their own brothers.

On the advice of the PR consultant, they had postponed launching the fund drive until the city returned to normal. But Klein upended that plan. After sitting on his exclusive for weeks, he broke the story without warning. The Chancery viewed it as a scurrilous, irresponsible hatchet-job which (among other things) took the Archbishop sternly to task for failing to make public disclosure of its finances, the results of past fund drives. The *Star* and *Post* were miffed by the scooplet. Those papers buried the story on the Saturday religion page. After this debacle, Prial dismissed the PR consultant. He then personally composed the article for the archdiocese paper, the *Weekly Messenger,* giving it front-page play beneath an eight-column banner headline. That, at least, brought a smile of pleasure to McInnerney's lips. But, all in all, it had been a fumbling start.

They had no sooner got started than Robert Kennedy was shot in Los Angeles. With his death, the funeral train, the burial, Washington was once again paralyzed, the clergy and the laity diverted by a new horror. The Archbishop had assisted in the Funeral Mass in New York, serving Cardinal Cooke as he served Cardinal Cushing at John Kennedy's funeral. The Chancery was overwhelmed by visiting Catholic potentates who came for the burial service at Arlington Cemetery. Prial and the staff were busy finding accommodations and transportation. The Chancery was in turmoil for almost two weeks.

In the meantime, Monsignor Ryan had discovered, the general economic picture could not have been darker. The war was playing hob with money. Interest rates were soaring. Money was tight, held down by the Federal Reserve to curb inflation, cool the economy. The city of Washington, particularly, was hard-pressed. The riots and burning in the ghetto had frightened off tourists. The hotels were almost empty. After tourism, the city's biggest "industry," home-building, was stymied by a critical shortage of mortgage money. The businessmen Ryan called on pleaded poverty. They, and the financial council, advised Ryan to wait a year.

Like many Americans, the Archbishop was stunned by the violence of those weeks. He heard on television and read in newspapers the pronouncements of the psychiatrists and political pundits that the country had gone mad. That society was crumbling, reverting to savage primitivism, perhaps even to total anarchy. He fell into a period of profoundest soul-searching. Much of this took place in his small private chapel. There, on the altar steps, he lay prostrate, often for hours, asking for guidance, inspiration from the Divine Family, believing the nation was teetering on the brink of disaster. At times, he remembered, with admiration and despair, Helen Hanrahan's vision. She had foretold it all. The death, violence, burning, chaos. She had been mistaken, he believed, in relating him directly to the events. He was convinced that the religious message of the vision related to Martin Luther King and the black problem.

The soul-searching led him to one firm resolution, surely divinely inspired. Regardless of the times, the uncertainty, he must push ahead with all energy on the theological center. He became utterly persuaded that half the trouble in America—half the chaos—had been brought about by an epic failure of religion, by the systematic undermining of authority and teaching in the Catholic Church—dissent, brought on by Pope John and the Vatican Council. Religion, McInnerney knew, was the binding force of any society. Take it away, allow men to question it, ridicule it, blaspheme it, and chaos followed, as day into night. That was true all through history. Hadn't Europe exploded in chaos and violence and war in the wake of Martin Luther? The center was *the* one hope of restoring cohesion, authority, and discipline in the Church. It must be built without delay—before disaster overtook them all.

So convinced, the Archbishop was almost overcome by joy when, in early July, he received a warm, personal letter from Pope Paul. Taking note of the violence in America, Paul, exactly expressing McInnerney's sentiments, put most of the blame on the recent erosion of the Church. He was severely critical of those he termed "dabbling theologians," megalomaniacs who dared challenge the body of Church teaching that had sprung from the Word of God Himself. The letter had another purpose, too. It was a notice to McInnerney that "shortly" Paul would hand down an encyclical on contraception that would settle, once and for all, this "disputatious" matter. Paul would not follow the recommendations of his commission. He would stick by the continuous body of Church teaching, would reaffirm the principles of Pius's *Casti Connubii*. He thought McInnerney, and other American bishops, might like to have this advance warning in order to prepare proper written material for distribution to the faithful. This message—Paul's decision—gave McInnerney renewed hope.

Taking a chair before the Archbishop's desk, Monsignor Ryan felt a terrible compulsion to flee the room. His latest report on the fund drive, tucked in a leather folder in his right hand, was nothing less than disastrous. Knowing that it would be, Ryan had not slept well for a week. He had lost confidence in himself, the drive. Everything they had done, it seemed, had backfired.

What hurt most—or what gnawed at Ryan most—was the fact that All Saints' was not setting the example for the archdiocese. The performance in this super-parish was, in a word, miserable. More than that. It was a disaster, like the whole drive. This, in spite of daily calls to Father Daugherty and Bob Favrot, the senior fund captain. There was no leadership at All Saints'. Daugherty did not understand the problem. He was financially uneducable. He had not inflamed his captains. There had been no ringing support from the pulpit. Instead, as Mrs. Munally whispered to Ryan on the telephone, Daugherty's were vague, lofty sermons (many "pro-nigger") which left Mrs. Munally disheartened, puzzled, and, occasionally, frightened. Lately, she reported, the young priest was closeted in his room "scribbling" his sermons, and had been refusing calls at the rectory. Mrs. Munally was worried that Daugherty might be "cracking up." All this had profoundly depressed Monsignor Ryan. It had led to his decision to request a return to All Saints'.

"Good morning all," McInnerney said, still cheery, lighting a cigarette. "Let's get the bad news out of the way and see what we can do to overturn it. Tom? Don't look so glum. Let's see."

He reached for the folder. Ryan extended it reluctantly. The Archbishop ran his eye down the column of figures.

"Ah!" he said. "Here's a bright spot. St. Anne's. Not bad, not bad."

"Let's see," Prial said, reaching for the folder.

He studied the figures. He saw no reason for cheer. St. Anne's showed an almost imperceptible rise. Up (by Prial's rapid calculation) three hundredths of a percent. He laid the folder on the desk with a derisive grunt.

Monsignor Ryan, feeling his courage slipping, believing that it was now or never, that in a moment he might become reinfected with the Archbishop's unflagging zeal, seized the floor. He cleared his throat, ran his hand through silver hair.

"Your Excellency," he said. "I don't like to add to your problems —become a part of the problem—but I want to ask a favor."

"Sure, Tom," McInnerney said. "Go on. Ask."

"I want to go back to All Saints'."

Archbishop McInnerney smiled warmly. "We need you very badly, Tom. You know that better than anyone."

"I know you do," Ryan said, rushing on. "I want to help. But I feel I'm needed back in my own parish. More there than here. I've set up the program. Anybody can run it. From now on, it's purely administrative. I had hoped that All Saints' would be the pace-setter, but now I find they're thirty-six percent behind my initial forecast . . . lagging badly. If I could get back there, I could put some steam into the thing . . . set an example. If we can't put it across in All Saints', I fear we can't put it across at all."

The Archbishop sighed, clasped his hands on the desk.

"Also," Monsignor Ryan went on, "I'm worried about my parishioners. There is discontent. Daugherty can't seem to pull them together. His heart isn't in the drive. Besides that, his sermons . . . from what I hear, they're far out and confusing. I told you in the beginning I didn't think he could pull his oar. I think he's . . . he's . . . well, frankly, dangerous."

The Archbishop was not surprised by this. He had been expecting such from Ryan for several days. He seriously considered returning Ryan to his parish, but it always came back to the same point. There was no one in the archdiocese better equipped—and more loyal—than Ryan, for the job. It was no time to experiment.

"Have we failed you in any way?" McInnerney said.

Feeling guilty, Ryan responded eagerly: "Oh, no! No indeed. I've . . . I've had the *complete* support of the Chancery staff. I couldn't ask for another thing. Honestly."

"Times will get better," the Archbishop said, "as soon as we get rolling. As for Daugherty, frankly, Tom, is he any worse than anybody else in his crop?"

Ryan thought about that. All the young priests who had fled the Church to marry—ten thousand, he had read somewhere. The rebels in the ghetto, like Groppi. By comparison, Daugherty was conservative. At least as far as Ryan knew. Most of the younger priests were pro-Negro these days. Mrs. Munally could have been exaggerating.

"Dangerous is a pretty strong word," Prial said.

Ryan's face colored.

"I'm sorry for that," he said. "I should have said unorthodox. Anyway, that's only one point. The parish is not coming up financially. That's the central point. If I could get out there, put some steam into . . ."

"A general doesn't fight his division on the front, Tom," Prial said gently. "At least, not a good general."

"He can't fight it from supreme headquarters either," Ryan said glumly.

"Tom," McInnerney said, with understanding. "Don't despair. Not yet anyway. God will provide. You'll see. There is something in the wind—I'm sorry I can't tell you about it today—that's going to change all this. Everything. Make your job much easier. Something *very* important. Something that will bring cohesion and an end to these stupid internal disputes . . . so you and I can get on with our jobs. Will you take my word for that? Help me a little longer . . . at least until we're out of the woods?"

Prial looked at his superior curiously. What secret was he holding back?

"All right," Ryan said, bending under the force of this appeal, then yielding.

"That-a-boy," Prial said.

"Conned again," Ryan said weakly, smiling.

"By the master," Prial said, removing his cigar, studying the hot ash, still curious about the secret. Then to Ryan: "You want me to call Daugherty and tell him to straighten up and fly right?"

"No . . . no," Ryan said slowly, thinking. "I . . . I might have been judging him too harshly. I shouldn't have said that. I'll talk to him privately."

"All right," McInnerney said, crushing out his cigarette. "Well, now! That crisis passed, let us get down to business." He turned to Prial. "Is there anything new on the deal?"

The "deal"—the sale of St. Luke's—had dragged slowly, in spite of Prial's effort. There had been, to date, one hundred and sixty-three revisions or additions to the contract. For all his priestly patience, Prial's contempt for lawyers had now reached a state of hot rage. The lawyers had delayed them. Then the riots and burning. The blacks had devastated the blocks surrounding St. Luke's. As Prial saw it, the devastation was actually fortuitous. The homes and stores would not be rebuilt. The IDA building would not "deprive" anybody. It would fill a gutted gap with new purpose—and jobs. But IDA had paused to study the new situation, to let the fires die, tempers cool.

"I'm very happy to announce that our closing is set for next week . . . a week from Thursday."

He turned to smile at Monsignor Ryan.

"Good," Ryan said. Was this the secret the Archbishop was withholding?

"I'll walk away from the table with five million and change," Prial added, unnecessarily.

"Tremendous!" the Archbishop exulted. "Simply tremendous. See, Tom? I told you not to despair. The Lord *will* provide."

"Proving again," Prial said, "the power of unrelenting prayer."

"And financial dexterity," the Archbishop said.

"This is off the record, Tom," Prial said. "They don't want any publicity on it for two or three weeks. They've got a whole basketful of PR problems to iron out. They want to play it just right. It's sort of delicate, sticking a quasi-war agency into the ghetto. Especially now that the war has heated up again. They want to emphasize the urban renewal angle, faith in center-city resurgence and all that. That plus the four hundred new jobs and so forth."

"I understand," Ryan said, drawing a finger across his lips.

"Which reminds me," the Archbishop said. "Did Seymour Jones vacate the gym?"

"Tomorrow or the next day . . . Friday deadline," Prial said.

"You couldn't find him anything else?"

"Not after the riots. I gave up."

"Yes," the Archbishop said thoughtfully. "He's going quietly?"

"Hopefully. He's been forgotten—I hope. Klein's been too busy with King and the riots and Columbia University and Kennedy and a hundred other causes. Let's all pray we've heard the last of Klein."

The Archbishop turned to Ryan.

"Anything else, Tom?"

That was a polite signal of dismissal. Ryan rose, scooping up his papers, and left the room.

"He'll be all right," McInnerney said, winking. "He just needs an occasional push. Like all of us."

"What's the big secret you're keeping?" Prial said, relighting his cigar. "Or were you just bluffing?"

"A letter from Paul," McInnerney said. He unlocked his desk drawer, withdrew an envelope. "Read it."

Prial opened the letter, unfolded the stiff, heavy stationery, and read, eyes growing wider with each line.

"So," he said, inhaling deeply. *"Finally."*

"I'm glad," McInnerney said. "Now that's settled, at least. No more debate. No more dissent. No more fresh winds. No more divisiveness. The talk's all over. The Pope, the Church, rules. Now sanity will return. Let those who disagree get out."

Prial chose his words carefully.

"I hope you're right."

"I *know* I'm right," McInnerney said. "The people *want* the issue decided. You'll see."

"I wish he could have waited . . ."

"The longer he waited, the worse it would be."

". . . at least until the drive is done."

"The drive? . . . why the drive?"

"Your Excellency," Prial said, very stiffly, "I took a poll—a confidential poll—of the women in the archdiocese—on how the women in this area feel on the matter of birth control."

"A poll!"

The Archbishop's eyes clouded. Prial hurried on:

"Merely in the interest of ascertaining a true picture of the frame of mind . . ."

"The Catholic Church is *not* a democracy," the Archbishop said sharply. "On this matter or any other."

"I'm aware of that," Prial said coolly. "But, Your Excellency, you know better than I that hard intelligence is a valuable management tool. Better to know precisely what we're dealing with than to go about with our heads in a cloud. You remember the Lou Harris poll? The nationwide one? Where Catholic American women favored some form of contraception seven to ten? I frankly couldn't believe the figures. So I hired a local polling firm—very reliable and very WASPish—to get our own sample. I thought it was important. I had a theory that our declining revenues are directly related to attitudes . . ."

"Yes," the Archbishop sighed. "Of course. Go on. What did they come up with?"

Prial opened a manila folder. His eyes told the Archbishop the news would not be favorable.

"Generally, about the same," he said, reading. "Seven out of ten favor some form of artificial contraception."

The Archbishop's face sagged.

"You know," he said sadly, "this is a tragedy. A real tragedy. What's *wrong* with the women of this generation? Where is the moral fiber? Where is the willingness to sacrifice? Where is the duty to God? To the Commandments? They *give* less. Less money. Less prayer. Less devotion. They don't teach their children . . ."

He threw up his hands in despair. He had said it all before. Many times. A few times from the pulpit. More often in the privacy of his chambers.

"There is more to the poll," Prial said. "Shall I go on?"

"Go on."

"The sampling also indicates that approximately forty percent of the

Catholic women in the archdiocese are *already* practicing some form of artificial contraception."

"*Forty* percent?" the Archbishop said hollowly.

"Yes. I was rather surprised by *that.*"

"I'm stunned," the Archbishop said, slumping in his chair. "Forty percent of our female population living in mortal sin? Why? Jesus, Mary, and Joseph! *Why?*"

"I don't know. Probably because they thought the Pope would approve it, at least in some form."

"Madness! Sheer madness. John perhaps. Not Paul, thank God!"

"The attitude on birth control in the archdiocese," Prial went on, "probably accounts for the attitude toward the fund drive and the collection plate. I have no scientific data. But it seems a reasonable speculation. I don't believe it's a downright boycott—far from it—but rather a deep psychological backlash. Our women control the donations, usually from household budgets. They are dissatisfied. It is only natural, I believe, that they would unconsciously, or perhaps consciously, contribute less and less. The usual excuse, of course, is that money is tight, the budget doesn't go as far, it costs money to raise kids . . . on and on."

The Archbishop folded his hands on the desk. His mouth was drawn firm in disapproval.

He rose suddenly and paced the floor near the window giving on the back-yard gardens. He clasped his hands behind his back. His lips moved, as though in prayer. He stopped pacing and faced the Vicar General.

"The rampant discussion," McInnerney said, "has led to confusion and misconception. The liberals hoped the discussion—the talk itself —would lead to a change. They misled many into believing there *would* be a change. That in itself is a mortal sin. That is why these women are doing it. They *know* it's a mortal sin. They feel guilty. It is *guilt* that makes them withhold, can't you see that? Now, our job is to help Paul put things aright. We must prepare pamphlets and other material to straighten this thing out, once and for all. Once we do, everything will return to normal. You'll see. The women will go back to . . . to rational behavior. They will not feel guilt. They will confess. The contributions will begin flowing again. There will be cohesion, a sense of belonging. Then we will build the theological center! And *never again* will this church, at least not in this country, permit itself to be rocked and challenged as it has been these last years.

Nate, don't present me with any more polls. We're not politicians. We rule with authority, by ukase. Not by democratic consensus."

He paused to shuffle through the papers on his desk. He held one up.

"Here," he said. "This is something I scribbled last night, guidelines for the preparation of the pamphlets. Let me read it to you:

"In matters of faith and morals, the bishops speak in the name of Christ, and the faithful are to accept their teaching and adhere to it with a religious assent of souls. This religious submission of will and mind must be shown in a special way to the authentic teaching authority of the Roman Pontiff, even when he is not speaking *ex cathedra*. That is, it must be shown in such a way that his supreme magisterium is acknowledged with reverence, the judgments made by him are sincerely adhered to, according to his manifest mind and will. Pope Paul's encyclical gives the authentic teaching of the Church, which is binding on conscience. While it does not preclude theological discussion, no one can either publicly question or preach doctrines which are not in conformity with the said authentic teaching. Neither may one counsel penitents contrary to that same authentic teaching."

The Archbishop laid the document aside.

"Pretty blunt," the Vicar General said.

"It's time for bluntness."

"I'm not sure," Prial said, relighting his cigar. "I have a feeling in my bones this encyclical is going to be . . . going to be dynamite. It's going to be a shock, believe me. Times have changed. We live in a revolutionary environment. I'm not sure the people—especially the young people—want it or will accept it. If we're not careful, we might have a full-scale revolt on our hands. I agree we're not a democracy. But this poll tells us something. Maybe we should listen."

"There's going to be *no* debate on this matter in this archdiocese," McInnerney said firmly. "That's why I wrote that statement. The Pope speaks. We speak for him. If anyone violates the policy, I feel we have the right to resort to disciplinary measures. These people—these dissidents—are like children. It's time we treated them as children. If we have a crisis of obedience, then let us act like a firm father. Let us accept that responsibility. Spare the rod and spoil the child. Let us show the world that the time has come to stop this nonsense. Let us stand firm behind the Holy Father in Rome."

The Vicar General stood, paced the floor, smoking his cigar. His mind was troubled.

"There will be a vast sigh of relief when the encyclical is released," McInnerney insisted.

"Or a massive cry of outrage," Prial said. "I frankly don't know which. I pray. One minute I think one way, the other the next. If it leads to . . . to a financial boycott—never mind the fund drive—it could destroy us."

"It will *not* destroy us," the Archbishop said. "Nothing can destroy this Chancery or the Church. It has stood for two millennia."

"Except ideas," Prial said. "Ideas can destroy any institution. The right idea at the right time. Freedom . . . the idea of freedom . . . has leveled the mightiest institutions. The idea of religious freedom is abroad today."

"Are you trying to change my mind?" the Archbishop smiled.

"No. It's your decision. I don't *want* to influence you. I merely wanted to point out pitfalls, relay sentiment. That's my job. My final conclusion is you must be prepared for an all-out fight. Perhaps total war."

"So be it," the Archbishop said.

II

In his bedroom at the All Saints' rectory, Father Daugherty worked at his desk, polishing what he thought of as the best of his series of "tunneling from within" sermons. Certainly it was his most thoughtful —and provocative. He could hear male voices downstairs. The fund drive captains were assembling for the weekly meeting. He glanced at his wristwatch. Six ten. He had run out of time. The sermon would have to go as it was.

He hurried to the bathroom to wash his face in cold water. The water was refreshing, yet not enough to force him back to reality. He was still "in the sermon," as he thought of it, the ideas and phrases cascading through his mind like a well-ordered brook. Returning to his desk, he picked up the first page again, let his eye run down the lines of scribbled words. He penciled out one. Then he put on his rabat and collar, black jacket, and left the room, descending the steps two at a time.

Father Daugherty had been moving at a dead run for the last twelve weeks—since the day Monsignor Ryan departed for the Chancery. It had been a frantic time, with no chance to plan, to really think. No time for self-pity or analysis. No time even for tennis. His spiritual crisis had been left in mid-air—held in abeyance, pending Pope Paul's forthcoming decision on contraception.

Lately, Daugherty had spoken by telephone several times with Le-Guiese regarding this. The Catholic liberal, intellectual community was still optimistic. The encyclical was expected almost any day now. It would be *the* historical turning point in Roman Catholicism, the first major change in nine hundred years. It would bring in its wake a sweeping modernization of the Church's outlook on man's sexuality. LeGuiese was certain—in spite of Paul's continuing statements to the contrary—that in not too long, the celibacy rule would also be struck down. Married priests would be a commonplace, as they were in the Catholic Eastern rite. The Pauline texts would be burned.

The Mary Murray affair, too, was still suspended in mid-air. In the two months between Dr. King's funeral and Bob Kennedy's funeral Dan and Mary had seen each other regularly at Halfway House. What was there, between them, had grown—awkwardly, somewhat confusedly. They had not yet talked in concrete terms about their feelings for one another. Yet what was there—and growing—was clear to both, in glances, overtones, the occasional touch. They had both talked—individually—to LeGuiese about it. If he was shocked, he concealed it well. He had advised that they stop seeing each other for at least six weeks. It was routine counsel for what LeGuiese believed to be a routine—and commonplace—aberration in the Church these days, ever since the nuns had left the cloistered life of the convents to work in the "real world."

Dan and Mary had attended the Kennedy memorial service together at St. Matthew's Cathedral. Afterward, watching the funeral on TV at Halfway House, when they were engulfed in grief and despair that the man for whom they hoped to cast a vote in November had been brutally snatched away, they had decided to begin the "separation." Mary would be busy with her orals and thesis anyway, the final details of her two-year course of study at CU. Daugherty was desperately

busy with June weddings, pre-Cana instruction, the coming summer
CYO camp program, and the Archbishop's fund drive.

They stuck by the agreement to the letter. No meetings. No phone
calls. No letters. For Daugherty, the experience had been painful, an
agony, as though a limb had been torn from his body. Not an hour
passed that he did not think of Mary. He curtailed his visits to Halfway
House. It seemed empty there without her. Those days, he had little
time for the runaway kids anyway. In bed at night, in the lonely,
sterile, dehumanizing rectory bedroom, he told himself he loved Mary.
He must marry her. If LeGuiese's optimism was justified, it would be
possible, perhaps soon, for Daugherty to have his cake and eat it too.
He could remain a priest in a sensibly modern, relevant church,
with a wife. Such was his current hope. That hope gave him energy
for his tunneling from within.

The long empty separation had "expired" that morning. Immediately after eight o'clock Mass, Daugherty returned to his bedroom and
telephoned Mary. Yes, she said, it had been ghastly. It had not proved
a thing. But they were glad they had done it. They owed everybody—
parents, friends, associates, LeGuiese, themselves—that much. Then
they talked about little details—updating. No, she had not found a
new place for her school. Neither had Seymour Jones. He was moving
out, lock, stock, and barrel, Friday. Yes, she finished her thesis and
her orals. She thought she had done "all right." The thesis might even
be published by the CU Press. Oh! She had received a letter from the
Provincial, requesting an interview in New York, Friday afternoon, "to
discuss her future."

This last news struck Daugherty hard. Friday? He must see her
before then—immediately. Halfway House? No. There were too many
kids around. They could not be alone. They would inevitably become
swept up in the problems down there. The kids' problems. They had
their own thing to discuss. Where, then? A restaurant? The CU Union?
No, too public. Having no better idea, Daugherty had proposed that
Mary drive over to All Saints'—the church, not the rectory. He was
finishing his best sermon to date. He'd like her to hear a "dry run."
Afterward, they could talk. Surely no one would see them there. If
they did, they had an excuse. Fine. She would be there at eight o'clock.

Mrs. Munally met Daugherty at the foot of the stairs. Her manner
now was total business. She resented Daugherty. She missed Monsignor
Ryan.

"Telephone," she said.

"Who is it?" Daugherty asked, a trifle curtly, matching her mood.

"Monsignor Ryan."

He resented her too—talking to Ryan on the telephone all the time. Daugherty knew she was passing along rectory business, parish business. He waved his hand toward the living room.

"Did you tell him I had a meeting?"

"Yes. He knows. He says it's urgent."

Daugherty hurried into the den, picked up the phone. He waited for Mrs. Munally to hang up the kitchen extension.

"I've *got* it," he said.

She hung up.

"Dan?" Monsignor Ryan said.

"Hello," Daugherty said, sitting down on the hassock.

"I won't keep you but a second," Ryan said. "I got the monthly fund report from your parish. For June. It doesn't look good. Besides that, you were late getting it in."

"I know," Daugherty said, frowning.

"Are you giving it the time you should?" Ryan asked.

"I'm giving it all the time I *can,*" Daugherty said coldly. "You forget I was pretty busy last month. I had . . . let's see . . . twenty-four weddings since mid-May. Every night, two or three couples for pre-Cana. Then the CYO summer camp. That didn't organize itself, you know. Fortunately the funerals have tapered off . . ."

"They're always worse in March," Ryan said.

"My fund captains are here right this minute," Daugherty said, impatiently.

"I know. Well, I just wanted to check in. We're counting on you to set the example, you know. This thing is very dear to the Archbishop. Very dear. The whole Chancery is looking to you. To your men. Make sure they get a kick in the pants. They're good people. This is a time for bringing in cash, not composing immortal homiletics."

Daugherty seethed. So Mrs. Munally had been reporting his every move! He would damned well speak to her sharply.

"Where the hell is that help I'm supposed to get?" Daugherty said, angrily.

"It didn't show up. They're short everywhere."

"I can sure understand why," Daugherty said, only half-jokingly. "Nobody in his right mind would take a job like this."

And not many were seeking it, apparently. That morning Daugherty

had seen a story in the *Washington Post* under the headline: ENROLL-
MENT IN SEMINARIES SLIPPING. The story said the 530 Catholic seminaries in the United States reported a decrease in enrollment—down
5,846 to a total of 33,990. Nuns too: 5,887 fewer novices enrolled
this year. All the clergy chart-lines plunging downward, the number
of Catholics zooming upward. It was crazy.

"Organize your time," Ryan said testily. "Delegate—"

"Delegate to whom?" Daugherty replied angrily. "I've got to go.
Goodbye." He set the phone in the cradle. He would put a stop to
these daily calls from Ryan. Starting tomorrow. He was not a child.

He went to the living room to meet with his fund captains. They
were solid, sober businessmen of the parish, plus a few lawyers like
Bob Favrot. They greeted Daugherty perfunctorily. They did not know
the acting pastor well. To many he was merely a figure they saw on
Sunday at the altar, in the pulpit, very young, a tennis player with
long sideburns like a movie star. Daugherty invited them to take seats.
Then he distributed the memo from the Chancery. Monsignor Ryan
had computerized the archdiocese lists. From now on, a blizzard of
direct mail, extolling the theological center, would fall on the Catholic
homes. The solicitation calls were to be "coordinated" with the direct
mailings. The memorandum from Ryan, outlining the strategy, termed
this a "sophisticated approach" for a "sophisticated objective." Father
Daugherty inwardly winced at the phrases.

One of the men, a young dentist, was first to speak.

"Father," he said earnestly, "I hope this works. But I have my
doubts, I feel, so far, like I'm wasting my time. I make these calls
with Cooper and we spend nine tenths of our time explaining things.
They want to know what the Pope is going to do about the pill. And
when! Hell! What can I say? Then they want to know what did the
Chancery do about the blacks? I've got the fact sheet on that. But
it isn't convincing. Then they say what about the schools? Hospitals?
Then they want to know if we're putting through a pay raise for the lay
teachers? How do we expect to get good teachers if we don't pay a
living wage? All that. It's the same in every home. The exact same
questions, as though some advance man was going in front of me,
planting them. By the time we get through all that, hours pass. Then,
they don't want to contribute. Not to some nebulous thing like a theological center. It's too blue sky. If we were collecting directly for black
charity, I could raise a fortune."

Daugherty nodded. He had been told this before. Not once, a dozen times. The other men agreed with the dentist. They had all run into the same wall.

"Tell you what we've got to do," Bob Favrot said, crossing his fat legs with effort. "You've got to give them the word from the pulpit, Dan. Sock it to 'em. Tell them how much we've done in the ghetto. Try to relate the center personally. Tell them how important it is for their spiritual well-being, the well-being of the whole Church. It's got to be in concrete terms, somehow, so they relate. Don't you agree, fellows?"

"I certainly do," the dentist said. "They've got to be educated."

"Maybe these direct mailings from the Chancery will help," Daugherty said. He did not believe they would.

"They better," the dentist said. "But we've still got to get it on a personal level. From you, Father. From the pulpit. Person to person."

"I've certainly touched on it often enough," Daugherty said defensively.

"Put *punch* in it," Favrot said.

Daugherty wanted to say: I can't put punch into something I don't believe. But he kept his counsel. He thought about Mary. His heart leaped.

"Sometimes I think we better go back to the drawing board," the dentist said, casting aside the Chancery memo.

"It's too late for that," Favrot said. "We're committed. If we fall on our face, we can't try it again. It was uninspired to launch this thing at this time."

"We all agree on *that,*" Daugherty said somberly. "But let's all do the best we can."

They discussed strategy and technique. After an hour, the meeting broke up. The men set off on their dunning calls. Bob Favrot was the last to leave. At the door, he said:

"I'd like a private word with you, Dan."

"Certainly, Bob. What's on your mind?"

Father Daugherty did not want to talk to Bob Favrot. He was too busy, his mind elsewhere. On Mary. He glanced at his watch. In an hour, she would be here.

"What do you think the Pope will decide?" Bob said.

"I haven't the foggiest."

"You've seen the leaks from Rome?"

"Yes."

"How do you feel about it personally?"

Father Daugherty sat down in a leather chair. He leaned his forehead against his hand. There came to him a picture—the endless procession of parish mothers, wives, teen-agers, those already taking the pill, guilt-ridden and frustrated, seeking permission, or some words of hope. Except for Jean, Father Daugherty had given neither. Bob Favrot was fishing. He must be careful.

"I don't have a personal opinion," Father Daugherty said. "I am bound by Rome."

"A lot of priests don't seem to be."

"No. I know it. Bishops too. Those in Belgium, Holland, Canada. It's a strange religion. If you live here, contraception is absolutely forbidden. If you move to Holland—eight hours away by jet—it isn't, apparently. It is unofficially condoned. The Pope has got to clear the air. He will."

"I don't think he'll authorize contraception," Bob said. "But you know, I think Jean really wants to take the pill."

Father Daugherty had not seen Jean Favrot to talk to since that day in the confessional. She had resigned from the census-taking and all other volunteer work, vanished into the air. He assumed, but did not know, that she was still seeing Dr. Cantor.

"That's her—your—decision," he said.

"I think it's wrong. A mortal sin. Don't you agree?"

"I told you, Bob. I don't have a personal opinion. You've read the Archbishop's letters on the subject."

"She doesn't seem like the same woman anymore," Bob said morosely. "Do you know she's typing a book? Neglecting her family, the children?"

"No, I didn't, Bob. I haven't seen her. Why don't you ask her to drop over? Will you please excuse me? I've got a sermon to work on."

"Of course," Bob said. "I'm sorry. I just wanted to talk. I appreciate the time. I'm glad to know where you stand. With Monsignor Ryan, there was no question, of course. But you're different. Your sermons . . . sometimes seem a bit . . . far out. But I see, you're not really all that radical. Well, good night."

Father Daugherty climbed the stairs to his room. His breath came short. He was slipping, physically. He would *have* to find time for exercise, for tennis. He must call Klein. He glanced at his sermon one last time. So Jean was typing a book! That explained her disappearance. He must find time to telephone her, invite her over.

Daugherty changed into informal clothes—a sport shirt, tight chinos. He picked up the pages of the sermon, went back downstairs to the dining room, sat down. Mrs. Munally appeared at the kitchen door. She returned in a moment, carrying his dinner.

"Fried chicken," she said unnecessarily.

Daugherty was famished. He devoured the chicken, potatoes, peas, then went to the kitchen for seconds. The custodian, John Joseph Scafidi, was sitting at the kitchen table, eating his dinner. Since Ryan had left for the Chancery, Scafidi (Daugherty had observed) had not been to Communion. Nor confession. Daugherty wanted to say something—offer his services. But he did not. If Scafidi would not deign to seek them, he was damned if he would go out of his way to offer them. Scafidi was a strange duck, Daugherty thought. He felt compelled to speak to the bent shaggy head at the table.

"Hey," Daugherty said, forcing cheer. "I understand you're quite an expert on flying saucers."

Scafidi's head jerked up, as though he had been stabbed. His eyes were dark, moody.

"Who told you that?" he said, voice low.

"I don't remember," Daugherty said, evading.

Scafidi boiled. It enraged him to know that his secret had leaked out—prematurely. That this smart-aleck priest, of all people, should know it and was now ridiculing him. How did he know? Oh, yes . . .

"That old Zancwski woman over on the lane," he muttered, bringing his eyes back to his plate.

"Her daughter," Daugherty corrected.

"She had a lot of crazy notions," Scafidi said, returning to his food.

Daugherty let it drop. He accepted second helpings from Mrs. Munally, who beamed as she handed him the plate.

"My star boarder," she chucked. "My *big* eater."

Daugherty ate his second helping slowly, in solitude, thinking. Scafidi made him uneasy. There was something not quite right. Why had he refused that coat last March? God knows, he needed it. Maybe the guy is paranoid. Someone should have checked him out. He carried his plate to the kitchen.

"I'm going over to the church for a while," he said to Mrs. Munally. "Please note the calls."

She frowned. "I always note the calls," she said archly.

"Of course, Mrs. Munally . . . I didn't mean to imply you didn't. My mind is going on me . . . giving out."

"We could use some help around here," Mrs. Munally said, with feeling. "*That's* what we could use."

"I'll say," Daugherty replied, smiling. "Maybe Ryan will be coming back soon."

"I hope so," she said, wiping her hands on her apron.

Hearing the name, Scafidi looked up. His eyes mirrored her sentiments.

Daugherty crossed the parking lot to the church. It was still false-light, a cool evening. He unlocked the door, sat in a rear pew, head bowed, legs crossed. He asked the Holy Spirit to give him courage—and patience. He was deep in prayer and thought when Mary arrived.

She came into the foyer, dipped her fingers in holy water, made the sign of the cross, and genuflected to the red light—the Eternal Presence —on the altar. Except for the light, the church was now pitch-black. She waited for her eyes to adjust to the dark. Then she saw his form in the pew. She walked there and placed her hand on his shoulder. He started, as though he had been sleeping, looking at his wristwatch.

"Mary! Is it eight already?"

"Yes," she said.

"Well . . . how . . . how *are* you?"

In the dimness, in her custom designed habit, she looked fetching, a portrait of innocence and beauty. Daugherty felt pain in his chest—the familiar tension, the heart-thud. Nothing, not a thing had changed. It was still the same. He turned away, momentarily at sea.

"I'm fine, Dan. And you?"

Her voice was melodic, soft. It said much more than the words. Nothing had changed for her.

"Fine," he said, turning to face her. "Mary . . . damnit . . . I missed you."

"Me too," she said, looking directly into his eyes.

They were both silent.

"My goodness," she said, breaking the spell. "Is there a light in here?"

"Yes. Excuse me. I didn't want to draw unnecessary attention."

He walked to the foyer, snapped a switch. From the ceiling over the altar, a thin, strong beam of light focused on the pulpit. He locked the front door.

"Very dramatic," Mary said, eyes roving around the church. "Very impressive."

"All the latest conveniences. All we lack is a neon sign on the roof, with a flashing arrow pointing to the door, blinking: Pray. Pray."

Mary laughed quietly. "You nut."

"Come on down front. Take a seat and listen to Bishop Fulton Sheen, the second."

They walked to the altar rail. Daugherty genuflected, crossed himself, ·
and mounted the four steps to the pulpit. Mary sat down in the front
pew. The beam of light was now focused on Daugherty's face, a strik-
ing vision. He was handsome, virile! Mary felt a chill up her spine, a
speeding-up of her heartbeat. The scene reminded her of Josh White, the
folk singer. The way he launched his performance before an audience
that almost feared to breathe. There was so much to talk about—
later.

Daugherty set the pages on the lectern. The light was blinding. He
could not see Mary. But he could feel her presence, and he imagined her.
He set his wristwatch on the lectern. The sermon should not exceed
fifteen minutes. That was his self-imposed rule. No one, he thought,
could listen to anyone else for longer than that without mentally
wandering off.

The idea for this sermon had come indirectly from LeGuiese. He had
suggested that Daugherty read Dostoyevsky, particularly *The Brothers
Karamazov,* noting especially the Grand Inquisitor scene, told by
the skeptic, Ivan. In this imaginary, ironic passage, Christ reappears on
earth in seventeenth-century Spain. There, the people are held in the
grip of an absolute, authoritarian Church, denied all freedom and choice,
free will. In the view of the ecclesiastical hierarchy, the people are
happy. Now, with Christ's reappearance, preaching freedom, there is
consternation in the Church. Christ is seen as a menace, a threat to their
well-ordered world. The Grand Inquisitor arrests Christ, orders him to
be executed, explaining that the people could not endure freedom. The
Church had spent sixteen centuries spiritually harnessing man, making
him happy and content. Now all that work had been thrown into jeopardy. To Daugherty, the passage seemed relevant to today's Church,
worth repeating.

While Daugherty spoke to Mary from the pulpit, John Joseph Scafidi
crossed the parking lot from the rectory to the church, going back to
put away the cleaning equipment. He unlocked and entered a side door
leading into the sacristy. He was about to turn on the light, when he
heard Daugherty's voice. His hand fell away from the light switch. He
dragged himself quietly into the sacristy until he could see Daugherty
through the door leading to the altar. Transfixed, Scafidi stood in the
darkness, listening carefully.

When Daugherty had finished—fourteen minutes by the watch—he
descended the steps to the altar rail. Mary came from the pew. Her
hands came up to meet his.

From his place of concealment, Scafidi looked on in astonishment. He had not heard the beginning of the sermon, so he did not grasp its detail. Yet he understood its thrust. It was revolutionary! And now, in the church, a *woman*! The priest, addressing her from the pulpit, now *holding hands!* His eyes narrowed, crossing the dimness. His mouth worked, his teeth ground. Anger rose in his temples. He backed away, into the shadows, overcome by a sensation of suffocation. Dirty priest! *Spoiled priest!*

"Dan," Mary said. "Oh, Dan! It's good."

They stood, holding hands in the dimness. Daugherty was conscious of her smell. It was a young smell, like the smell of the girls who came to the confessional, more penetrating even than the varnish smell of the pews and the altar rail. It was a very personal smell, something that should belong to him. They went to a pew in the rear of the church and sat down.

In the sacristy, Scafidi stood behind the open door leading to the aisle. He could see their heads dimly. He wanted to move closer—to hear the conversation. But he dared not.

Sitting side by side in the pew, Daugherty and Mary talked for a long time—around the point. About friends—LeGuiese, Seymour Jones, politics—the forthcoming political conventions. War—the new militant peace groups springing up across the country. The latest clergy dropouts, books by or about them: Father Longo and Father Girandola; Father Kavanaugh's new book; the big *Life* article on Father Terry Netter who had left to marry.

"Our spoiled priests are becoming minor folk heroes," Daugherty chuckled.

Then they edged cautiously to the central point.

"What are you going to do, Mary," Daugherty asked. "What are you going to tell the Provincial?"

She inhaled deeply, then sighed.

"I'm certain she wants me to go back to the novitiate and teach philosophy to the novices," she said, sighing again, wringing her hands. "So, I have made up my mind to resign. In any case . . ."

"I love you, Mary," Daugherty said, turning to face her. "I love you very, very much."

"I love you too, Dan. That's why I'm leaving. That's the real reason."

"I know," he replied.

"I'll petition to be released from my vows," she went on—in a cheerier tone. "These days, maybe you know, it's almost automatically granted. You get released in a few weeks. No more anguished hearings. It's really quite simple. I'll ask for a leave of absence until the papers come through. So, as they say, Friday is my last day."

"I'm sure you know what you're doing."

"I'm sure. Regardless of what happens with us, I know I must leave the order."

"Have you told LeGuiese?"

"No. I have an appointment to see him tomorrow."

"That's good," he said. "Last time I talked to him, he had a pretty solid rumor from a friend in Rome that Paul would soon hand down the encyclical on contraception. After that, LeGuiese believes, the Vatican will completely rethink its policy on celibacy—the whole sex thing. He thinks they will drop the celibacy rule, and that we'll have married priests."

Mary thought about that, silently. Then she said:

"Is that what you want?"

"Yes," he said. "I think so. If—a big if—the Church comes around—changes across the board."

"I think you are being pretty optimistic," she said. "I wouldn't count on it. It may take years—decades."

"I don't think so," he said. "The pressures for change are too great. The seminary enrollments are falling off . . ."

"And if *I'm* right?"

He shrugged and threw up his hands. In the sacristy, Scafidi strained to hear. The voices were unintelligible—a low murmur.

"I don't know."

"You ought to consider the alternative," she said.

"I have," he said. "I'll leave. We'll get married. Then I'll petition to be released from my vows."

"It won't be granted."

"I heard of a case the other day. Some guy in Germany. I've been trying to get some details."

"I'm sure it was a very special case. You know the story. You'll petition and you'll never hear from Rome. That's the way it goes ordinarily."

"I know."

"Would you apply for laicization?"

"No. Why go through all that painful business? The papers would say *'castitate semper servate'*—chastity being always observed—anyway. So what's the point? I'm sure it'll be returned marked *'pereat'*—let him perish. I'll just send a letter, resign, then petition direct to Rome to be released. I don't care if I ever hear from them. Mary, isn't it awful that canon law imposes no specific punishment for clerical fornication, adultery, sodomy, promiscuity, or any sexual aberration—not even concubinage? That for a priest to 'commit' honorable matrimony brings instant dismissal and excommunication? That before you can petition Rome, you have to break the law first? There is no way to arbitrate, no way to appeal, no one to go to. It's an absolute monarchy."

"Did you read the Girandola book?" she said.

"Yes."

"He seems to have gone through hell. The divorce from the Church part, I mean. So did Longo."

"They all do. What kind of Christian institution is this, anyway, that would so crush a man?"

Mary rose suddenly.

"I really must be going," she said. "By the way, do I gather from all this that you are proposing?"

Daugherty looked up, astonished.

"Of course! I thought that was understood!"

"Dan, I don't want it to be 'understood.' I want to be asked."

"I'm sorry. Will you marry me?"

"Yes."

They stood together and kissed. Not long, but tenderly and lovingly. Seeing them rise in the dimness, Scafidi slipped out the sacristy door, limping toward the rectory.

"There is much to be worked out," Mary said, breaking away, holding his hand. "But henceforth I'll consider myself engaged. I hope it won't be a long engagement. I don't quite fancy myself waiting for Rome to cancel the celibacy rule."

Daugherty laughed.

"Will you let me know right away what happens in New York?" he said. They walked toward the foyer. Dan shut off the pulpit light. They went outside. He locked the door.

"I'm almost afraid to ask what's new at Halfway House," he said. "God, I feel terrible about that."

"So do I," she said. "I don't know what's going to happen."

"Have you seen Sharon?"

"Not lately."

"We *can't* let that drift," he said.

"I know," she said sadly.

They walked toward the VW. In the dimness, Dan saw, at the other end of the lot, the custodian, Scafidi, climbing into his battered Ford. He was late tonight, he thought. Mary followed his eyes.

"Who's *that?*" she said.

"Our custodian, Scafidi. He eats in the rectory on his work nights. Very strange fellow. Crippled."

"Oh," she said, hand on the VW door handle.

Then Dan saw light at the kitchen door. Mrs. Munally descended the steps, walking briskly across the lot toward them. What did she want? *Damnit to hell.* The busybody! One more piece of gossip to carry to Ryan. She approached the car as though she did not see them. Then she stopped, a look of astonishment on her face. It seemed forced.

"Oh!" she exclaimed. "I didn't see you! I thought I saw a light in the church. I thought I'd better have a look . . . someone breaking into the poor box . . ."

She spoke her disjointed, obviously rehearsed words, then laughed heartily.

"This is Sister Mary Murray," he said, concealing his anger. "Mary, this is our ubiquitous housekeeper, Mrs. Munally."

"How do you do?" Mary said, in a calm, matter-of-fact voice, extending her hand.

"She came to hear a dry run on my Sunday sermon," Father Daugherty explained.

"I forgot you were there," Mrs. Munally lied.

"I locked up," Daugherty said. "Don't worry."

Mrs. Munally returned to the rectory. Dan watched her silently, knowing she had come to look at Mary, to find out who she was.

"That won't look good," Mary said.

"No," Dan said.

"I hope she doesn't . . ."

"Don't worry. It doesn't matter. Well, thank you for coming. You are a very kind critic. Good luck in New York."

"Thank you for asking me," Mary said. "I'll call you . . . Good night."

She opened the door and got behind the wheel. She fumbled with the large ignition key, making several attempts before she found the slot. She drove away hurriedly, the small tires squealing on the macadam. Dan watched her circle through the empty lot. Then he walked toward the rectory.

III

In the privacy of her bathroom, door locked, Jean Favrot swallowed her birth control pill, washing it down with a glass of water. She put the little white plastic case back in the drawer, behind her bag of hair curlers, safe from Bob's eyes. It was a simple act, simply undertaken. But how the tiny white chemicals had changed her life!

She might never have done it alone. She had been led to it, first by Father Daugherty, then Dr. Cantor, then Margo and Joan, the whole group-shrink (as she called her therapy) crowd. Rome, too. She had read the "leaks" in the papers predicting that Pope Paul was soon to rule on the pill, almost certainly in favor, or at least for some limited form of contraception. There was no point in waiting for the encyclica, a mere piece of paper.

She had lived with fear of pregnancy for seventeen years. It was not fear of the pregnancy itself—as Bob often said, Jean was built like a peasant—but the worry and the demands yet another baby brought on. Dirty diapers. Struggling up for the two o'clock feeding. Putting away all the fragile bric-a-brac in the living room. The constant need to keep an eye out. The worry that he would run into the street. Fall into a neighbor's pool. Get into poison, like Chris. (The memory of that near-disaster still brought on cold chills.) And, beyond all that, the still unanswered question of how could they afford to send them to college.

All that would soon be behind her. She had only to worry the baby, John, through. Then she was done. Finished. Hallelujah!

She returned to the bedroom. Bob was still sleeping, flat on his back, mouth open. She shook him roughly. He jerked stiffly, pawed the air, chewed.

"Reveille!" she said.

She went to the kitchen. Emma was there, pulling out the cereal boxes. Five-six-seven. The children each liked a different cereal. Jean said good morning, then poured a cup of coffee. Now that school was out, the children slept an hour later. They were geared for summer routine. Nancy was a counselor at the CYO summer camp. The boys—Paul,

Bob, Joe, Chris, Mike, Bill—were signed up for the community pool club—swimming and tennis. They spent the day there, working out with the swim team, taking tennis lessons, lifesaving, running up exorbitant bills at the snack bar. She must speak sternly to all of them about that. They ought to take their own lunch, sandwiches anyway.

She jotted reminder notes on a pad, marveling at her new efficiency. These days everything was attended to promptly. Decisions came easily. For the first time in years her mind seemed uncluttered, turning like a jeweled watch. She poured a second cup of coffee, sat at her desk to write two or three checks. Bills were now paid promptly. No more tart "reminders" from the department stores.

Then she read the *Washington Post,* feeling a compulsion to be well informed. Bob came from the bedroom. He was clean-shaven but red-eyed—hung over again. He coughed, a smoker's hack. He nodded to Emma and sat at the kitchen table. Jean passed him the paper. He scanned the front page, scowling.

In all his years in politics, Bob Favrot had never seen anything like the year 1968. His party, the Democratic party, was split wide open. Everybody seemed to be going mad. First the curious and unexpected McCarthy race—a direct challenge to the party chief, Lyndon Johnson. Then Bobby plunging, ruthlessly muscling McCarthy aside. Lyndon bowing out—really meaning it—to search for peace. Then, on the heels of the Martin Luther Coon murder, Bobby shot down in his prime. George Wallace campaigning for blue collar votes in the North! And now, inconceivably, Hubert Humphrey emerging with the prize! The tableau made Bob's head swim.

And now, he thought, the goddamned niggers camped on the Mall! Resurrection City! Wooden shacks in a sea of mud. Defacing government property, a national shrine. Garbage piled up to the roofs. Militants stealing and causing trouble. Reading, Bob mumbled:

"They ought to shoot that son of a bitch, too."

' Who?" Jean said.

"Abernathy," Bob said. "I'll tell you this. It was a big mistake. It's backfired on them. The people don't want it."

He turned, looked over his shoulder at Emma. She was, in Bob's phrase, a "good nigger." No airs. Knew her place.

"Isn't that so, Emma?"

"Yas *suh,*" Emma said. "People down there, I hear, don have nothing to eat."

Jean withheld comment. They had been through the Negro thing last month. In the wake of the rioting in the Washington ghetto, a controversy arose over the government's policy toward looters. Following the Kerner Report guidelines, the government had ordered the police to be "lenient" with looters, not to shoot. The businessmen who suffered in the riots denounced this new policy, holding that the lenient stand encouraged more looting and stealing. In the future, they said, the government should adopt the attitude of Mayor Daley of Chicago: shoot all looters on sight. Bob agreed with Daley. Jean did not. She believed the lenient policy had saved lives. She found herself, for the first time, wholly and passionately on the side of the blacks and the liberals.

"He gets his orders from Castro," Bob said. "Like all of 'em." He ate his eggs. Emma left to care for the baby. When she was gone, Bob laid aside the paper.

"Can't you speak?" he said.

"I was thinking about something else."

"Well, sometime today I want you to get those pledge cards organized for me."

"I don't have time."

Bob turned to face his wife angrily.

"You don't have time for anything important anymore. I want you to give up typing that book. You're neglecting the children, the house, everything. Look at the kids' report cards! Disgraceful! Now when it gets to the point you can't spare an hour to help your own church, you're in serious trouble."

"*You're* the captain of the fund drive," she said icily. "Not me."

"Well, for Christ's sweet sake! Now listen to me. I didn't ask for this job. I don't like to go out every night, putting the screws to these people. The least you can do is . . ."

"You don't like to go out because it cuts into your drinking time. That's the truth of it."

She got up, went to the sink, seething.

"I want you to give up that stupid job," Bob said, crashing his cup into the saucer. "And take those boys to get a haircut. TODAY!"

"Don't raise your voice to me."

"And do those pledge cards."

"I will *not* do the pledge cards. That's final. I will *not* quit my job. The boys do *not* need a haircut."

"Well, *shit!*"

"Shit yourself."

Bob looked at Jean, astonished. Jean was not a little amazed at herself. She had never said that word before. It just popped out. Shaken, Bob rose from the table, put his arm around Jean, and said tenderly:

"Honey, what's come over you? Are you feeling all right?"

Jean moved away, to the sink. She did not like his touch. She thought of Kenneth, in group-shrink. His phobia. Was it contagious? Bob slammed the kitchen door shut. He turned on Jean, eyes popping with rage.

"I want to know what the hell's come over you."

She did not reply. She stood at the sink, sipping her coffee, staring defiantly over the rim of the cup.

"I think you're cracking up," he said.

She sipped silently, glowering.

"I'll tell you what's the matter," he snarled. "I know. Don't think I *don't* know. You may think you have a secret, but I've known right along."

Jean set the cup on the sideboard with trembling fingers. She felt panic rising in her throat. So he knew about the group! The Jew doctor, he would say. His own wife, going to a goddamned quack psychiatrist! She had (with shudders) anticipated it all. She had meant to confront him. But it had been easier not to.

"What . . . what secret?" she said, voice faltering.

"The pill!"

She collapsed in the chair laughing. She felt relieved. In her mind, this deceit loomed smaller than the other.

"What's so goddamned funny, I'd like to know?" Bob raved on. "I found the box the other night in your drawer. You're not kidding anybody. Not me, anyway. I . . . I . . . I don't know what to say! I couldn't believe it. You can't do that without asking me. Did Daugherty OK this?"

"No, Daugherty did not OK this," Jean shouted, turning in anger. "I OK'd it myself."

"I's a mortal sin. Murder!"

"Oh, for God's sake, shut up! Everybody takes the pill, you stupid *fool.*"

"Everybody does *not* take the pill!"

"They will be soon. The Pope's going to approve it. So why should I wait?"

"The commission may approve," Bob said calmly, "but the Pope himself will make the final decision."

"He won't overrule his own commission."

"Don't bet on it."

Jean was calmer now, too. "In my judgment," she said, "we have enough children. Too many."

Bob looked at his wife.

"Which ones would you like to give back? Who's going to take care of you in your old age?"

"Certainly not my children," Jean said, ignoring his first question. I'll go in a home before I intrude . . . ruin any of their lives."

Bob got his boater and seersucker jacket from the front hall closet. He stood in the doorway.

"We'll discuss this further. I've got to go make a living. Will you please do the pledge cards?"

"No."

Bob stormed out the front door, slamming it behind him. The noise drove straight into Jean's heart. She felt distressed, guilty, no longer defiant, strong. She should have discussed the pill thing with him calmly, intelligently. She should not have deceived him. She had better tell him about group-shrink before he found that out, too. She would ask Dr. Cantor about that.

She went to the dining room. The rented electric typewriter with the pica typeface was on the table, with the paper, carbons, the rough draft. She could get in a solid hour before the kids got up. She had been at it many weeks now. Her speed and rhythm were good, as good as they were likely to get. She made few mistakes. Without interruption, she could grind out four double-spaced pages in an hour.

She turned on the light and fell to work. To Jean, it was a fascinating project, much different from what she had imagined. There was very little math in the book. It was mostly a story about people, biographies about mathematicians. She did not hold herself to be a good judge of writing, but she thought Bill did very well. The people came to life on the pages (and such lives!). In places, the book was amusing, lighthearted. It jumped from person to person, century to century. Exploring all those places and times excited Jean. It reminded her that she, too, was living several different lives now. The old one with Bob, the new one with group, and the one with Bill.

The new life with Bill was mostly in her mind. She thought about him often, wondering what he might be doing in his apartment (aside from writing), at his office. She wondered too about his kids and Angela. They had not talked much beyond the ground they covered the first day. When she called to pick up or deliver manuscript, Jean remained, rather circumspectly, near the front door. He had not again asked her to sit, or to have coffee. Yet, as his typist, the only other person to have read his manuscript, she felt a certain proprietary kinship. As though, between them, there was a very precious secret.

At noon, long after all the kids were gone, she finished the work for the day. She proofed it, finding only two typos in eight pages. Good! She gathered up the manuscript and shoved it carefully into a brown manila envelope. Then she went to her room. She brushed her hair, put on colorless lipstick, bell-bottom slacks, a frilly blouse, thick-chained pendant, bracelet, a dab of Arpege. She felt very good, very trim. The diet had knocked off twelve pounds; the exercise had tightened her stomach, the little tummy-hump was gone. The pill (she believed) had filled out her bosom and somehow added luster to her hair. Thanks to the typing, her closet was full of new, stylish clothes. In all, she felt ten years younger.

She drove to Bill's apartment. The motor, everything, seemed to be running smoother. Even the air-conditioner, which last year leaked Freon gas. It was a sparkling day. She remembered her horoscope. She was a Virgo. It said, "Take advantage of new opportunities that will come your way. Act impulsively without fear of consequences." She remembered, too, something Dr. Cantor had told the weepy Joan last week. "So what's wrong, for God's sake, in seizing a moment of intimate pleasure? Are you so hungup on the Judeo-Christian ethic that every thought you have is sin? Do you realize that as I look at you right now, I am subconsciously appraising you, perhaps with the idea of balling you? I do that five, ten times a day. Nothing more ever comes of it. But I don't feel guilty about it. I don't think it's a sin."

Jean now ranked Dr. Cantor among the most fascinating men she ever met. He was so iconoclastic! He accepted absolutely nothing as finite. No rule, belief, dogma, law, tradition, nothing. He held open season on anybody who did. They had learned in group that he was very happily married to a psychologist! They both lived the same life. There were no pretenses, no fronts, a total community of interest. Group-shrink was no longer an awkward confessional. They were all going at each other now, tooth and nail, tearing away layers and layers of defenses and styles and put-ons. Jean was beginning to see—albeit dimly —what it all meant.

Bill Clark, waiting in his apartment for Jean, had made a decision. He would invite her in and offer her a drink. He had finished Part One that morning. It was a logical time to pause and talk. He wanted to know more about her. Besides, he felt like celebrating. The book was going well. Much better than he dreamed. He would tell her exactly how much her little daily visits meant to him, how he looked forward to seeing her, even briefly.

In the kitchen, he cracked ice, made a gin martini, with a tiny dash of vermouth, carried it to the living room. He sat down carefully on the couch, thinking about his kids. They were out of school now, going to camp. Perhaps there some counselor would *force* them to write him. So far, there had not been a single letter except the usual bitter ones from Angela about the money, this or that. She was turning the children against him, he was certain. It always happened, in spite of well-meant intentions not to. He was being shut out. He was no longer consulted on decisions about schools, camps, bicycles. He felt an intense, deep loneliness.

Jean must be very busy, of course. With nine kids to look after! Probably up to her eyeballs in political activity. Or what-not. She seems to have lost weight. That lovely, musical voice! Should he ask her what she thought of the book? She had never said one word. Perhaps she thought he would not value her opinion. Or that he might even take offense. Yes, he would ask.

The door chimes sang. He rose, casually, dipping his head to see himself in the mirror. He smoothed his hair, needlessly brushed the front of his gray slacks. He opened the door with a genial smile. She stood there, envelope in hand, as always, smiling that wide Cajun smile, wearing those dazzlingly bright mod clothes.

"Hi," he said.

"Hey," she responded. "Beautiful day. Just gorgeous. You ought to get out of here and take a look."

"Maybe I will, later" he said. "Won't you come in?"

Jean stood on the threshold, hesitant, confused. He seemed very different today, very relaxed.

"Come on in," he repeated.

"All right," she said. "Just for a minute."

They went into the living room. Jean perched on the edge of the couch. Bill slumped into an easy chair. Jean noticed the martini on the table. It was full. He saw her eyes.

"I was celebrating," he said. "I wrote the last word of Part One this morning. I thought maybe it's a good place to take a break."

"Oh, that's *great,*" Jean said. "May I see how you finished? I'm really very involved. It's like a mystery story. I want to see how it comes out."

"Certainly," he said, rising, walking to his desk, immensely pleased. Over his shoulder: "I didn't know you were *that* involved."

Jean blushed. Her hand went to her lips.

"It's quite good," she said. "So different from anything I expected."

He returned to the couch with the manuscript, passing it eagerly, almost gratefully. Jean began reading without pause, hurrying through to the end. When she finished, she laid it aside.

"Oh, I think it's *great!*" she exclaimed. "I hope it sells."

"Me too," he said, beaming. "Jean, may I get you a drink?"

"Oh . . . no thank you. I . . . I can't stay, really. I . . ."

"It won't take a minute. Relax. Make yourself comfortable." He smiled warmly.

Jean's head swirled. She felt butterflies in her stomach. She wanted to stay and talk. But . . . well, gosh, why not?

"Not a martini," she said. "I can't drink gin. It goes straight to my head. One drink . . . whoooooof."

She laughed happily.

"Name your poison," he said.

"Would a daiquiri be too much trouble?"

"Not at all. Plain or frozen?"

"Plain, please."

He went into the kitchen. Jean got up—feeling restless—and walked to the bookcase to reexamine the titles. There were so many she had never read but always meant to. She *must* begin reading again.

Bill came from the kitchen with a cocktail tray bearing her daiquiri, cocktail napkins.

"Here we are," he said cheerily.

She returned to the couch, sipped her drink. Bill rambled on about the riots at Columbia, the SDS, and Tom Hayden's "Port Huron Statement," about which Jean knew nothing. She listened carefully. Bill sympathized with the kids, actually, but believed they needed organization and solid purpose, as did any protest or revolution. A program. A deep ideological base. They appeared to be flailing purposelessly. Eugene McCarthy might have provided that ideology, an articulation, but he was peculiarly ineffective, Bill said. Too much the poet, too much the friend of Robert Lowell and all that. Maybe a lightweight.

Jean was fascinated by Bill's eyes. He was sitting so the sun from the window struck obliquely, giving them a brilliant cast. She could feel the daiquiri. She ought not to drink on an empty stomach. Ought not.

Ought not. Ought not. How much of her life had she frittered away ought-notting? When she should have been living she was ought-notting. Seize a moment of intimate pleasure, Cantor said. Survive!

"Do you believe in Hell?" Jean said, cutting into Bill's monologue. His eyes darted to her, amused.

"I mean," Jean rushed on, "last Sunday Father Daugherty—you remember my telling you about him—gave this absolutely stunning sermon about Hell. I almost came out of my pew. He said . . . I can't remember his words exactly . . . but, in effect, he said there was no Hell at all. He said that our old concept of a vengeful God—and a flaming Hell—was ridiculous. That Hell was right here. The suffering and all. He quoted a lot of far-out . . . I shouldn't say far-out but maybe modern . . . theologians—Catholic theologians—to prove Christ never said, specifically, anything about Hell as such. That it was Old Testament folklore and so on. And that nobody was to get uptight—he actually used the word—about going to Hell. That, as I say, *this* is Hell right here, and that if we help our fellowman through Hell, then we will experience the Heaven part too. He said the best theologians had even gone *beyond* that concept."

"To where?" Bill said, lighting his pipe.

"He didn't say. That comes next week. I do wish you'd go over and hear him. You'd be fascinated."

She felt lighthearted, gay.

"Perhaps I'll look in," Bill said.

He knew he wouldn't, that it was pointless. There was no place in the Roman Catholic Church for a man divorced, no matter how devout, how much he may have loved the Church or needed it. No matter how misguided a marriage might be, once entered into—sexually consummated—it was spiritually binding. If he remarried, the Church did not recognize the second marriage. It made no difference, ecclesiastically. He might attend Mass, but he could not take Communion. He was an outcast, with no second chance. He would be living in sin—mortal sin —destined to spend eternity in Hell. That one in four marriages now ended in divorce, that probably one in two were miserable unions, seemed not to matter. It was—in contrast to Christ—an unforgiving Church. It made him bitter, sad.

"May I get you another?" he said.

Jean looked at her glass. It was empty. She was horrified.

"I got carried away," she laughed. "I shouldn't chug-a-lug. I ought to be going . . ."

Ought not to stay, she thought. Ought-not. Ought-not.

He put the glasses on a tray and went to the kitchen. Jean hummed to herself, swinging her leg. It was a good leg. Trim. Slim. He returned with the tray and a bowl of Do-Dads.

"I hope all this isn't too obvious," Bill said, sitting down again.

"What?" Jean said.

"I planned this," Bill said, smiling.

Jean blushed. She pushed at her hair. She sipped her new drink. What did it matter? She wanted to talk too.

"You mean you laid a *trap?*" she said, feigning terror.

"Yes."

She laughed.

"For *me?*" she asked, seemingly incredulous, actually much pleased, flattered. Wait until she told Margo! Margo had said it would happen— in time. They would come face to face with it—the eternal question: to screw or not to screw. (Margo used words like a sailor.)

"For you," Bill said. He raised his glass.

"You couldn't want *me,* for Lord's sake," Jean protested, chuckling. "You want a *young* girl. Not the mother of nine!"

"I enjoy your visits," he said, ignoring her coquettishness. "I wish they were longer."

"You're very lonely, aren't you?" Jean said.

"I suppose so," he said. "Yes. To be frank, I am."

"You need to get out more," she said. "You'll go stir-crazy if you don't. Go to the beach. Do a little girl-watching."

"The worst part," Bill said, "is I never hear from my kids unless I telephone. The phone bill is fantastic."

"Tell me about them," Jean said.

He did. As Jean suspected, there had been another woman. This news, thought expected, brought a stab of pain. It confused her. She felt jealous. But he made light of the girl. She had run off to Seattle. Never heard from again. The "usual" story, Bill added. There had been trouble all along with Angela. They married impulsively, without really knowing one another. Too young. Immature. Nor had he appreciated the whole thing about contraceptives. She wouldn't use one. They had six kids—bang, bang, bang—and Angela was really frigid! Got nothing out of sex. Did not want it. Conceived as a duty. They grew apart, had nothing in common, except the children. He went elsewhere for affection, for sex. Then he met the girl. Angela found out. Was unforgiving.

Made his life so miserable, he couldn't keep up his work. Got fired . . . divorced . . . moved.

"In effect," Bill concluded, "I'm beginning life all over."

"Wow," Jean said sadly. "I'm *terribly* sorry . . ."

"It's all done now," he said brightly. "Water over the dam. Hell of a lot of water. I'll get another drink. I really didn't mean to run on like that."

"I asked," Jean said, lifting her empty glass.

He went to the kitchen. Jean stared dazedly out the window. She was light-headed, getting sleepy. She *must* not be sleepy! She sat up stiffly, swung her legs. Get the blood moving. Ought-not to have another. Ought-not. Heck . . .

"Did you get some professional help?" she said, accepting the new drink.

"Oh yes," he said, nodding grimly. "Thousands down the tube for shrinks. Hers. Mine. The kids. The shrinks and the lawyers cleaned me out."

"Did they help? The shrinks, I mean."

"They opened my eyes," he said. "But not hers."

"Did you . . . did you . . . go *deep?*"

"Oh, yes," he said. "Very deep. My guy took me completely apart."

"Fascinating," Jean said.

"But I don't think he finished putting me back together right," Bill said. "He left a lot of holes."

Jean looked puzzled.

"It's too long a story," he said.

"*I'm* in a group," she said proudly.

"*You* are?" he said, incredulous.

"I am," she replied. "Don't you think everybody should . . .?"

"But you. I mean, if ever I met a normal person!"

"What's normal?" she laughed.

"OK. Touché. I meant, you seem very well adjusted. Very strong."

Jean talked about herself. Her kids. Bob. She spoke with a new sense of freedom, the group-therapy type freedom. She felt compelled to confide, to be honest and open. Two hours slipped by. They were both high.

"Would you mind some music?" he said during a pause in her recitation. He walked to the stereo. "I must warn you, my taste runs to the simple. Do you mind Glen Campbell?"

"*Mind* him?" Jean said, voice lilting. "I *love* him. Do you have 'By the Time I Get to Phoenix'?"

"I do. The album."

"Play that."

He put the record on the player and adjusted the volume and tone balance. Jean sat, swinging her leg, staring out the window, enchanted. Bob had never understood music. He was tone deaf. When he was drunk, he sang "Dixie" and "The Eyes of Texas" in a swaggering voice, exaggeratedly southern. He ridiculed her love of opera.

"May I have this dance?" Bill said, leaning over her in a mock-bow.

Jean felt a panic rising. He had read her mind! She had been too obvious, making a fool of herself. Drinking at midday. Alone with a bachelor! A divorced man! Neglecting her children. Going to that crazy shrink. Yes, truly she had lost her marbles. Gone round the bend. Next stop, little girl, the funny farm. Ought-not. *Seize!*

She stood. She was light-headed. He put his arms around her. They danced, stiff at first, then comfortably, then cheek to cheek. "You're an excellent dancer," Jean said, her voice barely audible.

"I'm inspired," he murmured.

He held her close. They danced for a long time. Jean's mind wandered to a strange, exotic place. It was cloudlike and feathery. Everything soft and dimly lit, very peaceful. She felt his cheek against hers, and then his lips, and then his lips against hers, very softly. She held him tight, clinging to the peace, the serenity. His hand on her breast made her feel secure, needed, loved. Her heart thudded in her ears.

The hall walls passed in a haze. Then the bedroom, his fingers on her buttons. She removed the rest with feverish energy, sensing rather than seeing that he had turned down the covers on the enormous bed. She felt no shame. She lay beside him and felt his hand, gentle, caressing. He did things with his fingernails that made her body moist, pulsating, hungry. He was not in a hurry, like Bob. He withheld, lovingly, tenderly until she could wait no longer. She brought him into her, and put her arms around him. His penis was small and gentle. He did not lunge. He held it near the surface, undulating slowly. Her body trembled and jerked in exquisite ecstasy. She came to orgasm before he fully entered her. Then, as he gently took his pleasure, she came again, and then once more, with him. Then she slept, holding him close.

IV

Marvin Klein sat at his desk in the *Tribune* city room, staring at the reminder on his spindle: CALL PRIAL RE: JONES AND GYM.

The St. Luke's matter had been pushed to a back burner for weeks. There had been no time for a *Catholic* revolution. Klein and his reporters had been absorbed with another revolution, exploding under their noses. The ghetto fires had licked within two blocks of the Tribune Building. On some days, they had merely to look out the window to cover the story—the looting and sniping, the police and soldiers, the chaos.

They had done their job well. Klein was certain George Emerson, his star reporter, would be nominated for a Pulitzer Prize. Emerson had tracked down the hard-core black militants, the organizers, and had persuaded them to tell him everything—anonymously. They had. The burning of Washington, they revealed, had not been a spontaneous gesture of sympathy for Dr. King. It was carefully planned, diabolical act of violence. The ringleaders had seized upon Dr. King's murder as a provocation. It was no accident that H. Rap Brown and Stokely Carmichael had appeared, almost magically, on the ghetto streets, shouting: "Get your guns. Kill Whitey. Kill . . . kill . . ."

Emerson's interview with the plotters, the smell of smoke and death (blessedly little, thanks to the lenient government policy) had profoundly shaken Marvin Klein. That and the gangs of young blacks roving his own neighborhood. Klein did not believe in violence. Violence in the war or violence in the ghetto. The burning of the Washington ghetto—an arrogant, calculated act of violence—forced him to reappraise his views of the Problem. The militants had overreached, overstepped, overacted. They had, among other things burned their own people out of their homes and stores. Klein felt responsible, in part. Guilty. Perhaps, as Serena had chided all along, the *Tribune* had been too inflammatory, had brushed some things under the rug they should have reported. From this reappraisal, Klein emerged with an old belief, very much reinforced: nonviolent blacks like Charles Seymour Jones *must* be encouraged to seek positions of leadership of their people. They—not the militants—must lead the blacks from deprivation and inequality through tough—but not violent—protest and demonstration, the courts, the Congress. They must also be discouraged from futile and ineffective action, like Abernathy's Resurrection City, a disorganized, pitiful mess that had served no purpose other than to raise hackles on the Hill and turn away many middle-of-the-roaders. Lawmakers and citizens alike. But the Joneses were not easy to find these days.

Klein picked up the telephone, asked the operator to connect him with Vicar General Prial at the Chancery. In a moment Prial came on the line, cold, distant.

"I'm checking you to see what, if anything, has been done to defer the eviction of Seymour Jones from the St. Luke's gym," Klein said, wiggling his pencil in the air.

"We've done all we could," Prial said. "I told your reporter—what's-his-name—that some weeks ago."

"Emerson," Klein said. "George Emerson."

"I talked to him for an hour," Prial said.

"I know. But now that the deadline has come up, we're rechecking," Klein said. "We want to do a piece tomorrow."

"Is that *really* necessary?" Prial said irritably. "Don't you have enough to write about in the ghetto without stirring up more trouble?"

"We don't stir trouble," Klein said icily. "We report trouble when we find it."

"That's *your* opinion," Prial said.

"It's a fact, not opinion."

"Did you read the Kerner Report?" Prial said. "The part about the role of the press?"

"I did," Klein said. "I don't agree that the press is being used by the dissidents. We merely report an existing climate. Anyway, that's beside the point."

"I don't think it is," Prial insisted.

"Are you evading my question?" Klein asked.

"No. The answer is the same. We did all we could. I said all along—and Jones knows full well—it was a temporary deal. We've turned the Chancery inside out trying to help him."

"You know he'll probably lose his OEO grant?"

"I'm sorry about that. But . . ."

"Does the Church realize that it is better for everybody in the

long run to help people like Seymour? If we kick the moderates in the
face, we'll alienate them too. Drive them over to the militants."

"Mr. Klein," Prial said, "the business of the Church is not primarily
concerned with life on this earth—no matter how deprived some lives
may be—but rather with the life hereafter. I wish you people could
understand that. We're not sociologists. We're not even psychologists.
Temporal matters are not our primary business. We're not trained for
it. We leave all that to you people who can do a better job."

"What about missionaries?" Klein needled. "I thought the Church was
big on missionary work."

"It is. Bringing the Word of Christ to heathens."

"They also cure the sick."

"True. But they don't get involved in welfare problems, OEO grants
. . . the economic structure. That is the business of the state. You
certainly wouldn't want us transgressing into the state's business, would
you? I thought you stood for absolute separatism."

"You're being Jesuitical again," Klein said.

"I believe we have reached a *reducio ad absurdum,*" Prial said.
"Can I help you with anything else?"

"How's the fund drive coming?"

"Fine," Prial said cheerily. "In spite of your story. So far, we couldn't
be more pleased."

"How much have you raised?"

"If you'll come over, we'll give you a complete story."

"Later, maybe."

They hung up. Klein rose, stretched. The Vicar General was lying.
Daugherty had told him last week the drive was sagging. He must remember to call Daugherty, see if he could shake loose for some tennis. He
walked back into the city room to the desk of George Emerson. The
reporter was reclining in his chair, head far back on the rim of the
chair, studying a photostat of a legal document.

"George," Klein said. "May I interrupt you a moment?"

Emerson swung forward in the chair, laid the photostat on his desk.
He removed his horn-rimmed glasses. Klein sat on the edge of the
desk.

"Jones moves out of the St. Luke's gym tomorrow," Klein said. "You
want to do the piece?"

"I just got back to that St. Luke's deal this week," Emerson said,
pointing to the photostat. "I think I've smoked out a rat."

"What's the deal?"

Emerson told his story. Before the riots, the land adjacent to St. Luke's had been bought up by a corporation calling itself the District Land Development Corporation. Emerson had dug out the incorporation records of that company, the list of directors. It was a new corporation. It was held by yet another corporation, with headquarters in New York. Searching back through records on file in the District Building, Emerson had ascertained that the apparent tycoon behind the labyrinth of corporations was a single man. His name was John Carter. One of the corporation papers listed an address for a John Carter, a Washington street. Emerson had gone to this address. He found a discount appliance store, one of a Washington chain. He called on John Carter, president. Carter conceded that he had bought property in the block, but would not reveal his reasons, other than for "investment" purposes. Digging through the *Tribune* morgue, Emerson found many clips on Carter. He was quite active in civic affairs. One clip announced Carter's appointment to Archbishop McInnerney's financial council.

"What's the financial council?" Klein said.

"A business advisory group for McInnerney," Emerson said. "Lot of big Washington businessmen."

"Hmmmmmmmm," Klein said, scratching his head vigorously.

"That's what I thought," Emerson said. "Odd coincidence."

"I don't believe in coincidence."

George Emerson smiled. "There's a problem. His appliance chain is Eliott's TV. A very large advertiser."

Emerson tapped a copy of the *Tribune* on his desk. It was opened to the Eliott TV ad, a standard, thrice-weekly full-page spread, shrilly promoting discounts, no down-payment, easy payments, warehouses jammed full of appliances that must be moved this week! It was an ad conceived for and directed to the *Tribune*'s large black readership. They would flock to the stores by the dozens, hungry for the fruits of the free enterprise system, sign notes with usurious interest rates. Many would wake up to find they could not pay. They would wind up, bewildered, in small claim's court, incurring exorbitant legal fees, saddled with hopeless judgments, or they would lose the fruit through repossession. It was a criminal system, Klein thought, and he, the *Tribune,* as purveyer of the ad, was as guilty as the merchants. Yet, without the ads, the *Tribune* could not survive, not within the existing economic framework of newspaper publishing.

"If it won't put your nose out of joint," Klein said, "I'd like to double back on this Carter. Do you have his address?"

"He'll be impressed."

"I don't want to put you in an awkward position," Klein said. "If we get a backlash from the ad department, it will be all my responsibility. OK?"

"Fine by me."

Later, Klein left by cab for Carter's headquarters. He arrived unannounced. He gave his card to a secretary in the waiting room. An hour later, Klein was admitted to the inner office, a vast room with tasteless modern furniture, a large, garish blue-green marlin mounted on the wall behind Carter's desk. Carter, blond, boyish-looking, was anything but cordial.

"What do you want?" he said bluntly, not offering a chair.

Klein sat down. He took out a notebook, ballpoint pen.

"We want to know why you bought up property around St. Luke's," he said.

"I told that reporter of yours it was an investment," Carter said. "Other than that I am not prepared to say."

"Do you intend to build there?"

"Maybe. Maybe a warehouse."

"Warehouse?" Klein said. "But that's residential property. You'd have to get it rezoned industrial or semi-industrial."

"I didn't *say* I was going to build a warehouse," Carter glowered.

"But . . ."

"I said maybe."

"Why are you giving me the run-around?" Klein said.

"You invited yourself here," Carter said. "I don't feel obligated to you."

"You have an obligation to the public," Klein said.

"Damn the public. What I do with my personal business is none of their business."

"What a white businessman does in the ghetto is the public's concern," Klein said. "Especially if he intends to build a warehouse."

"If you print that, you'll find yourself in serious trouble," Carter said. "I'll pull my ad accounts."

Klein almost said: "Pull them." Instead, he asked, "Why did you buy through a corporate front?"

"I conduct all my business through corporations," Carter said, boyish face red. "For tax purposes. On the advice of my accountants and lawyers. There's nothing unusual in that."

"Did you know that just across the street the Chancery had evicted an OEO neighborhood center from the St. Luke's gymnasium?"

"No. I know nothing about that."

"Yet you serve on the Archbishop's financial council?"

"We don't get into details like that. It's a high-level financial policy-making body. An advisory body."

"Is there a connection between the eviction and your buying property?"

"I told you I knew nothing about the eviction," Carter said thunderously, angrily. "And if you so much as hint that I do, I'll sue you for every penny that paper's got."

"I see no reason to sue," Klein said deferentially. "Unless you know something I don't."

"I bought that property and look what happened," Carter said, almost shouting. "The goddamned niggers burned it down!"

"If you're going to build a warehouse," Klein replied, "they saved you the work of clearing and demolition. I assume your property was insured?"

"That's none of your business," Carter exploded.

"Was it?"

Carter evaded. "I didn't say I was going to build a warehouse."

"What *are* you going to build?"

"None of your business," Carter repeated, rising. "Now get out of here. I'm calling your ad department right now."

"Go ahead," Klein said.

He departed Carter's office swiftly. Emerson was right. There was a rat in the woodwork. Perhaps a major scandal. He flagged a cab, returned to the Tribune Building. He arrived at his desk to find the telephone ringing. He picked up the receiver. It was a stranger.

"Mr. Klein? This is Roger Croft. I represent Mr. Carter. He called me after you left. He was quite upset. One of those things. Ah, it occurred to me you might want to make a deal."

"A deal?"

"A swap. I'll give you something in return for something from you."

"Be specific."

"I can shed light on the St. Luke's situation, provided you do us a favor. Leave out anything about Mr. Carter's investment."

"I don't make editorial deals," Klein said coolly.

"It could make quite a story for you."

"I have all the stories I need. I'm not so sure we don't have a good one, right here."

"Let me put it this way. I know how you feel. I understand perfectly. Suppose I say this: please consider leaving us out of it? And by the same token, we will, of course, consider leaving our ad schedule in the *Tribune.*"

"All right," Klein said, now very curious. "I'll consider."

"Our part is a small one," Croft said in silky tones. "Hardly newsworthy."

"I'll be the judge of that. Now what's with St. Luke's?"

"It's to be sold."

"Sold! The cathedral?"

"All the St. Luke's property."

"To whom? To you?"

"No. To a quasi-governmental agency."

"Why?"

"The cathedral will be torn down. A new structure will go there."

"What quasi-governmental agency?"

"This is strictly not for attribution?"

"Strictly."

"Then . . . it's IDA."

"You must be kidding!" Klein said, lowering his voice.

"No. HUD is providing funds under Title B, as we understand it. Is that a story for you?"

"It sure as hell is!"

"So that our little operation is insignificant by comparison?"

"By comparison, yes. Maybe. But . . ."

"Mr. Carter will be happy to hear that. Good-bye now."

Klein hung up. He waved Emerson to his desk. He talked fast, concisely, concluding:

"Get over to HUD. See if you can nail it down."

Emerson listened, eyes growing wide.

"Fantastic," he said. "Are you sure?"

"Ninety percent. But let's get something official from HUD."

Emerson left for HUD. Klein, shucking his jacket, telephoned Vicar General Prial.

"You again?" Prial said.

"We have it on good authority that St. Luke's will be sold to IDA," Klein said.

"Who told you *that?*" the Vicar General said.

"Never mind. Will you confirm it?"

"No." His tone was indignant, thunderous.

"I'm going to print it anyway," Klein said quietly.

"If you do, the Chancery door will be closed to you forever. And all other doors in the archdiocese."

"I'm used to closed doors."

"You know what you are?" Prial said levelly. "You're anti-Catholic. You're a Jew troublemaker."

Klein heard the click as the Vicar General hung up. He lowered the receiver into the cradle gently, the Vicar General's words burning into his mind. So be it, he thought. A man is as a man does. Klein was first, foremost, a journalist. They must move carefully, slowly. Get all the facts. So. A war agency for the ghetto! Carter, with inside information, buying up land! He pulled on his jacket again, picked up the telephone, spoke to the operator.

"I'm going out for a while. If Emerson calls, tell him I'm at Seymour Jones's gym. Got that?"

"Yes, sir," the operator said cheerily.

Charles Seymour Jones sat alone in his office in the neighborhood center, listening to the thump-thump of the basketballs on the gym floor, the shrill, happy cries. On the floor, behind the desk, were two small cardboard boxes filled with records and official papers. He had stopped packing, thinking he might as well throw it all away. He got up and walked to the sooty window. He saw the young blacks in the street, knocking a can along with a stick, pushing, shoving. Beyond them, rubble, where once had stood a row of houses. During the fire, the chaos, the people had come here, to the gym. It had been a haven. Later it had been a collection and distribution point for food, clothing, water, protected by a company of the Fifth National Guard Battalion, Second Regiment, Twenty-sixth Division. It was a nightmare Seymour would never forget.

The episode had sickened him. He was ashamed of his own people. Especially the young kids—many of *his* kids—running amuck in the streets, carting off TV's, women's clothes, chairs, tables, irons, transistor radios. Anything they could carry. The older ones, drunk, smashing windows, taunting the police, the soldiers, anybody in authority.

Clowning for TV cameras, spreading false rumors. And above all, the hypocrisy! All that destruction in the name of Dr. King, a man many, if not most, did not know, had never seen, couldn't care less if he had been shot in Memphis. They had played the fool nigger. Mr. Bones. Step'n Fetchit, gone berserk. All that Dr. King, and in his small way, Charles Seymour Jones, had worked for, torn down in a single, insane childish carnival. It had set the cause back ten years. Watching it, Jones himself had been utterly demoralized, as though King had died in *his* arms on the balcony at the Lorraine Motel. Now Abernathy with this confused, stupid—even dangerous—house of cards on the Mall. And Bobby Kennedy dead.

Caught in the eddies of these waves, Jones had made no further effort to relocate the neighborhood center. To hell with OEO, Prial, the Chancery. He finished his studies for the year, formed no plans beyond a vague notion of going to Memphis to visit King's shrine in the Lorraine, and his grave in Atlanta, a trip he was sure would never occur because it was fundamentally too sentimental and impractical, not to say expensive.

He returned to his deak. He sat down, thumbed through the mail, the underground newspapers, the mailers from the Liberation News Service. There were appeals, demanding freedom for Huey P. Newton, Eldridge Cleaver, Rap Brown, Harlem Five, Harlem Six, all black prisoners, Timothy Leary, the Oakland Seven, all drug prisoners, all draft resisters, Benjamin Spock, Jeff Segal, Martin Kenner, Fort Hood Forty-three, Catonsville Nine, Milwaukee Fourteen . . . the list seemed endless. And stupid.

Marvin Klein appeared in the doorway, like an apparition.

"Marv!" Jones said, jumping up.

"Hello, Seymour. What's new?" Klein said, taking off his jacket. "Christ! It's hot in here."

"We disconnected the air-conditioning," Jones joked.

Klein sat down in a rickety chair. He had not seen Jones in a long time, not since the riots.

"I didn't want you to think I forgot you," he said, sweeping a hand toward the gym. "I was on the horn to Prial right up to the end. Today, in fact."

"I appreciate that," Jones said.

"It was a waste of time. But we did find out some information. *Why* they're evicting you."

"That should be interesting," Jones said.

"I'll say," Klein said, leaning forward, lowering his voice to a confidential level. "Can you keep it under your hat until we break it?"

"Sure."

"Absolutely off the record?" Klein said.

"Absolutely. Man, who would *I* tell?"

"All right. They've sold off the cathedral, the land. IDA is going to put a headquarters building in here under Urban Renewal."

"IDA! Man, you're putting me on."

"No. It's true."

"A war agency in the ghetto? Have they blown their mind?"

"Yes."

Jones rolled his eyes in mock-delight, inhaled deeply.

"So . . ." he exclaimed, exhaling. "Oh, wow! Beautiful! What are *they* smoking?"

"I have an idea," Klein said, ignoring the question, voice mounting in intensity.

"I'll bet," Jones chuckled.

"You stay put," Klein said. "Don't move out."

Jones seemed puzzled.

"Let them forcibly evict you."

"Who?"

"Either one. The Chancery or IDA. Either way, you win."

"Win what?" Jones said skeptically.

"Well . . . attention. By refusing to move, you protest, peacefully, nonviolently, this act of arrogance. Selling off a church—depriving blacks of a house of worship—to make way for a war agency."

"Protest to what end?" Jones said wearily. "Man, I've got no bread. We can't operate. OEO will cut us off like that, especially if we're blocking a HUD renewal project."

"Maybe, maybe not. Maybe the government's left hand won't know what the right hand's doing. It wouldn't be the first time."

"Still . . ."

"You asked about the end. The goal. Well, Seymour, if you don't do it, you know who will?"

Seymour thought. He knew very well. The militants, the men who burned down the ghetto. That might lead to almost anything.

"If you stake the first claim," Klein said, "the militants might be frozen out. You could become a real hero . . . I mean a *real* leader."

"Or a martyr."

Jones, thinking, shuffled through the list of appeals on his desk. The list needed, above all, organization, he thought. It was a Coxey's army, like Nat Turner's. Sometime soon, someone, somewhere, would step forward to lead, to replace King. To finish what King had begun. The man would artfully combine oratorical ability with a genius for organizational detail. He would rise spectacularly from a single act, a single episode, to lead, to unfold a plan, to execute the plan. He would be a man of passion, yet of discretion. No Cleaver or Brown or Carmichael. He would not overreach; he would not underreach. He would not kill. Burn. He would not be stampeded by emotion. He would not foolishly attempt to create events, or dam or divert the flow of history. He would ride that flow skillfully, and—above all—survive. Survival was the key; martyrs furnished old shrines to venerate and speeches to quote, useful tools. But they did not survive to lead, to create that which had to be created. The new political order. The new political power.

"What do you think?" Klein pressed.

"I think I might get killed," Jones grinned.

"That's a risk, I guess," Klein said, lighting a cigarette, looking away.

"Not a risk these days," Jones said. "A real, real possibility . . . maybe probability."

"I leave that to you."

"When are you going to uncork this monster?" Jones said.

"I don't know. Week. Maybe two. We've got to nail this down, very solid. George Emerson's working on it. Before we're finished, I'm going to drive this right through the heart of that damned Prial. When you strike a king . . ."

"I know."

Jones drew a finger across his throat.

"Exactly."

Yes, Jones thought, a man would arise. Cleaver, with his brilliant acid pen, would denounce him, as he had denounced King and Baldwin, for being Whitey's patsy. The Establishment's boy. But Cleaver was a nut, a fanatic. He was in exile. Because Cleaver did not understand how to use the system for one's own ends. Compromise, gradualism, politics as the art of the possible, these were foreign words and concepts to Cleaver. He did not understand that revenge could be exacted slowly as well as quickly. Jones looked at Klein, his sponsor, the liberal white Establishment, asking his help.

"Let me think about it," he said. "I'll call you tomorrow."

"OK," Klein said, extending his hand.

They rose, shook hands, Jones thinking he would very much like to see the expression on Prial's face, if . . .

Klein departed, walking slowly toward the street. The more he thought about his hurriedly conceived—but inspired—plan, the better he liked it. It would be a sensational story.

He walked to his car, eyeing the cathedral, with its ancient, grotesque spires, gargoyles, minarets, heavy Vermont slate roof. It was a monstrosity, no doubt some long-ago bishop's concept of solidarity, strength, power. There were half a dozen young blacks gathered at the rear of his Jag, looking at the bumper stickers, the old ones for Kennedy and McCarthy, the new one in the middle: "Boycott Grapes." Klein routinely checked to see if his hub caps, radio antenna were still in place. One of the young blacks ran up, shouting.

"What dat, mister? Dat Grapes?"

Klein unlocked and opened the door, sat behind the wheel pensively. He turned to the young boy.

"It's too long a story."

"Is he running against Nixon?"

Klein chuckled.

"No. No. Well . . . maybe. In a way."

He started the motor, put the car in gear, drove back to the Tribune Building. George Emerson was still out. Klein peeled out of his jacket again, returned to his role as editor.

The desk telephone jangled. Klein snatched it up, pencil poised on copy paper.

"Klein here," he barked.

"Marv? This is Ken. Ah . . . would you mind sitting in briefly with my staff? We have some problems here that I think you ought to know about."

Kenneth Penn was the *Tribune* advertising manager. He was young, able, dedicated, part of the new management team. Klein had little to do with the man, believing as he did that a blank wall should exist between editorial and the business side of the paper. Klein laid aside his pencil.

"I'm pretty busy," Klein said. "Can it wait?"

Penn hesitated only a moment.

"It's important," he said. "You know I wouldn't bother you if it weren't."

That was true, Klein knew.

"OK. I'll be up in a minute or two."

He left the city room, caught the elevator to the top floor of the Tribune Building. He found Penn and his staff—the key sales executives—in the conference room, sprawled in chairs around the long, polished table. Penn rose to greet him warmly.

"You've met these fellows? Patrick? Bache? Stone? Kantor?"

Klein shook hands. Then he sat down. The tabletop was cluttered with old clippings from the *Tribune*. Klein noted the headlines, many his own creations: POPE REPORTED FAVORING PILL. EX-PRIEST WEDS EX-NUN. EX-PRIEST BOOK TELLS IT LIKE IT IS. REBELLION AT PAPAL DOORS. CHANCERY LAUNCHES UNPOPULAR FUND DRIVE FOR "BLUE SKY" THEOLOGICAL CENTER. UNREST SWEEPS CHURCH. CHANCERY FUNDS CHANNELED TO AFFLUENT SUBURBS. WHITE PRIESTS STILL CONTROL GHETTO CHURCHES. POLL SHOWS CATHOLIC MOTHERS FAVOR BIRTH CONTROL.

"You can see what we've been discussing," Penn said solemnly. "Have you seen this?"

He handed Klein a piece of paper, a press release. It bore the date for the following day and a note—"For immediate release." It was on the letterhead of the archdiocese of Washington. It stated that the Archbishop of Washington had publicly denounced *The Washington Tribune* as reckless and irresponsible, divisive and unethical. He called on all good Catholics to boycott the paper until it was "disposed to report the affairs of this Catholic archdiocese, and the Church at large, with objectivity and fairness." At present, the release stated, "The editors of the *Tribune* deceive their Catholic readers and do a great disservice to ecumenism."

Klein read the release, seething. The words of Vicar General Prial hung in his mind: Jew troublemaker. He laid the release on the table.

"That's pretty strong stuff," Penn said.

"Bastards," Klein spit.

"The Chancery's bringing pressure to bear on our advertisers through the back door," Penn said carefully. "We've had three ad schedules canceled already in the last two weeks. Two of them substantial enough to cause us real trouble. We expect more."

"How do you know they canceled because of pressure?" Klein said.

"Because my salesmen know. They were told. The advertisers don't want to be involved in a religious controversy."

"A newspaper *is* controversy, Penn," Klein said. "You've got to roll with the punch. You win some, you lose some. That's the nature

of the beast. They're overreacting now. But wait and see. Our advertisers need us more than we need them."

"I wish I could be sure of that," Penn said. "Can't we cool it for a
while? Let this thing die down? You've been covering the Chancery
like it was the only story in town."

Klein bit his lip, fighting back words of anger. He spoke coolly.

"Those are old clips, Penn," he said. "We haven't done a thing on
the Church for weeks. But we *are* going to, I'll tell you that. When
centuries and centuries of unrest in the Catholic Church blows beneath
your nose, that could be the biggest story in town. The unrest in the
Catholic Church, the challenge to authority, the decay and corruption
of institutional power is maybe one of the biggest stories of the century.
That and the black revolt. I'm happy to say my staff's on top of both."

"But it seems to me," Penn protested politely, "you and your reporters are blowing this thing out of proportion. You're inflaming it.
Is that the responsibility of journalism?"

"Are you trying to tell me how to run my paper?" Klein said.

"I point out to you that it is *our* paper," Penn said calmly. "We
have a big stake in this thing too."

"I meant the editorial side," Klein said.

He felt the blood draining from his face. This was interference from
the business side that no editor would tolerate. But he kept his temper.

"Damnit, Penn. Aren't you straying out of line? I don't tell you
how to run your shop. Don't tell me how to run mine."

Penn seemed not to have heard. He waved toward the pile of clips,
as if offering positive, conclusive proof.

"We're being blackmailed," Klein replied. "By the Chancery . . .
the financial council of the Chancery . . . that arrogant bastard Prial,
the Vicar General."

Penn did not appear convinced.

"I got a call a while ago from Jack Carter, Eliott TV," he said.
"Our biggest local advertiser. It was a very strange call. He wanted
to reassure me he was sticking with his schedule."

Klein trembled inside. So Carter was blackmailing too.

"It was curious," Penn went on, "because we never had any indica-
tion the schedule was in trouble."

"So, what has that got to do with me?" Klein said.

"He said you had come by to see him," Penn said.

"Oh," Klein replied.

"You're not doing a piece on *him* are you?" Penn said.

"No. Not him, exactly. We're looking into something that may involve him indirectly."

"I hope you handle him with kid gloves."

"Oh, yes," Klein said, forming the headline in his mind: INSIDER PROFITS ON ST. LUKE'S LAND SALE.

"He's Catholic," Penn said.

"I know," Klein said. "A member of the Chancery financial council."

"Yes," Penn said, looking pained.

"Anything else?" Klein said, rising to leave.

"No, Marv," Penn said. "Look, I hope you understand our position. We've worked pretty hard to get where we are. It's been a team effort all the way. We've stuck by you, taken our lumps, and will continue to take them as the case may be. All we ask is consideration for what *we* have to do."

"I understand," Klein said.

"We're not trying to bring pressure or to influence editorial."

"You're not?" Klein said, smirking.

He left the conference room amid saccharine so-longs from the admen. A despicable crew, Klein thought. Would sell their own grandmothers for a fifteen percent commission, bonus, trip to Nassau. Sanctimonious disavowals! Spineless wonders. Jellyfish. Wait until they found out what editorial had in store next.

V

Sister Mary had packed the evening before, leaving only her toilet articles and hot plate to go into the cardboard carton. She awoke with cramps. This was a shock. She had lost track of her cycle. Damnation, she thought. Of all days! She got up, made hot tea, took two Excedrin, then lay on the hard bed another half hour, waiting for the pain to subside, going over the half dozen important things she had to do that day before setting off on the drive to New York. Among other things, she *must* remember to check the oil in the VW.

She rose and dressed in regulation Sacred Heart habit. She tucked away the last items in the box of books, carried it downstairs first. She had given away most of the books, saving only her prized paperbacks—Camus, Sartre, J. F. Powers, Ellison, Mailer, Styron, Bellow, Malamud, Norman O. Brown, Paul Goodman, John Holt. She set the box in the back seat, then returned for her suitcase. The dorm was deserted: the other girls had left in ones and twos during the week. She closed the latch on the suitcase, looked again in the closet, found nothing, left, struggling down the steps with the heavy suitcase.

The motor started without effort. She listened for a moment to see if it were running smoothly. Then she opened her purse and Scotch-taped her reminder list to the dashboard. Many things had been done: check cashed, bank account closed, library books returned, postman notified, phone disconnected. First on the list for the morning was a stop at the St. Luke's gym to see Seymour, make sure he would (without fail) move the Montessori apparatus from its storage there to the basement of Halfway House. She pulled away from the curb, away from the university, her home for two years, feeling a catch in her throat. She blinked away a tear, chastising herself for invariably being weepy when she got her period.

She drove away from the campus, down through the northeast section to the ghetto. It was a scorching hot day. It would be blistering on the turnpike. She drove fast—too fast, like most VW drivers—weaving through traffic. In the ghetto, she noted the progress of the cleanup. Slow. The streets were still littered with glass and debris, the bulldozers were still pushing at the rubble that had once been houses, homes. There was much work to be accomplished here, she thought, much more than clearing rubble.

She parked in front of the gym, glancing sideways at the padlocked parochial school. So much for that era. She hurried up the walk, smiling to the young black boys. Inside the gym, she saw boys playing basketball. That was odd. Why weren't they packing? She hurried along the sidelines to Seymour's office. She found him very comfortably established behind his desk.

"Seymour Jones!" Mary said with mock-sternness, hands on hips. "Why aren't you packing?"

Seymour rose from the desk, smiling happily.

"We're not moving," he said.

"Not moving?" she echoed. "Hurray! What happened?"

"Nothing," Jones said solemnly. "We're just not moving, that's all."

Mary nodded her head slowly, as if absorbing a profound idea. Weighing the pros and cons. Thinking, too, of her apparatus. Imported from Holland, it had cost more than $2,000. She must be certain it was safe.

"So," she said. "You're going to defy the Chancery?"

"Yes," Jones said. "They're going to have to move us bodily."

She chuckled. "What a splendid idea! I wish I had thought of it."

It was hot in the office, almost sweltering. Mary felt suddenly light-headed, woozy. She must get a sandwich. She sat in the rickety chair, dabbed her brow with a handkerchief.

"All those clothes," Seymour said sympathetically. "You must be wilting."

"I am."

"Where you going, all dressed up?"

"New York. To the home office."

"A career conference with personnel, I'll bet," Seymour said.

"Exactly."

"How does it feel to have that parchment?"

"I don't really have it yet," she said. "They're mailing it. At least, I *hope* they mail it."

"Do we call you Doctor now?" Seymour joked. "Doctor-sister or Sister-doctor?"

Mary smiled. She was very glad to have the degree. Knowing that it was there, on her record, gave her a tremendous sense of accomplishment, of having done something important and done it well. It was security, too. Something to fall back on. It could never be taken away. She had been officially certified an expert. If the worst came to the worst, she could always get a good job doing something interesting. She turned to Seymour:

"How were your grades?"

"All right," he said in a kidding tone. "I passed."

"Squeaked through again," she bantered.

"*Talked* my way through."

"How long do you think you can hold off the Chancery?"

"How many divisions does the Pope have?" Seymour grinned.

"I wish I could be here for the first encounter," she replied. "The confrontation with Prial."

"We already had it—this morning on the telephone."

"What did he say?"

"He was completely thrown. Hopping mad. An hour later, the cops came."

"They *did?*"

"Oh yes," Seymour said. "The fuzz and the *Tribune* photographers. Both left. I don't think the fuzz wants to get mixed up in this affair, not yet anyway."

"Holy Toledo," she sighed.

"I sent some of the boys up to picket the Chancery," Jones said, with pride. That had been his own idea. He did it mainly for Klein's photographers who said they needed something "visual."

"Marvelous!" Sister Mary chortled. "Absolutely marvelous! Picketing the Chancery! Oh, I just *love* that."

"You are a rebel at heart, aren't you?"

"I guess I am. Now, Seymour, what about my apparatus? I assume you haven't moved it?"

"It can stay right here with us."

"I want to be sure it's safe. That it doesn't get damaged."

"It's fine," Jones said. "I'll look after it, personally."

"If you do have to vacate, will you promise me you'll move it to Halfway House?"

"If we have to vacate, yes. But I don't think it'll come to that. I think they'll back down."

He ached to tell her the full story, the dimension of the battle that lay ahead, the IDA explosion. But he had given his word to Klein. Until it all broke in the *Tribune,* it was top secret—or top sacred, as Klein had joked.

"They may get an injunction, or some legal thing," Mary said.

"In that case, I'll move the gear," Jones said. "Don't worry about it. Anyway, you'll be back in a few days, won't you?"

Mary felt the catch in her throat again. She would not cry, not in front of Seymour.

"I . . . I . . . I don't know."

"You don't know! You mean you may not be coming back?"

"Maybe not," Mary said. "I may wind up in the Congo."

"But you *have* to come back," Seymour said. "You belong here. What they gonna do, put you away in some cloister? You don't belong in a place like that. Hell, Mary, this is where the action is. We need you here."

"I don't really have much choice. You go where they want you to go."

Seymour Jones thought about that. He remembered vividly the crippled black children in her classroom, happy, hopeful, so very much cared for. He spoke agitatedly:

"Mary, you come back here. I promise you this, I can't tell you the whole deal, but I promise you that by the time I finish with Prial and his gang, you'll have enough space for *ten* schools. No bull. I'm gonna run him right out of town. You can count on that. Believe me."

"I appreciate that very much, Seymour. Very, very much. I . . . I . . . I'll try. I'm . . . I'm very much up in the air . . . very uncertain . . . but please. Don't feel I'm running away."

"You run away? Don't be funny. And don't let those old hens in the home office push you around. You got more guts, more talent, more hip than the whole bunch put together."

She rose, beaming.

"Thanks for that," she said, extending her hand. Seymour shook it warmly.

"Don't worry about your gear."

"I'll keep in touch. Good luck."

"You too."

She returned to the car, blinking away the tears. She must remember to check the oil. She drove away, thinking about Prial, the Chancery, laughing to herself. How would they deal with *that!* Good for Seymour. He was going to be big one of these days. What would Klein call it? A gym-in? She reached with a pencil, crossed out the top item on her reminder list. She drove to Halfway House, parked opposite.

She had not been there for a week. It was not right to let it drift along, unsupervised, but she was only one person. She couldn't be in two places at the same time. The wind-up at CU had taken priority; that and her own problems. Maybe Dan could get down more often now that she was going north. No, he was too busy, drafting radical sermons! And now (as he had told her excitedly last night on the phone) his big "Folk Mass" next week. Wait'll Prial heard about that! Oh wow!

She crossed the street, giddy from the heat. Three, smelly, overflowing cans of trash stood on the curb. Uncollected! Probably not put out in time. She must speak to Sharon about that.

It was cooler inside the foyer. She paused to catch her breath. Then she went inside calling: "Sharon! Sharon!"

Sharon came from the kitchen. She looked a mess. Hair scraggly, eyes tired and swollen, barefoot, jeans. Her belly poking out, six months gone. She seemed depressed.

"Hi," Mary said cheerily.

" 'Lo," Sharon replied, eyes downcast. Then she buried her face in her hands and sobbed.

"What is it?" Mary said, rushing forward, taking Sharon by the shoulders. "What's the matter, love?"

"Peter," she wailed.

"What's the matter?"

"He left," she cried out.

"Come on," Mary said, leading her back to the kitchen. "Sit down. Tell me all about it. Here . . . here . . . stop crying. Now, that's better. What happened?"

Sharon choked back her sobs and told it all in a rush: "The other night, Dad got juiced, got in another rage, and got in the car and went to Peter's house. Oh, God! It must have been awful. He stormed in and started denouncing Peter to his parents and all and they had no idea . . . you know. They're very strict Baptists and all that, and they almost passed out. They didn't *know*. So Peter comes down . . . and Daddy turned on him and wanted to kill him . . . so they called the police and when they came Daddy told them—cops and everybody— that Peter was going to marry me—right now—Daddy was going to make an honest woman out of me, that bit, with the cops standing there, jaws hanging open and all, and Peter's parents telling the cops he tried to kill Peter and demanding they arrest him—Daddy—and . . . let's see . . . the cops then shouting for everybody to shut up . . . one talk at a time."

"Oh, Sharon," Mary said. "I'm *so* sorry."

"Thanks. Well, everybody cooled off. The cops left saying they were shorthanded that night and had some emergencies and for them to all sit down quietly and see if they could work it out and then if anybody wanted to file charges, come down to the station and do it tomorrow, you know. Well, Daddy left, and Peter's parents raked *him* over the coals and all . . . and got him so uptight, he left. Ran away."

"Where to?"

"I don't know," Sharon cried again, deep, heaving sobs.

"Sharon. Sharon. Don't cry. Please . . ."

"He's not coming back!" she gasped.

"How do you know?"

"He called me. Told me what happened. I pleaded . . . I begged . . . but he was scared."

"He didn't say where he was going?"

"He didn't know. He had twenty dollars. He was just . . . just heading west."

"Oh, dear," Mary said.

"He's never coming back, I know."

"Now, Sharon. I'm sure . . ."

"No. No. I know it's true. He's not coming back!"

She laid her head in her arms and sobbed. Mary stroked her hair, patted her back. Damn, damn, damn, she thought. If she had been there, this might not have happened. If Dan had been there, had had time to talk further with her parents! Stupid, boorish father! A criminal thing to do.

"Sharon," Mary said, suddenly firm. "Get a grip on yourself. Come on, now. It's not all that disastrous. You're not the first—"

"I *hate* him!" Sharon said. "Hate him."

"Hate who?"

"Peter. I don't want to have his baby. I don't want anything to remind me of him. Ever."

She sat up now, dry-eyed, defiant.

"I can understand . . . but . . ."

"But what? What do you know about babies?"

Mary flushed.

"I was one once," she said, seeing it was useless to argue now. Later, when tempers cooled, she (she—from New York?) could deal with the matter.

"He'll be back," Mary said.

"No, he won't!" Sharon wailed. "What am I going to do? What will happen to me?" burying her face again.

"Nothing. Nothing right now. Get a grip on yourself. Calm down."

"I'm afraid."

"There's nothing to be afraid of," Mary said.

"You're going away too," Sharon said, wiping her eyes.

"I'll be back . . . I'm just going to New York . . ."

Be back? Would she be back? Mary thought.

"Dan never comes anymore," Sharon said. "Why doesn't he come?"

"Because he's very busy," Mary said. "Running that whole parish by himself. They won't give him any help. They don't *want* to give him any help. Here, love, let's have some coffee."

Mary turned on the flame beneath the tea kettle. When it whistled, she poured two cups. Sharon was more subdued. She sipped the hot coffee carefully.

"Sorry," she said. "I blew my cool. I was lonely. I didn't have anybody to talk to. I'll be all right now."

"Good girl. Where're the other kids?"

"Didn't you know?"

"No. Know what?"

"They went to the Eastern Shore to start a commune."

"Commune? Oh, no! Really? I can't believe it."

"They did."

"Does Dan know?"

"I don't think so. They just left last night. Just like that!"

"I'll be darned," Mary said. "Well, Sharon, you certainly can't stay here by yourself."

"Some other kids are moving in."

"Who?"

"Some fellows and girls I met at DuPont Circle."

"Who? Who are they?"

"I don't know much about them, really. They needed a place to eat and sleep. I thought it would be all right."

"Are they heads?"

"I don't know. I don't think so."

"Dan ought to talk to them, interview them."

"When?"

"I don't know." She looked at her watch. Time was flying! She must leave this minute. "Sharon, I've *got* to run. I have an appointment in New York this afternoon. Do me a favor, please. Call Father Daugherty. Tell him these new kids are checking in and to do everything in the world to get down here tonight. Will you please do that for me?"

"Sure. When are you coming back?"

"I'm not sure," Mary said, voice trailing off. "It depends . . ."

"On what?"

"A lot of things."

"Dan?"

Mary blushed. "What do you mean?"

"Oh, you know," Sharon smiled knowingly.

"Sharon! Don't tell anybody *else* you think that. Another thing. The Montessori apparatus won't be coming over today. Seymour isn't moving out of the gym, so I'll leave the gear there for the time being. And . . . *when* did you put the trash out?"

"This morning," Sharon said, turning her eyes away.

"They come Tuesdays and Thursdays."

"I know. I goofed."

"Well . . . that's all right. I hope the dogs don't knock it over."

She rose, kissed Sharon good-bye. She fled down the hall to the

front door, down the stoop, around the garbage cans, across the street
to her car. Sharon stood in the doorway, waving, as Mary ground the
gears and roared on, crossing yet another item off her list.

She drove through the downtown section, around the Capitol, then
toward Baltimore. She stopped for gas—and to check the oil, pencil-
ing off another item. Then she took the parkway, a narrow, bumpy,
dangerous road leading to the Baltimore tunnel. The tunnel was hot,
the exhaust fumes almost overpowering. Beyond the tunnel, on the
Kennedy Memorial Highway, the best and most beautiful section
of the drive, she floorboarded the accelerator, watched the needle
climb to eighty miles an hour. The cramps were easing. She pulled
off her veil and laid it on the seat, letting the wind whip through her
hair.

She thought now about her long talk with LeGuiese. This time, he
had not been so cordial. He had put much faith in the separation. It
had failed. They were now eyeball to eyeball with the grit, reality.
What they had to do was untangle the problem. Separate—and deal
with—its many parts. First, *she* must decide, independently of any
feeling for Dan, whether or not she had a vocation. If she decided she
truly did not, then she must resign—ask to be released from her perpetual vows of poverty, obedience, chastity—the order. In reaching
this decision, she must remember she was an exceptional person, that
the order had invested not only much hope but also money in ad-
vancing her vocation. The order—the whole Church—needed good
people like Mary Murray. If all the Mary Murrays decided to walk
out overnight, what then of the Church? Who would inherit it?

She must remember that Dan's situation was different, much different. He was a priest. "Thou art a priest forever—according to the
order of Melchizedek," he quoted. The Church did not so easily turn
loose its priests. It would probably never release him from his vow of
chastity. He refused to consider being laicized. If Dan married her, he
would be automatically excommunicated, cut off from the Church and
sacraments forever. A spiritual outcast. She also would be excommunicated. Technically, if she married him after she had been released
from her vows, she would be committing sin. Not a healthy situation,
at best. Would God bless such a marriage? LeGuiese didn't know.
If they insisted on going through with it, it might be better if they
merely lived together for a year or so, until the dust settled, the hurricane of emotions died down. And, above all, she must not influence
Dan one way or the other. She must hold herself apart, let him separate

his own problem into its individual parts, and deal with them, one by one. Dan was being unrealistic to place any hope on Pope Paul relaxing the celibacy rule. . . .

Lost in these reveries, Mary did not see the state police cruiser immediately behind her, blue dome lights flashing. She sped onward, downhill and up, going wide open. The trooper pulled from behind, then abreast. Mary glanced sideways. The trooper pointed to the shoulder with authoritative forefinger. Heart sinking, Mary took her foot off the accelerator, braked, pulled off the road, stopped. Her cramps returned with new force. The cruiser followed her to the shoulder. The trooper climbed from the car, walked to her window. Mary fumbled in her purse for her license, berated herself for this delay which might make her late in New York.

The trooper bent down, looked into her window. He gawked, astonished, when he saw Mary's habit. He had patrolled the road since it opened. He had passed many nuns, sitting primly in station wagons, usually four to six to a car. But he had never seen a nun alone. Especially not a speeding nun, driving a Chinese-red VW. Mary looked up, noted his surprise, smiled innocently. She handed him her license. The trooper studied it, eyes shifting from the plastic card to Mary.

"Sister," he said at last, "you shouldn't drive that bug so fast. It's not safe at high speed. You hit a cross-wind, you're going to rock, lose control, and maybe flip."

He returned the license. He was not going to write a ticket, Mary knew. She had been unnecessarily panicky. Police never gave tickets to religious. She had never known it to happen, anywhere, no matter how grave the infraction. That was one of the emoluments . . . a small thing. A token of respect. On the outside, she would not be entitled to that, philosophy degree or no philosophy degree.

"You're right," she said. "I was daydreaming."

"You've got to *drive* these roads," he said. "For yourself and everybody else."

"I know."

"Where are you headed?"

"New York."

"Well, take it easy."

"Yes, sir. Thank you very much."

"Pleasure," he said, tipping his hat.

Mary sat, watching him return to the cruiser. She put on her veil.

Then she drove off, slowly, carefully, exaggerating caution. She kept within the speed limit, crossed the high Delaware Memorial Bridge, then entered the long, boring, sleep-inducing Jersey Turnpike. She stopped once for a sandwich and coffee in a plaza, named for an American poet. At the exit, she paid the toll, then found the approach to the George Washington Bridge. She crossed it, closing her window because the height made her uneasy, then made her way through upper Manhattan to her appointment on 91st Street, parking in a prohibited zone before a large, dirty granite mansion.

It was cooler in New York, much cooler inside the dark, cavernous Sacred Heart Convent. She crossed the Oriental rugs to the office of the Provincial, announcing herself to the young Novices who were working as secretaries in the outer office. They spoke quietly, almost in whispers. Mary found herself (against her will) lowering her voice, injecting a note of respectfulness, almost reverence, which she did not really feel. The whole place struck her as too gloomy, unreal, far removed from the St. Luke's gym, the Halfway House, Sharon. She sat down to wait, feeling her cramps again.

By her watch she was five minutes late. By the old grandfather clock in the office she was five minutes early. At exactly four o'clock by the grandfather clock, one of the Novices, with a soft rustle of muslin, led Mary into the inner office. It was dark, foreboding, like a crypt. The Provincial sat behind a huge mahogany desk, piled high with papers and books. She was old—Mary had no idea how old. Her face was white as bond paper. Beneath it, her soft, flabby chins were pushed up by the neck-choking habit. She looked up from her desk, smiling sweetly, then rose, softly, easily. Mary bowed and clasped her hands in front of her as she had been trained.

"Dear!" the Provincial said. "How *nice* to see you again. It's been so long. Please sit down. Would you like lemonade?"

"No . . . no, thank you," Mary said, feeling a curious sensation of comfort and security. Perhaps even serenity. She had but to say the word and she could remain forever behind these thick, solid, cold walls, aloof from temporal affairs—war, revolution, crime, drugs, political murder, blacks, angry kids, the upheaval and flames of the modern America. She could pad softly through these unreal corridors, straight up the staircase to the Gates of Heaven. Spare herself, forever, the emotional crisis which lay yawning ahead like the jaws of a tiger. It would be very, very easy.

"I see you've had your share of excitement in Washington," the Provincial said, sitting down. "They spared us this time. I believe that was because of Lindsay. He made friends in Harlem."

Mary was stunned by this comment. Until then she had believed the Provincial ignorant of Harlem, its problems. Not ignorant, but indifferent. Mary smiled.

"Now if he can work out the garbage collection," the Provincial went on, "New York might be livable again. I doubt that though. I believe the city's gotten beyond human control. Was your school burned?"

"No, ma'am. I had closed it . . . before the riots. Or rather, it had been closed by the city. I believe I wrote you, didn't I? In any case, it . . . St. Luke's was spared."

"Must be on its last legs. I remember going there as a small girl. It was quite *the* place, then. Of course now . . ."

"One hundred percent black," Mary said, thinking of Seymour. Wondering how his act of defiance was progressing, if the police had returned, if Prial was at wit's end.

"Congratulations on your work at CU," the Provincial said. "I have several fine letters . . . one from Monsignor LeGuiese."

The mention of his name made her uneasy. He had not told her he would write. How *much* had he told?

"He's very brilliant . . . was very helpful to me," Mary stammered.

"He's very complimentary of your work," the Provincial said. "Extremely."

Mary blushed.

"Is he a pal of Father Curran's?" she said.

"Pal" seemed to Mary unforgivably slangy. What had happened to the Provincial? Was she trying to be "modern"?

"He's an *associate* of his," Mary said, more lamely than she intended.

"Was he involved in the demonstration against the Chancery . . . the board of regents?"

"Indirectly, I believe," Mary said, remembering, too, that tumultuous time last year on the CU campus, the student uprising, the faculty strike, the pickets, sit-ins, the exciting turmoil. And LeGuiese's latest academe joke: One college student to the other: What are you taking this fall? Other student: the Ad Building. Chuckling, she told the Provincial the joke.

"I'm waiting for that at Rye," she replied half-seriously.

"That'll be the day," Mary said.

"You've been exposed to some pretty radical thinking," the Provincial said. "How did you react to it? I suppose you're ready to chuck it all, now. Go back and work in the ghetto?"

Mary sat up, suddenly astounded. How? . . . how? Had LeGuiese told her?

"As a matter of fact . . ." Mary said, summoning courage for a frontal attack. There was no point in putting it off. If the Provincial had not been forewarned, then she was a mind-reader. "As a matter of face, that is precisely what I want to do."

"The seven-year itch," the Provincial said lightly, as though dealing with an everyday problem. "When I was your age, I had it too."

Mary raised her guard.

"Of course," the Provincial continued, "when I was your age, we didn't have all the free and easy routine. Temptation was harder to come by. But we found it nonetheless."

She said the last proudly, as though it were an achievement of high order. Mary waited for her to add: "And we overcame it." But she said:

"Many of us didn't overcome it."

Mary hesitated, regrouping for the attack. She was being outflanked, outwitted. It was not at all like she anticipated.

"Today," the Provincial said, "overcoming it really means something, don't you think? It must require incredible determination, especially for a pretty girl like you. That makes it ten times harder. You didn't hide in here because you were a wallflower."

"I . . . I . . ." Mary stumbled. "I don't think the Church is relevant anymore, that's all."

"Neither do I," the Provincial said. "I thought the Council would help."

She seemed sad. Mary stared uneasily. What was this? Was she serious or was she being clever? The Provincial leaned forward, handed Mary a letter. It was from Vicar General Prial. It suggested that Mary be recalled. Mary read, seething. She looked at the date, remembering. It was the day she had gone calling at the Chancery, asking help. The hypocrite!

"Don't let it upset you," the Provincial said. "He's a monumental fool. The Church is full of them. Ambitious, scheming. I knew him well when he worked for the Cardinal up here. He would steal pennies from the eyes of a dead man. Tried to get us to sign over property as though we were children! McInnerney is worse. A dull-witted, ambitious Irishman, the worst possible combination. They want you out of the archdiocese because they're afraid of the fresh winds, the searching minds. I see he's begun a fund drive in the midst of all that trouble down there. Now that makes a lot of sense, doesn't it?"

"It's stupid," Mary said.

"Worse," the Provincial said. "It will turn people. He doesn't have the imagination to see that. Never mind, I hear on good authority that your thesis might be published by CU Press. That's very exciting. It is a very good, very sound piece of work. Mary, we're proud of you. You have been a credit to your order, your friends, your family. I suspect that when you get some experience dealing with people, on a financial level, you might very well someday inherit this chair."

Mary recoiled inwardly. The cramps came on now, severe, like a hammer blow. The pain was so intense, she bent over.

"I'm sorry," she said. "My period came today . . . of all days!"

"Why don't you go lie down?" the Provincial said. "You've had a long trip."

"No . . . no . . . I want to . . . I'll be all right. I want to finish. Say what I have to say. Get it over with. I've made up my mind . . ."

"Here, have some water."

She offered a glass, with ice, from the silver carafe on her desk. Mary drank gratefully.

"Thank you," she said, replacing the glass on the tray. "I feel better."

"Good. Now you were saying . . . ?"

Mary composed herself. The stabbing pain subsided.

"Back in Washington, I've been working in this place we have . . . sort of a home for runaways . . . good kids. You see . . . after my school was closed. Today, I left behind this girl, seventeen. She's from a good family, very wealthy family in Potomac, a dropout from Stone Ridge."

"Sharon McFee?" the Provincial said.

"Yes!" Mary said, astonished. "How did you know?"

"I know the McFees. All about them. I taught her mother. We've talked lately."

"I see," Mary said, wondering if it were true. "Anyway, Sharon's a runaway, and pregnant!"

"I heard."

"Well . . . you did? . . . Anyway, I've been working with her, bringing her along. Today, when I left, I was overcome. I feel I cannot leave her. I've got to go back."

"And how does she differ from our girls at King Street? St. Louis? Philadelphia? Coconut Grove? Boston? What is so much more appealing there?"

"Her family . . ."

"Don't you know about families in Rye and Greenwich? Certainly you haven't forgotten your own home town. Today it's a thousand times worse. The blacks need help, I agree. They need money, jobs, dignity, equality. But there is another kind of deprivation—the deprivation of the affluent. In many cases, they are more needy. To have achieved all the fruits and benefits of our society, and then, after the striving, find life hollow and meaningless, that is a serious matter indeed, maybe the ultimate frustration. That is where we come in. Helping those people is our mission."

"But . . ."

"Mary, you are a mature woman. You have a gifted mind. You have a degree in philosophy. You have an innate gift of leadership. You are dedicated. I want to talk to you like a real woman. This order, like all others, is in trouble. Serious trouble. Look at the dropout figures. Last year, a hundred and fifty-one. This year already a hundred and forty-seven. Good people, trained at huge expense, leaving. It's almost like a foot race for the gate. You think you could possibly arrive here today with something that could surprise me? Believe me, Mary, I've heard everything. Everything! Half of them think they're in love with priests! Tomorrow, it will be a different story."

The cramps returned, suddenly, violently. Mary felt faint, cold with terror. She could not have guessed that! LeGuiese had not told her—had not broken the seal of the confessional. Or had he?

"I won't bore you now with my financial problems," the Provincial said. "Just this: I can't make ends meet. We're going deeper into the hole every week. Look at these bills!"

She pointed to a stack of envelopes, unopened.

"We're facing a major crisis," she went on. "I need your help. I want you to work with me, right here in my office, as an administrative assistant. I want you to help me develop a program for our young people *and* the old people! They're more trouble than the young. We've got to find a way for the two to work side by side, tolerating each other. We cannot survive with the atmosphere we have inside these walls. We've got to tear down the walls. Make this order relevant to society, to our mission. I want you to help me do that."

Mary slumped in her chair. Visions now of the cloistered, monkish cell, the silent meals, the boring recitation of group prayer, shot away. In place of that, a new vision of Mary the executive, a financial wheeler-dealer. Impossible!

"Mary, I want you to help restore *my* faith."

The feeling of unreality returned. She must be dreaming. A nightmare! Visions of Dan, her room at CU, the crippled children in her classroom, Seymour Jones, the fires in the ghetto comingled in her mind, confusing her. How could she possibly help this woman's faith?

"I want you to help lead this order out of trouble," the Provincial continued. "If we can't do that, we've had it. We might as well bolt the door."

"I'm not sure I'm qualified," Mary stammered. "Even if I . . ."

"I *am* . . . with time. It can't be done overnight. We don't want revolution, but evolution. We've got to revise everything: curriculum, recruiting, training, policy . . ."

The words came as from afar. Mary stopped listening. She sat dazedly, thinking about Dan. She had to get away. Leave this room, this person, this crazy old woman. She rose unsteadily.

"Will you excuse me . . . please. I'm sorry . . ."

The Provincial came from behind her desk, put her arm around Mary's shoulder, comforting, tenderly.

"I'm sorry," she said. "I shouldn't have . . . not today. But I've been so eager, so wrapped up in it . . . so anxious to talk to you. Go away . . . go up to the Kenwood retreat house . . . it's very pleasant there this time of year. Very cool. Take a week. Two weeks. Sit, look at the mountains, the clouds and sky. Meditate. Pray. Pray for my faith."

"Yes . . ." Mary said, voice trailing. "I will. I shall go there. First, I want to see my mother. Tonight. I'll stop there and then go on up tomorrow."

"Good. I'll call ahead for you."

"Oh no! That's all right. I'll manage."

"No trouble. Thank you, dear, for stopping in."

Mary turned, tears in her eyes.

"You know what I thought?" she said to the Provincial. "I thought you were going to send me to the convent to teach the novitiates philosophy."

"Mary!" the Provincial laughed. "I've got a *dozen* girls who can do that! Philosophy! What is philosophy these days? Hairsplitting. Semantics. Dull-witted idiots. Gosh, we might even abolish philosophy. And Latin and Greek and . . ."

Mary dried her eyes with a Kleenex, completely confused.

"Have a good time," the Provincial said. "Pray for me."

Mary left the office, trying to compose her gyrating thoughts. She hurried to her VW. She pulled away from the curb, eastbound to the FDR Drive, the Triborough Bridge. She reached the drive only to be caught up in a titanic traffic jam. She crept along, bumper-to-bumper, windows tightly shut to keep out the impure air, the troubling noise of the city, thinking back on the interview, one moment swelling with pride, the next, dissolving in tears. Feeling guilty, depressed that she had withheld the most important thing, that she was such a sniveling, irresolute person after all, a phony.

The traffic broke beyond Bruckner Expressway. She picked her way into the fast lane, turned on the Connecticut Turnpike. Three toll gates later, she pulled off into sleepy, beautiful Greenwich, heart throbbing with excitement at the familiar surroundings. She had not been back for over a year. She took North Street, crossed Putnam Avenue, turned left off North up her—*their* street. She turned sharply into the drive, pulled the emergency brake up, killed the engine. Her mother, gray-haired, well groomed, appeared at the front door.

"Mary!" she cried running into the yard. "What a pleasant surprise!"

"Hi, Mums," Mary said, opening the door. The cramps struck again. She doubled over. Her mother helped her to the house.

"What a ghastly day," Mary said. "Do you have any Excedrin?"

"Aspirin," her mother said. "Two?"

"Please."

Mary took off her veil, kicked off her shoes, flopped on the couch. Her mother brought the aspirin, water. Mary gulped down the pills. She felt better immediately.

"I'm on my way up to Albany," she said. "Where *is* everybody?"

"Well, your father's in town, the kids are . . . scattered here and there. Pat will be here for dinner, I think. You never know with Pat anymore. *Very* independent!"

"Aren't we all."

"We received a very nice letter from the dean," her mother said. "Congratulations. I wish we could have come down."

"There was nothing to come down *to*," Mary said.

"Still . . . What happens now? Where will you go?"

Mary looked away.

"I don't know," she said, voice hollow. "I . . . I may not be going anywhere. I saw the Provincial today. I told her I wanted to leave."

Mary's mother took the news calmly.

"Are you positive of that?" she said.

"No," Mary said, crying again. "Damnit! I have my period. Nowadays I get weepy."

"Natural," her mother said thoughtfully. "But tell me . . ."

"I can't," Mary said. "It's too complicated. I had my mind firmly made up. I've grown apart from the Church, the formal Church. I can't accept a lot of it, especially the hypocrisy, the dishonesty, the irrelevance. But today the Mother Superior asked *my* help. The order's in serious trouble, she said. She wants me to help fix it."

"That's quite a tribute, at your age," her mother said.

"It's probably a ploy," Mary said. "Her technique for heading me off. It's a very serious thing. Already, I think she said, about a hundred and fifty have left this year."

"Well, Mary," her mother said. "I want you to know how your father and I feel about it. Frankly, we were never sure you had a true vocation. Somehow, it didn't seem the thing to do. We didn't try to dissuade you beyond the normal request for careful thought, as you may remember. We've often discussed it since. To us, you seem much more interested in . . . well, you know, the social action spectrum. Your little Montessori school and all that. Remember that summer you spent in Harlem? I don't think I've ever seen you happier. Anyway, I just want you to know that your father and I would not be angry if you decided to break your vows and leave. Many girls, as you say, find the life incompatible nowadays. As you say, irrelevant. There is satisfaction, too, in raising a healthy, stable bunch of kids. I should know. I can tell you all about that."

"I feel like a heel," Mary said, angry with herself. "They spent all that money to send me to school, then when I've got what I want, I walk out."

"That's a risk they take," her mother said. "A reasonable business risk, as your father might say. Money, I should think, the Church doesn't worry about."

"Oh, they *do*," Mary protested. "They're going bankrupt all over."

"Anyway . . . if you want to talk . . . the old shoulder is still here, Babes. Right here."

Mary cried, hiding her face in her hands. Her mother leaned forward and stroked her head.

"Tell me all about it," she said. "Go on, let it go. You've been under such a strain . . . all that studying . . . losing your school . . . a decision like this is not easy."

"Oh, Mother!" Mary exclaimed suddenly. "I feel like a *whore.*"

"Oh, my pretty little girl," her mother said. "Dear girl. Is there . . . is there . . . is there a man?"

"Yes!" Mary exploded. "Yes . . . a *priest!*"

"Well now, that *is* a problem," her mother said, adroitly concealing the shock. "Suppose you tell mums all about it."

VI

The Archbishop ate a spare breakfast, as usual, tea and toast, small glass of vegetable juice. Afterward he dressed in his working clothes, then paused at the window to stare down into the street. The Seymour Jones pickets were there, four or five blacks with Afro hair and curious clothes, picket signs slung carelessly over their shoulders, shuffling back and forth. Stupid! McInnerney said, aloud. Young kids! They ought to be working in a supermarket, sacking groceries.

The Vicar General arrived for the morning conference in a high state of agitation, angrily denouncing Klein, the *Tribune,* the whole "liberal" press establishment. Not a single newspaper had carried the Chancery press release assailing the *Tribune,* proving (if more proof were needed) once and for all that, as Prial expressed it, the Jews had seized all the important communication outlets in America, that (somewhere behind the scenes) they had joined hands, pledged themselves in a sinister back-scratching, self-preserving cabal, to do everything possible to undermine the Catholic Church. Every day, there was a new revelation of trouble in the Church—reported sensationally.

Klein had the story on the sale of St. Luke's in his hip pocket.

He had not yet published the story, but the mere fact it had leaked had caused Prial no end of anguish. Klein was sure to slant it against them. The day before yesterday, he had published the story of Seymour Jones under a big, black headline: BLACK LEADER DEFIES CHANCERY. Yesterday there had been a follow-up story on the pickets in front of the Chancery. The other papers had jumped on the story. The news-magazines and TV networks were calling for a Chancery statement, interviews with McInnerney, which had been refused. Prial's policy for dealing with the matter was to ignore it publicly. They would not be drawn into a name-calling contest with Charles Seymour Jones. Now, immediately ahead, lay a much more serious problem: what would the Jewish-controlled press do when Pope Paul handed down the en-cyclical reaffirming the ban on artificial contraception? There was no telling.

Prial sat down in his chair with a jar so forceful it bunched the carpet. He lit his cigar, blew smoke in the room.

"I've been on the horn to the public affairs man at HUD," he said. "I'm happy to say, they're cool-headed over there, not a sign of panic. I also talked to IDA. They're not upset someone leaked to Klein, or about Jones either. The deal is still set. The HUD man says, in effect, brazen it out. They deal with this sensitive stuff all day long. Routine. When the dust settles, we'll get an injunction against Jones. The point is, if you yield, you give in here, the line breaks all along. You get overwhelmed. At the same time, he felt some kind of gesture was in order. I'll get back to that. Meanwhile, the all-important thing is to beat Klein to the punch. Get the release hammered out, let it go, be-fore Klein can break the thing in his twisted way. We must put a *positive* cast to it."

"Of course," the Archbishop said. "What kind of gesture did he have in mind?"

"Well, his idea was that you go down to St. Luke's yourself, on a Sunday, say Mass, then, from the pulpit, announce what's going to happen. You give a little background on what we've done for the black community, à la the fact sheet. You give a little history on St. Luke's, how it helped the community. Then you discuss the specific problems of St. Luke's—the sagging foundations, the bad roof—paint-ing a real horror story, which will only be slight exaggeration. Then you give them the IDA pitch—how this will bring a new industry to the area, four hundred-odd jobs, so on and so forth, à la the draft proposal for the IDA press release. We have a copy here someplace.

You also touch on Seymour Jones—sympathetically—tell what a good job he's done (with *our* facility as a donation), pull the rug from under him. Smother him with kindness. Then, last, you tell them we're going to erect a new church nearby. That's *very* important."

"What *new* church?"

"Well, I didn't say *when*. You don't even have to say church. Just something like, 'their spiritual needs will be taken care of.' We'll work out the language. You can't leave them hanging."

"There isn't enough income to justify a new church down there."

"I know," Prial said, a trifle impatiently. "We leave that part vague. But it *must* be dealt with."

"Yes," the Archbishop said. "You're right."

"HUD and IDA will contact the press, TV and all that," Prial went on, consulting notes. "You'll get a lot of live TV coverage. A chance to get your—our—points across before Klein and the newspaper boys put a negative twist into it. TV is pretty good about that."

"Speaking of the press," the Archbishop said. "Are you getting anywhere with the *Tribune* advertisers?"

"I'm making haste slowly," Prial said. "Our staff has sent every advertiser—a list laboriously compiled by going through all the *Tribune* issues this year—a copy of our press release. I've made some personal calls to members of the financial council that I think have done some good. Yesterday I called John Carter, for example. He's calling me back today. His situation is rather complicated, he says. All his store managers are Jews. They depend on the ads for floor traffic, new bait. They have to have this high-volume traffic. Not so much to move the merchandise, as I learned, but to sell on credit. Get the 'paper,' as he called it. They make more on the interest on the paper than they do on profit on the merchandise, which was news to me. (And a lesson we might try to apply in our operation, somehow.) Anyway, they have to have a constant source of new names for new paper. So they need the *Tribune* ads. Also, as he says, his managers *like* the *Tribune,* its viewpoint. They think like Klein. So he's got to be damned careful, telling them what to do."

"He owns the company, doesn't he?" the Archbishop said, somewhat perplexed.

"Yes. But this isn't the nineteenth century—unfortunately! Good managers are hard to find."

"Did you check into the ownership of the paper? That New York syndicate?"

"All Jews. Solidly behind Klein."

"We might make some calls to the New York Chancery."

"No. No. That's too complicated."

"A friendly call from Cardinal Cooke to the president of the syndicate . . . maybe an invitation to lunch?"

"No," Prial said emphatically. "We lose control if you get the New York Chancery involved. Our best bet is to fight on a local level. Besides, we don't want New York to think they have to fight *our* battles. That makes us look weak. If Spellman were still there, yes. He could do it with a phone call. I certainly wouldn't mind asking *him*. But, with Cooke, I'd be leery. You know how unpredictable he can be at times."

"All right. But we must get rid of Klein."

"I am dedicated to that goal, believe me."

"That's a very good idea, going down to St. Luke's," the Archbishop said, reflecting. "I would like to do that. I *want* to do that. We owe them that much."

"I think so. It will be a controlled situation. Very good image-wise."

"You don't think there might be trouble?"

"Don't worry. We'll have the police there in force."

"No violence."

"They have the ghetto under control now. Better, they say, than ever before. Riot troopers. Special equipment, the antipersonnel vehicles —those little tanks—Mace, and jeeps with barbed wire. The men are well trained. Besides, I don't think they'd provoke any violence in church. At least, so far the churches have been spared."

"I wasn't thinking of myself, of course," the Archbishop said. "I don't want anybody to get hurt."

"I understand that perfectly," Prial said, shuffling through his folder. "Now, next item. The advance printed material for Paul's encyclical."

"Yes. I read it last night. I especially liked the one, *Sex in Marriage* —what was the subtitle?"

"Love-giving, Life-giving."

"That's it. Who wrote that?"

"Well, I didn't tell you, but I trapped two Franciscans who were passing through, sightseeing."

"Franciscans!"

"Very bright young men."

"I changed a few words, but not enough to notice," the Archbishop said. "I assume these will go to the printer today? We ought to have them in the parishes by next week, latest. Will we get them there on time?"

"I've been giving the encyclical a lot of thought," Prial said, examining the end of his cigar. "As I'm sure you have. I wonder if, at this time, we're wise to take a hard-line stand? I think the press might jump on us very hard. We could avoid that if we let it slide without comment."

"I think that needs explaining," the Archbishop said curtly. "Perhaps a *lot* of explaining. If you're suggesting we not back up Paul . . ."

"I didn't *say* that," Prial said impatiently.

"Go on."

"I merely raise the possibility that we could let it go without comment," Prial said. "Without waving a red flag in everybody's face. A viewpoint we ought to consider."

"Absolutely not," the Archbishop said. "Not while I have the breath in my lungs. To sit here and say nothing is tantamount to . . . it implies disagreement on our part."

"Not necessarily," Prial said. "Anyway, I wish he had waited. We've got revolution enough on our hands—at least in this country. Kids taking over universities. Blacks challenging us on all fronts. Massive dissent over the war. A confused, explosive political year. I fear that, as they say, there is revolution in the air, that the spirit infects everybody, that the encyclical will come as one more uncompromising edict from the Establishment, one more act of arrogance, and that in the general air of rebellion, we're very likely to find ourselves in a full-scale war."

"With whom?"

"Everybody. I hear along the grapevine that Curran and LeGuiese at CU, Dupre and others at Georgetown, the bunch at Notre Dame and Fordham, are stockpiling ammo. They know it's coming and they're getting set. They're thirsting for a showdown."

"Then we'll give it to them," the Archbishop said angrily. "They want a fight, we'll give them a fight."

"I'm worried about the young priests in the archdiocese, the Daughertys."

"If they speak up, we'll chop off their heads."

"It may not be so easy."

"I've told you before, the Church is not a democracy. We don't set policy by consensus."

"I know . . . I know. I'm also worried about the laity—the women. That poll scares me. I have a feeling opinion may be much more explosive than the poll reflected. If the theologians, the young priests, the laity—especially the women—band together in unholy alliance, conceivably we could find ourselves in a very tough position. Very tough. Especially with the black situation—Seymour Jones—the way it is and Klein and the press hunting for trouble."

"The Church is unassailable," the Archbishop said. "We shall not yield on this, Nate. Not an inch. Prepare the documents for the printer. Let them go. Sandbag the doors and windows and let them open fire."

"In a sense," the Archbishop went on, "If it has to happen, I'm glad it's happening here, in Washington, in our baliwick. The city has become the symbol of power in the free world. If we're to have a showdown over power and obedience in the Catholic Church—and essentially that's what it's all about—then what better place than Washington?"

"That's fine—if we win."

"Now, speaking of trouble," Prial said, returning to his agenda, "here is one more flyspeck. But I thought you ought to know since it involves our friend Daugherty indirectly."

"What has he done now?"

"Nothing. You remember you asked me to get Donovan down at the precinct to keep an eye on Halfway House? Well, he has. He reports that the old bunch of kids moved out and a new bunch moved in. He suspects this new bunch may be taking narcotics, maybe hard drugs. Nothing solid to go on, just a suspicion. He's put one of his young undercover agents into the group. The problem is, as he puts it, there is no longer any supervision down there. Daugherty hasn't been there in days, maybe weeks. Sister Mary has gone back to New York."

"Is she mixed up with Halfway House too?"

"Apparently. To what extent, I don't know. Anyway, she's out of the picture now."

"We certainly must take every pain to disassociate ourselves from that place," the Archbishop said.

"It'll be hard," Prial said. "It has a Catholic image, thanks to Marvin Klein. But don't worry, Donovan and I are right on top of the situation. Now, let's see, what else?"

They discussed the other items, mostly financial. The fund drive—lagging badly. School operating expenditures, going up sharply, with inflation. Collection plate revenues, down, down, down. The Washington lay association now presenting a formal demand for a teacher salary increase.

"Damn the lay association," McInnerney said, the pent-up anger exploding. "We won't accept ultimatums from them, or anybody else."

He had been strongly opposed at the Vatican Council to encouraging greater lay participation in the operation of the Church. Why invite uninformed laymen to meddle in serious affairs? The Church was *not* a democracy.

They turned to other matters. There was no end of problems. Finally it was done. Prial rose to leave. McInnerney had a final word:

"Nate, thank you. Thank you for my faith."

"And thank you for mine," Prial said.

"It's worth fighting for."

"Of course. Nothing good comes easy in this world, it seems."

After Prial had left, there was a telephone call from Helen Hanrahan. McInnerney accepted it—almost with reluctance, knowing in advance what she would say. He was right. She was calling with another warning. Armageddon. Cancel the fund drive. The same story. He accepted her words, invited her to visit soon for a long talk, promised to proceed with care, then hung up with a polite good-bye. Afterward, he was deeply troubled. His own unshakable confidence, shaken.

He took time off from temporal business to visit his private chapel. He closed and locked the door. He knelt on the altar steps, hands clasped, head bowed low. He prayed to God the Father, God the Son, and God the Holy Ghost. He prayed for a long time, finding strength and inspiration. His mind cleared, and he was certain his prayers had brought him these words:

Do not despair. Do not be frightened. God has appeared to Helen Hanrahan. He has told her many things that are authentic. He has, lately, presented these visions. They were meant, not as she interpreted them, but as a warning. A dire warning. If the Church does not take steps to clean its own house, He will appear again, sadly, to do what man was not able to do, even with His boundless love and inspiration. You appeared in the vision because you were chosen to lead the Church back to its proper place. You must heal the schism, wipe out heresy, restore order and obedience, bring the people to their senses. Death, blood, violence hover near you because these will be necessary before you complete your task. The battleground will be your archdiocese. You will take a stand. You will inspire the Church and the world. You will save the Pope, the Church, and the world from the Armageddon foretold in the final vision. You will bring peace and tranquility to the world. You will, ultimately, unite the Church, mankind, and then there will be no reason for the Saviour to come again. Be forthright. Be strong. Go with Christ.

The Archbishop lay prostrate on the altar steps for a long while. When he left the chapel, he was still shaken, humble. Humble yet bursting with resolve and newfound strength, given him by the Holy Family.

After supper in the Chancery dining room that evening, Monsignor Ryan retired to his third-floor room, a monastic cell, whitewashed, with bare floors, sparse furnishings. He knelt and read his breviary, with a Special Intention directed for the seven automobile dealers who had denied him a dozen cars for the fund drive raffle. A dozen cars! The dealers had exploded! Didn't Ryan know money was tighter than a tick's ass? They could barely finance their own floor inventories, let alone float a dozen cars with no profit in sight on any of them. Did Ryan realize the profit margin they were now operating on? They were all skirting bankruptcy. Chapter Eleven. Ryan lay on the hard bunk, looking at the ceiling. They would need an authentic miracle to pull off this fund drive!

His telephone rang twice. It was the receptionist downstairs, very polite, solicitous.

"There's a lady to see you, a Mrs. Munally."

"Oh?" Ryan said, surprised. He added: "I'll . . . I'll be right down. Please show her to the library."

Ryan put on his collar and jacket, took the elevator to the main floor, then walked to the library. It was a huge room, dimly lighted, jammed with rows and rows of books on church history, philosophy, theology, a very good, very thorough Chancery library which was seldom used, not by Ryan anyway. It smelled of stale tobacco smoke and old leather. The rows of books he had never read depressed him. He was not a book man. He had not read much of anything since the seminary.

Mrs. Munally stood by the floor lamp, waiting. It had taken all her courage to come to the Chancery, to get in her car, to drive downtown, to ring the front bell. Now she was not so certain she should have come. Her presence was probably not wanted. Ryan, she was sure, had problems enough without her adding more.

"Good evening, Bridget," Ryan said, extending his hand. "This *is* a surprise. Good to see you."

"Good evening," she said, taking his hand. "I hope I didn't disturb anything important."

"I was just taking my ease," he said kindly, "after another fruitless day."

"It's not going well?" she asked.

"Not at all. Please sit down. How are things? How's Father Daugherty?"

Mrs. Munally hesitated.

"Could we close the door?"

"Certainly," Ryan said, going back, pushing the great oak door closed. "Now . . ."

"I shouldn't have come like this without warning," Mrs. Munally said in a distraught tone. "If I didn't think it was important, I wouldn't have."

"What is it?"

She sat in a deep green leather chair by the lamp. Ryan took the adjoining chair, facing her.

"It's Father Daugherty," Mrs. Munally said. "I don't want to be a gossip. If I hadn't searched my conscience, I wouldn't be here. My conscience told me to come. The Blessed Mother told me to come."

"Of course," Ryan said gently. "Go on—please."

"I don't think I'm being a gossip."

"Knowing you all these years, Bridget," Ryan said, "I'm sure you'd be the last person on earth to bear false witness."

"Thank you," she said, brushing a tear. Then going on: "The whole parish is a mess! They're upset by the sermons. They were bad enough to begin with. Then he started with the Russian thing—that writer—and they've been getting crazier ever since. I can't understand a word he's saying . . . I understand the words, I mean, but to me it's all crazy. He says there's no Hell. No Purgatory. No Limbo. No Heaven! There's too much pressure on him. I'm afraid he's going crazy. Really losing his mind . . ."

"Is there anything . . . anything specific you could tell me, beyond the sermons?" Ryan asked carefully.

"Yes!" she blurted. "Yes, there is. Not long ago—one night last week—Scafidi went back to the church to get something and found him, in the dark, giving a sermon to one person!"

"Really? Who was that?"

"A nun. Sister Mary Frances Murray."

"Is that so?" Ryan said, sitting back, stroking his chin, concealing the shock. "How do you know who it was?"

"Because Scafidi—poor man—came hobbling back to tell me. I don't know if he was scared or angry or both. I have never seen anybody so upset. His eyes were glassy and his hands were trembling."

"It might have been from the exertion."

"It might have been, yes. Anyway, I went out to see who it was, playing like I was going to church. I met her at her car—a *red* Volkswagen! She, all alone. Wearing one of those fancy-pantsy modern habits, her hair showing, too."

"I see," Ryan said. "And the implication is?"

"*I'm* not implying anything," Mrs. Munally said. "But Scafidi saw them in the church, holding hands!"

Her voice dropped to a whisper. Monsignor Ryan had leaned forward to catch the last words. He remained in that position, elbows on his knees, eyes on the Oriental carpet.

"I thought you said the church was dark?" he said.

"There was the pulpit light," Mrs. Munally said. "That's all."

"And where was Scafidi?"

"In the sacristy. Standing in the door."

"Is he absolutely certain?"

"He is," she said emphatically. "I questioned him very thoroughly."

"Holding hands? I mean, *actually* holding hands?"

"Yes," she said sadly.

"I don't think Scafidi likes Father Daugherty," Monsignor Ryan said judiciously. "It's possible he made it up, or misinterpreted something."

"That's possible," she said. "But I don't think he would make up a thing like that."

"Legally, it's only hearsay."

"I don't understand."

"Never mind. Is there . . . is there anything else?"

"Just the thing yesterday. The eleven o'clock Mass."

"What happened?" Ryan said, holding his breath, not wanting to hear more.

"He had a nigger guitar player there," Mrs. Munally said.

"A *Negro* guitar player?" Ryan repeated incredulously. "Jesus, Mary, Joseph. Who was it?"

"The one who telephones him. The one from Halfway House. Charles Seymour Jones."

"Are you absolutely certain of that?" Ryan asked, sucking in his breath.

"That's the way he introduced him from the pulpit," Mrs. Munally said.

"Oh, God!" Ryan groaned. "He *introduced* him!"

"It was a sort of Folk Mass," she went on. "Very informal, lot of talking."

"An honest-to-God Folk Mass?" Ryan asked.

"To tell the truth, I don't know what a Folk Mass really is," she said. "But it was all very different. The congregation was confused. Some were . . . they didn't *like* it."

Ryan slumped in his chair. He was silent now, weighing her information, accusations. Any . . . *all* . . . were dynamite. McInnerney had outlawed Folk Masses. And Jones! His own pickets blocking the Chancery door. Truly, Mrs. Munally was right! Daugherty had cracked up, was having a nervous breakdown. Either that, or he was picking a fight.

"Is that everything?" he said finally.

"All the important things," she said. "Oh. There was a newspaper photographer at the Mass, taking pictures, standing big-as-you-please right in front of the Blessed Sacrament, as though *It* weren't even there."

"Where was he from?" Ryan said.

"I didn't ask. But I didn't think it was right, taking pictures on the altar."

"Well, Pope Paul was on television in Shea Stadium," Ryan said. "So I guess maybe that's not a sacrilege anymore. Now, Bridget, let's be frank. What you bring tonight is very, very serious. I don't have to tell you that. It's not merely his reputation, but his career, his life work that is placed in jeopardy."

"I understand, sir," she said. "If I wasn't so worried about the parish, all the people, I wouldn't have come. I was hoping that maybe you could find a way to send him someplace, to a home or someplace, where he could get some rest. I think it must be the pressure . . ."

"I'll have to talk to Scafidi. If a formal accusation is to be brought, I will need a signed statement from him."

"I'll tell him."

"No. Don't tell him anything. Don't tell him you were here. Not him or anybody. You keep this strictly to yourself. I'll deal with it from here on out. That's perfectly clear, isn't it?"

"Perfectly," she said. "Now, as for Scafidi, I don't know. I'm worried about him, too. Ever since that night . . . he's been talking real strange. Talking against Father Daugherty. His voice sort of goes high and crazy-like. He thinks Father Daugherty is a *devil*. Really."

"Try to discourage Scafidi from discussing him. It can't do any good. I'll speak to Scafidi. Soon. Tomorrow. Meanwhile, I want to thank you very much."

"I hate this," she said.

"So do I," Ryan said.

VII

Jean Favrot left her house, feeling momentarily like a thief. She was leaving too much to Emma, poor soul. But Emma had not complained —not yet. She was willing, a good person. That morning, Jean had almost told her, or rather, had felt a compelling urge to tell. If Emma knew, she might understand, as a woman. It must have happened to Emma at some point in her life. She would understand and not feel put upon. No. She could never tell Emma.

Bob was away on a business trip, down South in Louisiana, delegate-hunting with Senator Root. The South was in political upheaval, being courted by all the candidates—Wallace, Nixon, Humphrey, Reagan. It was a good time for making deals, extracting promises. Bob had been gone five days. He would be back tonight or tomorrow.

She got in the car, started the air-conditioner, raised the tailgate window, drifted back along the drive, watching the rear-view mirror. Suddenly, she felt a metallic crunch. She slammed on the brakes, pulled on the emergency, jumped out, ran behind the car. There she found Chris's bike, with a mangled rear wheel. Damn! she said silently. How many times have I told him not to leave it in the drive! Now it would be back to the bike shop, two weeks wait, another expensive repair bill.

She dragged the bike on the grass, got back in the car. She backed into the street, eyes on the disabled bike, disturbed now because Chris would be so saddened when he saw it—saddened and guilty.

Such a sweet child! How he loved that bike! She must take it to the repair shop tomorrow . . . no, now.

She pulled back into the drive. She lifted the bike into the back deck, soiling her hands and pink shift. Then she drove to the shop in Vienna, fighting traffic. As she thought, it would be two weeks, not less than $22, depending on what could be salvaged. She drove straight from Vienna to Bill Clark's apartment, faster than she should. She was late. He opened the door before she pushed the bell, as though he had been waiting, listening for her footfall.

She slammed the door and threw herself into his arms. They kissed. Jean tingled all over, feeling the pulsing in her groin, the insatiable lust. They stumbled backward, feet intertwined, toward the couch, where they flopped side by side. Then he was in her, throbbing, hot, yet gentle. She came to orgasm, an explosive venting of tension, sublime, intense, savage. She held him tight, crushing him against her chest. After he came, they lay together for a long while, not talking, breathing in one another's ear.

The sex had gone like this for ten days. Jean hurried to Bill's every morning without qualm, as though her conscience had fled with the wind. On the first two days they had paused to have a mild drink. After that, as soon as Jean arrived, they went straight to the couch or to the bed, or both. They stayed in bed all morning, noon, and early afternoon, making love. They would make love and then nap. Eat a snack (in bed), then make love again. The whole time, stark naked. In between, they would lie together in the bed, caressing one another, exploring bodies, smelling the smells of rising and spent love. They bantered and smelled and touched and tingled, unrestrained, uninhibited. And even after all that, each day, they could not bear to part. So they kissed and touched and felt and whispered down the hall to the living room to the foyer to the door. As Bill often said, it was unreal.

The work on the book had come to a standstill. Bill had not even outlined Book Two. Nor did he go to the office. The office was still a shambles of disorganization, the computer now completely out of commission, torn apart by the IBM technicians, who worked methodically but slowly, only a few hours a day. Bill was not missed. No one seemed to care if he appeared or didn't. He didn't care either. Nothing like this encounter with Jean Favrot had ever happened to him before. Surely, in all history, there had never been anything to match it in intensity, totality, euphoria. It had swept away his blue funk, his depression, his concern for his children, religion. In this time and place in the brief, incoherent, inexplicable history of his life, Jean Favrot was exactly what he needed.

"Did you hear from Bob?" Bill said afterward.

"Yes," Jean said, eyes closed, drawing her mouth into a pucker. "He called last night."

"When's he coming back?"

"Tonight."

"Will he take some days off?" Bill said.

"I *hope* not," she said. "Wouldn't that be ghastly?"

She regretted these words instantly. True, she had confided much to Bill, criticizing Bob more than she ought. But she had never gone this far.

"We could work around him," Bill said. But his voice lacked conviction. Working around Bob Favrot might be dangerous. If he were at all suspicious, he might come calling, any hour of the day. Maybe with a gun . . .

"I don't think he can take time off," she said. "They're up to their eyeballs in deals. Anyway, let's don't talk about Bob. Look, I know what we should do. Let's go on a picnic! I know the perfect place."

"Where?" Bill said, liking this proposal very much. He had hardly been out of the apartment for ten days. It was a beautiful day, warm but clear.

"Harper's Ferry," Jean said, eyes lighting up. She had been thinking about this for two days. Last year, she had taken the children to Harper's Ferry. She found it enchanting, fascinating, a crucible of history plus interesting old architecture and fantastic views of the Potomac and Shenandoah rivers from the lofty brows and cliffs. She remembered particularly one high grassy knoll, just above the old cemetery. You could see for miles and miles, straight down the Potomac, churning white and foamy through the rocks. She had weighed the risk of being seen by someone they knew and found it to be negligible. Harper's Ferry was a touristy place, not likely, in this July heat, to attract anyone she knew.

"Well, let's get on it." Bill said, rising, collecting his clothes, then pausing to look down on Jean. He bent down and kissed her. Jean shuddered.

"I suppose I'm turning into a middle-aged nymphomaniac," she said wistfully. "But why not?"

"If I could think of a reason, I wouldn't tell."

"Oh, God, I feel good!"

"Me too."

"I'll fix lunch."

Bill packed a pipe and sat in his easy chair, listening to Jean scurry around in his kitchen. She was great! So full of life. *Joie de vivre!* The pill, he thought. That gave her the release she needed. Emancipated her. Did they all react like this when they got on the pill? He had never read anything about *that*. But it must be so. Or was it the forty thing, the last fling?

They took Jean's car. Bill's car, a creaking 1962 Buick Special Wagon, salvaged in his property settlement with Angela, was no longer roadworthy. Leaving the apartment parking lot, they drove to the state liquor store in the shopping center to pick up a bottle of Lancer's Rosé. Jean sat in the closed car, air-conditioning high, idly listening to WMAL, then playing Campbell's "Gentle on My Mind," "their" song. So absorbed, Jean did not see her next-door neighbor, Annie Shields, approaching. When Annie knocked on the window, Jean jumped in fright. She turned in her seat, heart pounding.

"Jeanie!" Annie shouted at the window. "What are you doing sitting here?"

Eyes darting from Annie to the state store, Jean cranked down the window, desperately racking her mind for a plausible lie. Waiting for one of the children? No. Annie would know they were at the pool with her children. Then *what?* God, Bill! Don't come out. Don't come out!

Damned stupid, coming to the shopping center. *Any*body might see her. A picnic basket sitting on the back seat!

"I just stopped," she said, "to hear this song. Glenn Campbell's latest. Isn't it beautiful?"

She turned up the volume. Annie stared at Jean, puzzled, not quite sure. She pretended to listen. Her eyes wandered to the rear seat, to the picnic basket. Jean had certainly been acting queerly lately. Gone all day. Where? Kids running loose. Poor Emma. Bob down South.

Jean kept her head low, as though listening to the music, but her eyes, turned away from Annie, were glued on the state store. Oh, God, she said silently. Get me out of this! God, I swear, I promise. Oh, my God, I'm heartily sorry for having offended Thee. I detest all my sins because . . .

Bill came jauntily from the liquor store, small brown bag tucked lovingly in the crook of his arm. He stepped from the sidewalk to the curb, searching the parking lot for Jean's car. Jean started her motor. turned casually to Annie:

"Well, that's it. Isn't it beautiful? I've got to run. Million things to do . . . see you later."

She cranked up the window and moved off, leaving Annie standing in the empty place. Jean did not know what to do. She must get away from Annie, move the car away. She drove along the rows of cars, watching Bill, who was shading his eyes with his hand like an Indian, searching.

God, let him understand, Jean said.

He did. He understood at once. He stepped back to the sidewalk, walking casually in the direction Jean was moving. He passed Peoples Drug Store, the Super Giant, dodging shopping carts, busy housewives with their hair up in curlers. Jean turned behind the corner of the Super Giant. Bill walked steadily ahead. He turned the corner. Jean was there, waiting. He leaped into the car. Jean gunned down the side alley.

"Stay down," she hissed. "Hunch down."

Bill slid to the floor.

"Down," she said.

"I'm *down,* damnit."

"That was Annie. Did you see her?"

"Your next-door neighbor?"

"Yes. What a fool thing to do! It *would* be her! She's got a nose like a bloodhound. Her husband's a spook—for CIA. Had something to do with the U-2 and the *Pueblo.* He doesn't talk about it. Says he works for the State Department. Annie thrives on that cloak-and-dagger stuff. She's probably been *following* me for days."

"Now, Jean," he said jocularly. "You're getting paranoid."

"I have a right."

"Can I get up now?"

"Wait till I get . . . wait a minute. Oh, wow! That was too close."

"Would she . . . she . . . talk?"

"Are you kidding? She and Bob are like that."

She held up crossed fingers.

"You mean . . ."

"Hell no," she replied. "That *prude.* Certainly not with Bob. Ugh! They talk politics."

"I've heard that before," Bill said. "Now can I get up?"

"All right. I guess so. This is madness!"

She turned to him. smiling. She kissed him through the air. She added:

"But I love you."

"Crazy, man," Bill said, backing up on the seat.

"Beautiful," she said, resorting to Nancy's jargon, which seemed peculiarly appropriate. "Groovy."

Bill drew the Lancer's from the paper bag, held it aloft. She smiled appreciatively. It was, as he knew, her favorite wine. The sight calmed her. She turned on the road to Harper's Ferry, a sleepy two-lane macadam, winding away from McLean, into the verdant foothills. She thought: Have I really gone mad? What am I doing in this car with this man? This foolish, crazy, wonderful, divorced man, going to Harper's Ferry, taking God-knows-what risks? If Annie had seen, had told, then what? She remembered, too, her promise to God.

They were soon in the Blue Ridge Foothills, following the river, looking up at the shale cliffs. It was a beautiful drive.

"Have you been in the Rockies?" Jean said, not wanting to talk about Annie anymore.

"Yes. Fantastic."

"I'd like to see them," she said.

"I'd like to take you."

That would be fun, Jean thought. She could learn to ski, in Snowmass and Aspen and Sun Valley. They could be ski bums, going from resort to resort. No. That was a dream. Who would take care of the children? She might dream, but the dream must be limited. Limited to what? To his apartment? Harper's Ferry? It must end. But she did not want to think about that either.

"When are you going to tell me what your shrink told you?" Jean said.

"That would take hours."

"Can't you boil it down?"

"No. It's too complicated."

She thought about group, Margo's hysterical laughter when Jean told them, confessed all about Bill. It seemed like months ago. Yet it was only two nights ago.

"I did what you said," Jean said. "I told the group."

"Ah!" Bill said. "What happened?"

"Well, Margo laughed her head off. It was *quite* an evening. Took up the whole session again."

"What was the consensus?"

"Generally they approved. Margo. Joan. Mack. Even Kenneth. Mike didn't."

"Why?" Bill said.

"He said it was irresponsible," Jean said. "He said: 'Where will it end?' Not a bad question."

"No," Bill said. "Not bad."

"How *will* it end, Bill?"

"I don't know," Bill replied. "Why talk about that?"

"He said someone was going to get hurt," Jean said.

"This Mike is omniscient?" Bill said.

"No," Jean said, lowering her voice.

As they rounded a curve, she suddenly said, "There it is!" The roadside was dense with oaks and elms. Bill could see nothing.

"Where?"

"Over the bridge."

They crossed the Potomac River over a new, low, modern bridge. Then they turned, following an old barge canal with ancient wooden locks, into the town. It was like a movie set, curiously deserted, with tiny, steep winding streets, Federalist houses abutting the broken sidewalks. Behind the town, perched on the bank of the river, the hills rose steeply, breathtakingly.

"Isn't it neat?" Jean said, swinging into a tourist parking lot, a modern facility appended by the park service.

"Quaint," Bill said.

"You know why it's famous?" Jean said, parking, killing the engine, reaching for the picnic basket.

"Not exactly," Bill said. "A Civil War battle?"

"John Brown," she said. "He was caught here, raiding the federal arsenal. They hanged him."

"John Brown's body lies a-moldering in the grave?"

"Yes. Did you read Stephen Vincent Benét?"

"No."

"I love that. You know who caught Brown? Who conducted the trial?"

"No, who?" Bill said, getting out, sucking in the pure air, admiring the old homes and shops, the view.

"Robert E. Lee," Jean said, locking the car door.

"I'll be damned," Bill said, enlightened.

"Come on," she said. "Let's go see the ruins of the arsenal. Nothing left but the old stone foundation."

They went to look. They found the foundation, almost overgrown by grass. Bill remarked that it all seemed impossible—incredible that this little place provided the spark that ignited the Civil War.

They followed the steep sidewalks into the village, peering in the shop windows, the wax museum. Then they climbed the sidewalk stairway to the old Episcopal church and beyond that, the Catholic church, a gutted ruin. They stood in the roofless area, reading the graffiti scratched on the walls: "Sue loves Charlie, 1959."

"You wouldn't think there were enough Catholics for this size church," Bill said. "What were Catholics doing here?"

"From Maryland—next door."

"Oh," Bill said.

They climbed the pathway, still higher, huffing. Then they came to a space on a cliff, a gigantic flat slab of granite, almost overhanging. It was Jefferson Rock. A tourist sign quoted Jefferson as saying that the view from this spot was worth a voyage across the Atlantic.

The view was awesome. They could see the confluence of the Potomac and Shenandoah far below, the rocks and rushing water, the valley receding in the distance. Jean climbed to the top of the rock for a better look. Bill hung back, feeling a surge of panic—the terror of acrophobia. He turned away.

"Come on," she called.

"I'm bushed," he said.

She climbed down.

"Don't you like it?"

"It's great. But I don't like heights."

"It's not high," she insisted. "Look over the edge. It's not sheer. The ground slopes away."

She pulled him toward the rock. He broke her grip with a desperate motion, drawing back to safety. She stood on the edge of the precipice, looking puzzled.

"Then how can you go skiing?" she said.

"I don't know," he said. "It's different."

"Don't you go up high in a chair lift?"

"Most of them are not really high—not far from the ground. Jean, I'm sorry. This is stupid."

"No it isn't," she said. "Come on, let's go. I'm starved. Let's eat."

They walked uphill to a grassy meadow beyond the old cemetery. There were no steep cliffs here, rather a gentle fall. They found a scarred picnic table beneath an old oak. Jean spread the lunch. They ate the sandwiches and drank rosé from paper cups. Then they lay on the grass, watching the clouds march overhead, listening to the birds calling. It was peaceful and free. A dream. Jean had never felt so relaxed and safe. The wine made her sleepy. She did not fight it. She closed her eyes and let her mind drift to faraway, dreamy places—ski slopes, Caribbean islands, ancient ruins on the Acropolis, lush gardens in Hawaii.

Afterward, they walked back to the village, going through the cemetery, checking the tombstones for familiar names. They found five Clarks, including one who died in 1783. Bill stood looking at the faint inscription, mind clouding with somber thoughts of his children. He pointed to the grave.

"Do you think it all stops here?" he said.

"I don't know," she said, eyes following his finger. "I wish I knew."

"Don't we all," Bill said sadly.

The new questions that had recently been gnawing at Jean came suddenly: Why are we here? What is the point? So, you live and die. For what purpose? What was one life, more or less? Who would remember, forty years from now? She would be swallowed up in the mists of history, like old man Clark, d. 1783. Only the children . . .

She was suddenly depressed.

"Let's go," she said. She was sorry now that they had come to the cemetery.

"All right," Bill said.

They drove home, down through the foothills to the large roads and the speeding cars, the afternoon traffic. It was late—after five when they reached the parking lot of Bill's apartment. Jean did not think she should go in again. But Bill was depressed. He insisted. She sensed that he needed her—her body. Inside, they made love. But Jean's heart was not in it. She did not come to orgasm. She was worried about the children, their dinner.

"I'm sorry," Bill said.

"Sorry?" she said, lying against his warm body.

"You didn't come."

"Oh, Bill. I don't come *every* time. I . . . I wasn't in the mood. I'm worried about dinner."

He handed her the telephone.

"Call Nancy," he said. "Tell her to get it started."

"Oh, Bill. I *can't*. I've got to get home. Honestly."

"Go on," he said firmly.

"Oh, all right."

She dialed her home. Nancy answered. In the background she could hear the other children, shouting, fighting. She *must* get home.

"Nancy dear, this is Mums. Will you start dinner?"

"Mums! Where are you? Do you know what happened? Chris's bike got stolen. Right out of the yard. Mrs. Shields came over and called the police. They came and talked to Chris. It was so exciting!"

"The *police?* Oh golly! The bike *wasn't* stolen. I backed over it and bent the wheel. I took it to the shop."

"Oh *no!"* Nancy groaned.

Damnit to hell, Jean thought. She should have told Chris or Emma. And damn that nosy Annie. Cloak-and-dagger! Police in her home! God! Now the whole neighborhood would be on full alert: Where had Jean been all day? Oh, God! What am I doing, lying here naked?

"Nancy," she said sternly. "Put the potatoes in the oven. Put Chris on the line. I'll be home in half an hour."

"Where are you?" Nancy repeated.

"In Bethesda, playing bridge."

Chris came on the line. Jean's heart collapsed at the sound of his voice.

"Never mind, honey," she said, interrupting his long and melodramatic story, "it's *not* stolen. I ran over it and took it to the shop. I should have told you. Go watch TV or something. I'll be right home."

She hung up, verging on despair. She *had* to get out of there, *right now*. God. Bob coming home tonight, too! She jumped up, dressed quickly. Bill watched her from the bed.

"Trouble?" he said carefully.

"Oh . . . yes and no. Nothing serious. But I've got to hurry."

"Will I see you tomorrow?" he said.

"If I can . . ."

"What do you mean . . . *if?*"

She didn't know what she meant or why she had said that. The walls were closing in around her. They must have a talk. Yes. She would come tomorrow, if possible. But they must talk. She hurried home.

When she turned in the drive, her heart froze in terror. Bob's car, a beat-up Chevvy, was parked in the drive. Oh-God-oh-God-oh-God, Jean moaned silently, beating the steering wheel with her fist. She parked, half in panic. She ran into the house. The kids were in the living room, gathered around Bob, who was doling out small gifts. Jean stood by the door, watching. When he saw her, Bob did not speak. His eyes were sullen, angry.

Jean went to the kitchen. Nothing had been done. She put the hamburgers on to cook. The wall telephone rang. Jean, alerted by a sixth sense, snatched it from the cradle.

"Jean?" It was Bill.

"I can't talk," she whispered frantically. "Bob's home."

"OK. 'Bye."

Jean hung up, faint with fear. Bill had never called before. What a stupid thing to do! She knew why. It had not been right at the apartment. He was worried and depressed. Otherwise he would not have called.

Bob strolled casually into the kitchen.

"Pretty late bridge game," he said.

"I got caught in the beltway traffic," she said.

"I hear the police were here," Bob said, mixing a vodka-tonic.

"Can't you even say hello-how-are-you?" Jean said snappishly. "You're early."

"We got in sooner than I thought."

"How was the trip?" she said.

"Good. We worked like hell as usual. Nancy says you've been away almost every day."

"I keep busy," Jean said. "It's good for my mind."

Bob left the room without another word. Jean put the dinner on. Afterward, she cleaned the kitchen and lashed the boys into the tub and saw them to bed, in ones and twos. All the while, she thought about Bill, wondering why he had taken that desperate chance, what might have happened if Bob had not been holding the children's attention in the living room, if Nancy had answered instead . . . if . . . if. Then she went to bed, exhausted. She lay down and closed her eyes.

Bob came in, carrying a fresh drink. He closed the door. Jean felt trapped. He was suspicious. He *sensed* something. He was going to worm it out of her, unless she diverted him to something else. Something big. Group!

"I think we ought to talk," Bob said, sitting on the edge of the bed.

"Go on," she said arrogantly. "Talk."

"I want to ask you what's come over you," he said gently. "What do you *do* all day?"

"What's come over me?" Jean echoed sarcastically. "Don't you *know* what's come over me? I'm losing my mind. That's what's come over me. Isn't it apparent?"

"Jean, I'm trying to be serious."

"I *am* serious, goddamnit!" Jean shouted, sitting up against the headboard. "I'm going out of my mind and I am going to a shrink. To group therapy."

Bob fixed his eyes on the liquid in his glass.

"Group therapy?" he said softly. "Where?"

"At the McLean Guidance Center. Dr. Cantor."

"Dr. Cantor? Who's he?"

"A psychologist. We have a group of ten people. We sit around and discuss our problems. It is very . . . very enlightening."

Bob sipped his drink slowly.

"What problems?" he said.

"I'm . . . I'm not supposed to talk about it outside the group. We have this covenant. If you talk about it outside, it destroys the purity of the group."

"It does, eh?" Bob said, standing up suddenly, shouting. "Well, Jesus H. Christ! You go down there and talk to a bunch of perfect strangers about problems you can't even discuss with your own husband? Jean, for God's sake, I have to know what's come over you. I don't understand you. We've grown poles apart. Sometimes I think I don't know you at all anymore."

"That may be true. I don't think I understood myself until I joined the group."

"But . . . tell me, for God's sake. What do you talk about? What do you *do?*"

"Talk. About sex mostly. Various hangups."

"Sex! Hangups! You talk about *sex* to perfect strangers?"

"They're not perfect strangers. We're like a . . . like a little family. A hungup-type family. We criticize each other and . . ."

"Family! My God in Heaven, what is this world coming to? Don't you have family enough? You don't really believe in that horseshit, do you? You're not nuts. You don't need a head-shrinker. Jesus! If you're not normal, who is? If you think you got problems, what about *me?*"

"Your defenses are OK. I don't worry about you."

"Defenses? What *defenses?*"

"Your ego. Very strong. If I hadn't gone there, I might have been sent away, to St. Elizabeth's."

Bob looked at his wife, disbelieving. Tears filmed his eyes. His voice was halting, uncertain.

"Jean . . . darling. What's happened to us? I don't understand anything anymore. I don't understand one goddamned little thing anymore.

You think my ego is up? You're crazy. If anybody is having a nervous breakdown around here, it's me. We can't afford that bullshit. How do you pay for it?"

"From the money I make typing the book."

Bob winced. He wiped the tears from his eyes. He tossed off his drink in one gulp.

"If you weren't taking that pill and feeling so guilty about it you wouldn't be all screwed up," he said. He squinted his eyes. "And why *do* you take the pill? We haven't had sex for six months. Or is it longer?"

"It's good for me. It regulates my period. I feel better physically. And I never know when you'll be in the mood."

She looked at him coyly and smiled. He turned away. He made another drink, returned silently, undressed for bed. Jean watched—revolted by his potbelly, his baggy pajamas. She went to the bathroom, undressed, put on her nightgown, slipped back in bed.

She read two chapters of *Anna Karenina,* a book she had borrowed from Bill's library. He had suggested it as a starter for her new reading kick. She was now deep in the novel. It had excited her at first— Anna's decision, her fling. Now it depressed her. Anna's life seemed hollow, empty, obviously foredoomed. She put the book on the night table and snapped off the bedside light.

"Why are you reading that book?" Bob said, voice booming from the darkness.

"It's a great novel. Tolstoy. I'm rereading the classics."

"Why?"

"To improve my mind."

"Your mind is OK. I wish you'd get that through your head. If you'd go back to what you were, everything would be fine."

"I'm not going back there. That life was slow suicide."

"Your new life is fast suicide."

"Go to sleep, Bob. I'm very tired."

She felt his hand on her stomach. She rolled over, and the hand fell away. She lay with her back to him. She closed her eyes and thought about Bill, seeing him now at the tiller of a sailboat, spray slashing his strong jaw, the pipe, the hood of his yellow northeaster, wind billowing a gaudy-colored spinnaker.

"Jean," Bob said. "Don't go to sleep yet. I want to tell you something."

"What?"

He rolled up on his elbow, caressed her shoulder with his finger. She shivered. Tonight, of all nights, she did not want his rough, tearing sex. "I love you," he said gently. "I don't care what you do. Go to group. I'll pay for it. Mold yourself into another person. But, please, honey. Don't forget me. The children. We need you, more than you will ever know. I need you, especially. I'm not strong anymore. Sometimes I can't seem to go on. If I didn't have my faith, I couldn't. Don't take that from me. I may be stupid, fat, lecherous, inconsiderate, old-fashioned, Neanderthal. But I'm your husband and I care about you more than anything in the world. I'd do anything if I thought it would make you happy."

He cried unashamedly, shoulders jerking. Jean closed her eyes and cried, too, biting her fist to hold back the sobs.

VIII

Father Daugherty shuffled through the stack of mail on the rectory table. In the last three days the mail had been heavy—mostly anonymous letters protesting the so-called Folk Mass. Many of the letters seemed to make almost exactly the same point, as though they were products of an organized campaign, directed by a single mind. Others, laced with raw threats such as: KEEP THAT NIGGER OUT OF OUR PARISH —OR ELSE!, were, Daugherty thought, from crackpots. The flow of letters had been evoked, he believed, by the publicity in the *Tribune*. Klein had overplayed the story with a "scare" headline: GHETTO HERO BRINGS SOUL TO SUBURBS. There had been pictures of Seymour Jones and Father Daugherty (a profile shot, showing his sideburns) and a purplish text, overdramatizing the Mass as "experimental." Daugherty had been flattered that what he said or did might be worthy of public notice, but now he believed it was a mistake to permit the photographers and reporters in the church. The publicity was doing more harm than good.

Among the mail there was a letter marked "Personal." It was addressed in green ink in a backward-sloping, neat, feminine hand, vaguely familiar. Daughtery turned the envelope over, noting the return address:

M. Murray
206 Cedar Street
Greenwich, Conn.

Daugherty slit open the flap. Leaning against the door jamb, he read:

Dear Dan,

I hope this finds you well. I have resigned from the order. I did this entirely on my own, without—I believe—any other consideration than my own, somewhat turbulent, personal relationship to the Church. I believe I had firmly made up my mind—with LeGuiese's help—before I arrived in New York. My reception there could not have been nicer—I was offered a tremendously interesting new job and challenge. I went up to the mountaintop and thought about it very earnestly—and also prayed. I decided that while the new challenge was tempting beyond words, my basic break with the Church still remained, deep down, and that was really the crux.

It was not an easy decision, as I'm sure you understand. I am now back in Greenwich with my family—temporarily. I'm not sure just yet what I plan to do. I want to get back to my work of bringing Montessori to the ghetto deprived. Yesterday, the good folks at Whitby offered me a job teaching there at a good salary. It's a great place and great people, but I still can't see myself happy with all those indescribably affluent kids. That's just not my bag. I may hit up some of the foundations. The word is they're hungry for worthy projects. In the meantime, this summer, I may volunteer for some work in the ghetto.

Meanwhile, I cannot get Halfway House out of my mind. The day I left I saw Sharon. She was down, down. Peter bugged out on her, headed "west." The other kids had left for a commune on the Eastern Shore. Sharon had made contact with a new bunch about which she knew little. I am worried about her and the new kids. I know you are busy as you can be, but please try to look in to see how they're doing. I miss Sharon very much and feel that I deserted her. I hope she understands what I have been going through and that, for once, I had to counsel *myself*. If you can get down there, do so.

Mother and I have had many long, girlish chats. For the first
time in my life I feel I really know her. Now we talk about *real*
things—not just the weather or my studies or the order. She has
a lot more to her than I thought. Her advice has been good.
She's provided a strong shoulder. One piece of her advice was
that I should not return immediately to Washington. She feels
that you have your own troubles and problems to work out either
alone or with LeGuiese without any unnecessary distraction provided by me, and I think she's right. When you have made up
your mind, let me know. So for now, good-bye and good luck. I
mean that sincerely, Dan. You are a wonderful person with
tremendous qualities to do good. Whatever you decide, I will
understand.

In Christ,

Mary

Daugherty, shaken, confused, reread the letter with an overwhelming sense of loss.

Mary had called him that Friday night from Greenwich, after her
talk with the Provincial. She had been somewhat vague, understandably
distressed and uncertain. She said she was going away a few days to
think. That she would call or write soon. This was his first word from
her since that call.

He made his way to the den in a daze. He sat down, read the letter
a third time, the last paragraph again and again. She did not categor-
ically say she loved him. Yet she must! She had told him so. That's
why she resigned. It was there, between the lines. God! He must call
her—telephone tonight. Get her back. Harlem! She was just losing
herself probably, trying to forget. I must meet her mother, try to
explain. She was probably furious.

Lost in thought, Daugherty was not aware of the jangling telephone.
Mrs. Munally appeared in the doorway.

"Excuse me," she said. "Telephone."

Daugherty snapped back to reality.

"Who is it?"

"The Chancery," Mrs. Munally said. "The Vicar General."

She left the den. Daugherty lifted the telephone gingerly. He had
been half-expecting the call—ever since the story in the *Tribune.*

"This is Father Daugherty," he said, aware that Mrs. Munally had
not hung up the kitchen phone.

"Prial here," the Vicar General said. "The Archbishop would like to see you this afternoon. Could you make it about three o'clock?"

"What's it all about?" Daugherty said.

"I should think you'd have some inkling," the Vicar General said.

"All right." Daugherty said, sighing. "I'll be there."

He hung up. Almost immediately, Mrs. Munally reappeared in the doorway, in a highly agitated state.

"You heard?" Father Daugherty said, annoyed.

"I wanted to be sure you were on," she said lamely. She advanced hesitantly into the den. "There is something I'd like to say," she added, almost in a whisper.

"Yes?" he said.

"It's about Scafidi . . ." Mrs. Munally said. "He's . . . I'm *very* worried about him."

"What's he done?"

"Nothing. Nothing specific. It's just that he's been talking sort of crazy-like."

"About what?"

"You."

"*Me?*" Daugherty said. "Why me?"

"He doesn't like you."

"Believe me, the feeling is mutual," Daugherty said. "I've told you that all along. We ought to let him go and get someone else. What, specifically, has he been saying about me?"

"You remember . . . the night . . . Sister Mary Murray came by?"

"Yes. Certainly."

"He said he saw you inside the church with her."

"Oh?" Daugherty said, suddenly very angry. Scafidi had been eavesdropping! Scafidi, of all people on the face of the earth! A sneak. A *crazy* sneak. A dangerous man.

"It may be why the Chancery called," she said, voice falling to despair.

"What do you mean?"

"He may have said something to Monsignor Ryan. He was his confessor, you know."

"Said *what* to Monsignor Ryan?" Daugherty said angrily.

"That . . . you know . . . that . . ."

"Come to the point quickly, Mrs. Munally."

She burst into tears and fled from the room. Daugherty, astonished by this, stared after her, thinking. He must find Scafidi, right now, have a good, long, tough talk. If he had prattled to Ryan! God! But Ryan would not pass on a thing like that to Prial—or McInnerney. Not without proof.

He ran from the rectory to his MG. He drove fast through the sub-divisions to the dirt lane, pulling into Scafidi's drive in a cloud of dust. He banged on the door. There was no answer, no sign of life. He peered in the window, astonished by the sight of the wooden crates jammed with books and pamphlets. Was this Everest of work all flying saucers? Crazy! Mad!

He drove back to the rectory, anger slowly deflating, questions rising. Why had Mrs. Munally seemed so agitated? Of course! *She* had gossiped to Ryan! Not Scafidi. That night when Mary was here. *She* had come into the parking lot, obviously spying. *She* talked to Ryan every day. The letter! Damn. He had left it on his desk in the rectory. He must destroy the letter.

The letter was undisturbed—just where he left it. He read it one last time, then set a match to it in the den fireplace. He sat thinking again of Mary, her decision, his own decision, the call from Prial. The call must be about the *Tribune* publicity. It could not possibly be any-thing about Mary.

He ate lunch alone in the rectory. Mrs. Munally served it, trying very hard to please. Watching her, Daugherty convinced himself she had betrayed him to Ryan. A hopeless gossip. He would not say any-thing. Not now. She might call Ryan again, raising the wrong issue at the wrong time. Later he would deal with her disloyalty.

After lunch, he went up to his room to read his breviary and to think, watching the time carefully. He must call Mary as soon as pos-sible, find time to drop by Halfway House. At two thirty Mrs. Munally called up the stairway.

"You have a visitor."

"Visitor?" Daugherty said, coming from his room, looking at his wristwatch. "I don't have time to see anybody. I have to leave for the Chancery."

"She said it wouldn't take a minute."

"Who is it? Can she come back tonight?"

"It's Mrs. Favrot," Mrs. Munally said.

"Oh," Daugherty said.

It must be important. After that brief chat with Bob, he had meant to call Dr. Cantor to see how she was doing. But there had been no time. No time to do anything properly.

"Tell her to have a seat," he said. "I'll be right down."

He hurried back into his room, put on his collar and rabat, thoughts returning to Mary. He would call tonight, after the rates dropped. Then he skipped down the steps, two at a time, a feat of agility that reminded him that—no matter what—he must take drastic steps to get back into shape. Call Marv Klein about tennis . . .

He found Jean Favrot in the den, examining the pathetically thin rectory bookshelf. She seemed radiantly beautiful, brimming with health and vitality, thinner and tanned, eyes clear and sparkling. There was no trace of the old weariness, the fatigue lines on her face. Dr. Cantor must have done a good job.

"Jean!" he exclaimed. "You look marvelous!"

"Hi," she said cheerily. "I hope I'm not interrupting . . ."

"As a matter of fact," Daugherty said sadly, looking at his watch, "I'm due at the Chancery for an appointment with the Archbishop in twenty-five minutes. I'm sorry. I'd be more than happy to see you tonight after supper . . ."

"Oh, no!" Jean said, blushing. "*I'm* sorry. I should have called. I just came . . . on impulse."

Her eyes fell to the floor.

"Is there something wrong, Jean?" Daugherty said, his tone professionally gentle.

She lifted her eyes. They were brimming.

"Yes . . . !" she stammered. "There is . . . I'm terribly confused . . . all mixed up. I've been trying to do . . . trying my best to do the right thing. I'm in a group. My whole life has changed . . . I . . . I . . . But. . ."

She stopped. Daugherty encouraged her: "Go on, let it out."

"It's a long story," she said, composing herself. "Perhaps I'd better come back when . . ."

"Tell me the heart of it," Daugherty said.

Jean paused, as though gathering her thoughts. Then she said:

"I feel like I'm being torn in two. The group tells me one thing. Bob . . . my conscience tells me another . . . I can't reconcile . . . I don't know if I should be taking the pill or not."

"You *are* taking it?" Daugherty said.

"Yes!" Jean blurted. "Yes . . . and that's not all . . ."

"Does Bob know?"

"Yes. Oh yes. *I'll* say he does."

"He doesn't approve?"

"Not basically. He doesn't approve of group either."

"You told him about that?"

"I had to."

"Of course. Well, Jean. I wish I could talk. Any other time . . ."

"You go on. I'll come back. Maybe tonight."

Daugherty saw from her tone that she would not be back tonight, perhaps not ever. She was here now because she was desperate. Desperate *again*. She needed help. He must find time to help her. He had not helped her. He had merely fobbed her off on Dr. Cantor. Her religion, her whole spiritual life, was in crisis. If he couldn't help her, then he was surely a failure. Bob was angry. They *both* needed help. If he could talk to them together, perhaps . . .

"I better not keep McInnerney waiting," Daugherty said, again glancing at his watch. "I have a feeling he's not in the best of moods. I don't think he was too happy about Seymour Jones being out here."

"Well, you can tell him my teen-age daughter liked him," Jean said. "She's still talking. Telling all her Protestant friends . . . bragging as though we'd had the Monkees here. The other kids are quite impressed."

"I'll tell him that," Daugherty said ironically. "As a last resort. Jean, will you please come by tonight?"

"I'll try," she said.

"If you can't make it," he said, "I'll call you tomorrow."

"All right. Good luck."

"My regards to Bob."

She preceded him to the front door. He left immediately afterward in the chromeless rectory Chevvy. Downtown, he parked on a side street, walked the half block to the Chancery. Four of Seymour Jones's young pickets were on duty, sitting on the grass in the shade, almost out of sight, looking bored. Daugherty waved to them, entered the Chancery without ringing the bell. A maid showed him to a chair in the long foyer. He sat, listening to the clatter of typewriters, the ring of telephones echoing against the marble floor, the hushed conversation of the staff.

He felt very much the stranger. He had been to the Chancery one or two times before on routine business. Each time, he had the same feeling. The Chancery was a thing removed from him, with no real connection with his work, or All Saints'. It was a vague, distant place from which pastoral letters and other communications emanated, like the federal government. He had met McInnerney several times over the last two years at Church functions, always formally and distantly. Mc-

Innerney was his spiritual leader, in theory, his teacher, yet they had never exchanged a close word. He knew nothing about the man, really, except the pious platitudes he had heard from Ryan, and the public image of a stern, ascetic prelate.

Vicar General Prial came striding down the corridor, escorting Helen Hanrahan, talking animatedly. The woman looked familiar. Daugherty recognized her face but could not remember her name. Somebody he had seen on TV? He rose from the chair. Prial introduced Helen Hanrahan.

"I read your column faithfully," Daugherty said. This was not pure truth. He dipped in it occasionally, always skeptically.

"You're the young dissident, I take it," she said, looking grave. "I saw your picture in the paper."

"Dissident?" Daugherty said.

"The *modern* priest, then," she said, smiling.

"The Archbishop was telling Helen about you," Prial said.

"Not *all* bad I hope," Daugherty said, smiling uneasily.

"Don't go through with it," Helen Hanrahan said, suddenly quite grave. "Give it up. If you don't, there's going to be trouble."

"Give *what* up?" Daugherty said.

"Remember your vow of obedience," she said, walking away, toward the door. Prial followed her, opened the door with an unctuous bow. Then he returned.

"Let's go on up," Prial said. "But—fair warning. He's in a crusty mood."

"Thank you," Daugherty said.

They went toward the elevator, Prial leading. There was something about Prial Daugherty admired. He could not put his finger on it. He was, at least, open and friendly. Not devious. In the elevator, Daugherty said:

"Has anybody ever compiled a box score on Hanrahan's predictions?"

"The Archbishop is a firm believer," Prial said. "She sure called the tune on Dr. King. Predicted his assassination."

"Oh?" Daugherty said.

"Uncanny," Prial said. "And a very devout Catholic. Very devout. I wish I had the strength of her faith."

"I didn't know that," Daugherty said.

Prial knocked on the Archbishop's door. McInnerney opened it, stepping back. Daugherty knelt, kissed the ring, not in true reverence, but because custom demanded it.

"Come in and sit down, son," the Archbishop said gently. "You remember your pastor?"

He swept a hand toward the couch. Monsignor Ryan sat in a corner, very solemn. Daugherty smiled hello. Inside he felt his chest go tight. Why was Ryan here? Ryan returned the greeting, but did not speak. Daugherty sat on a chair by the couch. The Archbishop and Prial sat on the couch with Ryan. Daugherty studied the Archbishop's impassive face for clues to his humor. He found none. The Vicar General lighted a cigar.

"Have you seen the paper, the *Tribune?*" the Archbishop said.

"Yes," Daugherty said, relieved. So it would be Seymour Jones—not Mary.

"The editor, this Klein, is a friend of yours, isn't he?" McInnerney said, adopting the tone of a prosecutor.

"I know him pretty well," Daugherty said. "We used to play tennis regularly. But I hardly see him anymore."

"Tom told us you were tennis pals," Prial said. "I assume he plays a deadly game."

"Pretty fair," Daugherty said.

The Archbishop lifted a copy of the *Tribune* from the coffee table. It was fresh—the early edition. He pointed to a story, gave the paper to Daugherty. It was a photograph and a piece about Charles Seymour Jones picketing the Chancery. The placard he carried in the photo read:

WE WANT BLACK PRIESTS
IN THE GHETTO
Why are black priests relegated
to menial tasks? Where are the
black pastors?

Daugherty returned the paper without comment.

"This Jones is a friend of yours too, isn't he?" McInnerney said.

"I know him quite well, yes."

"I understand he participated in an unauthorized Mass at All Saints'," McInnerney said.

"It was not an unauthorized Mass," Daugherty replied, determined not to lose his temper, to respond to any charges put to him concisely, legalistically. "It was an ordinary Mass with Jones playing music. The *Tribune* story was exaggerated. It was not an experimental Mass."

"He has also played at your so-called Halfway House, has he not?" McInnerney said.

Damn! Daugherty thought. Who told them that?

"Yes," Daugherty replied, without elaboration. He would restrict himself to monosyllables, if necessary.

"Who invited the reporters to All Saints'?" the Archbishop asked, changing to a gentle tone.

"I don't know," Daugherty said. "I didn't. Maybe Jones did."

"You didn't?" Prial said, as though nailing down a point in his favor.

"I didn't," Daugherty repeated. Then turning to McInnerney, "And, may I ask, why is Halfway House referred to here as so-called? It *is* a halfway house. It has accomplished a good deal—without any help from this Chancery."

"We'll return to that later," McInnerney said. "Now, back to the *Tribune*. Are you aware that your pal Klein, your tennis opponent, is embarked on a systematic crusade to destroy the Church, and this Chancery specifically?"

"No," Daugherty said coolly. "I was not aware of that."

"In league with Jones," McInnerney continued, as though unfolding a vast conspiracy. *"Your* guest at All Saints'. *Your* guest at Halfway House."

"I don't believe either man is systematically trying to destroy the Church," Daugherty said. "Klein is merely reporting an existing climate of opinion . . . since the Council. All the press is—"

"Do you realize," the Archbishop went on, "this dope addict, Jones, Klein's hero, is organizing pickets all over the ghetto? Did you see them downstairs? It's an outrage for you to invite this enemy to All Saints'. A personal insult. Jones is irresponsible. He has no right to picket us. *I* desegregated the archdiocesan schools *four years* before the Supreme Court ruling. *I* mounted a special drive in 1952 to recruit black priests. *I* authorized my priests to participate in the march on Selma. We have black pastors in a third of the ghetto churches. As fast as we can train them, and promote them, we're replacing the white pastors. But you can't do this overnight. They aren't ready. They don't have the education, the experience. Many of them don't want the responsibility. They're lazy."

Daugherty shifted uncomfortably in his chair. "Is this what you wanted to see me about?" he said.

"We think it's very dangerous that Jones is your friend, Klein is your friend," McInnerney resumed. "We want you to stop seeing them."

Daugherty glared. Rage pounded his temples.

"Helen Hanrahan just stopped by to see me," the Archbishop said, making a church with his fingers. "She is very upset. She has had a vision. An armageddon, related somehow to this archdiocese. I believe I understand her, have interpreted the vision properly."

The Archbishop let his eyes fall on Daugherty, who could scarcely believe his ears. The Archbishop taking that woman and her predictions seriously!

"The Church is verging on crisis," the Archbishop went on. "It is besieged from all sides by . . . by people like Klein and Jones. Probably never before in history has it been so absolutely necessary for us to close ranks, stand back to back, and fight off the enemy. Do I make myself clear?"

He raised an eyebrow.

"I'm following," Daugherty said, smothering anger.

"I will not tolerate any further dissent, black or white," the Archbishop said. "The pendulum has swung too far to the left. We are going to swing it back to the right. If Jones doesn't vacate the gym and call off his pickets, I'll simply padlock *all* the ghetto churches *and* get a legal injunction to remove him from the gym. We keep those churches going at a sacrifice, a financial loss. Jones doesn't realize that, of course. Or wouldn't accept it if he knew. We're having the lawyers go over the *Tribune*. We may file a libel suit against the paper if this assault keeps up.

"As for life in the ghetto, let me tell you something, young man. I was *born* in a ghetto. A white ghetto on the South Side of Boston. I grew up in a ghetto. During my young years as a priest, I worked in a ghetto, helping to organize unions. *I* instituted the rule in this archdiocese that all lay employees must be union men. In New York I helped integrate the Puerto Rican population into the city and the Church. I did all this while you were raised in the lap of Main Line luxury. You rich young people grow up feeling guilty. You spend a few weeks in a ghetto working off that guilt. Then you think you know all about discrimination and poverty. You think you've discovered something brand-new."

Daugherty bit his lips.

"Another thing," the Archbishop continued, "I've been hearing about your sermons. Dostoyevsky! The Grand Inquisitor! You're talking rot. Dostoyevsky was a Russian! A nihilist. A madman and a criminal. A revolutionary. His books helped bring on the Communist takeover of Russia, the enslavement of hundreds of millions of people, the abolition of the Church. There is no room in this Church for Dostoyevsky."

Daugherty leaped to his feet.

"Dostoyevsky was a Christian!" he said, remembering LeGuiese's estimate. "A great Christian. He understood the poor! He lived in a house of the condemned! A political prisoner. No man had a deeper or more profound belief in God."

"Rubbish," McInnerney said, dismissing the subject. "And let me tell you another thing, young man. I want this talk about artificial contraception stopped. *Paul is not going to rule in favor.* The women of this archdiocese are living in mortal sin. Nearly half the women! I want you to stop reading Dostoyevsky and do your duty . . . the duty you learned in the seminary. Your duty is to save souls, save these sinners. My mother . . . my own dear mother raised ten children. She was a laundress. *Ten* moral, healthy children, none of whom took dope, or ran away, or ever broke the law, or used a pill."

At the mention of the Pope, Daugherty's mind reeled—a confused jumble of images. He found his voice.

"How do you know he . . . the Pope . . . Paul . . . is not going to rule in favor of artificial contraception?" he asked, voice wavering.

"Because he wrote me. The encyclical will be released any day now."

"But . . ." Daugherty managed, groping for words, not believing. "All the stories from Rome . . ."

"The press is wrong, as usual," McInnerney said.

"I can't . . . I can't believe it," Daugherty said. His thoughts were running wild. He grasped one: "Doesn't he understand about the population bomb? That by the year 2000 there won't be room on earth for the people, that the rivers and lakes and oceans will be polluted . . . that we won't be able to breathe the air . . . or grow enough food? That three and a half million children a year are already dying of malnutrition? That we'll have famines! Epidemics! For God's sake, what does he want, what does he expect of us?"

"My dear young man," McInnerney replied quietly. "I have been hearing that nonsense all my life. Man has always found a way to clothe and feed himself. If he can't, God will provide. That's a lot of anti-Catholic propaganda. The press has very cleverly mobilized the conservationists against us, along with other liberal elements, don't you see that?"

"But the biologists . . . the statisticians . . ."

"You can prove—or disprove—anything with figures. You ought to know that."

"Your Excellency, I'm afraid . . ." Daugherty began.

"And I want these Folk Masses stopped," the Archbishop went on. "I want you to get a haircut! Shave off those sideburns! No more gimmicks. They cause trouble. We must close ranks! Throw out the dissidents. The freaks. Solidarity is what preserved the Church for two thousand years. Not disobedience. Ecclesiastic, civil, or otherwise."

"Christ's life was a great example of civil disobedience . . ." Daugherty heard himself saying unthinkingly. It was stupid to argue.

The Archbishop threw up his arms. He raised his eyes toward Heaven.

"God help us," he said. "God, give me strength to show these young people." Then, turning to Daugherty, he said with sudden humility:

"Pray for me, Father. And forgive me. The pressures. They go hard on an old man. Often, at night, I think I should step aside, make way. I pray. I am told to stay put, for the time being. There is important work to be done here. Vital work. I must somehow show you young men why you are wrong. I must make you understand. God has picked this archdiocese as a testing ground. I want you to help me, not fight me."

Daugherty stared in astonishment. Forgive him! Help him! What kind of man was this?

Prial blew cigar smoke at the ceiling. The Archbishop cleared his throat and embarked on a new subject.

"Tom tells us All Saints' is lagging on the fund drive," he said. "Perhaps if you spent more time on that and less on writing lofty—and confusing—sermons, you'd be showing better results."

At the mention of his name, Monsignor Ryan, squeezed between McInnerney and Prial on the couch, drew himself up, tugging at his trouser creases at the knee. He was uncomfortable, both physically and spiritually. He had been invited out of courtesy, because Daugherty was technically still his subordinate. Yet he felt out of place, a supernumerary. He did not like scenes. This one, particularly. He felt a dangerous undercurrent, an irreconcilable division which might lead to a fatal explosion. The Archbishop, Ryan thought, was pressing too hard. Ryan felt sympathy for Daugherty, a paternalistic instinct. For all his faults, Daugherty was his boy. With age, he might be brought along. The Seymour Jones incident, like the Sister Mary episode (which Ryan had dismissed, not wishing to further inflame Scafidi) had been a regrettable lapse in judgment, worth perhaps a friendly word of caution. But not the third degree. The fund drive mess was not Daugherty's fault. Even Bob Favrot, Ryan's champion fund captain, had finally declared the matter hopeless—in a private telephone call to Ryan. Ryan, then, was tempted to speak up, to enter the conversation as mediator. But silence seemed the better course. There was no sense in prolonging the discomfort with yet another viewpoint. McInnerney would cool off in time. So would Daugherty.

"I've done everything possible," Daugherty said, determined now to leave at once, see LeGuiese. Later—tonight—he would call Mary. He added angrily:

"The fund drive is a colossal piece of stupidity. Theological center! Twenty million for a boondoggle like that when the blacks are starving and burning down the city! You people have lost touch with reality."

The Archbishop flushed with anger. He did not respond. He rose, walked to his credenza, took a blue pamphlet from a large stack. He returned to Daugherty, leafing through the pamphlet.

"You'll be receiving these for distribution to your parishioners in a few days." he said. "I want you to read it carefully yourself and see that you preach exactly according to these guidelines."

Daugherty accepted the pamphlet, reading the title: *Sex in Marriage. Love-giving, Life-giving.* He knew without reading what it contained.

Without further word, the Archbishop terminated the meeting. Daugherty put the pamphlet in his pocket, shook hands with Ryan, but did not kiss McInnerney's ring. He nodded good-bye and left the room, Prial behind him. In the elevator, Prial said:

"Sorry, that was a rough one."

Surprised by Prial's solicitous tone, Daugherty responded feebly:

"Thanks."

"Klein is out to nail us," Prial said, chewing his dead cigar. "He's got his teeth into something else that could really hurt."

"What's that?" Daugherty said.

"You'll see in a few days," Prial said. "If you keep reading the *Tribune.*"

He obviously did not wish to say more. Daugherty, preoccupied with more pressing thoughts, did not pursue it. Going down the hall, Prial said:

"By the way, have you been down to Halfway House lately?"

"No," Daugherty said, pleased to see Prial had dropped the disparaging "so-called."

"We're getting some bad playback from down there," Prial continued.

"What kind?"

"Dope maybe."

"It's not permitted," Daugherty said firmly.

"Maybe you ought to have a look-see," Prial said.

At the doorway, Daugherty paused, confused.

"Does the Archbishop really believe that Hanrahan stuff?" he said.

"Emphatically," Prial said. "They can't seem to agree on what the vision means, but yes, he does believe."

"And you?"

"I don't know what to believe anymore," Prial said, smiling genially. "About anything."

Daugherty walked into the warm afternoon air puzzled by Prial's parting comment. Was it meant as an overture? A plea for help or forgiveness? A veiled criticism of McInnerney? Or was he just conning? Trying to keep peace? Be everybody's friend? He felt his pocket. The pamphlet was still there. He would drive straight to LeGuiese's. There was plenty to talk about now. But first he would stop by Halfway House. It was on the way.

He drove down Massachusetts Avenue, swung around DuPont Circle, cut down a side street. He had not been in the neighborhood in many days—or was it weeks? He could not remember. He turned the corner, slowing to avoid a clutch of hippies sauntering across the street against the light. Then he saw two police cars, blue dome-lights flashing, parked in front of Halfway House. Surely not, he thought. Not today. All this could not happen to him in one day! He parked and ran along the sidewalk. On the front stoop, talking to two uniformed patrolmen, Daugherty saw a familiar face, Detective-Sergeant Patrick Donovan. The detective looked up, surprised.

"Father!" he said. "I've been trying to get you."

"What happened, Pat?" Daugherty said, looking into the rear seats of the patrol cars. The seats were empty.

"All kinds of bad news," Donovan said, frowning, tucking his notebook in his back pocket. The patrolmen went inside the house.

"One of your kids . . . girl named Sharon. Had a real bad trip. Went wild in the streets . . . we busted her. She's in bad shape. Did you know she was pregnant? We found a big batch of stuff in the house. More kids freaked out. I'm afraid I've got to shut it down."

"Oh, God!" Daugherty groaned.

"We found out who she was and notified her parents. They took her to St. Elizabeth's," Donovan said.

"What did she take?"

"LSD, I think. My boys think so anyway. Who knows? They take anything they can lay their hands on. Maybe she was chewing banana peel."

"She didn't have a record," Daugherty said. "No evidence whatsoever she was a user. She was a good kid."

"We found five pounds of grass upstairs," Donovan said.

"It's a damned shame," Daugherty said. "A damned shame. Pat, I feel responsible. It . . . it just makes me sick. This was a new bunch. I didn't have the time to work with them."

"Dan, you can't do everything. I don't know why you waste time on these kids anyway. Bunch of goddamned nuts. If I had my way, I'd lock 'em all up and throw away the key. Throw the damned book at 'em. I don't know what the country's coming to. It's one hell of a mess. I'm sorry about this. But I can't leave this place wide open. If you can find some adult to live down here, maybe I can talk to the captain. But he's plenty upset—I can tell you that."

An adult, Daugherty thought. But who? Mary maybe? If she would come back . . .

"Can you keep it out of the papers, Pat?" he said.

"I can try. But I doubt it."

"It'll ruin the house," Daugherty said, thinking of Prial, the Chancery. "I think I might know someone who could take over full-time. Give us a second chance."

"I'll try like hell. Dan. I know what this means to you. But I have my own duty—to uphold the law."

"Of course," Daugherty said. "I understand that, Pat."

"I got to get back to the station. Can I count on you to lock this place? You have a key?"

"Yes, I have a key."

"Good. When the fingerprint boys finish, lock it up tight."

"All right."

"I'll tell you one thing for your own good, Dan," Donovan said, lowering his voice, glancing up and down the sidewalk. "The Chancery won't be sorry to hear this place has been shut down."

"How come?" Daugherty said, knowing the answer.

"They've been leaning all over the captain for weeks," Donovan said. "Hell, we've had this place under twenty-four-hour surveillance. Just waiting. Now I wish we'd moved before that kid tripped out like that. She looked bad. Real bad. Well, be seeing you."

"Thank you," Daugherty said.

He waited on the stoop until the fingerprint men finished, thinking of McInnerney now as a Gestapo agent. Then he went inside. The place was a shambles. Dirt, rags, paper scattered everywhere, windows filthy, candlewax spilled and caked on the rug. The rooms smelled of body sweat and urine. He closed the front door behind him quickly, locked it as though shutting out a nightmare.

He returned to the car, spirits crushed. He would not see LeGuiese today. To hell with that. What could LeGuiese tell him now? He would go home—home—to the rectory, call St. Elizabeth's, get a medical report on Sharon, then call her parents, then call Mary. He must take time to think. The whole evening, if necessary. Telephone Jean Favrot, tell her not to come. She would probably not come anyway. Think it all out carefully. Step by step. Without emotion, without panic. It was his life, his future.

Mrs. Munally met him at the door.

"A Detective Donovan has been trying to reach you," she said, avoiding his eye.

"I know. I saw him."

"Is there something wrong?" she said.

"They closed Halfway House," Daugherty said.

"Oh, I'm so sorry," Mrs. Munally said. "Is that what the Chancery . . .?"

"No, it was not, Mrs. Munally."

"Scafidi?" she blurted.

"No. Seymour Jones."

"Oh," she said, sighing audibly. In the excitement, that minor sacrilegious episode had fled her mind.

Daugherty hurried up to his room. He telephoned St. Elizabeth's. The news was not good. Sharon had had a psychotic reaction to the drug. She must have been latent schizo, the doctor said, and tripped all the way out. He had no way of knowing if she would return to normal. He knew of cases that had lasted ten–twelve months. The baby—the fetus—might be damaged by the drug. Nothing could be done. Daugherty hung up in despair. He would have to call Sharon's parents—tomorrow. They would blame him.

Seldom had Daugherty felt so angry. The Archbishop, his *spiritual* teacher, had treated him like a child. Get a haircut! Shave his sideburns! Hell, he would grow a beard—like Christ. He picked up the pamphlet, read McInnerney's introductory remarks: no one would preach or teach against the word of Rome. It was, without qualification, a hard-line stand.

And the encyclical. Paul was crazy. They were all crazy, living in an Alice-in-Wonderland world. LeGuiese, too, lived in a fantasy. Words. Canon law. He was wrong. Dead wrong. The whole intellectual community was wrong. Maybe LeGuiese was working with McInnerney, conning him! There would be no shift in Church policy on sexuality. They would *never* drop the celibacy rule. And Mary! Sitting up there, defrocked, waiting his decision. He must call her, tell her. *At once!*

He went to the kitchen for ice. He told Mrs. Munally he would skip dinner. He returned to his room, poured a stiff drink. Then another. He picked up the pamphlet, flung it at the wall. Madness! he exclaimed to himself. *All madness!* Klein and Jones in a conspiracy to destroy the Church! They were paranoid. The Church was committing suicide. Spying on Halfway House. Closing it down. A fund drive for a theological center. He would not raise another penny for this crazy Church. He poured a new drink, gulped it down.

Excommunication! What did that mean anymore? Excommunication from what? They—those crazy people—could not separate him from his God. Who did they think they were? It was nothing. *Nothing!* A piece of paper.

"Thou art a priest forever . . ."

He picked up the telephone, placed a person-to-person call to Mary.

IX

Mary Frances Murray looked at herself in the full-length mirror on the back of her bathroom door. The skirt was short, so short it made her uneasy. She felt naked from the waist down. Was she too old? The salesgirl at Saks had tried to sell her a miniskirt! The young girls on the streets of New York were wearing *micro*skirts. How did they sit down? Mary turned, looked over her shoulder. Her legs were lanky and trim. She looked young for her age. But she did not want to shock. She examined her nails. They were growing—slowly.

The other new dresses were spread out on the bed, grouped around
her new suitcase. My trousseau! she thought, smiling to herself. The
colors, the styles were wild! Next year, probably, hemlines would fall
to the ankle. Then what would she do? She folded the dresses carefully,
delicately, placed them neatly in the suitcase. Then the underthings,
the shoes, belts, one of her pocketbooks, the plastic bag with the hair
curlers. She returned to the mirror to observe, again, the lift the dress
gave her bosom. This worried her too. But, she thought, why not?
When you've got it, flaunt it!

She snapped the latches on the suitcase. She lifted it from the bed to
the floor, placing it in line with the dome-shaped portable hair dryer
and the makeup bag that matched the suitcase. She carried the two
smaller bags downstairs, out the front door to the VW. Her mother,
who could not abide teary good-byes, had gone out. The house was
empty, silent.

She sat behind the wheel a moment, mentally checking. The car
was gassed, oiled. Her father had done that for her last night. She had
clothes, toilet articles, accessories—all new, gifts from her mother. She
had money—$500 from her father, "to launch you into a new life." She
had her driver's license, registration. She had a written leave of absence
from the Mother General. The formal papers had been sent to Rome;
they should be returned, approved, in two or three weeks.

She pulled out of the drive, thinking now of Dan, what lay ahead
five hours from now. The telephone call night before last had come as
a shock. Before it came, she had convinced herself that Dan would go
about his disengagement slowly and logically, taking one step at a time,
as LeGuiese had advised. His voice was emotional, at times incoherent,
his reasons illogical. But his message had been clear: he was leaving
the Church now—this week—and he wanted to marry her, right
away. To hell with this waiting! Please come back—live at Halfway
House. Now. What had brought him so suddenly and swiftly to his
decision, she did not know.

Afterward, in the long talk with her parents in the library, Mary had
not once been uncertain. She would go back. It was all very well for
LeGuiese to recommend this and that—that was his job. But it was
really quite impossible to follow his advice. How did one separate the
heart from the mind? They had left it up to her. She was a mature
woman. It was her life, to lead as she chose.

She parked three cars down from Halfway House, behind a battered Ford with Virginia plates. She opened the door, climbed out slowly, exposing too much thigh. She locked the door and walked up the sidewalk, trembling with excitement. Then suddenly she felt a tidal wave of doubt. Dan had been drinking. What if it was whiskey talk? What if the door was locked?

The door was not locked. It was standing open. Mounting the steps, Mary heard the high-pitched whir of a vacuum cleaner. It was a new instrument, not the low moan of the Hoover. The doubt fled. He was here, cleaning! She ran up the last two steps, into the foyer, the living room. In the far corner she saw a man—not Dan—working with an Electrolux, bent over, preoccupied, lamely dragging one foot. It was, who? What's-his-face? The custodian at All Saints'.

Scafidi did not hear Mary enter the room. Rather, he sensed her eyes on the back of his neck. He turned and saw a strikingly beautiful girl wearing a short New York dress. She was standing by the door, as though looking for someone—Daugherty? Barely pausing, Scafidi pointed toward the ceiling—meaning look upstairs. Then he returned to the machine.

Mary mounted the steps to the second floor, calling:

"Dan? Dan?"

He appeared suddenly, peering over the hall rail. He was bare-chested. His hair was disheveled, matted down by sweat, which trickled through his sideburns to his ears. He was more manly than she had ever seen him.

"You're early!" he shouted, beaming with joy, rushing down the rail, rounding the corner, coming down the stairs. He was barefooted, wearing chinos, rolled up above his ankles.

They met face to face on the stairway, he towering above her. stopping, looking down. The clothes. The hair. The soft skin. She was a vision. Fantastic! His impulse was to lift her, sweep her off her feet, smother her with kisses. But no. Later. Don't frighten her. Don't soil that crazy dress! He held out his right hand, leaning down, holding the banister with his left.

"You look fabulous," he said.

Mary felt blood rushing to her temples. His hand was wet, firm, yet tender. A perfect fit. She looked down at her hemline.

"Is it too short?"

"Very stylish," Dan said. "You look like you were born for that."

"I guess I was," she said uncertainly.

"Come on up," he said, turning, mounting the stairs.

They went to the front room. Dan sat on the windowsill, by the open window. Mary perched on the edge of an old chair, crossing her ankles underneath, tugging at the skirt. Dan lit a cigarette.

"I'm sorry," he said. "I had hoped to have it ready when you came. It was a shambles. Once we got started . . . Oh, hell. We'll have it ready before dark, I think."

"It looks lovely," she said. "It'll be fine. Now, before we say another word, I want to ask you one question."

"Shoot," he said.

"Are you sure you know what you're doing?"

"Yes. Yes, I'm sure."

"What happened?"

"Well," he said inhaling, frowning. "It's a long story. In a word, I got called down to the Chancery, chewed out for . . . for, among other things, not having a haircut! While I was there, McInnerney told me Paul was going to hand down his encyclical on contraception—disapproving the commission—in a few days . . . he had a letter from Paul. McInnerney already had some propaganda printed up . . . the old party-line. So . . ."

"You mean Paul is . . . ????"

Her hand went to her mouth. Daugherty nodded glumly.

"That's what McInnerney said."

"It's true, I suppose?" she asked.

"I don't think he'd lie, do you?"

"No."

"Oh, my God!" she said, sitting back, eyes going to the ceiling. Then she looked at Dan. "What have you done officially? Did you tell them?"

"No . . . I wrote this letter. One paragraph. I took it out to show LeGuiese. A courtesy—I thought I owed him that much. But he was in New York yesterday. Coming back tonight, I think. So I thought I better get this damned place shaped up. I picked up Scafidi, and we started in yesterday. That's really all I've done since I talked to you . . ."

Scafidi appeared in the doorway.

"Downstairs finished," he said sullenly. "What's next?"

Daugherty reached in his tight trousers' pocket and pulled out a crumpled, sweat-stained list. He ran his finger down the items.

"We've got to wash the bathrooms and the bottom shelves in the kitchen and replace the lining on the shelves. I brought some of that adhering shelf paper. It's on the sideboard."

"I'll change clothes and get to work." Mary said, getting up.

Scafidi appeared perplexed. Who was this woman?

"Oh, John," Dan said. "This is Mary Murray. Mary, this is our custodian, John Scafidi."

"How do you do?" Mary said pleasantly.

"Fine," Scafidi said. "Considering the heat."

"Yesterday was worse," Daugherty said to Mary. "The place was shut tight. Like an oven. Stunk like a . . . you know."

"Garbage dump," Scafidi said.

"Mary's going to be living here," Daugherty said to Scafidi. "And looking after the kids."

Scafidi studied the young girl intently. So she was the reason! She seemed vaguely familiar. Where had he seen her? At Mass at All Saints'? Not Mass! She was the one . . . that night . . . in the church. But she was a nun!

"Where are you from?" Scafidi said carefully.

"From?" Mary said, taken off guard. "Well, I was born in Connecticut. Grew up there and . . . well, lived there until I went into the order."

Yes! Scafidi thought. It was the same one. The one he held hands with that night in the church. Now she was fallen. A fallen nun! A spoiled nun. A sorceress. A devil! In Scafidi's gallery of evil, there was no greater menace, no more disgraceful monster.

He turned without another word, went downstairs.

"Ugh!" Mary said. "Cheery soul."

"He's seen you before," Dan said, inhaling the cigarette. "The night you came out to hear my Grand Inquisitor bit. He was hiding in the sacristy, spying."

"How do you know?"

"He told Munally, who told Ryan."

"Dan! Why didn't you tell me this before?"

"You had enough on your mind. Don't worry. Nothing came of it. Ryan doesn't believe everything he hears."

"Do you think it was wise to bring him down here?"

"It's all right. He's a damned good cleaner. Try to find one. Even a poor one."

"You're too trusting, Dan. Well . . . I . . ."

"Look, let's get this job finished. Get Scafidi out of here. Then we can lock the front door and have a good, long talk about everything."

"All right. Would you mind getting my suitcases?"

"Coming right up."

Daugherty fetched Mary's luggage from the car and put it in the front room. She shut the door and opened the suitcase, tugging a pair of new jeans and a blouse from the bottom. She lifted off her dress and hung it on a hanger in the closet, then stood for a moment, in bra and slip, feeling adventurous, sexy, letting her thoughts run free. It was strange to be standing there, almost naked, in Halfway House. Almost like being in his bedroom. If he came in now, he would see *most* of her in broad daylight! She stepped out of the slip, put on the jeans and blouse.

When the cleaning was finished, Halfway House was once more airy and habitable. The rancid smell was gone, replaced by the odor of ammonia and soap. The old porcelain bathroom fixtures gleamed, the worn kitchen linoleum shone with wax. Even Scafidi grudgingly conceded the thoroughness of the work. Mary, on the point of going to the grocery for food, said to him:

"Will you join us for dinner?"

Scafidi declined. He had seen what he had come to see. The house. The woman. The way she looked at the priest. The way Daugherty looked at her. There was evil—and scandal—brewing here. He wanted to see no more. Certainly he did not want to share their contaminated food. He accepted his money from Daugherty, picked up the All Saints' Electrolux, and departed.

They showered and changed clothes—Mary on the second floor, Daugherty on the third. In the privacy of her room, Mary unpacked, daubed herself with perfume, "Joy," another gift from her mother. She put on another new dress and some of the costume jewelry from Saks, a bracelet, pin, but no earrings. Then she made a list and went to the corner grocery, walking stiffly. Her muscles ached.

She cooked dinner and served it in the dining room, a simple meal of spaghetti with her special meat sauce, a green salad with Italian dressing, garlic bread, a half bottle of Chianti, coffee. During dinner, she told all that had happened to her. Then Dan recounted, in detail, the events of his last two days, dwelling on the scene at the Chancery with McInnerney, Prial, and Ryan. She listened attentively, eating slowly, delicately.

"So, I guess that did it," he concluded, lighting a cigarette. "By the way, a great dinner."

She said thank you, smiling. He reached for and held her hand. squeezing.

"So here we are," she laughed. "Alone. Now what do we do?"

"For one thing," Dan replied, "I've got to get my letter in the mail. Maybe I ought to call and see if LeGuiese is back. If he isn't back tonight, the heck with it. I'll take it by and give it to McInnerney."

"I'd like to read it."

"It's out at the rectory—locked in my drawer. It doesn't say much. I wrote a longer one—full of self-pity and criticism of the Church and all that, but I tore it up. The new one merely says that I cannot teach or preach what my conscience tells me is wrong and therefore I am separating from the Church."

"You didn't say you were getting married?"

"I didn't think that was McInnerney's business. Later, I'll petition Rome—after I've broken the law. Then I'll be excommunicated. 'Let him perish.' Mary, they're all sick. Let them go on with their Pauline views of sexuality—blind idiots. I've had it up to here. I don't give a damn."

"Are you absolutely sure?"

"Absolutely. Anyway—what means excommunication? No mere mortal can separate me from my God. Once a priest . . ."

"Will you remain a priest?" she asked uneasily.

"Of course. I mean . . . Yes. In a sense. I'll preach and teach on the side. For openers, we'll make what we can of this place. Then we'll branch out, see what happens. Maybe I can launch my priest-worker concept in the ghetto. By the way, I think I have a priest who'll marry us in the Church—secretly."

"Who?" she asked.

"I don't think you know him. Joe McDivitt, assistant pastor out at St. Jude's. Real fine guy. Classmate of mine in the seminary. Didn't I ever tell you about him? He was the guy who used to smuggle beer into the dorm and keep it in the toilet bowl tank. *Great* guy. Played first-string football at Notre Dame."

Mary hunched her eyebrows in deep thought.

"Dan. I don't mean to be a wet blanket. But . . . we've never really discussed this . . . What about money? How're we going to live?"

"I've been thinking about that," he said cheerily. "Maybe I can get an OEO grant to run this place. We could put your Montessori school in the basement and maybe you could get *your* grant renewed, now that you have quarters."

She pursed her lips.

"But Dan. When OEO finds out . . . we'll be controversial. They may be scared off. Besides, an OEO grant takes *time*."

Dan frowned.

"I can get a job, too," he said.

"Doing what?"

"Social work. Welfare counseling. Ex-priests are in great demand these days. Isn't that ironic?"

"You know what your take-home pay would be? It would hardly be worth your time."

"I could drive a cab. Mary. Stop worrying about money. The Lord will provide, as Ryan says."

They cleared the table and did the dishes, Mary washing, Dan wiping. Mary missed the convenience of her mother's dishwasher. The facilities at Halfway House were rather primitive. Nothing like the elegance of the Sacred Heart mansions. But, as Dan said, it was fun doing things with your hands. Together!

"I'll have to get some life insurance," Dan said, mind returning to economic matters. "That five-thousand-dollar policy I have has my seminary for a beneficiary. Very clever, these Chinese."

"Are you entitled to GI insurance?" Mary said.

"I don't know. I'll have to find out."

"You mean you don't *know?*"

"What did I need with GI insurance? If I left it to my parents, it would only cause them a tax problem or something."

"You won't miss the soft life of a priest?" Mary said. "I saw somewhere that a priest lives, economically, like a bachelor earning twenty-five thousand a year."

"We'll make out."

After the dishes, they went to the living room. It was cooler than the kitchen, swept by a gentle breeze from the open windows. Mary tuned the battered radio to soft music on WMAL. Dan sat in the dimness smoking, thinking. She sat beside him, taking his hand.

"Are you sure, Dan?" she said.

"Positive."

Her body was soft, tender, warm. Dan stroked her silky hair with his fingers, not talking, yet feeling the bond, close, deep, intimate. Something—a feeling of contentment and safeness that he could not put in words, lover's words, which were foreign to him, and would sound shallow and trite, too limp for the occasion. He held her hands, intertwining fingers. He kissed her, a strange taste, like a copper penny. Her lips were soft. They kissed again for a long time.

"Oh, darling, darling," Mary said, pausing for breath. "I *want* you. Darling . . ."

The words came like thunder.

"I want you too," he whispered. It was all right now. The decisions had been made. The letter would go tomorrow. They would be married by Joe McDivitt soon. There was no point in waiting, no merit in discretion. They went to her room.

Mary did not know what to do about the light. Or about the clothes she wore. She stood, frozen in uncertainty, until he snapped off the light, until she felt his fingers on the back of her dress. Dan proceeded fearfully, blindly, confused by the intricate, unfamiliar lashing of her dress, her bra. Then it was dark and they were both naked, standing kissing, loving.

He led her to the bed. They lay down, side by side, kissing and gasping, body-heat radiating. He felt her mound, experimentally, like an explorer in dark continents. Her pulsating response frightened him. Then he felt her fingers on his sex, embryo fingernails, childlike, hurting. And then, without warning, a sudden sublime eruption, a cascade of shivering ecstasy, into her palm, her fingers. The fear, tightness seeping away.

"Damn," he whispered into her ear. "Amateur. I'm sorry."

She held him tight.

"Wait," she whispered.

And, intertwined in the dark, they waited.

On the street below a dark figure hunched behind the wheel in a battered Ford parked opposite, eyes on the second-floor window of Halfway House. Scafidi had left but he had not gone home. Instead, he had gone to a nearby White Tower for a hamburger. There, he had sat on a stool at the counter, reading the *Evening Star*. Not ordinarily a follower of current events, Scafidi had nonetheless been hypnotized by a profile of Sirhan Sirhan, Robert Kennedy's assassin. This wide-ranging biography also spoke of Dr. King's killer, James Earl Ray, and of John Kennedy's murderer, Lee Harvey Oswald. In one bold attempt to explain the inexplicable, a noted psychiatrist speculated that all the murders came about for common cause: man's innate frustration and primitive hostility, his lack of identity in our dehumanizing computer society, his loss of individuality, these culminating in twisted minds with such intensity it led to a compelling desire to act in a single decisive, dramatic act. To right in one blow all the wrongs of a sick society. There had been pictures of Sirhan, Ray, and Oswald, all in a row, all similar. Scafidi had torn these from the paper and tucked them in his wallet.

After the hamburger, he had driven to Haines Point, a public park on the Potomac. There he had wandered along the stone wall, listened to the gurgle of the water, watched the skies. In summer, he often watched the skies. In those warm months, UFO's stepped up activity and boldness. A sharp observer who knew the heavens, who could discriminate, might easily see a gleaming object, might even be lucky, like many, to be contacted or signaled. The Venusians were exceptionally active this summer. There had been countless sightings plus the observed landing in Canada.

But Scafidi's luck was poor this night. He saw nothing.

Headed homeward, he was mysteriously drawn back to Halfway House, as though he had left unfinished business there. He parked and peered intently into the dark. He saw *her* VW, *his* MG, both parked where he had last seen them. Then he saw the shadowy figures in the living room, then in the front bedroom, the light going out, the whole house dark. Having seen all this, he started his car, drove off slowly, lights extinguished, mind seething with rage . . .

X

Marvin Klein read George Emerson's copy on the St. Luke's sale slowly and admiringly, feeling the onrush of excitement that came when, as a reporter, he got his teeth into a good exclusive. Emerson had pried the key element from HUD: an official statement confirming that IDA would purchase the cathedral grounds, plus "improvements thereto" under urban development Title B Funding. It was a long piece, thorough, incisive, with only one or two holes: it lacked a pompous justification from the Chancery and "angry reaction" from outraged Catholic clergy. Klein put a piece of copy paper in his typewriter, stared moodily at the keys, then wrote the headline:

WAR AGENCY FOR GHETTO!
CATHOLIC LANDMARK GIVES WAY TO IDA

He called George Emerson to his desk.

"Beautiful job," Klein said, showing the headline.

"Thanks," Emerson said. "I like that."

"Ah . . . good," Klein said carefully, not wishing to offend or imply criticism of Emerson's reporting or writing. "I think we could use one or two more details. We need a quote from the Chancery and reaction from a dissident priest—somebody like my friend Daugherty at All Saints'."

"We don't have much time," Emerson said. "HUD says they will hold this for us twenty-four hours, not a second longer. They mean it."

"It won't take long. I'll get it for you. In fact, what would you say to a sidebar on McInnerney? A Man in the News Profile?"

"You know I can't write a profile," Emerson said.

"I'll do it," Klein said. "I'll call him and go see him."

"I thought that door was closed."

"I've got something that may open it—the Carter deal."

Emerson looked doubtful.

"Maybe one thing at a time," he said.

But Klein, picturing the front page, had made up his mind. He glanced at his watch. There was not much time. No time for sparring with Prial on the telephone. He would jump in a cab and go straight to the Chancery.

"Send this on to Composing," Klein said. "I'll make a run at the Chancery and see what happens. At least they can't claim we didn't go to them for their side. I'll call my friend Daugherty. I've got to call him anyway to make a tennis date."

"All right," Emerson said. without enthusiasm. He was not anxious to encourage anything that would take away from his own piece, or rob it of space.

"Don't worry, George," Klein said, sensing this. "We'll run your piece in full. It's beautiful."

Klein departed in a rush. He flagged a cab and rode to the Chancery, transported now by the electricity of the story, the exclusive, the impending battle, revenge.

He debarked from the cab, observing with satisfaction Seymour Jones's desultory pickets. He rang the bell and opened the door without waiting. He walked directly to the receptionist.

"My name is Marvin Klein," he said. "I'm with the *Tribune*. I'd like to see the Archbishop, please."

"Will you have a seat?" the girl said politely.

Klein consulted his wristwatch with an urgent movement.

"I'm rushed," he said. "I have a deadline."

"Do you have an appointment?" the girl said.

"No. No." Klein said impatiently.

"Then please be seated. I'll tell the Vicar General you're here."

She turned her attention to the PBX. Klein did not sit. He paced the marble floor, angry for the delay. He did not want to see Prial. That would mean further delay. A minute ticked by . . . two . . . three.

Vicar General Prial was in his office, working in a cloud of dense cigar smoke. The priority task confronting him was the Archbishop's appearance at St. Luke's Cathedral, only six days away. Prial himself was composing the statement McInnerney would give from the pulpit, the announcement of the sale. He had "coordinated" through the public affair offices of HUD and IDA. The latter would make the necessary media contacts. There had been no hint to him from either HUD or IDA that an official statement had already been provided George Emerson of the *Tribune*. As far as Prial knew, his strategy of bringing pressure on *Tribune* advertisers had worked. Klein had evidently dropped the story.

He was seated at his typewriter, slowly pecking out the Archbishop's forthcoming words, when the call came from the receptionist announcing the presence (in the Chancery!) of Marvin Klein, who wanted to see his Excellency! Jesus, Mary, and Joseph, Prial thought. What now! He put on his jacket and left his office. He walked down the corridor, swiftly. There must be some mistake. Certainly Marvin Klein was not waiting in the foyer to see the Archbishop! But yes. There he was.

"Good morning, Mr. Klein," Prial said coldly.

"Good morning," Klein replied, matching Prial's tone. "I would like to see the Archbishop briefly, if that is convenient."

"What about?" Prial said.

"The St. Luke's situation."

"We have nothing further to say about St. Luke's," Prial returned, seething. So. He had not given up after all. "At least we have nothing to say to the *Tribune*. Now, would you be so good as to leave?"

"More specifically," Klein said, "I would like to inquire as to Mr. John Carter's role in the St. Luke's affair."

"Mr. Carter's role? He has no role."

"He serves on the financial council, does he not?"

"Yes, he does."

"And the council was informed, I take it, in advance of the IDA deal?"

"I'm afraid that's none of your business."

"I'm afraid it is," Klein said. "Mr. Carter has bought up considerable land surrounding St. Luke's, for what he described to me as investment purposes. It cannot be coincidence that he bought in that particular area. He took advantage of inside information received while serving on the council. In my book, to use your own favorite words, this is irresponsible, divisive, reckless, and unethical."

The words sliced into Prial like a hail of knives. It couldn't be true! Not John Carter. Or could it? Did that explain his reluctance to withdraw Eliott TV advertising from the *Tribune*? Blamed it on his district managers. This was dynamite—if true. He must find out more—what, precisely, Carter had done, what precisely Klein intended to do with his information.

"Come on in my office," Prial said.

"I'd rather discuss this directly with the Archbishop, if you don't mind," Klein said.

"I'll see what I can do," Prial said.

He left Klein standing in the foyer. In the privacy of his office, he telephoned the Archbishop, relaying the news. He recommended that he see Klein—briefly. Then Prial returned to the corridor.

"Let's go on up," he said.

They rode the elevator in silence. Prial pushed open the Archbishop's door. McInnerney was waiting, standing by his desk, pleasant, uneasy, as though confronting the Devil.

Prial made the introductions. Klein shook hands, compiling a mental picture for his Profile: Irish, firm handshake, clear eyes, flinty, stubborn. Establishment. The Archbishop invited Klein to sit.

"Now, Mr. Klein," McInnerney said politely, "the Vicar General tells me you bring news of Mr. Carter. I was not aware of his . . . I'm not aware of his *personal* financial transactions. He has served ably on the council, has rendered valuable service to this Chancery and the community for a number of years. Very valuable. Perhaps you can enlighten us?"

Klein told all that he knew about John Carter's real estate purchases: the corporation fronts, the buying up of the land, Carter's suggestion that he might build a "warehouse." As he talked, the Archbishop and Prial listened attentively, deadpan. Mentally, Klein made further notes on McInnerney: pasty-faced, feminine hands, chainsmoker (Camels). Then he was finished.

"Do you intend to publish that?" Prial said, sitting on the couch, lighting a cigar, concealing his worry. A Carter expose might torpedo all his carefully laid plans for the Archbishop's visit to St. Luke's.

"Maybe," Klein said.

"What do you have against this Chancery?" McInnerney said, smiling genially.

"I have nothing against the Chancery," Klein said. "Or rather, I didn't until you called for a boycott of my paper—which I consider blackmail. Beyond that, I question the wisdom of selling off St. Luke's to IDA at a time like this. Only a few weeks ago, the militant blacks were burning down the ghetto. This could touch off a new wave of violence."

"If you and the other media wish to provoke it," McInnerney said calmly, "then I suppose there's a danger of violence."

"The media does not provoke violence," Klein said. "As I tried to explain before to the Vicar General, we merely report a climate that exists."

"You fellows inflame them," McInnerney rejoined. "They *perform* for you and TV. Look how you've egged on this boy Seymour Jones. Where would he be without your publicity?"

"I don't think so," Klein said. "He's a very able man. We need people like that to provide leadership in the ghetto. They should be supported. *You* should support him."

"We've done quite a lot for him," McInnerney said. "*And* his people. That's what I can't understand. Now he has *pickets* downstairs. Little boys who should be doing more constructive things."

The Archbishop rose and returned to his desk, withdrew a fact sheet from the drawer. He gave it to Klein, who glanced at it curiously, then returned it.

"I have one," he said.

"Keep it," Prial said. "We've got more."

Klein folded the fact sheet and put it in his pocket.

"Where will the St. Luke's blacks worship?" he said.

"We're going to take care of them," Prial said.

"With a new church," McInnerney said.

"Where will that be and when?" Klein said, withdrawing a notebook. If true, it must be noted in the story.

"We're not prepared to say just now," Prial said. "We're negotiating for the land. We don't want them to know who we are. Otherwise the price will double on us."

This went into Klein's notebook as: vague plans, new church. Prial lying? McInnerney actually gentle man. Heart of steel maybe. Not contentious.

"We'd rather you didn't mention the new church," Prial said, glancing uneasily at Klein's notebook.

"Why?"

"We want to make an announcement down there at the right time and circumstance," Prial said, "to avoid undue adverse reaction, any distortion . . ."

"I think you better hurry," Klein said. "I'm running my IDA story tomorrow."

"Tomorrow?" Prial exclaimed, disbelieving.

"Tomorrow. I have an official statement from HUD."

Klein withdrew a Xerox of the statement from his pocket. He passed it to Prial, who snatched it eagerly. He read the official document with anxious eyes, grasping, yet failing to grasp. The duplicity! HUD had given this to Klein for what reason? Why hadn't they told them? Klein would tear down every constructive brick they had mortared in place. The HUD people did not understand that. They were out of their minds. Crazy.

"Where did you get this?" he demanded, passing the paper to McInnerney.

"We have good friends there," Klein said. "The doors over there are not closed."

So, Prial thought. Some damned fourth-echelon bureaucrat, somebody in the public affairs department, currying favor with Klein. Buying protection by tossing out a bone. Wait until he got them on the telephone! He'd go right to the top with this, by God. They would not push him, McInnerney, the Church, around like this. They were making a fool of the Chancery. Now, on top of it, John Carter!

"Are you putting Carter in your story?" Prial asked.

"No," Klein said. "I'm saving that for later."

"I see," McInnerney said, returning the HUD statement.

"We don't know anything whatsoever about the Carter thing," Prial said quickly, emphatically.

"I understand that," Klein said. "I believe you. I wonder if you stopped to think he might have been doing that for years?"

"Doing what?" McInnerney said.

"Using his position on the council to better himself personally."

"I don't believe that," McInnerney said. "Not John Carter."

"There's nothing wrong with it anyway," Prial said. "Nothing il-legal."

"I didn't say illegal," Klein said. "I said unethical."

"He's one of your great supporters," Prial said.

"You mean you couldn't pressure him to pull his ad schedules?" Klein said.

Prial seethed. Why were they wasting their time with this jerk?

"Is there anything else?" Prial said curtly, ostentatiously looking at his watch.

"I came primarily to inform you of our story on St. Luke's and to get a statement," Klein said.

"I told you we have nothing to say."

"Then I guess we're all wasting each other's time," Klein said.

The Archbishop's phone jangled softly.

"Excuse me," he said to Klein, lifting the receiver. It was the Pope's Nuncio, calling with an urgent message. McInnerney accepted the call. The Nuncio was calling to inform him that, within the hour, the Vatican would be releasing Pope Paul's encyclical, *Humanæ Vitae* (Of Human Life), dealing with artificial contraception and other matters concern-ing the Sacrament of Matrimony. McInnerney, glancing with alarm at Klein, replied guardedly, thanking the Nuncio for this courtesy. Then he hung up. Prial stared curiously, seeking some sign to explain the call. McInnerney gave none. He turned to Klein:

"Before you leave, there is something I would like to say, Mr. Klein. I would like to make a direct and candid appeal to you. If there is any way possible, I would like to heal the unfortunate breach that has come between us. We have large and continuing interests—and problems—in the ghetto. Just as, I take it, you do. There is a common interest. It seems to me we'd both be better off if we worked together, rather than being at each other's throats. We have done much for the blacks—read the fact sheet—and we will continue to do much. You have somehow gotten the impression that we're bigots, or indifferent, or both, that we're ogres. Nothing could be farther from the truth. Actually, we're Shepherds of Christ. I am a bishop, a teacher. I am not skilled in slick public relations. I have done my share in the field of social problems. But you must try to understand this simple fact: here, in this Chancery, in Rome, we are concerned first and foremost with saving men's souls. We are not—and should not be—social activists. Our concern is the spiritual life of mankind. We are having family squabbles over certain matters, not all of them minor. We sincerely ask you, in the Name of Christ, to let us thrash them out in private. I implore you from the bottom of my heart not to publish your St. Luke's article. It may do us untold harm. You simply can't realize how much needless trouble it will cause us. We desperately need our time and attention for more pressing problems."

Rising from his chair, Klein found himself touched by the sincerity and humility of the Archbishop's words. Not merely touched, but thrown off stride. He barely managed to mumble:

"Yes . . . there is a common interest . . . but sometimes I feel that I am fighting all alone . . ."

He composed himself for his departure. He smiled, shook hands with both men. Then he left, hurrying to the elevator, leaving Prial behind in the Archbishop's chambers.

Returning to the office by cab, Klein recalled Serena's accusation: that he was meddling unnecessarily in Church affairs. The ad manager, Kenneth Penn, had said much the same. Perhaps they were right. Maybe he had been overdoing it. It was a thin line. Maybe he ought to tone down Emerson's copy—at least scrap the scare headline. He would not kill the story. Emerson had worked too hard for it. But they might angle it differently . . .

He came into the city room, peeling off his coat. There, he noticed unusual activity at the city desk, felt a new electric current in the air. Something big was coming over the ticker—a bulletin. Seeing Klein, the copy editor, Jim Cunningham, a potbellied, florid-faced journalist of the old school, came waddling to meet him, carrying a swatch of ticker, chewing an old cigar.

"Bulletin from the Vatican, Chief," Cunningham said. "The Pope's encyclical. Released about an hour ago. According to a Vatican spokesman, it's a hard-line, anti-pill stand."

Klein froze midway to his desk. He snatched the ticker, scanned it, disbelieving. He read it twice, shaking his head. It was true. He turned to Cunningham.

"What do you think, Joe?"

Joe Cunningham, Klein knew, was orthodox Catholic, father of eight.

"What can I say?" he replied, shifting the cigar in his mouth. "A lot of people are going to be very unhappy. But a lot of people will be happy."

"Who?" Klein said.

"People like my wife. She figures *she* had to do it, so why should the next generation get off scot-free?"

Klein shook his head. Cunningham spoke again, lowering his voice:

"But, tell you the truth, Chief, I think it's criminal. It's gonna blow the Church wide open."

Klein went to his desk, feeling a sudden surge of rage. At Pope Paul. Then McInnerney. The telephone call to McInnerney! That must have been a tip-off. Why hadn't he mentioned it? How long had he known? They were conning him again—like the day they staged the lunch for the theological center briefing. Why couldn't they play open and aboveboard? Why this slipping around? Why couldn't they be honest?

He sat, staring out the window, thinking. Beyond all that—the duplicity—what was wrong with Pope Paul? The encyclical was madness. Pure madness. Millions in Africa, India, Latin America already starving. Populations exploding. The world's food supply shrinking drastically. Now, by order of the one man who could have done most to stop it, six hundred million of Catholics—one fifth of the earth's population —must go on propagating at a furious rate, *encouraging* others to follow their example. Was Paul blind to reality? How could he be? He had traveled—the first Pope to leave Italy since 1812. New York. The Holy Land. Bogotá. He *could not* be unaware. He *must* know. Then why?

Impulsively Klein picked up the telephone, dialed All Saints' rectory, asked for Father Daugherty. The woman on the telephone seemed vague, distressed by the question. Father Daugherty was not there. She did not know where he could be reached. Would he care to leave a message? Klein said no thanks, hung up feeling a monumental frustration. He turned back to his work.

He turned to his typewriter to compose an editorial. He began with the headline: THE DEATH OF MANKIND. It grew in intensity as he typed. When it was finished, he sent it to Jim Cunningham, who returned it immediately with a comment scrawled in red grease pencil: TOO STRONG. Meanwhile, other editors shaped the encyclical story for the front page. The Emerson piece on St. Luke's was rescheduled for the following day. It would not do to overload one edition with anti-Catholic stories.

Klein left the office that day still angry. As an editor, he had done all that he could. He had brought the word, the pronouncement from

Rome, and added a dissenting comment—vastly toned down from the first draft. They would stay on the story—ride it as long as the readers were interested. All week, if necessary. Then, like all stories, it would fade from the front pages, replaced by a new outrage of mankind, a new folly.

Turning out of the parking lot, he jammed on the brakes, remembering that he had meant to call Seymour Jones, tip him that the Chancery planned some kind of show at St. Luke's, an official ceremony putting a good face on the sale. He turned his car north, toward the ghetto, St. Luke's. He would deliver the message in person.

He found Jones in his "office" behind the gym, reading *Soul on Ice.* Jones laid the book aside.

"What's the matter with you?" Jones said. "You look pissed off at the world."

Klein grumbled, laid the afternoon *Tribune* on Jones's desk. The headline was bold and black: POPE BANS PILL. While Jones scanned the story, Klein sat down in a rickety chair, tilted back precariously.

"The Chancery will like that," Jones commented, folding, returning the paper.

"Keep it," Klein said.

"So what else is new?" Jones asked. "When are you going to do your St. Luke's–IDA story?"

"Tomorrow."

"I been thinking on that," Jones said, suddenly rising.

"Thinking what?"

"That maybe I ought to do something."

"Such as?"

"Such as—I ask myself—what would Dr. King do in my place?"

"And?"

"I think he might have a staged a protest, some kind of nonviolent thing."

"Well . . . you may be interested," Klein said, tilting his chair forward. "I came by to tell you I picked up a hint at the Chancery today. They're probably planning a little show down there. Something ceremonial probably, to put a good face on the announcement of the sale. I would say quite soon, maybe this weekend."

"I think you're right," Jones said quickly. "*Something's* going on over there. The pastor's been running around like a chicken with his head cut off."

"That's probably it. What were you thinking?"

"I had this idea. I was thinking maybe I might do something more than picket. I tell you, I'm having a hell of a job recruiting pickets. It's too hot. They're lazy. They don't want to do it."

"What's your idea?"

"Well, inasmuch as this cathedral was built by black money—that is, going back to slave days—then why not ask the Church to give the blacks the money from the sale? It's a black parish, supported by a black community. All they're going to do, now, is take the money and put it out in the white suburbs. Right? But suppose I stand up and demand the money?"

Klein thought about that. Seymour's logic was faulty. The sins of the fathers ought not to be visited on the sons. If that were the case, the whole world would be guilty. On the other hand, it was not a bad idea. It would make a story, a headline. The Chancery would be hard-pressed to find reasons to deny the request. After all, it *was* a black community. Yet . . .

'I don't think it will work," Klein said. "I mean, I don't think they'd give you the money."

"I *know* that," Jones said, airily. "But it might scare the hell out of them. And . . ." he paused. "It might put me in a good bargaining position. With this, I put them on the defensive. Then maybe I quietly drop the demand in return for permission to stay here in the gym."

"They're going to tear the gym down."

"Maybe. Maybe not. Maybe I can get them to give me enough money to build a brand-new neighborhood center."

Klein thought about that. Jones was dreaming. Yet why kill a dream? As though reading his thoughts, Jones quoted:

"I have a dream . . ."

"That's all it is," Klein said.

"Will you send somebody to cover it?" Jones asked. "Can you find out if the Archbishop's really coming down here? And, if so, exactly when? If he is coming, I might just face him, right across the communion rail. Eyeball to eyeball, like Dr. King.

"I'll find out," Klein said. "I'll give you a call."

Klein drove off, thinking of McInnerney, Prial, the Pope, the encyclical. The editorial, the headline, had not discharged all his spleen. It had been a long time since he had been so thoroughly aroused. He felt an overpowering desire to do something more. To mobilize. To fight. Seeing a public telephone, he swung the car to the curb, jumped out, again called Father Daugherty at All Saints'. This time the woman said, no, she had not seen Father Daugherty, but if it were urgent, he might try calling Halfway House.

Klein hung up, puzzled. Halfway House was shut down, he thought. He searched in his pocket for another dime. He was out.

"Oh, hell!" he said, returning to the car. Halfway House was not far—less than ten blocks. He would drive there.

He gunned off, taking the shortest way. Coming opposite the house, he stopped, peering from the street. The front door was closed. It seemed deserted. Yet, there was Daugherty's MG. He parked, picked up the paper, hurried up the front stoop, ringing the bell, waited.

He heard noises inside. Good. In a moment, Daugherty, sleepy-eyed, unchained the door, peeped out.

"Dan!" Klein said. "I saw your car . . . I thought I'd stop in."

Daugherty swung the door open. He was only partly dressed. Mary was still upstairs, in bed. Damn, he thought, of all people! Did he also know Mary's car? No.

"May I come in?" Klein said.

"Sure . . . sure. Come in. I was taking a nap. Been working like hell. Cleaning this joint. Getting it in shape."

They went inside. Daugherty slammed the door, spoke in a loud voice, to warn Mary. Klein unfolded the paper, showed Daugherty the headline.

Seeing the news, officially, in cold type, brought back the rage in Daugherty's chest. The *ignorance* and *arrogance!* Paul, there in the Vatican, living in wondrous pomp on his golden throne, as far removed from reality as man could be, advised by sick, doddering reactionaries in the Curia, a dungheap of corruption, body stink, and foul breath. There, dining on plates of gold, Paul had spoken, and he had said, once again, let them eat cake. Daugherty wanted to scream his outrage. Instead, he returned the paper.

"Yes. I'd heard about that. It's sick. I . . . I just don't know what to say. There's no explaining it, except to conclude they're all madmen."

"That was my reaction," Klein said.

"Yes," Daugherty said. "Madness."

They stood, awkwardly.

"Would you like some coffee?"

Daugherty went toward the kitchen. Klein came behind, saying:

"I'll help you."

"That's all right," Daugherty replied, remembering the luncheon dishes on the counter. Dishes for two. "I can manage."

But Klein followed him to the kitchen. The dishes were just as they left them on the table. Two places. Klein saw them at once. Daugherty turned on the gas beneath the tea kettle, spooned instant coffee into mugs.

"What are you going to do about it?" Klein persisted.

Daugherty turned to Klein, searching his eyes.

"I don't know," he said quietly.

"You don't sound like the old rebel I used to know. Dan, is there something wrong?"

The kettle whistled. Daugherty poured and stirred the water. He handed Klein a mug.

"No," he said, blowing on his coffee. "Nothing wrong."

"What are you doing here? I thought this place was shut down."

"I'm . . . I'm reopening it. Uh . . . oh, hell. Marv. Come in the living room. I've got something to tell you."

It was pointless—and possibly dangerous—for him to deceive Marvin Klein. Better to confide, put it off the record. They went to the living room.

"You remember Mary Murray? Her Montessori school?"

"Certainly."

"Well, off the record, she left the order and she's coming back to run it. We hope to set it up here. Maybe."

"Really?" Klein said. "Why?"

"A lot of reasons. They wanted to pull her back into the home office in an administrative job. She wanted to keep working with the kids, the blacks."

"A good yarn," Klein said, making a mental note. "When's she coming?"

"Aw . . . oh, hell, Marv. She's here now."

Daugherty looked at Klein earnestly. He added: "There's a lot I have to tell you—off the record. Can I do it that way?"

"Sure," Klein said, now very curious.

"Wait a minute."

Daugherty went to the hall, called Mary's name. Then added:

"We have a visitor. Come on down."

Mary came down the stairs, into the room, looking sheepish, embarrassed, yet very pretty without makeup.

"Hi, Mary," Klein said. "Dan just told me the news. Off the record."

Mary's eyes grew wide.

"*What* news?"

"That you're . . . that you've leaped the wall . . . that you're coming down here to run this joint."

"Oh," she said. "Yes."

"There's more," Daugherty said, going to Mary's side, arms encircling her waist. "Also off the record."

"Well, I'll be damned," Klein said. "Stupid me. Crack reporter? Christ, I'm blind as a bat."

Mary turned suddenly to Klein, eyes fearful.

"Marv, don't you dare print it."

Klein smiled.

"I'm sorry. We're off the record completely. I won't print it until *you* want it printed. *If* you want it printed."

Mary sighed.

"We don't want to deceive you," she said. "But I was telling Dan last night. I don't want the public life. Not the Netter or the Kavanaugh or the Girandola or the Longo bit. If it has to be—and we're at your mercy—let us get our own lives adjusted first. This isn't easy."

"Naturally," Klein said. "I'll bury it, with one condition. I want to be at the wedding. Have you really resigned, Dan?"

"Not officially. My letter goes to the Chancery today."

"We're going to move in here," Mary said, "and reopen the house. Work with the runaways. I'm going to start up my school again—in the basement. Dan hopes to divide his time between here and welfare work in the ghetto. The kind of work he loves."

"I don't suppose I could write that you both resigned because of . . . in protest against the encyclical?" Klein smiled—showing Mary his headline.

"Don't be foolish," Mary smiled back. "It goes much deeper than that."

She took the paper and read avidly.

"And not celibacy either," Daugherty put in. "It's the whole thing. It's rather difficult . . . complicated . . . to explain."

"I understand," Klein said. "But what I don't understand is why so many of you are quitting. Just lying down and playing dead."

"We're not going to lie down and play dead," Mary said, looking up from the paper. "We're going to do our part, in the best way we can."

"I mean in the organized structure," Klein persisted. "If enough of you stood up . . . made your views known, they'd *have* to come around."

"Don't count on it," Daugherty laughed sarcastically. "Not after this. Paul really means it. I mean . . . this is the signal. He's going to take us back to pre-Council, to . . . to . . . *Trent,* for God's sake."

Klein was silent a moment, then said: "I thought the Council gave the bishops, the laity, all kinds of new authority and power . . . the synod of bishops . . ."

"Don't delude yourself, Marv," Daugherty replied. "As McInnerney says, the Church is not a democracy. All that talk of delegating power was just that—talk . . . lip service . . . done with mirrors. Paul appointed a commission to study artificial contraception. From what I heard, it voted to change the rule—to permit some forms of birth control under some circumstances. But now look. You see what good it did. So what good does it do to speak of synods, councils, associations, and so on? The man is arrogant. He rules arrogantly, like an absolute monarch. There is no way to negotiate, influence, or appeal a decision by him. All his thinking is governed by those stupid octogenarians in the Curia. That's the reality of it. You might as well face it."

Klein drew himself up, a trifle pompously.

"The birth control decision," he said, "is not merely . . . is no longer just a *Catholic* matter. I think it is fair to say that with his decision, he is tampering with the fate of mankind. You know the statistics on population. Already six hundred million Catholics! When the Pope tampers with the future of mankind, then he is open game, for anybody. McInnerney asked me not to meddle in the private affairs of the Church. But, as I see it, it is no longer a strictly private affair. The Pope cannot arrogantly dispose like a monarch, when the fate of man is in the balance. That custom went out quite some time ago."

"So what do you intend to do?" Mary said.

"Fight," Klein said grimly. "In every way I know how. Educate the people. When educated, they have a way of overthrowing blind and arrogant monarchs. There aren't many left in the world."

"That's true," Daugherty said, "but the Pope is pretty solidly entrenched."

"Not so solid as you might think," Klein said. "They said that of the Hapsburgs, the Czars of Russia, the Bourbons. They didn't get away with it. Really, I'm serious."

"But you're *one* man," Mary said, sighing. "What can *you* do?"

"I am the press," Klein said, more pompously than he intended.

"And my job is to safeguard the public interest. I *wish* I could get help from people like you."

"Considering the circumstances," Daugherty said, sweeping his hand around the room, shrugging helplessly, "we're not exactly the best troops to send into the field against the Pope. I'd say we were pretty vulnerable. Soft targets. Wouldn't you?"

"No," Klein replied.

"How so?" Mary said.

"You said you hadn't sent in your letter yet," Klein replied coolly. "That means you're still on the inside. Before you leave, you could stand up and shout. Be counted. Hang in there long enough to get something rolling."

"Get *what* rolling?" Daugherty said.

"I don't know. Something. We can think of something. Maybe the St. Luke's deal. Did I tell you McInnerney had sold St. Luke's to IDA? They're going to tear it down and put up a headquarters office building. The blacks down there are on the warpath. Seymour Jones is going to demand the Chancery give the money from the sale to the blacks. Maybe you could go down there and pitch in."

"No, no," Daugherty said impatiently. "That's the wrong issue. Who wants that damned cathedral? Any cathedral? They won't give Seymour a dime. McInnerney desperately needs that money for the theological center. Now . . . *there's* something you could take issue on . . ."

"Dan," Mary said quietly. "You said . . ."

"I know," Daugherty replied, biting his lip. "I . . . well. Anyway, St. Luke's is *definitely* the wrong thing . . . a sideshow. A tempest in a teapot."

"It's a good local story," Klein said. "And maybe a national story— if Seymour demands the money. That could spin heads in Chanceries all over the world. Put them on notice that they're accountable. If you could plant that idea—the idea of accountability . . ."

"Still . . ." Dan said. "Look, Marv. You need somebody who isn't so vulnerable. Frankly, we've got our own problems to work out. Big problems. I'm sure you understand. I'll give you a couple of names. Very savvy young priest named Joe McDivitt out at St. Jude's. I'll give him a ring for you. Then, let's see. You ought to go see Monsignor LeGuiese at CU, a pal of Curran's. Very top-notch guy. In fact, you ought to *start* with LeGuiese."

"How do you spell it?" Klein pulled out his notebook, pencil poised.

XI

Jean Favrot sat at the kitchen table, drinking coffee in early morning solitude, reading the *Washington Post*. The story was there at great length: a special report from Rome, a partial text of the encyclical, *Humanae Vitae*, a background piece on the Pope's commission on birth control, "reaction" statements from Catholics, Protestants, Jews the world over. All the reactions were unanimously disapproving. She devoured every word, including a local story which summarized the contents of a new "guideline" pamphlet for Washington Catholics, issued by Archbishop McInnerney, entitled *Sex in Marriage,* which indicated, the *Post* story speculated, that McInnerney was "solidly behind" the Roman Pontiff.

Jean poured a second cup of coffee. As she read on, she felt she was smothering—suffocating. The second cup jangled her nerves, opened her eyes. Rage engulfed her. If Pope Paul walked through the door she would spit in his face. Her eldest, named Paul! By God, she would take steps to change his name legally. No. That was insane. Bob would fight her. Paul too, probably. He would be the butt of too many jokes.

Bob came from the bedroom, digging fists into puffy eyes. He poured coffee sleepily, then sat down, picked up the paper. Tapping the table-top with her forefinger, Jean awaited his reaction. It was surprisingly mild.

"I guess that's that," he said.

Jean glowered.

"Now maybe the bleeding hearts will shut up and go back to work," Bob went on.

"I think it's terribly unfair," Jean said. "And besides that, I don't think he can make it stick."

Bob sipped his coffee, reading the partial text.

"It's not infallible," Jean said. "It says so right there."

"It doesn't have to be infallible," Bob said. "It's still binding on all Catholics."

"It's just a rule."

"It's a papal pronouncement," Bob said, looking up. "A clear and unequivocal order. It *must* be obeyed."

"But the Vatican spokesman said the Pope did not prohibit theological discussion," Jean insisted. "That means . . ."

"That's just a technicality," Bob said. "They always do that. They'll nit-pick for years in the theological journals. It gives the ivory-tower boys something to do. But for us, this is the final word."

"I think he's going to be sorry."

"What are you going to do?" Bob said, laying the paper aside.

"I don't know," Jean said. "I want to talk to somebody."

"Why don't you call Monsignor Ryan?"

"Ryan!" she shouted. "That old fogy!"

"He's our pastor."

"Daugherty's our pastor."

"Acting pastor," Bob corrected.

"What do you want to do, have five more kids?" Jean shouted.

Bob looked up quietly. He said nothing.

In truth, he wanted no more children. The load on Jean was too much. She was clearly at the end of her rope. The cost of living was soaring out of sight. By the time Chris reached college age, it would cost $5,000 a year tuition and board. They couldn't afford that on civil service pay, even with cost-of-living raises. But she must stop taking the pill. It was now unequivocally a mortal sin, and dangerous medically. They would have to abstain from sex, that was all. No more Vatican roulette.

"I read last night the FDA was doing a new study on the side effects of the pill," Bob said. "Some women are developing blood clots."

"A *tiny* percentage," Jean retorted. "Those with a history of clotting. My history's OK. More people die from bee stings."

"Hmmmmmm," Bob said, picking up the paper again. "Do we have a copy of this new booklet from the Chancery—*Sex in Marriage?*"

"No."

"It says here they've been distributed to the local parishes. Why don't you drop over and pick one up?"

"I know what it says."

"I'd like to read all of it."

"Then you pick it up, if you're so interested."

She rose, stalked from the kitchen. She went to the bedroom and fell on the bed, burying her face in the pillow. She remained there, dry-eyed, angry, until she heard Bob leave for work. Then she went to the kitchen for the paper and returned to the bedroom. She reread the excerpts of the complete text, searching vainly for loopholes. There were none. It was a thoughtful, elegantly composed, lucid document— but stupid. She would go over and talk to Daugherty. If he wouldn't give her an OK, she would damned well find a priest who would.

She could hear the children in the kitchen, shouting, fighting, beyond doubt spilling orange juice, cereal, sugar, milk. Then she heard Emma's commanding hush-nows-and-eat. Good old Emma, she thought, the last of the breed. In a few years, help would be a quaint memory. None of them (Emma told her) wanted to do housework. Nancy would raise her children without help. They would read about domestics in history books. The Pope didn't have to worry about that. He had dozens of servants, Swiss Guards in pantaloons, carrying their ceremonial halberds. What did *he* know about raising kids. Hah!

She leaned over, dialed the All Saints' rectory. The housekeeper, Mrs. Munally, answered. Jean identified herself, asked for Father Daugherty. He was not in. Did she care to leave a message? When was he expected? Lord only knows, Mrs. Munally said, a hint of distress in her voice. Jean would call back, thanks. Not at all.

Daugherty—she thought—was probably down at the Chancery again, sounding off. She hoped so. If the Daughertys of the world united, they could change the Pope's mind. But what chance did he have against that Chancery crowd? McInnerney was strictly hard-line. A Spellman man. Another McIntyre, Ritter. They were all cut from the same cloth in the New York Chancery. Wops in the Vatican. Irish in New York. Damned Irish! Couldn't make it anywhere except in the Church, on the police force, or in politics.

When the children had left for the swim club, Jean had yet another cup of coffee in the kitchen, with Emma.

"I seen the paper," Emma said. "Seems like it was the wrong thing to do."

"It was," Jean said.

"Got too many kids running wild now," Emma said. "Got to stop that. No men in the house. All our women on relief. Having more and more babies so they can git bigger relief checks. It just ain't right. It robs people of their pride. You got to work to keep pride."

"Yes," Jean said.

"He some kinda powerful man, that Pope," Emma said. "But I think he done wrong this time. What do you suppose he's aiming at? Half the world already starving."

"He thinks the Bible says birth control is wrong."

"The Bible don't say no such thing," Emma said testily. "I know that for sho. I *knows* my Bible."

"He thinks it's killing."

"Huh! Ain't no killin'. Killin' gon' come later when all these people try to find someplace to breathe, a little piece of land to work. If I were you, I'd write him and tell him what the truth!"

"I might just do that," Jean smiled.

"You sho' got plenty. You got a right to speak yo' mind."

"What's left of it."

"You feelin' poorly, Mrs. Favrot? I worry about you. You don't seem too happy lately. You seem to be runnin' hard just to stay in place. Maybe you ought to take it easy for a while?"

"For a while, I thought I was going out of my mind."

"I thought so too."

"Truly."

"I know. I seen you, gon' in circles. Eating like a humming bird. Not sleepin' good. That happens to everybody from time to time. Just get so you think you gonna scream. Then you got to back down and take it easy. Take a deep breath and start all over. That's the way life is. Right into the grave."

"I suppose so. When I was very young, there was so much I wanted to do."

"We all like that."

"I felt trapped."

"You got nine healthy children," Emma said. "That's more than most can say. They take care of you when you get old, at least. Somebody to look after you."

"Yes," Jean said, tears brimming.

She returned to her room. Damnit! she swore silently. What do You want of me, God?

Her thoughts turned to Bill Clark. He had not yet started on Part Two. There was no manuscript flowing to Jean, no typing, no income to pay the bill at Lord and Taylor's. Maybe it was *her* fault. Maybe she ought to suggest they get back to work. Without the work, their meetings no longer had a business pretext. It was pure, raw sex. Day after day. Raw and risky with that damned snoop, Annie Shields, next door, asking pointed questions all the time. Bob suspicious. Maybe comparing notes with Annie. Even Nancy wondering where she spent her time . . . Plunging on like this with no foreseeable conclusion, no answer to Mike's question: Where will it end?

She did not want it to end. She dressed and drove to his apartment, faster than usual, hungry for his arms. God, she was hungry! He was waiting behind the door. She fell into his arms, sobbing, hugging him tight.

"What's the matter, honey?" he said.

"I don't know," she said, holding him. "Love me."

They went to the bedroom. He had not made the bed. It was rumpled. The sheets were dirty. She could see the stains, the spilled seed. It seemed sordid. She undressed slowly. He crawled in bed, beneath the sheet, waiting, watching her.

Suddenly she was no longer in the mood. It was not the answer, not this morning. She felt cold, distant. She was a long time warming. She was tight and dry. Bill was patient and careful and eager, shifting position, probing her ear with his tongue. She pumped hard. Her back ached, her muscles throbbed. She helped him, knowing she would not come to orgasm, not today. At last he erupted, moaning, gasping, withdrawing, falling away. Then napping. Jean lay beside him, wide awake, eyes open, thinking about her conversation with Emma. Poor old woman, she thought. I must stop loading her with work, the children.

Feeling a disturbing restlessness, Jean eased back the sheet, rose quietly, and dressed. She wandered into the living room, to Bill's desk. There was a silver-framed color photograph of Bill and the six children, posed in ski gear on the slope of a mountain. She studied the faces. They were handsome children, blond, blue-eyed, healthy—fatherless. She felt sorry for them. She remembered the scene from her novel, the desperate, heart-wrenching, furtive meeting between Anna and her son on his birthday. Soon it would be Joe's birthday. She should be planning a party, be thinking of a present, something new and different that would last a long time.

She looked up to see Bill standing in the doorway.

"What's the matter?" he said.

He walked to the desk, looked down. Jean set the picture back on the desk, shook her head from side to side, tears brimming again.

"Your kids need you," she sobbed. "I *hate* her."

He put a hand on her shoulder, squeezed.

"Who?" he said quietly.

"Angela," she said.

"Why?"

"I don't know," she blurted. "She had no right . . ."

"You're upset about the Pope's thing, aren't you?"

She buried her face in her hands.

"Yes . . . yes. I . . . I was *sure* he would go the other way. Now . . . What am I going to do?"

Bill sat down in an easy chair, crossed his legs, filled his pipe. Thinking: How alike all women are. Illogical, emotional, sentimental, touchy, children.

"You thought if he OK'd the pill, he would in effect be OK'ing this relationship, didn't you?" he said slowly, carefully.

"No. Don't be silly."

"I'm not being silly. I'm dead serious. You identify me in your mind with the pill—don't you?"

"Don't give me any of your Freud baloney," Jean said uneasily.

"This is not Freud baloney. This is just common sense. You wanted the Pope to confirm the sexual revolution. He didn't, so now you're all upset."

"Let's not talk about it."

"I think it would help," Bill said. "When you get uptight, it always helps to talk it out. Doesn't it?"

"Yes. You're right. But let's not talk about it. The encyclical is stupid."

"I agree. If I were you, I'd ignore it."

"How can I just *ignore* it?" she said, voice plaintive.

"Would you like a daiquiri?" he said, puffing on his pipe.

"No. God no! Bill, look. You know what's really bugging me? I'm worried about the book. Why have you stopped writing?"

"I'm waiting for the well to refill."

"How long does *that* take?"

"I don't know. I'm new at this."

"Well . . . can't we talk about it? Make an outline? What comes next? Don't you have some general idea or plan?"

She rose, fitfully paced the floor, wringing her hands. She felt oddly light-headed, disassociated, confused. As though she were enclosed in a glass cylinder. Like the day she ran out of gas in McLean. God!

"Why don't you just sit down and relax?" he said.

"I *can't.*"

"Well, why don't you call Daugherty? See what he has to say?"

"I did. He wasn't there. Besides, I'm uptight about the money. Yesterday I got a second notice—very polite—from Lord and Taylor. I owe them a small fortune. I've got to send something. But if you're not typing . . ."

"Writing, you mean."

"Writing. Then I don't get paid. I'll have to look for something else to do."

"Stop being ridiculous," Bill said firmly. "Sit down and take it easy. Why didn't you tell me you needed money? I can advance you money against future work. How much do you need?"

The question angered her. She did not like her position. She was *dependent.* Now he was offering money, without work. What did he think she was—a whore? That's all she meant to him. Sex. Maybe he doesn't even intend to finish the book. Just using it as an excuse.

"Let me get you a drink," Bill said, rising. "Please."

"No," she said, subdued. "No thanks . . . sit down. Let's talk without liquor. Bill, we've got to deal with the question. Where is this leading? What are we doing?"

Bill looked at his pipe pensively.

"I don't know," he said glumly. "I don't know."

"We've *got* to talk about it," she hissed.

"It's not the best time . . ."

"You don't seem to understand. I have nine children. *Nine!*"

"Jean. Please. You're . . . you're upset."

"I'm leaving."

She rose.

"Jean!" Bill said, rising, going to her. "Please!"

"I'm just your paid whore, aren't I?" she shouted.

"Jean. Jean. I love you."

"Let me go. I want to go home."

She pulled away, toward the door, feeling panic.

"Call me," he said at the door, behind her.

"All right," she said weakly, leaving, pulling the door closed behind her, going blindly toward the parking lot, the car. On the walk, she almost collided with Annie Shields.

"Jean! What are you doing here?"

Jean stopped, frozen. So! Just as she thought. This damned bitch had been following her all along. Following her and running to Bob. Tearing her apart, night after night, under the guise of talking politics.

"I just dropped off some typing," Jean said, composing herself. "What are *you* doing here?"

"Calling on some new people—from the outfit. Just back from Hong Kong. A boy that works with Pete. Very nice young couple. Why don't you join us for coffee?"

Jean huffed inwardly. That was a likely story.

"I've got to get back," she said, voice wavering.

"Is there something wrong, Jean? Are you all right?"

"Yes. Yes. I'm all right. God, it's hot. Let's not stand in the sun. I'll see you later. OK?"

"OK, Jean," Annie said. Then added: "Jean. Wait. Just a sec. Jean, I've hardly had time to say boo to you for the last . . . I don't know how long. Let me give you some unsolicited advice. Give up this stupid job. You're running yourself ragged. You've got too much responsibility. I *know* it would make Bob happier."

Jean glowered. So it was true! They had been talking secretly behind her back! The rage rose, erupted.

"You stay away from Bob," she snarled. "Just stay the hell away from him. You hear? I'm sick and tired of your snooping into my life. Those confidential talks with Bob. Just stay in your own back yard. Mind your own business!"

Jean walked away swiftly, overwhelmed with dizziness. Annie stared after her, half in amazement, half in pity. She went to the pay telephone on the wall.

Jean, smoldering, defiant, drove directly to All Saints'. She rang the rectory bell. Mrs. Munally came to the door. No, Father Daugherty was not back yet. No, she didn't know where he was or when he might be back. She had not seen him since he said the Masses Sunday—then vanished again. Jean said she would come in and wait. She went into the living room, sat down, lit a cigarette, found a copy of the booklet, *Sex in Marriage,* on the coffee table. She tried to read but the words blurred, the ideas, the arguments made no sense.

She waited an hour, two. A strange priest in cassock came into the room, asked if he could be of service. He seemed to look at her in an odd way, as though she were dangerous, perhaps needed watching.

Jean reassured him that she was fine, that she attended group therapy once a week with Dr. Cantor. She dug into her purse to find his business card—the solid proof. It was not there. She smiled sheepishly at the strange priest, who left the room, unctuously excusing himself.

Sometime later, she forgot when, she left the rectory. She drove more or less toward home. Turning in the drive, she saw Bob's car. He was home early. Very early. Her heart pounded. Why? Annie Shields! She went into the house slowly, warily. He was sitting in the living room alone, waiting.

"Jean! Where have you been?"

"Why are you home?" she said.

"Answer *my* question," Bob said coldly.

"I've been at All Saints' trying to find Daugherty. By the way, here's your damned pamphlet."

She hurled the small blue booklet across the room. Bob watched it flutter to the floor. He stooped, huffing, and picked it up.

"All right," he said, laying the pamphlet on the mantle. "Why did you go to Bill Clark's today? You haven't been typing lately. You haven't even been home."

"I knew that damned bitch would call you," Jean hissed. "Goddamned sneak!"

"She's not a sneak. She's concerned about you . . . the children. Answer my question. Why did you go there?"

She did not reply.

"He's your lover, isn't he?"

She glowered defiantly, not speaking.

"Isn't he? *Answer* me."

"You know all the answers. Answer yourself."

"I want to talk," he said. "We're going to have a long, serious talk about you, your lover, Bill Clark. Go to the bedroom. I'll be there in a minute."

Jean turned and walked down the hall to the bedroom. She could not think clearly. Could not think at all. Her mind swirled with wild, shapeless images. She flopped on the bed and buried her face in a pillow. She did not hear Bob close the door.

"If I believed in divorce, I'd file," he said. "I'm tempted to anyway, goddamnit. Maybe I could persuade your modern pal, Daugherty, to approve it. No, I'm not going to do that. For the children's sake. I'm going to teach you a lesson. Do you hear me? Sit up and listen to me."

In the distance, Jean heard the front door slamming, the children home from the club, running to their rooms, the kitchen. One tried the bedroom door, but it was locked. The child kicked at the door.

"Stay out," Bob shouted. "Your mother and I are talking."

"I'm hungry." It was Mike.

"Get some milk," Bob said through the door. "Leave us alone. Tell the other kids to go outside and play. And *no* fighting."

He turned back to Jean.

"Now what do you have to say for yourself?"

She did not move.

"Answer me, goddamnit. We're going to have this thing out, once and for all."

She did not move. She lay, frightened, feeling the panic.

"If you don't answer me," Bob hissed, "I'm going right down to his apartment and blow his brains out. And there's not a jury in the world that would convict me."

She sat up, turned and glared at him through puffy eyes.

"You wouldn't dare."

"Oh, wouldn't I? Don't press me. All it would take, would be . . ." He snapped his fingers. "So explain yourself," he said coldly.

"I don't have to explain myself. I *can't* explain myself. Maybe I'm just crazy."

"Like that Jew shrink, and your group. Is that what they tell you to do there? Is this the approved formula for normality? Committing adultery?"

"Shut up."

Another of the children knocked loudly on the door.

"Go away," Bob shouted. "We're talking."

"Can I go to Gene's?" It was Joe.

"Yes. Yes," Bob shouted irritably. "Be home by six."

"OK."

Keds crashed down the hallway. Bob turned back to Jean.

"Where was I?"

Another knock at the door. Bob lunged for the knob, unlocked the door, flung it open, shouted at the hall:

"Goddamnit, stop knocking on this door. Your mother and I are talking."

Nancy shrank down the hallway. Bob slammed the door again, locking it. Jean rose from the bed, dabbing her eyes with her fist. She walked toward the door.

"Where are you going?" Bob glared.

"To fix the children a snack."

"Let Emma do it."

"I'll help her."

"Let Nancy help her. She can do something around here besides talk on the telephone and run up the charge accounts."

"Stop shouting at me. I'm not an animal."

"Aren't you?" Bob said. "Isn't that, in fact, precisely what you are?"

He grabbed her dress at the neck. He shoved her across the room. She fell backward on the bed, reeling in terror.

"Stop that!" she cried. "Have you lost your mind?"

"Maybe I have. Don't I have the right?"

"You don't have a right to strike me."

"I didn't strike you."

"*Or* throw me down."

"Shit!" he shouted.

"You're making accusations . . . false accusations," she said, voice low, cool. "I didn't say I was . . . that I was having an affair with him."

"But you are, aren't you?"

"No."

"Don't lie to me."

"You're paranoid."

"So what?"

Jean turned and lay with her face in the pillow. She sobbed. Tears gushed from her eyes. She felt empty, insane.

"I'm going down there," Bob said, "and ask him face to face."

"No. No. Don't . . . don't make a fool of yourself."

Bob tore off his jacket, flung it in a corner. He jerked down his tie.

"Sister, you have this thing all twisted in your mind. It's *you* who's making a fool of *me*. The laughingstock of the neighborhood . . . the whole world. Now, if you won't admit it, I'm going to beat it out of him. We'll see how he looks, down on his knees with a gun barrel at his head. We'll see how old lover-boy reacts. Haw!"

Jean sat up straight, holding her head with her hands. Bob walked toward the door.

"You really would, wouldn't you?" she hissed. "You'd *kill* him, wouldn't you?"

"Yes," Bob said.

"And never mind the consequences . . . the effect on the children!"

"Your newfound concern for the children is very touching."

Jean rubbed her eyes. She lit a cigarette.

"All right," she said. "If you give me your word you won't go over
there, I'll tell you about it. Anything you want to know."

Bob let his hand fall from the doorknob. He walked to the bed, sat
down.

"All right. I'm listening."

She told him the story from the beginning: how she had blown her
mind the day she ran out of gas, how she had screamed in the confessional, how she had gone to Dr. Cantor and group, then Bill and the
affair. It took her more than an hour to tell it all, including one trip
to the bathroom to take two aspirin. She did not cry during her story.
But when she was finished, she sobbed again and threw herself on
the pillow. Bob did not speak for a long time. Finally, he said, as
though he had struck upon a new and profound insight:

"Life is tough."

"Dehumanizing," she said. "The world is dehumanizing."

"You didn't say you were sorry."

She did not reply.

"Aren't you sorry? Aren't you going to at least apologize?"

"I don't feel I owe you an apology. I'm really not sorry."

He put his hand on hers. She pulled away.

"I'll not be blackmailed," she said. "Our relationship remains essentially unchanged."

"Except I'm a cuckold. What am I to do, roll over and play dead,
for Christ's sake?"

"I told the group . . . I don't like you to touch me. It's repulsive
. . . I can't stand it."

"How long have you felt like that?"

"A long time. Since our honeymoon."

"You told those strangers *that?*"

"I told you, they're not strangers."

"Which reminds me. I'm going to call Dr. Cantor right now. You're
resigning from that group, first of all. Then we'll get to the next thing."

He fished the telephone from the bedside table. He dialed Dr. Cantor's office. Dr. Cantor was with a patient, could not be disturbed, the
receptionist said. He would call back.

"You tell him to call me in five minutes," Bob said angrily, "or
I'll be over there."

Dr. Cantor returned the call immediately.

"Cantor? This is Bob Favrot, Jean Favrot's husband. My wife is resigning from group therapy immediately. I think you people are out of your goddamned minds. Do you realize we have nine children? You got her sleeping all over town, destroying herself . . . I ought to sue you for malpractice."

He slammed down the telephone.

"Now . . ."

"I'm not resigning from the group," she said, eyes defiant.

"You're going to do exactly as I say, or lover-boy is going to face the consequences."

"You said you wouldn't . . . you gave me your word."

"I didn't say I was going to kill him. Maybe just have a long, cozy chat. You poor girl. Poor little lovesick girl. Tell me, does he have a good pecker? Bigger than mine? Is that his secret?"

"Shut up."

"I'm repulsive to you, eh? All these years, you didn't tell *me* that. All the time I thought you liked it. You sure fooled me. Hell, I thought for a while I had a nympho on my hands. The first year and a half."

"I was doing what was expected of me."

"Big sacrifice, eh? Joan of Arc bit. A martyr."

"Don't be melodramatic."

"And not even an apology?"

"No. I told you. I'm not sorry."

There was a crash in the kitchen. Bob stopped to listen.

"That was glass," he said. "I'll go see about it. Then I've got to get back to the office. We can resume this discussion later tonight, after you've had time to think on it a while. I don't know what I'm going to do. But before I leave here, I want one thing from you. I want your word that you will never see him again. Do I have that?"

Jean turned, buried her face again in the pillow.

"I want your word."

"We'll talk about it when you get back."

Bob opened the door and hurried to the kitchen. Jean got up, closed the door, locked it. She took off her clothes and put on her nightgown. She crawled into bed and stared at the ceiling through a film of tears. She dialed Bill, fingers trembling violently.

"Bill?" she said, almost whispering. "This is Jean. Bob was home when I came in. He knows everything. Be careful. He's in a rage. At first he said he would kill you. Then I told him everything . . ."

She burst into tears and hung up the phone, turned off the bell.

"Mother?" Nancy said through the door. "Are you all right?"

"Yes," Jean said, between sobs. "I'm all right. I'm tired. I want to take a nap. Will you see about the children for me? Give them some milk. Tell Emma to cook the roast for dinner."

"All right, Mum."

Jean closed her eyes. She felt drowsy, then dead tired. She fell asleep. She had ghastly nightmares. In one, she wrecked her station wagon, killed five of her children. She awoke from that, knowing that she had been screaming hysterically. She lay quietly, hands wet with perspiration. She could hear the kids in the kitchen eating dinner. They were safe, after all.

She fell asleep again. It was a light sleep, interrupted several times by noises in the house. Once she heard Bob's car in the drive, pulling in, racing the motor as he always did before turning off the key. It was ten after eleven when she awoke again. Again, she felt strange, light-headed, unreal, as though her spirit had separated from her body. Her chest ached, somewhere deep inside. She felt terrible, as though weighted down by chains of lead.

She got up and went to the bathroom. She weaved, as though she were drunk. She stared into the medicine cabinet mirror, shocked by the horrible image that stared back at her. She clawed at her hair with her fingers. Her eyes were red and swollen. She shouted at the mirror:

"You tramp!"

She sat on the toilet and cried. She beat her fists on her knees. Then she leaped up hysterically, flung open the medicine cabinet, found her birth control pills, flushed them down the toilet. Her eyes returned to the cabinet, a haze of bottles. She saw Bob's bottle of Tuinal, half full. She seized the bottle, dumped the pills in her hand, counting. Twenty-two. She filled a glass with water and started taking the pills, one by one.

After she swallowed the twelfth pill, hands trembling, she paused to take stock. Nothing had happened yet. She was not even sleepy. Her heart thudded in her chest. Then, suddenly, panic overwhelmed her. The room spun round and round. She steadied herself on the sink. She looked in the mirror again, appalled by her tortured, anguished face.

"What have I done?" she screamed. "The children!!"

She half-staggered from the bathroom, lunging for the bedroom door. She jerked it open, fell into the hallway, screaming:

"Bob! Bob!"

Bob was asleep on the living room couch. He woke suddenly, leaped to his feet, and ran toward the bedroom. He saw his wife sprawled on the floor, clutching the empty bottle in a tight fist.

"Jesus God!" he said.

He ran to the bedside telephone. He dialed the rescue squad. Then he ran back to his wife. He picked her up and dragged her to the bed. He felt her pulse. Strong. He put her head over the edge of the bed, stuck his finger down her throat. She vomited.

Father Daugherty had been in his rectory room for two hours, door locked, phone extension shut off, packing his personal belongings. First he had placed his most valuable papers in a small, blue steel box with a combination lock. These included the letter he was going to take to the Chancery, his Navy discharge papers, his high school, college, and seminary diplomas, the papers he received when he was ordained (and the news clips extolling this event), a few keepsake letters, other odds and ends. He packed his chalice, pictures, books, and tennis gear in cardboard cartons. Then his clothes in two suitcases. Mary was parked downstairs in the lot, waiting in the VW. Between the two cars, they would transport this meager freight to Halfway House.

He heard the telephone ring downstairs. It was quite late. It must be an emergency, a sick call, or an accident. Well, he would let the Maryknoll missionary handle it. It would broaden him to administer extreme unction to a teen-ager lying on the shoulder of the beltway beside the wreckage of his car. Something different from beri-beri and scurvy and jungle rot and the other stuff Daugherty supposed he was used to.

There came an insistent rapping on his door.

"Father Daugherty?"

It was Mrs. Munally. Her voice had an urgent tone. He did not want to see her or her to see his boxes and suitcases, all packed. There might be a scene. He wanted to leave quietly, silently.

"Yes?" he spoke through the door.

"There's an emergency. Can you get the telephone?"

"Who is it?"

"Mr. Favrot, calling from the hospital. Something happened to his wife."

Oh, God! Daugherty thought, leaning against the door jamb. Jean Favrot! She had been by the rectory that morning to see him, Mrs.

Munally had said earlier. She seemed to be acting queerly. Had she totaled her car or something?

"Yes. I've got it."

He leaped to the telephone extension on his desk.

"This is Father Daugherty."

"Dan, this is Bob Favrot. I'm over at the hospital. The emergency room. Jean's . . . Jean tried to kill herself. I think they caught it in time, but . . . can you please come over and bring your things?"

No! Daugherty sat down heavily in his chair, mind reeling. This was *his* fault. She had come by last week, asking help. Then again today. He had not provided help. He had been too busy! Running to the Chancery on a fool's errand. Indulging himself at Halfway House. There was no time, these days, for the Jean Favrots of the Church. No one looking out for them. He spoke into the mouthpiece:

"I'll be right there, Bob. Five minutes."

He hung up quickly, gathered up his black case, and unlocked the door. He pulled it closed, locking it again. He flew down the stairs. Mrs. Munally was standing in the hallway, hair in curlers, ashen-faced.

"I heard," she said.

"I know you did," he replied curtly. "You always do, don't you?"

Daugherty ran into the night, around the rectory to the lot. In the shadows of the church, he found Mary in the VW.

"Drive me to the hospital—quick," he said, climbing in the cramped front seat. "I'll explain on the way."

She drove from the lot fast, following his clipped directions. On the way, he told her about Jean, the Favrots, as much as he could squeeze in during the short ride. At the emergency room door, Daugherty leaped out, pushed through the heavy swinging doors, ran down the corridor toward Bob Favrot, who was standing outside a closed door.

"In here?" Daugherty said needlessly.

Bob Favrot nodded. Daugherty brushed past him, went into the room, closed the door. Jean, covered to the chest by a white sheet, lay with her head on a pillow, the bed cranked high. Two nurses and a young intern hovered around her. The intern spoke quietly to Daugherty at the foot of the bed.

"She's OK, Father. Overdose of Tuinal. Pulse is strong, but if you want to do your thing, we'll get out."

Daugherty nodded, then stood to one side, watching, considering. Then he pursed his lips at the intern, indicating that he would perform the last rites, just to be on the safe side. The intern and the nurses left the room. Daugherty laid his black case on the bed, opened it and took out oil and the crucifix. He anointed Jean. Her eyes fluttered open. She saw him and smiled wanly. Then her eyes filled with terror when she saw the black case and the crucifix.

"Am I dying?" she whispered.

"No. You're all right. You're going to be fine."

"That's good," she said weakly.

Daugherty broke off the sacrament. It was pointless now, irrelevant. She was going to be fine. His heartbeat slowed. He packed everything back into the case. She watched silently, eyes following his hands.

"They wouldn't have buried me in hallowed ground, would they?" she said.

"I guess not," Daugherty said, setting the case on the floor, looking at her, moved by profoundest pity.

"It'd really be murder, too?" she said.

"Yes," he said.

"And no Funeral Mass?"

"That's right."

She smiled weakly.

"For one little mistake?" she said. "A few pills? The other kind?"

"That's the rule," Daugherty said, taking her hand. It was cold. She squeezed his hand. "Jean," he added, "do you feel all right?"

"Weak," she said.

"Don't try to talk."

"I *want* to talk. I was trying to find you all day. I waited . . ."

"I heard. Mrs. Munally told me. I'm sorry I missed you. Truly sorry. I was downtown. I . . ."

"That's all right. I wanted to tell you about Bill . . ."

"Who?" Daugherty said, knowing, dreading the rest.

"Bill Clark . . . a so-called writer. Actually, he's not a bad writer . . . when he writes."

Daugherty, still holding her hand tightly, reached back with his other hand and drew up a chair. He sat down. Jean told him everything in a voice just above a whisper. Daugherty listened to the all-too-familiar tale, thinking of other things: Pope Paul, McInnerney, Prial, Ryan, Mary . . . the encyclical . . . Halfway House . . . Sharon . . . Seymour Jones, his whole fantastic, unbelievable world, the fearful, violent, bitter vale of tears, created for what diabolical reason by whom? For whom? A Church that would not even have given Jean Favrot, who gave birth to nine souls, a Christian burial!

"Isn't that stupid?" she said, finishing her story.

"No, Jean. Not stupid. I feel that in many ways, it's my fault . . . that day you came to confession . . . I probably shouldn't have suggested Dr. Cantor . . . I don't know really. Do you want to say an Act of Contrition?"

"I guess so."

She did, Daugherty echoing in Latin. He blessed her, forgave her sins. He did not administer penance. She had already paid for her indiscretion, he knew, in pain and agony he could only vaguely imagine. He rose, picked up his case.

"Don't leave me," she said, pleading with her eyes.

"I'm not leaving you," he said. "Bob's right outside. Don't you want to see him?"

"Yes."

He called Bob Favrot into the room. Bob went to his wife, kissed her, picked up her cold hand, soothed her brow. Daugherty nodded to Bob gravely, then left the room. He walked slowly down the corridor, past the admitting desk, through the swinging doors into the warm night. No, he thought, scuffing along toward the VW, he would not leave her. He would not abandon her to McInnerney and the Chancery crowd—not yet. He had failed her and, in so doing, had failed himself and all the Jean Favrots the world over. If he abandoned her, he surely was a quitter, a spoiled rich kid, turning his back, selfishly doing his own thing. That must wait. Mary must wait. She would understand this one last thing. He would leave, yes. In time. But first he must find a way to take McInnerney and Prial and the whole pigheaded, superstitious bunch with him, if possible. Maybe even the Pope. If McInnerney were spoiling for a fight, by God, he would give him one. He walked faster.

He found Mary, the VW. He climbed in the front seat, sighing wearily.

"Is she . . ." Mary said softly, fearfully.

"No. She's all right. They caught it. Mary, let's go somewhere and find a pay phone. I want to talk to Marvin Klein. Right now. Let's find out how much fight he really has in him. OK?"

"OK," Mary said, starting the motor, putting the car in gear, understanding at once.

BOOK THREE

AUGUST, 1968

I

The air in the Washington Chancery, ordinarily sweetly serene, was now charged with electricity, like a newspaper city room. On Monday, Pope Paul's encyclical. On Tuesday, the *Tribune*'s inflammatory story on St. Luke's, the libelous profile of McInnerney. The PBX lit up like a Christmas tree, and stayed lit late into the night. By count of the frantic operators, near hysteria from the sudden onset of crisis, twenty-six reporters, nine TV newsmen, and four news-magazine writers had called, urgently demanding either a statement or an interview with McInnerney on Pope Paul's encyclical. All went unanswered, priority going to internal business of the Church—returning calls from Cardinals Cooke, Cushing, Ritter, McIntyre, other potentates, and to the key clergy in the Washington archdiocese, who wanted "guidance" on the encyclical, something more specific than the generalized doctrine of the Chancery pamphlet, *Sex in Marriage, Life-giving, Love-giving.*

Vicar General Prial, who until now believed he controlled events passably well, toiled in his office like a cornered rodent. Fortunately, by Friday, the Archbishop's sermon for the St. Luke's ceremony on Sunday had been finished, edited, retyped on the large-print typewriter. The major details of McInnerney's visit—the police escort, the coordination with the St. Luke's pastor, the invitations to the resident bishops to join in the Mass—had all been worked out in advance. As for the press and TV coverage, HUD and IDA were handling that. In the tornado that followed the news ticker from Rome, Prial had had no time to double back on these arrangements—or complain about the leak to the *Tribune*. Nor had he time to check into the John Carter business.

As for the *Tribune* story. When Prial first read it, he bridled, especially at the cruel portrait of his friend and boss of many years. The profile was full of factual errors (which Prial angrily underlined), scathing innuendo, irrelevant personal asides (such as the fact that McInnerney chain-smoked Camels). It painted McInnerney all-black, a dedicated, pro-war reactionary, opposed to all change—social, ecclesiastical, spiritual. No mention of the heroic work he had performed to integrate the Puerto Ricans into the New York diocese. No mention of his commendably liberal record in the Washington ghetto.

Prial had carried the paper to McInnerney in a smoldering rage. But the Archbishop was monumentally calm, covering his disappointment, if any, with amusement, first at Prial's excessive anger, then at the cartoonist's caricature of himself. He was not upset that the *Tribune* had prematurely broken the St. Luke's story. He rightly judged that the story would serve, ultimately, to heighten interest in St. Luke's, enlarge the press turnout for Sunday, and thereby provide them with a greater vehicle to get across their side of the story. On calmer reflection, Prial concluded the Archbishop's unflagging optimism was not misplaced. Perhaps that was what HUD and IDA had had in mind by leaking. There was much about news management he did not understand.

In truth, the St. Luke's problem had been roughly pushed into the background by Paul's encyclical. It was that document—not St. Luke's —that generated the flood of calls to the Chancery. In response to these urgent inquiries, McInnerney had decided by Tuesday noon, against Prial's advice, to deliver, along with the sermon at St. Luke's, a pastoral letter on the encyclical. It would be a firm, unequivocal statement supporting Rome, taking advantage, as he said, of the expected large media turnout at St. Luke's to get across their position on that point, too. Prial opposed this for two reasons. First, he still thought silence was the better policy on the encyclical. Second, to raise the encyclical at St. Luke's might confuse (or enrage) the laity, introduce excessive controversy into an already delicate situation.

Overruled, Prial waited until the last minute. He had spent Saturday afternoon, telephone shut off, cigar firmly clenched between his teeth, pecking out the pastoral letter on his typewriter. The text did not come easy, perhaps because he lacked conviction. Then there were constant interruptions by the staff. It was late Saturday evening when he finished, later still by the time McInnerney finished his editing, very late by the time the stoical typist completed her finished copy and ran off a hundred Xeroxed copies for distribution to the press and others. Too late, in fact, for distribution to the parish rectories and, therefore, too late for a general reading from all the archdiocese pulpits Sunday, an administrative untidiness that annoyed Prial no end, violated his well-developed sense of order. He slept fitfully and briefly, arising Sunday morning feeling drugged, a victim of battle fatigue.

The Archbishop, by contrast, was ebullient. He had slept soundly, confident that his day would go well, that many testy matters would finally be laid to rest. The air would be cleared. The encyclical, his positive teaching in the pastoral letter, left no room for doubt or discussion. Everybody would, at last, be relieved, reassured. Now that that bridge had been crossed, they could all get back to work on the main task, the theological center. For that project, never far from the forefront of his mind, McInnerney had conceived a bold new idea. Sometime in the immediate future—the sooner the better—he would stage a ground-breaking ceremony on the land at CU, to which he intended to invite all the princes of the American Catholic Church. The gathering would be an impressive display of unity, purpose, cohesion, solidarity. It would give the project a much-needed push—help establish it in the public's mind as an ongoing fact—and it might generate substantial financial contributions from sources outside the archdiocese. McInnerney had kept this idea to himself. He did not want to distract his overburdened staff with yet another major undertaking.

That Sunday morning, he dressed in his public vestments—the red cassocks, the zucchetto (his skull cap), and the pallium, the white neckpiece signifying his office. The pomp and ceremony of the public appearance were balm for the laity, reassuring. A reminder for them there was a purpose, a God-sent organized structure, proper supervision —teaching—which the garments symbolized.

He descended the elevator, looking forward to the day. The Vicar General, holding the Archbishop's ornate mitre, silver crozier—the crooked shepherd's staff—and was waiting in the foyer. The limousine, the police escort were parked in the drive.

"All set?" McInnerney said brightly.

"All set," Prial responded in a voice tinged with hoarseness.

They walked down the corridor to the door.

Charles Seymour Jones had slept fitfully, too. Three times during the early hours, he had awakened, got up, gone to his desk, and when his puffy eyes adjusted to the light, sat down and fiddled with the document he now entitled in bold print, MANIFESTO. In the last forty-eight hours that he had been composing the document, it had changed form many times as Seymour had struggled to compress within its pages a thousand years of black history, Catholic imperialism (reaching through centuries, from Castille to St. Luke's), harsh words of outrage and indignation suitably interspersed with lofty and noble sentiments and finally, the demand itself, presented in reasonable terms. Most of that depressing history had been struck away, thrown in the overflowing trash can. Now the document was brief, trenchant, a series of "whereases," set forth in a logical sequence, almost legalistic in effect, as though it were the work of an authorized body.

He had approached the blank paper with a feeling of elation, of sweet anticipation. Here was the idea by which Charles Seymour Jones might catapult himself from relative obscurity to the front rank of black nonviolent leadership. Arrive, like a thunderbolt on the horizon, in full battle dress, with an almost-perfect ploy, something utterly and confoundingly new, a near-unassailable issue. How it would have warmed the heart of Martin Luther King! Wait until the Browns and Carmichaels and the Cleavers read it. They would back-flip with jealousy.

But the intense concentration of the work raised doubt in his mind. It came midway, on Saturday. Who was he to make this bid for leadership? By what right could he assert this claim? What experience could he call upon? Where was his podium experience? Where was his education? The more he read, the less he felt he knew. The Browns and Cleavers were certain to lunge after him, the new target, with words, deeds, perhaps knives and guns. Where was the courage to face this assault? He was not a fighter in the usual sense. He was a cringer, deep in his soul, a coward. What did he care about St. Luke's? IDA? The war? The war was a white man's problem. Not a gut black issue. So was the fight with the Pope.

To dam his eroding level of resolution, Seymour had forced himself to remember the little crippled children in Sister Mary's padlocked school, his own good boys who would be on the streets now, if he had not already taken a first, hesitant step of defiance. He was committed. After dawn, he returned to his bed and slept well for three hours.

He arose, made coffee on his hot plate. Then he dressed, putting on his best conservative dark suit, with white shirt, somber tie. This day, he must dress like Dr. King, presenting an image of responsibility, seriousness, respectability, a man who would not be confused in the public mind with the dashiki and shade-wearing crazies. So turned out, he walked into the heat of the morning, the penciled draft of the manifesto folded in his pocket, to his gym office, where his boys were already gathering. They were feverish with excitement. Seymour set them to work printing placards with Magic Markers. The text was improvised by Seymour as they went along:

WHERE IS THE BLACK CHRIST?

GIVE ST. LUKE'S TO THE BLACKS

IN THE U.S.: 900 BLACK NUNS, 165 BLACK PRIESTS

NO CATHOLIC DISCRIMINATION?

And so on. He specifically forbade placards denouncing the war, or condemning IDA and other peripheral issues. He cautioned all his boys that there would be absolutely no violence, no cavorting for TV, no shouting, no threats, no provoking gestures, no clenched fists held to the sky.

When the placards were done, some twenty-five good specimens, Seymour dispatched the boys toward the cathedral, watching them depart from the gym door. By now, the large TV vans were already in place. There were also a half dozen police cruisers parked here and there, and a contingent of the riot squad with blue helmets, extra-large batons. The riot police directed his orderly picketers into a single circling line on the sidewalk opposite the cathedral. A few curious onlookers had gathered behind the roped-off aisle leading up the cathedral steps.

The Archbishop and his Vicar General rode to the cathedral in the rear seat of the limousine, windows tightly shut, air-conditioner humming. They did not speak. Their eyes watched the silent passing landscape, the rapid deterioration from the mansions of Massachusetts Avenue to the seedy row brownstones of the middle-class whites to the shabby wooden row shacks of the ghetto. Neither man had been there since the riots of April. They were moved by the sight of so many gutted houses, the many stores and shops boarded tight, the words "Soul Brother" crudely painted on doors and windows. It was, in truth, another world from their own.

By now there was a line of cars at the cathedral steps. As they inched forward in line, escorted by two motorcycle police with flashing red lights, they saw all that Seymour could see from the gym, and more. Gathered now at the head of the steps, at the cathedral door, was a cluster of Catholic hierarchy, priests, monsignors, the pastor and staff of the cathedral—the welcoming committee. When these caught sight of the limousine, there was a flurry, a forming up by rank and seniority like a military or diplomatic reception. McInnerney's attention was fixed on the pickets, the placards. Turning to Prial, he said:

"Is that right? Are there only nine hundred black nuns and 165 black priests? Is that all we have, nationwide?"

"I really don't know," the Vicar General said. "I'll check. It's probably an exaggeration."

"I fear it may be true," the Archbishop said.

"Me too," Prial said.

"Thank God, *this* pastor is black."

"Yes."

They debarked, door held obsequiously by the black pastor, who flashed dazzlingly white teeth, knelt, and kissed McInnerney's ring. As McInnerney moved away, mounted the steps, he carried his crozier in his left hand and held his pectoral cross out from his chest with his right, smiling benevolently to the black onlookers—benevolently and reassuringly. By now, the blue-helmeted police had formed a line behind the rope, and mixed with the onlookers. Across the street, Seymour's pickets marched slowly, silently. The TV cameras whirred.

Among the spectators, discreetly standing back from the rope, the camera eyes, was Mary Frances Murray. She was there, partly as observer, partly out of curiosity. She wanted to see Seymour's confrontation. She wanted to gauge, as best she could, McInnerney's reaction, the reaction of the parishioners, the press, TV, the blacks in the street. If they were going to make war, then it would be well to see the Chancery enemy—in a rare public appearance—close up.

She had come alone, from Halfway House, parking some distance away, walking the last three blocks, not without some apprehension. It was a strange, sullen neighborhood, a mean street. The blacks sitting on the front stoops and porches, some still drunk and bleary-eyed from Saturday night, did not know her. She was no longer Sister Mary in the red VW illegally parked in front of the school. She was a pretty, short-skirted white woman, all alone, deep in black territory.

Alone, without Dan, she felt uneasy. He was busy elsewhere. Tuesday night, after seeing Jean Favrot in the hospital, after calling Klein at home, Dan had returned to All Saints' rectory to unpack, and plan, work out what form his fight would take, how long it would go on. Mary had returned to empty Halfway House, which, she discovered, when all alone, creaked ominously in the night. During the next few days she had seen him only occasionally. All during Saturday, she had waited by the telephone for Dan to call, with a mounting sense of fear and uncertainty, her role in Dan's life, briefly clear, now murky. He had called, finally, from LeGuise's, where he had gone for conference. He was somewhat vague. There was still no concrete plan.

Dan would return to All Saints' that night and "play it by ear" through Sunday, at least. He had suggested that meanwhile, she "look in on the Seymour thing at St. Luke's," being sure to take a cab, an extravagant suggestion. They would get together at Halfway House later on Sunday, after he had said all the Masses, finished the baptisms. He did not mention the letter. Technically—legally—he was still very much a priest.

Mary watched McInnerney and Prial ascend the cathedral steps, the pomp and ceremony, the bedazzled expressions of the black spectators. Then, as the crowds of worshippers folded in behind the procession, she joined them, going up the steps, head turned away from the TV cameras, as though she were a CIA agent unwilling to reveal her cover. Inside the cool of the dark old building, she blessed herself with holy water, turned down a side aisle, edged into a pew which afforded a good view of the pulpit, communion rail, and middle aisle. She knelt, feeling blasphemous in her short skirt, said her Prayers before Mass, absently watching the archdiocese hierarchy take seats in the regal, hard-backed chairs and benches in the nave, the cherubic black boys gathering behind the organ in the elevated, baroque choir box, illuminated now by the brilliant, blinding glare of TV lights, beaming from the balcony.

Routinely saying her prayers, Mary reviewed her sins. This exercise, once so lightly embarked upon, now brought a jolt, a profound feeling of wretchedness. The scenes with Dan in the bedroom rose up, assaulted. No, she groaned inwardly, it *didn't* happen. But it had. There was no denying it. Reexamined now, in the cold light of day, she was horrified, swept by panic. She was really losing her mind! Walking out of the order. Going to bed with a priest. Knowingly joining in a conspiracy whose grandiose aim was nothing less than unseating the Pontiff, the rock of her own religion. She was here, in this House, unrepentant, unconfessed, conspiring, a brazen spy in another country, sauntering about in dangerous neighborhoods in a state of mortal sin, now facing Mass, unable, even, to take Communion! She bit her fist in despair.

Watching from the gym door, Seymour saw his time had come. His heartbeat surged, like an astronaut's at lift-off. Fingers trembling, he felt again the manifesto in his pocket. Almost unwillingly, his body cranked into motion, transporting him down the sidewalk to the street, around his line of pickets, for whom he had a careful smile, then across the street, between the ropes, up the steps, eyes straight, in all, a very proper, determined figure of a purposeful young black. He stopped at the cluster of newsmen at the door. One, George Emerson, wearing his horn-rimmed glasses, tan Dacron wash-and-wear suit, blue shirt, and tie, turned.

"Hi, Seymour."

"Hi, George," Seymour smiled.

Emerson shook hands. The other newsmen, mostly whites, looked at Seymour curiously. Emerson introduced him to the others. Seymour recognized some of the men. They regularly covered the ghetto, black protests, good works, riots, whatever the tide of ghetto history cast up.

"Do you have a copy of your statement?" Emerson said.

"What statement?" a white reporter asked quickly.

"No, I don't," Seymour said, tugging the manifesto from his pocket, unfolding it, holding it aloft. "I just finished it this morning."

"Too bad," Emerson said. "You should have had it run off."

"What statement?" the white reporter persisted.

Emerson deferred to Seymour, who refolded the manifesto, returning it to his pocket.

"There's going to be a little show inside," Seymour said.

"A walkout?" the reporter said.

"More than that."

"Like *what?*"

"Like, be patient. You'll see."

He went inside, waiting, watching the ponderous pageantry of High Mass, the chanting, the echoes, the organ. A half hour passed before Archbishop McInnerney mounted the steps to the pulpit to deliver his sermon.

In the pulpit, McInnerney, wearing his rimless glasses, turned with kindly eyes to address the congregation. He spoke into the mike, into the glaring lights, the red light on the front of the TV cameras.

"Distinguished visitors, dearly beloved . . .

"As I stand before you today, I recall a time, many years ago, so long ago it is almost dim in my memory, that I stood here before. On that Sunday, some of you may recall, I announced that the parochial schools in this archdiocese would be desegregated. It was the first time the Church had taken this step anywhere. Our Chancery led the United States by its example, even the Supreme Court. This is one of my fondest memories.

"I stand before you today, to celebrate the last Mass that will be said in this renowned cathedral. She has served out her time. She has served you well. But now she is old and decrepit. It is not economically sound to lift her face. She needs a new roof. The slate alone would cost upward of a million dollars. The Chancery, with the wise counsel of many businessmen, has made the decision to close it down. In its place, we have arranged to build an institution that will provide jobs—more than four hundred—for people in the neighborhood, the ghetto, the black community. The income from these jobs will amount to some two million dollars a year in direct pay, plus indirect benefits, including retirement, social security, hospitalization. In a sense, St. Luke's will go on working for your direct temporal benefit for years and years to come. As for your spiritual needs, they will, rest assured, be looked after—as we have done for so many decades."

He went on, gently, quietly, pleasantly, in the folksy pulpit style he had cultivated as a young priest. Simple, direct, sincere. No elaborate metaphors, no patronizing parables, no well-worked quotations from Scripture. He presented the essence of the fact sheet, a convincing history of good works by the Chancery in the ghetto. Winding up, he felt the congregation going with him, that his points had been well made. Now, pausing, he opened the leather letter-folder Prial had supplied him, removed a copy of his pastoral letter. He laid it on the lectern, fiddled with his glasses, cleared his throat, and resumed.

"Now, my friends, today, in this distinguished company, I want to talk to you on another subject. Obedience. As you know, these are troublesome times in the Church. Last Monday, the Pope issued his encyclical, *Humanae Vitae,* which means, Of Human Life . . ."

In the rear of the cathedral, Seymour Jones hunched his shoulders, strode stiffly down the center aisle toward the communion rail, into the glare of the TV lights. He looked straight ahead, toward the vast nave, the altar, the crucifix. At the communion rail, he stopped. He turned to face the large congregation, solemn, steady. McInnerney, who stopped speaking, looked down from the pulpit with a puzzled expression.

"What is it?" he said to Jones. "Who are you?"

"I am Charles Seymour Jones."

Seymour took the manifesto from his pocket. Two elderly black ushers came up the aisle. One spoke to Seymour:

"Will you please leave? You can't interrupt the Mass, the Archbishop, like this."

Seymour ignored him. The usher looked at McInnerney helplessly. McInnerney, still puzzled, returned his helpless look.

"Whereas," Seymour read, "for centuries the Catholic Church has exploited the black man, commencing with the slave trade in Africa, long before Columbus sailed west to America, and the Pope not only condoned but encouraged this slave trade in Europe and, later, in Latin America, and whereas through centuries the Catholic Church was the direct and largest beneficiary of the sweat of those black slaves . . ."

McInnerney looked around in confusion. His eyes went to the rear of the church, to the ushers, who had backed out of the lights. Then growing angry, he shouted down to the cameramen:

"Turn off those lights!"

The TV men did not hear him, or elected not to hear. They moved closer, focusing on Seymour Jones.

Seymour continued reading his momentous document. McInnerney now signaled to the organist. The organist energetically played thunderous deep chords. Seymour raised his voice to a shout. He could not be heard in the rear of the church. But he was heard by McInnerney, the distinguished visitors, and the television soundmen. He concluded:

"We therefore ask the Chancery office of Washington to turn over to the blacks of this neighborhood all the proceeds of the sale of St. Luke's. We estimate this sum to be ten million dollars. This money will be distributed in the black community for the purpose of creating meaningful employment for all the black people—industry, business, insurance, managed by black people."

Seymour folded the manifesto and put it in his pocket. He turned directly to the television cameras and spoke, clear-eyed, resolutely:

"We are dead serious about our demands."

An elderly black woman, wearing a floppy pink hat, rose suddenly from her pew, pushed by the cameras, walked toward Seymour. She raised a scolding finger.

"You are a disgrace to your race," she said. "You can't walk in here and interrupt a service like this. Not in the presence of Our Lord in the Tabernacle."

Seymour, ignoring her, now walked slowly down the center aisle.

The cameramen, hunkering low in front of him, backed toward the rear door. The church dignitaries on the altar were stony-faced. Many in mild shock. Vicar General Prial, standing openmouthed by the pulpit, looked on in amazement, then fear—that an explosion might occur, that his chief might be in physical danger. In the pulpit, McInnerney, now rendered speechless, held firm to the railing and watched the procession going down the aisle.

Midway to the rear, Seymour stopped. He faced the black congregation and shouted impulsively:

"Get off your knees, black people. It is better to die on your feet than live on your knees. Walk out of here with your heads high."

Seymour stood, chin held high, defiant. Several of the younger blacks, responding to his call, rose and slipped out of the pews. Then others.

"Come on," Seymour exhorted. "Right on."

Other young blacks followed the first. The cameramen parted to make way in the aisle. The organ thundered deep chords. Now the pews were emptying rapidly. Seymour passed through the front door. Outside, he reread his manifesto for the reporters and TV soundmen, to be certain the organ had not drowned out his message. The cameras whirred, the crowd gathered and pulsed, the police exchanged uneasy glances.

Inside the church, there was vast confusion and indecision about whether to continue the services. Prial made the decision swiftly. He darted up the pulpit steps, escorted McInnerney to the sacristy, where he sent a young priest to bring the limousine to the side door—with its police escort. The two men waited, ashen-faced.

Mary, forewarned, had watched Seymour from her pew, heart thudding, uneasy, as though she were not an observer, but a principal in the confrontation. As Seymour read his document, voice lost in the thunder of the organ, she pulled hard for him, silently saying: "Go, go, Seymour." But unease gave way to fear. Watching the old woman in the floppy hat, she felt they were treading the knife edge of violence. The direct confrontation was a mistake. It brought conflicting passion too close. This was not the intelligent way to make war.

She hurried from her pew, joining the throngs now pressing toward the rear, the door. Over her shoulder, she saw Prial, shouldering McInnerney down the pulpit steps, into the sacristy. Even from that distance, she could see the fear in McInnerney's eyes. That was not right, either. It was not right to physically frighten old men.

She followed a black throng out the door, into the glare of sunlight, blinking. She caught a glimpse of Seymour, standing on the front steps, almost lost in the crush of white reporters, TV cameras, a shouting, shoving confusion. A cameraman with a heavy shoulder-TV stepped back, lost his balance, and fell, crashing against the blacks. Those struck or brushed shouted angrily at the hapless TV-man, now lost from view. Following this, the riot police advanced resolutely with batons. The blacks backed up sullenly. A black police lieutenant with a bullhorn spoke authoritatively:

"All right. Clear this area. All of you. Go home. The Mass is over. Clear this area."

Across the street, Seymour's pickets stopped marching. They stared at the confusion, placards slung sloppily over their shoulders.

Mary edged down the steps to the sidewalk. She went into the street, between the yellow police sawhorses, hurrying now, away from the cathedral, toward her car. A block away, she threaded her way around a group of small black children, jumping up and down, raising clenched fists defiantly, hurling obscenities in the general direction of the cathedral, toward the riot police who were safely beyond earshot. She reached her car, quickly unlocked the door, got in without looking back, started the engine, and roared off.

Well into the white neighborhood, she pulled into a gasoline station, parked, and hurried to a public telephone. She fished out a dime. With trembling fingers, she dialed the All Saints' rectory. Mrs. Munally answered. Mary asked for Father Daugherty.

"He's eating his lunch," Mrs. Munally said coolly. "Can you please call back?"

"No, I'm sorry. It's important."

"I'll get him then," she said.

There had been no need to identify herself. When Dan answered, Mary let go:

"Dan . . . I've just come from St. Luke's . . . I feel lucky I got out alive . . . Nothing really happened. But you felt all along it was *about* to happen. Understand? Seymour was great. I mean . . . he *looked* very impressive. There was tremendous media coverage. Mc-Innerney seemed stunned. He tried to drown out Seymour with the organ. It broke up the Mass. I was almost sure there was going to be violence."

"Where are you now?" Dan said.

"In a gas station. Out of the ghetto."

"Good. Now . . . try to calm down. What was the . . . can you give me the general reaction?"

Mary paused.

"A combination of consternation and confusion. Maybe fear . . ."

"He got his point across?"

"Oh yes. I'll say. But, Dan . . . I don't know. I don't like it. It was . . . *dangerous*. McInnerney was frightened. So was I. There was this tension in the air. One spark, somebody could have been *killed*. Do you understand?"

"Yes. Of course. What . . ."

"Dan, we've got to talk, soon," she rushed on. "I don't like it. I mean . . . this is *not* the way to do it. For one thing, it's the *wrong* issue. It's the wrong weapon . . . St. Luke's is really a diversion."

"I know that," Dan cut in. "We discussed all that the other night. I never did buy St. Luke's as an issue."

"It mixed the black thing in, which is not really relevant."

"I know, I know. That's Klein's thing. Not ours."

"Well, Mr. Klein's got to stop running this show. I feel very strongly about that. It's too dangerous down there. And, as I say, we say, it's beside the point. We've got to have a *plan*."

"We have a plan," Dan said. "I worked one out with LeGuiese. Mr. Klein will not run this show. Mr. Klein will merely be a tool."

"When am *I* supposed to hear about it?" Mary said, in a tone that conveyed her general anxiety: what about me?

"Today. This afternoon. As soon as I can get away."

"It's got to be a better plan than this slap-dash stuff. Something intellectual, not physical. If you frighten these people physically, it's going to backfire."

"It's *plenty* intellectual," Dan said defensively. "Certainly it does not include violence, or even near-violence."

"All right. And another thing. I'm resigning my role as ghetto spy. I'm not cut out for this."

Daugherty chuckled. "OK."

"What *is* my role?" she said.

"We'll discuss that later—OK? My lunch is getting cold . . . I've got three baptisms."

"I'll be waiting," she said coolly. "As I have been, patiently, for days."

"Mary," Dan said firmly, "I'm sorry . . . it couldn't be helped."
"Never mind," she said, forcing cheer. "Can you abide spaghetti for dinner again?"
"Sure," he said. "See you in a little while."
" 'Bye."
She hung up and returned to the car.

II

Staring into the mirror of the bed table, Jean Favrot energetically scrubbed her face with cold cream. Color had returned to her cheeks. Her eyes were clear, her stomach settled. She felt fine, ready to go home—impatient, the way she had always been on the third day after each of her deliveries. Bored by the hospital routine, the dull food, the lying abed, hour after hour. Five days! This time—thank God—there would be no breast drying, no painful bindings, no stitches. She wiped her face with Kleenex, threw back the sheet, sat on the edge of the bed, eyes wandering to the vases of flowers, the little mason jar of wilting wildflowers Chris had sent. God! she thought. Then she cried.

Bob came through the door, carrying a small suitcase with her clothes. He had just finished at the cashier's cage, given the floor nurse the pink release slip. The bill for the five days had been $436.61. One more shocker, added to the others. Blue Cross covered much of it. The rest he paid by check. He set the suitcase on the bed.

"What's the matter?" he said, noting—with genuine alarm—Jean's tears.

"Nothing," she said, dabbing.

"Are you all right?" he said.

He had been asking that question of her all week, every time he saw her. He had come often, commuting between house and hospital, shopping center, All Saints', and God-knows-where-else. It had been a trying time. Annie Shields (who knew the truth) had helped Emma with the meals, getting the children ready for Mass, looking after the baby, and the creation of the "cover" story—ptomaine poisoning. But

Bob had done all the driving and shopping, an eye-opening experience. All week he had worried: that his anger had driven Jean to do it, that she might do it again. That was why he kept asking the question.

"I'm fine," Jean said, getting up, opening the suitcase, going into the bath with her clothes. "I'll be ready in a second."

Dressing quickly, she kept her mind fixed firmly on practical matters. A mental list of things that she must do. Go to market. See about the laundry. Take back the rental typewriter.

She returned to the room, folded her nightgown and bathrobe, placed these and her cosmetics in the suitcase, snapped the top closed.

"All set," she said cheerily.

"What about those?" Bob said, looking at the vases of flowers.

"Why don't we just leave them?" Jean said.

"OK."

Bob picked up the suitcase. They left the room, walking down the gleaming tiled corridor to the elevator. In the parking lot, Bob threw the suitcase into the deck, held the door for Jean. He had not done that for years.

"Thank you," she said, smiling, getting in.

"Welcome," Bob said, starting the car, the air-conditioning. He let his hands fall to his lap. He spoke quietly:

"Before we go home, I thought we'd better go by and see Dr. Cantor. I've been talking to him over the weekend."

"Oh? All right," she said.

Dr. Cantor had not come by the hospital. He had called Jean, a brief, routine how-are-you-feeling call, like the one from Annie Shields. He had said nothing to indicate he had been talking to Bob.

"He's a pretty sensible guy in some areas," Bob said.

He drove from the hospital to the McLean Clinic. Jean sat silently, thinking, letting her mind, for the first time, dwell on that night. Until now she had been drifting in a haze, letting people, events sweep her along. But now—as Dr. Cantor would say—she must face reality. Perhaps Bob really did want a divorce. They would talk about that, she supposed.

Bob interrupted her thoughts, offering a piece of paper.

"That's McInnerney's pastoral letter on the encyclical," he said. "You might want to glance at it. They're passing them out over at the church."

Jean read the letter. It was, as anyone would guess, an uncompromising endorsement for Rome. It contained no surprises. It did not

affect her one way or the other. In a sense, it seemed of no concern.
"What do you think of that?" Bob said.
"Oh . . . I don't know. What did you expect?"
Bob drove silently.
"Did you see him on television?" Jean said. "That thing at St.
Luke's?"
"Yes," Bob said. "It was on all the news . . . all afternoon and last
night."
"I know. I was watching."
"Fool thing for that crazy nigger kid to do," Bob said.
"Why? I thought it was clever."
"Apart from the arrogance and rudeness—disrupting the Mass—
the idea is farfetched. Why should McInnerney—or we—be held
responsible for Spanish imperialism and so on?"
"That wasn't the main point. If they're selling St. Luke's, the money
ought to be plowed back into the ghetto. That's not unreasonable."
"True. But . . . a big but. You can't have outsiders—minority
groups and street gangs—telling you how to run your business. Maybe
the Chancery needs the money for something else."
"Like a theological center? Boy, we really need that, now don't
we?"
Bob swung into the clinic parking lot. They went inside, sat down on
the hard, plastic waiting chairs, thumbing magazines.
Dr. Cantor came from his office. He was dressed in dark blue Palm
Beach suit, regimental tie, black shoes. He was short, dark, smiling.
"Hi," he said cheerily. "I'm sorry I kept you waiting. 'Lo, Jean. Bob?
I'm Dr. Cantor."
Bob rose. He shook hands, warily gauging the man, whom he knew
only by telephone voice. He was much younger, much, much younger
than he had imagined. Young—yet businesslike, precise in dress. A
good outward impression—yet a man to watch. They followed him to
his office, a small but substantial room with cork walls, bookshelves,
very comfortable lounge chairs, in all, a cozy, intimate place. They
took seats. On the wall behind the desk, Bob noted, there was a single
picture—a black and white line drawing—a profile of a man with a
Van Dyke beard, disturbing eyes. Cantor turned immediately to
administrative matters, his appointment calendar, which controlled his
life as rigidly as the timetable controls the airliner.
"Let's work out how we proceed time-wise," Cantor said, unscrewing

his fountain pen, poising it over the calendar. "Bob, you called me. What do you suggest?"

"Me?" Bob said, crossing his legs with effort. "Hell, you're the doctor. What do you suggest?"

It was true that Bob had telephoned Cantor. He had turned to the man, partly in desperation. The whole business had thrown him to an area of life about which he knew nothing, had had no practical experience, and which, as he confided to Annie Shields, after a few vodka-tonics, gave him the creeps. There was, he was certain, no history of . . . insanity . . . in Jean's family.

His first instinct had been to call Ryan, get the name of a Catholic head-shrinker. But Annie had advised the call to Cantor. After all, Cantor already knew Jean, the problems, the situation. To start from scratch, with a new shrink, would be time-consuming, redundant, and probably very expensive. Bob had been impressed on the first call, after he apologized for his own intemperate call, and language, the previous Tuesday afternoon. Cantor didn't snow him with mumbo-jumbo, nor try to sell him anything, as Bob had feared he might. Even so, Bob was not yet comfortable in the office of this non-Catholic shrink, and a little nonplussed that Cantor had turned the responsibility for the meeting back to him.

"I think that's mostly up to you and Jean," Cantor said. He turned to Jean. "Do you have any opinion?"

"I don't understand," Jean said.

"Oh?" Cantor said turning to Bob. "Didn't you tell her your thinking?"

"No," Bob said, uncrossing his legs. "I didn't have time."

Cantor looked from Jean to Bob.

"I think," he said, "for openers, it might be well to establish some communication link between you. Nothing exotic. Merely some primitive procedure."

"May I ask what this is all about?" Jean said.

"Suppose you tell her," Cantor said.

"Over the weekend, honey, Dr. Cantor and I were tossing this . . . your . . . uh . . ."

"Her theatrical pill-taking," Cantor interrupted. "Go on. . . ."

"Yes . . . tossing that around. *He* felt that perhaps it would be wise if you and I . . . if we *both* came to see him."

"Oh, I see," Jean said.

"Actually," Cantor said, "it was Bob's idea, not mine. Isn't that correct, Bob?"

"As a matter fact . . . yes. Not that it makes that much difference."

"On the contrary," Cantor said. "It is quite important."

"All right," Bob conceded. "It was *my* idea."

"How do you feel about it?" Cantor said to Jean.

"I don't know," Jean said. "All right, I guess."

"We'll withdraw you from group in place of these private sessions," Cantor said to Jean. "Inasmuch as group seems to be—at least for Bob —a point of contention, an abrasive. You understand that?

"Yes . . ." Jean said.

"I don't *suggest* you withdraw from group," Cantor said. "It's entirely up to you."

"I *like* group."

"And you're *good* for the group," Cantor said. "However, it may be that we can push this along faster and better in private session. I leave it up to you two. It is more expensive this way. . ."

"To hell with the expense," Bob said, thinking back on the hospital bill. Where would it end? Was this some kind of exotic con game?

"Then how do we do this?" Cantor said. "Shall I see you separately or together?"

Bob looked at Jean.

"I have no idea," Bob said.

"Jean?"

She shrugged her shoulders. Cantor thumbed his calendar, frowning.

"I can give you this hour every Monday until the fall," he said. "Actually, it's a cancellation. You could alternate, or I can see you together."

"I'll be traveling a lot," Bob said.

"Why don't we do this?" Cantor said. "I'll put you down for the hour. Today I will see you separately, briefly, then together at the end. Then, I'll see you jointly, if Bob can make it, is not traveling, or Jean alone. In other words, the hour is yours. The cost is thirty-five dollars an hour."

"OK," Bob said.

Cantor made a note on the calendar. Then he wrote out an appointment card, handed it to Bob. The card had no name, no mention of the clinic, only the date and time.

"Now then," Cantor said, looking at his wristwatch. "Time is running.

Suppose I start with Jean? Bob, would you mind waiting in the reception room? Thank you."

Bob left the office immediately. Jean set her purse on the floor, lit a cigarette. Cantor got up, partially closed the venetian blinds, returned to his swivel chair, reclined with his head far back.

"Well," he said. "You've certainly been busy."

"Yes," Jean said, inhaling. "It was sort of stupid."

"I had a nice long chat with Bill Clark," Cantor went on, ignoring this. "He stopped by Saturday morning and we had coffee."

"How did he hear?" Jean said.

"I called him."

"Oh."

"I liked him very much. Very bright guy, very nice. Honest. He's had a rough year . . . and I'm not sure he had the best professional advice out there. He certainly needed a good lawyer. That wife of his . . . ex-wife . . . was a real bitch. Didn't leave him a damned thing. Anyway, he is weighted down by guilt. First, his kids. Even Angela. Now you. But I told him, quite frankly, to forget you. That you were simply using him."

"That's *not* true," Jean said, angrily snubbing out her cigarette. "That's what Mike said and you said he was wrong."

"I didn't say that at all."

"You didn't?"

"Anyway, Jean, it's water over the dam."

"How is he?"

"He's fine now, I think. I have a new group forming up next week. So, *he's* going into that."

"How's his book?"

"He's going back to it this week."

"He needs a typist."

"Let *him* worry about that."

"Why do you now say I was using him? Using him how?"

"For sex. For . . . well, Jean. Let's go back a few months. Your life, for whatever reason, brought you up against a blank wall. The anxiety you felt, I firmly believe, was brought on by a kind of desperate need to explore yourself. Your religion wasn't enough. Isn't that what you said, in effect, the first night of group? You're not unique. Everybody who comes up on forty is swept by that same panic. You look back on those yawning years, that great abyss, think about all that *could* have been, what actually was, and it seems trivial, inconsequential, meaningless, even crazy . . . inexplicable. That's on the surface, then there are deeper needs. Childhood traumas, perhaps forced up by your own teen-age children, whose voices, problems remind you of your own . . . that sort of thing. Anyway, I don't want to go into that now. You were using Bill the way you used group. I think more than anything else, you believed he might help you to understand yourself."

"Is that so wrong?"

"Wrong? What is wrong?"

"I mean . . . Well, he told me he had been deep."

"And you hoped to take advantage of that. Play amateur psychiatry with him. True?"

"I don't know," Jean said, lighting another cigarette.

"Anyway, he's fine. He'll be all right. There is no need for you to feel sorry for him."

"I don't. Curiously . . ."

"And the sex was great, wasn't it?"

"Terrific," Jean said.

"You needed that. We all do—in spite of the Pope's idea."

"And how! But I don't want to be another Margo."

"You won't be. You *can't* be. It just isn't in the cards. One Olympian fling—a majestic encounter—and that's all. Now back to business."

"Why did I take the pills?"

"Guilt, goddamnit! Why does anybody do anything? Everybody do everything? That whole scene was inevitable. It's nothing to worry about. You won't do it again."

"Why did you say it was theatrical?"

"Because you didn't really mean it. It was a kind of . . . a catharsis. Purging yourself. Shutting out that old life, symbolically, bringing on the new. It was also a cry for help. To force Bob to concentrate on *your* problem. That's why, in effect, you're here today. Isn't it?"

"I suppose so. But . . . I *did* feel I meant it. I've read . . . you have to be careful. Suicides always telegraph . . . in advance . . . they make gestures to attract help."

"Bullshit! Jean, that's like saying all marijuana smokers turn into heroin addicts. It just isn't so. I wish I had a nickel for every patient of mine who took an overdose. I'd be a rich man."

"Doesn't speak well of your therapy," Jean smiled.

"Time's running out," Cantor said, glancing at his wristwatch. "I'm going on the assumption that you want to try to make a go with Bob."

"I guess so. If he does. He said he wanted a divorce."

"He doesn't. The marriage contract, as he says, is unbreakable. But it won't be easy. He's been hurt, very deeply. It's going to take time."

"I have to do it—for the children."

"No, Jean. Not the children. For *you*. Right?"

"All right."

"You'll have to find something to do with that fantastic energy of yours . . . some real, meaningful outside interest. And I don't mean parish censuses and stupid things like that."

"I couldn't go back to that."

"Get Bob. Later, we'll all talk."

Jean crushed out her cigarette, picked up her purse, went out to the reception room. Bob took her place. Cantor packed a pipe, lit it with his silver butane lighter. Bob watched this activity carefully. He was not yet sure about Cantor.

"She's all right," Cantor said, inhaling, then getting up, opening the window a crack.

"That's good," Bob said, leaning back, swinging his legs on an ottoman.

"Do you get any exercise?" Cantor said.

"What? Yes . . . I play golf."

"That's not *exercise*. You look forty pounds overweight to me."

"I'm a little heavy."

"How much do you drink?"

"Oh . . . a few, here and there."

"How many ounces a day?"

"Ounces? I don't know. I never counted ounces. I have a couple for lunch, a couple before dinner, a nightcap or two. . . ."

"Experience has led me to double these estimates," Cantor said. "You say six drinks a day. Would twelve be more accurate?"

Bob looked at the floor.

"I guess so."

"Two-ounce drinks? Twenty-four ounces a day? That would be very nearly a fifth, would it not?"

"Hell no! I'm not a fifth-a-day drinker."

Cantor passed over the pad on which he had been adding.

"You add it," he said, offering Bob the pad.

Bob stared at the figures. He returned the pad without comment.

"My job is to force people to face reality," Cantor said, "and then work out a way to cope with it. Have you ever thought of what you may be doing to your liver?"

"My liver's fine," Bob said. But, inwardly, he wondered, was it?

"Good. I hope it stays like that. I'd guess it was pretty ragged."

"For my age, I'm in damned good shape."

"You look like a flabby, middle-aged suburban type to me. No offense meant. That's the impression you convey. Think about it. Anyway, let's get down to business."

"All right," Bob said. "Fire away."

"I assume from your comments over the weekend you want to try to put this deal back together?"

"On my terms," Bob said. "First, I want her absolute assurance this won't happen again. She will never see that son of a bitch, or anybody else, again. Second, I want an apology. Some slight sign of remorse. Third, she's got to cut out all this outside intellectual nonsense—no more typing! And no more classic novels! For Christ's sake, I was looking at that book over the weekend. Do you know that gal threw herself under a train? No wonder . . ."

Cantor puffed on his pipe, weighing, thinking. This was not going to be easy. Bob Favrot would be tough, stubborn, rigid. He sat up, interrupted.

"That was before *him,*" he said, thrusting a thumb over his shoulder at the portrait behind him.

"Who's *that?*" Bob said.

"Freud."

Bob Favrot stared at the drawing. He knew Freud. In high school, the Jesuits had taught him about Freud. He was an atheist, a quack. Very clever, and, at root, anti-Catholic, the greatest threat to Roman Catholicism, the Jesuits had said, since Luther. But that was years ago, and times had changed. Or *were* changing, apparently.

"Let's back up a minute," Cantor said. "You might as well face some facts, Bob. I can't put a deal together with you coming on like this. Jean is a different person, for better or worse. Better, I believe, in spite of all. Her eyes are open, or at least opening. She's going to be her own person from now on, no matter what you think—or want. She's going to do more than change dirty diapers. You can't keep her down on the farm, like the old days. Now, can we proceed from that premise?"

"*She's* the guilty party," Bob said. "Not me. I have a right . . . I haven't done anything."

"Haven't you?"

"Certainly not. Not once in seventeen years."

"I didn't mean that."

"I don't follow you."

"Do you think of her as an equal?"

"Equal? Equal how?"

"Oh, say, a companion. A drinking buddy."

"No."

"You never talk about things that count?"

"I guess not."

"You have the southern view of womanhood, I take it. Her place is in the home, et cetera; women should be seen, not heard. All that old garbage."

"Certainly not."

"Think about it—later. I've got a lot of ground to cover in a hurry. Right now, yes or no, shall I try to put this deal together?"

"I said yes."

"You've got to meet her halfway. Right on the fifty-yard line. That means you've got to bend. First off, forget who is or who isn't guilty. This is not a divorce court. I'm not a lawyer. This is going to be hard. I need your *total* cooperation."

"OK. I'll do that. For the sake of the kids."

Cantor laid his pipe in the ashtray.

"Another thing. Let's get the kids thing straight. I don't want, ever again, to hear about those kids. We're not doing this for the kids. If we start on that premise, we'll never get anywhere. We're doing it for *your* sake, for Jean's. You each have a life of your own, separate and distinct from the children's. That is the life we're structuring here. Stop worrying about the children. You can deal with that later. Right now we're dealing with you and Jean—a matter of survival . . . of two adult human beings."

"All right," Bob said. "But she ought to apologize, at least."

"You're not living just to have children . . . there's more to life than that," Cantor said, ignoring Bob's renewed demand.

"It's important," Bob replied.

"But not controlling."

"If you say so."

"Why don't we call Jean? We only have ten minutes left. Is there anything else you'd like to tell me privately?"

"I can't think of anything."

"Did you give some thought to the booze?"

"Yes."

"What do you think?"

"I probably ought to cut down . . . been hitting it pretty heavy."

"Probably . . ." Cantor said.

Bob returned to the reception room to call Jean. They sat down again, facing Cantor.

"We've got a lot of work to do," he said, lighting his pipe again. "One thing I meant to ask both of you and forgot. What are we going to do about birth control? Bob?"

Bob pursed his lips, averted his eyes. Then he took out the pastoral letter, passed it to Cantor. Cantor read the letter swiftly.

"What do *you* think of that?" he said to Bob.

"It's binding," Bob said.

"Hmmmmmm," Cantor said. "Jean?"

"I think it's stupid."

"Bob," Cantor said, "don't you have enough kids? Haven't you done your duty? Maybe you've earned an exemption."

"It's not a matter of exemption, it's a matter of moral law."

"What does that mean?"

"Moral law? That means, oh, hell, you know what that means don't you? We don't have time to go into the whole moral law thing."

"Jean should never have another baby," Cantor said. "Don't you agree?"

"Yes," Bob said. "Absolutely. But . . ."

"You've got to educate the ones you have."

"I *know* that," Bob said impatiently.

"And Vatican roulette obviously doesn't work."

"Not always," Bob said.

"So if we have sex, then we must have the pill. It's that simple, isn't it?"

"Not quite . . ."

"Yes it is, Bob," Jean said. "It's really that simple."

"Look at it another way," Cantor said. "Do you *want* sex?"

"Certainly," Bob said.

"Then all you people have to change the Pope's mind."

"How?" Jean said.

"I don't know," Cantor said. "Didn't the Council give more power to the laity? Let the Pope hear from you—direct."

Jean laughed.

"Write him a letter," Cantor pressed, seriously. "Or run naked in the street. Organize. Get up petitions. Stone the Chancery. It's not my church. But you've got to let him know how you feel. Nothing in this world is immutable—except birth and death and guilt. Bob, you're a politician. Don't you spend all week changing laws?"

"Yes. But the Church is *not* a democracy."

"Why not?"

"Because it is founded on the Word of God. You don't vote . . . you don't change that."

"I can't believe God would want you to go on having babies or forswearing sex. I just can't believe it. Bob, why don't you take a highly personal point of view of the matter? Be selfish?"

"I have looked at it that way. But, in the Church, you either go along or get out. My faith means too much to me to get out. So I have to rock along like it is."

"Or change it," Cantor said. "It seems to me the climate is going to dictate change. The polls . . . about half the Catholic women use some form of birth control, don't they? I don't know of a single psychologist—Catholic or otherwise—who concurs with the Pope. Seems to me if you could mobilize all that opposition, forge it into some kind of effective weapon, you could bludgeon him into changing his mind. OK, let's concede both of you are over the hill. That you could survive without sex. I don't really believe that, but let's just say so. The real question is: Do you want to pass this can of worms on to your children? Do you want them to grow up all clutched sexually, like you two people?"

"No," Jean said angrily. "Absolutely not."

"Well, then," Cantor said. "You have to *do* something. I saw your Archbishop on TV last night. He seemed like a reasonable enough person, maybe a little dense selling off that church in the ghetto and touching off all that mess, but . . . why don't *you* go talk to him, Bob?"

"That would be the ultimate waste of time."

"Jean?"

"Me? Go see McInnerney? He wouldn't give me the time of day."

"I thought he was your spiritual teacher?"

"Yes, but . . ."

"What about this fellow Daugherty? He certainly couldn't buy all this?"

"I don't think he does," Jean said.

"He goes along," Bob said. "Or he has, up to now."

"Go have a good heart-to-heart with him," Cantor said. "The two of you. Well, time's up. I got into that because I think it is quite obviously core stuff for the three of us. We have to get that in focus before we can move on to the other stuff. OK?"

"OK," Bob said glumly.

They stood. Bob shook hands clumsily with Cantor. At the door, Cantor spoke up again.

"By the way. Wait a minute. Come here a minute."

They returned to the center of the office.

"How about you two facing each other."

Jean and Bob looked at him, puzzled. But they turned, standing face to face, like obedient schoolchildren, feeling foolish.

"Good," Cantor said. "Now, Bob, take Jean's hands in yours. That's right. Go on. Good."

Bob and Jean stood, face to face, holding hands, looking, for the first time in many years, directly and deep.

"How do you like *that?*" Cantor said.

"I feel a little stupid," Bob said.

Jean said nothing.

"Well, good-bye," Cantor said. "See you next week."

Jean and Bob left the office, walking slowly through the reception room, where two teen-agers were thumbing magazines in a desultory way, then out into the heat, to the station wagon, both silent, lost in private thought. Driving away, Bob said:

"This is what they call psychiatry?"

"He's not an MD. He's a psychologist."

"He's not a bad fella. Sure does like to go straight to the heart of things."

"He's very direct."

"I'll say. Stone the Chancery!"

"Maybe we should."

Bob thought about that.

III

Father Daugherty drove from All Saints' to Halfway House in an exalted mood. Things were moving! Boy, were they moving! His doubts about LeGuiese had been resolved that afternoon. LeGuiese was both thinker *and* fighter. The plan, still not refined, now at least had a hard core, a direction. Tonight he, McDivitt, Klein, would begin shaping a superstructure around the core.

It was a glorious summer evening. The cool spell was lingering on. Daugherty had put on khaki slacks and a knit sportshirt, lowered the shabby MG roof. He drove like a fanatic at LeMans, weaving, cornering, laying rubber at the traffic lights. The MG shuddered from the strain.

He must remember to reassure Mary. They must formulate their own private plan, to mesh with the larger plan. It was not right to leave her dangling, suspended in mid-air at Halfway House, getting more paranoid by the minute. She must be drawn into the plan, assigned a specific, important role, to keep her mind occupied. She would be valuable. She had more brains—and common sense—than all of them put together, excluding LeGuiese. Nobody had a better mind than LeGuiese. Tonight, after McDivitt and Klein left, they would talk.

He parked in a space opposite Halfway House. He stood by the MG for a moment, looking at the house, then he crossed the street, mounted the stoop. The screen door stood ajar. It needed a new spring. He pulled it tight behind him, then called down the hall:

"Mary! I'm here."

From the kitchen, Mary returned his call:

"Come on back. I'm in here."

He went down the corridor to the kitchen. She met him at the door, smiling, wearing a faded apron over her short cotton dress. They kissed, long, tenderly, passionately. It had been two—almost two—days. Then they sat down at the kitchen table.

"What a day!" Daugherty said, drumming his fingers on the table-top. "The whole town's exploding! LeGuiese is going to release the statement tomorrow morning. I brought a copy. Here, read it. No, wait. Later. It's all-out—no holds barred. You should have heard them fighting over the words! Words! Like a bunch of prima donnas with their eyes on history . . . anyway, let's see. Oh, yeah. You saw the papers? The news stories? The bishops in Canada, Belgium, Holland, where else? New Zealand or someplace down there. LeGuiese says the Georgetown bunch—the theology department—is going to come out the day after, supporting the statement . . . attacking McInnerney."

He paused, scratching his head.

"Dan?" Mary said calmly. "May I please have a drink?"

"Yes, of course," he replied sheepishly. "What do we have?"

"I bought a bottle of Scotch. In honor of the occasion. My first dinner party!"

"Can we afford it?"

"Why not? We only live once."

Daugherty went to the sink, poured two drinks, adding ice and water.

"Red Label!" he exclaimed, holding the bottle aloft.

"I didn't know what kind to get. The man said that was good. It cost a little more—but . . ."

"A toast," he said, giving her the drink. "To Success. No, wait. Better. Here's to Eve, the mother of our race, who always wore a fig leaf in the right place. Then here's to Adam, the father of us all, who was always Johnny-on-the-spot when the leaves began to fall."

"Oh, Dan! That's awful."

"Something I remembered from the seminary."

"It doesn't scan."

"I think I goofed. Let's see. Here's to Eve, the mother—"

"Never mind. Oh, before I forget, I must tell you. Guess who's back in town?"

"Judge Crater?"

"Can you be serious for a minute? Peter's back—Sharon's boyfriend."

"Ohhhh-ho! Did you see him?"

"No. The nurse said he was back, trying to see her. They won't let him near the place, of course. Not while she's showing improvement. She's much, much better today, they said. The treatment is really working. She's weak, but rational."

"Good. Good. Good."

He sipped his drink, remembering Sharon. So much had happened so fast.

"The nurse said she ought to be aborted."

"Yes," Daugherty said, frowning. "I suppose she ought to be, actually. Right?"

"I don't know. The fetus is fully formed. There's no danger to Sharon's health, of course. The fetus may be damaged, true. But . . ."

"We don't condone abortion, even if she could get one legally," Dan said, pressing his lips grimly.

"I suppose not. I . . . I don't know *how* I truly feel, frankly. It seems so drastic. It really does seem like murder, doesn't it?"

"Yes, it does. I . . . somehow I just can't go that far. Can you?"

"No. I really can't."

"Maybe we don't buy it because it hasn't become our problem. It *hasn't,* has it?"

Mary blushed and turned her head. She spoke in a low voice:

"I hope not! God, Dan. I've been worried *sick*. We took an awful chance."

"Yes," he said glumly, sipping his drink.

"So I went to see a doctor this morning," Mary said, still looking away.

"You did?" Daugherty said incredulously. "What did he say? Are you . . . ?"

"I don't *know*, silly. You can't tell right away. It takes . . . you have to wait until your next . . . your next time of the month. If it doesn't come . . ."

"Oh," Dan said. "With all the modern science around, you'd think they could give you some kind of test."

"Not this soon. Anyway, I asked him what I should do. I had no history of blood-clotting or kidney problems, so . . . he . . . he gave me a prescription for the pill."

"You're kidding," Daugherty said, draining his drink. Then he got up, made another drink, thinking that, somehow, it did not seem right that Mary should take the pill. Others, remote from his real experience, yes. But Mary!

"I'm not going to worry myself to death," she said. "We're not ready for a baby yet!"

"That's for damned sure," Dan said, returning to the table, sitting down. Until now, he had not given that possibility a thought. No, not ready now, not even soon. They had to get their own lives realigned before they could think of introducing a third. "Which reminds me," he added. "Jean Favrot came by the rectory this afternoon, just before I left for LeGuiese's."

"How is she?"

"Fine."

"Fine?"

"Well, determined, I'd say. She wanted to volunteer for some gutsy work. I couldn't tell her anything . . . yet. I told her there were some things cooking and I'd let her know. She could be very useful. She has a lot of respect in the parish, knows a lot of people."

"Did her husband come too?"

"No. But she said he was seeing the shrink. *That's* progress, believe me. She also asked me to OK the pill."

"What did you say?"

"I said OK. Morally, I suppose, there's not much difference between that and Sharon having an abortion, or for that matter, *you* taking the pill. Once you cross the line in your mind . . . Anyway, enough of this. What's for dinner? What's that I smell?"

"Meat loaf—with garlic," she smiled.

"I *love* meat loaf."

"I know. You told me. I just hope Klein and McDivitt do."

She jumped up to check the meat in the oven.

"I hope I don't burn it. There's no meat thermometer around here."

"Shall I go get one?"

"No," she said, closing the oven. "Let's live dangerously."

"As if we're not already," Dan said. "Don't be uptight. You'll like McDivitt. Very cool. *Very* handsome. Now, don't you go making a run . . ."

Mary blushed angrily. Then she glared at Daugherty.

"I'm sorry," he said quietly. "That *was* stupid."

He sipped his drink, berating himself. You don't joke around about some things. He was learning about nuances of life—slowly.

"Have you talked to him since . . ."

"Yes," Daugherty said. "Every day."

"What did you tell him about . . . us?"

"I told him we had postponed it temporarily, until this thing blew over."

"What did he say?" Mary said, sitting down.

"OK by him. He understands."

"I wonder," Mary said coolly. "I mean, really, Dan, can you go on dipping in and out of the priesthood like this, as the occasion requires?"

"No, Mary, of course not. But LeGuiese says hang in there, for a few weeks longer. At least help get the thing rolling. There has never been an opportunity like this."

"Did he clear you to take the sacraments?"

"Yes."

"You confessed?"

"Not exactly. It's sort of . . . sort of gray. He said it was OK to say Mass and all. Actually, we didn't have much time to talk about it."

They sat drinking, talking, like husband and wife. The lonely, neglected feeling—and the guilt about the pill—Mary had felt all day evaporated. The house now rang with laughter, talk, plans, ideas. She felt the euphoria of defiance, the thrill of impending battle, the reassurance of clear-cut and decisive action. Then, a sudden wave of doubt. Was she pushing Dan into battle for her own gain, to make certain he crossed that bridge, the point of no return? She must think about that, above all, not push.

They heard a booming cry in the front hall.

"Dan!"

"Hey, that's McDivitt!" Daugherty said, jumping up, kissing Mary on the forehead.

McDivitt boomed into the kitchen, almost on the heels of his greeting. He was a giant of a man, six-four, over two hundred well-tanned, well-shaped, muscular pounds squeezed into tight chinos, a white shirt, brown loafers, no socks. His face was square-jawed, his blond hair cropped short, like a military recruit. His glinting, quick blue eyes swept the room, taking in all, like a quarterback sizing up the downfield pass defense. He moved with the unhurried grace of an athlete. His eyes fell on Mary, fixed, friendly. She had seldom seen a man so prepossessing, so ruggedly handsome. Certainly never a priest.

"Mary, may I present Joe McDivitt. Joe, this is Mary Murray."

McDivitt smiled, a huge, enveloping smile, like Eisenhower's, truly meant.

"How do you do?" he said, in his low, booming voice. "I've been looking forward to this."

He stood back, admiring her. Mary blushed red, avoiding his eyes.

"How the hell do you get a drink in this joint?" McDivitt said, good-naturedly. Then to Mary:

"You know what this con man told me? He said you were an *intellectual*, a PhD in philosophy."

"Well," Mary said politely, "I *am*. Won't you sit down?"

"Thank you," McDivitt said, subdued by Mary's cool retort. He settled his bulk into a rickety chair, feet planted firmly on the floor.

"We have Scotch," Daugherty said, going to the sink.

"Good," McDivitt said. "By the way, Dan, have you seen the papers?"

"Yes," Daugherty said, returning with McDivitt's drink, a new one for himself and Mary.

"The phone's been jumping off the hook," McDivitt said. "I must have had a dozen calls from people all over. Two or three I hadn't heard from since the seminary. One guy, Italian type named Nalle Nalle—Nalle?—Malle, I mean—you remember him, Dan? Always sitting up in the john with the light on, cramming. Straight-A guy."

"I remember him," Daugherty said, sitting down beside Mary.

"Well, he's up in some damned dumpy parish in West Virginia. Said he was willing to lead a protest march right out of the hills, down to Washington. He was plenty burned up."

"I've been getting calls too," Daugherty said. "A dozen. Mostly around here—except from Seattle. From what's-his-name O'Brien?"

"Tim," McDivitt said.

"Yeah, Tim."

"He called me too," McDivitt said, sipping his drink. "What did you tell them?"

"To cool it—temporarily."

"I also got a call from Frank Hanson who's with that bunch in Detroit," McDivitt said. "They've got two hundred and fifty signatures on a petition to end celibacy."

"All priests?" Mary said.

"All," McDivitt said, draining his glass. He set it on the table. He wiped his mouth with his hand.

"Why do we sit in the kitchen?" Mary said. "It's so hot in here."

"Closer to the source," McDivitt joked, jerking his thumb toward the Scotch bottle.

"You want a refill?" Daugherty said.

"No thanks. I'll pass. Good Scotch."

"There's a bunch in Brooklyn with a petition," Daugherty said.

"McNulty's deal?" McDivitt said.

"Yes."

"I also got a conference call from Simon and Goodpastor in San Antonio," Daugherty said. "I usually say Simon and Garfunkel. Anyway, they've got a full-blown war on their hands down there. They told me they've written every order in the world asking them not to send replacements down there until Lucey resigns."

"Clever," McDivitt said. "The real trick is to get all this dissent organized, mobilized, and pointed in the right direction."

"By the way," Daugherty said, "I told you Klein was coming?"

"Yes. Good show."

"There's two sides to that coin," Mary said. "Klein is a good man, but I think he's getting carried away. In my opinion, it's a *great* mistake to drag the black issue into this one. The Seymour Jones thing. This is not a black fight."

"I agree," Daugherty said. "To a point. But—as LeGuiese says— Jones is very very useful as a diversion. While Jones keeps pressure on the eastern front, we sweep around from the north in an enveloping move. St. Luke's is a gut issue for the black community. The manifesto was ingenious. His diversion gives us time to mobilize and attack."

"But the important thing," Mary put in firmly, "is not to forget Jones *is* a diversion. This must be made clear to Klein. In addition, you also make it clear to Klein that *he* is not the general. He is—or should be—a war correspondent. So far, he has been playing general. He must be reduced to size. Right, Dan?"

"Right."

"Then do it, tonight," she said firmly.

"I will. I will."

"Who's going to be our general?" McDivitt said.

"I don't know," Daugherty said.

"Well, we better get *that* decided pretty soon," McDivitt said.

"Oh," Daugherty said. "By the way, I have copies of LeGuiese's statement. The LeGuiese document. Here, you guys, have a read."

He passed copies of the document to Mary and McDivitt.

The document was not long—two pages. In essence, it was a concise yet eloquent dissent against *Humanae Vitae*. It criticized Pope Paul for his high-handedness, his arrogance, for ignoring all the legitimate theological and scientific arguments that had been raised since *Casti Connubii*, against Rome's birth control policy, for being insensitive to the suffering of the poor and ignorant, as well as those families already overburdened with children, and for turning his back on the voices of concern raised at the Vatican Council and by his own commission on birth control. It said the encyclical was not infallible, and reminded all Catholics they had a legal and moral right to dissent if they wished.

It concluded: "Therefore, as Roman Catholic theologians, conscious of our duty and our limitations, we conclude that spouses may responsibly decide *according to their conscience* that artificial contraception in some circumstances is permissible and indeed necessary to preserve and foster the values and sacredness of marriage."

Mary and McDivitt read the statement twice, slowly, carefully. Mary spoke first.

"I guess that says it all," she sighed. "It certainly wraps up *my* feelings about it. It is a very beautiful, very powerful statement."

"You could build two dozen sermons on this," McDivitt said admiringly. "I never would have believed a bunch of ivory-tower theologians could say it so clearly and simply."

"That's LeGuiese's fine Belgian hand on the final draft," Dan said. "The first few drafts were unreadable, fifteen or twenty pages long."

"Why did they do it, Dan?" Mary said. "Why have they stormed out of their precious little journals into the open?"

"They're human, like all of us," Daugherty said. "They don't like the way things have been going since Paul, the way we're drifting from the religious freedom implied by the Council. Technically, I think, they resent the fact that Paul chose to ignore all the work they've done over the last twenty years to punch holes in the natural law arguments. They feel Paul is out of touch. Then, finally—and most important—they don't like the didactic tone of the encyclical, the way Paul—and then McInnerney—tries to give the impression the encyclical is an infallible document, the final word. They resent his ignoring the commission, not consulting the bishops before reaching his decision, and being told how to think. In short, of everybody being treated, more or less, like children."

"When are they going to let it go?" McDivitt said.

"In a day or so," Daugherty replied. "They're waiting so the copies they mailed around can arrive. They're lining up support at Georgetown, Fordham, Notre Dame, Holy Cross, and so on . . . the other theologians. Get them to put out supporting statements or sign this one. They're shooting for six hundred signatures."

"Wait till this hits the Chancery," McDivitt said. "Oh, boy! I wish I could see Prial's face!"

"I'm sure they've got a copy by now," Mary said.

"LeGuiese mailed them a bunch," Daugherty said.

"So," McDivitt said. "What do we do? Where do we come into all this?"

"That's entirely up to us," Daugherty said.

"What do you think, Dan?" the other priest asked.

"I think our best course is to mobilize public sentiment behind the theologians. Create a sort of public groundswell, here in Washington, which is as good a place to take a stand as I can think of, and maybe, because it's considered a kind of power center, the best. Besides that, McInnerney has been obstinate enough to go on record with a hard line, and that makes him a perfect target. In the words of Jean Favrot, we'll stone the Chancery!"

"Who's Jean Favrot?" McDivitt asked.

"A woman in my parish with nine kids. Now on the pill."

Daugherty tapped the theologian's statement with his forefinger. "As it says right here in the fine print, *'spouses may responsibly decide according to their conscience. . .'* "

"Those are the operative words," McDivitt said. "But how do we stone the Chancery? Anyway, is the Chancery the right target? Isn't Rome the target?"

"We start with the target at hand. Bring it to a head here, and build support."

"I think that's wise," Mary said.

"Those guys down in San Antonio didn't build much support," Mc-Divitt said.

"They didn't have this issue, this statement."

"True," McDivitt said.

"I intend to start by distributing a copy of this statement to all my parishioners, next Sunday," Daugherty said.

"How will McInnerney react?" McDivitt said, frowning, digging in his hip pocket, bringing out a copy of the Archbishop's pastoral letter. "It says here, quote: While this does not preclude theological discussion, no one can either publicly question or preach doctrines which are not said in conformity with the said authentic teaching. Unquote. That seems to put the theologians in the clear, but not us—not the pastors manning the public pulpits."

"In the first place," Daugherty said, "distributing this statement is not preaching against the encyclical. It's merely making available all the latest theological thinking . . ."

"Now that's really hairsplitting," McDivitt said, smiling ironically. "I *like* that . . . making available the latest theological thinking. . . . Dan, you're a shyster lawyer at heart. Go on."

"In the second place," Daugherty continued, "LeGuiese says there is a real canonical question here about whether McInnerney can forbid a priest to publicly take issue with an encyclical. Legally, anything that is not infallible can be questioned. We've been doing it for two thousand years, off and on. So, as LeGuiese says, who the hell is McInnerney to tell us how to think?"

"Your boss."

"There's that," Mary said.

McDivitt smiled and said:

"Having dinner with Klein isn't exactly what I'd call making the latest theological thinking available. That goes a little beyond that."

"True," Daugherty said. "But McInnerney doesn't have to know."

"He'll find out," McDivitt said.

"So be it," Daugherty sighed. "In any case, the battle will be launched on an intellectual plane. We'll fight it strictly on this conscience statement, the operative words."

"You're sure that LeGuiese and his crowd haven't conned you into being a fall guy?" McDivitt said. "I mean, they can sit back in their ivory towers and disagree on theological grounds and never get hurt. Maybe eventually come up smelling like a rose. But if you start passing this thing out and conspiring with Klein, you're going to get your neck cut off, I think."

"So be it," Daugherty repeated. "They didn't con me. I made my own decision. I'm doing this for all the Jean Favrots of the world."

"Now don't go getting sentimental on me, Dan. The Jean Favrots of the world! Holy Toledo!"

"He means it, Joe," Mary said.

They heard a banging on the screen door.

"Klein," Daugherty said.

He got up, walked down the hall to the foyer. He saw Klein through the screen, a shadowy figure in the twilight.

"Hi, Marv! Come on in. We're having a drink in the kitchen."

Klein shook hands.

"You want to hang your jacket in this closet?" Daugherty said. "It's a little warm."

"No, thanks," Klein said. "I'll wear it."

They joined the others in the kitchen. Klein, accepting his drink, hunched his jacket on his shoulders, looked at McDivitt. So, this was the Joe McDivitt. He didn't seem priestly. He looked more like a cross between Billy Graham and the Redskin linebacker, Chris Hamburger. Klein sat down opposite Mary. He now emptied his pockets of scraps of news ticker, spreading them on the table like playing cards.

"The Jones bit at St. Luke's is sweeping the country," he said, with pride. "Look. In Buffalo, somebody else did it in the Episcopal church. Here's one in Omaha. And Louisiana. A bunch of seminarians have seized the administration building. They want the diocese to turn over the seminary to the blacks."

Mary, Dan, and McDivitt picked up the scraps and read, exchanging as they finished.

"You people get out of here and go in the living room," Mary said, getting up, again checking the meat loaf. "I've got to have room to work. I hope you all like meat loaf."

"Crazy for it," McDivitt said.

"Yes," Klein said, without enthusiasm.

In the living room, Daugherty switched on a shabby lamp. They took chairs. Daugherty, leaning elbows on knees, now came to grips with the problems raised by the news stories on Jones.

"Marv," he said. "Look, we don't profess to be experts in the field of communications. But the whole Jones thing strikes us as a side issue. It's not core. I mean, as I told you last week, the *real* issue to carry this fight on is—or should be—the encyclical. That is a *white* fight, not black, as we see it. Understand me, I see your point about St. Luke's and all that. The publicity is fantastic. But . . ."

"Birth control *should* be a black issue," Klein said thoughtfully, twisting his glass in his hand. "The blacks, the Puerto Ricans, the Indians, the deprived, and so on, suffer most because of the Pope's position. Have you ever been in Spanish Harlem? You talk about over-population . . ."

"I don't deny that," Daugherty said. "But, really, how many *black* Catholics are there anyway? Let me show you what I think is the crux." He handed Klein a copy of the theologians' statement.

Klein read. He saw at once the statement was pure dynamite. Open rebellion. Revolt. The crisis of Catholic obedience now focused right here, in Washington, his territory.

"You see," Daugherty went on, carefully. "This is an intellectual argument. A theological dissent which takes us—or will take us—into an honest dispute with the powers that be. It is not an inflammatory thing, not emotional, like the St. Luke's thing. And it's not black, not . . . not violent . . . or even apt to be violent."

"Is this for general release?" Klein said, headlines forming in his mind.

"Yes."

"When?"

"Tomorrow or the next day."

"May I have this?" Klein said.

"Yes. I have another. Now do you see what I mean?"

"I sure do," Klein said, making plans, mentally deploying his troops.

"Well, that's what we have to talk about tonight."

Mary came from the kitchen. She had put away the apron, primped. She stood in the doorway, silhouetted by the flickering candles on the dining room table.

"Dinner is served, gentlemen," she said, forcing a casual tone. "Come along before it gets cold."

The three men adjourned to the dining room.

IV

Sunday afternoons at the Chancery had been, for as long as the oldest inhabitant could remember, a time for rest and meditation, for entertaining old friends, for catching up on personal correspondence. After midday dinner, usually a sleep-inducing feast served on gold-rimmed china, the kitchen help put a light supper in the refrigerator and left for the day. McInnerney, lulled by the dinner and wine, and the ponderous prose of the Sunday *New York Times,* napped most of the afternoon. Prial escaped to television, to watch sporting events, pro football, golf, baseball, Olympic Games, or whatever the season offered. The Chancery was almost tomblike, the staff reduced to a single girl on the PBX.

No more. That Sunday, the Chancery was fully manned, like the White House war room during an international crisis. The center of action had shifted to the second floor, to McInnerney's private office. The shift in Sunday routine at the Chancery was caused by the statement of the theologians. It had arrived in the mail on Friday, almost simultaneously with the afternoon *Tribune*, which had proclaimed, in shattering headlines:

CATHOLIC WAR ERUPTS IN D.C.

THEOLOGIANS DEFY PRELATE

The statement, the headlines had caught them flat-footed. Prial's instinct—and grapevine—told him to keep up his guard. But he was waiting for the first shot of the theologians where it had always come— in the theological journals or the *National Catholic Reporter* or *Commonweal* or *America*—not in screaming headlines in the *Tribune*. The statement, a declaration of war, had provoked yet another deluge of telephone calls at the Chancery, requests for press interviews, rebuttals.

McInnerney had laid low Saturday, bewildered, stunned, thinking, planning, ignoring all calls save one. Helen Hanrahan had called on the private line to volunteer help. Otherwise, he had kept his own counsel. The statement, McInnerney had concluded, was an act of treachery, disloyalty, disobedience, defiance without precedent in modern Church history. That it had occurred here, in his jurisdiction, seemed absolute confirmation of Helen Hanrahan's vision. McInnerney was more convinced than ever that he had been chosen by the Holy Family to defend the Church in a decisive showdown. By leaking to Klein, the theologians had set the tone of battle. It was scurrilous, dirty, unforgivable. The Chancery would take off the kid gloves. They would fight fire with fire. Sunday morning, shortly after Mass and breakfast, McInnerney had summoned Prial to proclaim that he was going to take a personal hand in the counterattack. They would cancel Sunday dinner, keep on a full staff.

By the time McInnerney and Prial met for private conference that afternoon, the Archbishop had produced a long list of moves. The first, always uppermost in his mind, concerned the theological center, the ground-breaking ceremony, which had now assumed majestic proportions in his mind. In the privacy of his office, he unveiled the idea for the first time to Prial, adding:

"I'll tell you this, Nate. If ever we needed proof of the need for this center, just reread this statement from our so-called theologians. Give Spellman his due. In spite of his cantankerousness, he foresaw this need very clearly, long before I did, anybody did. He was truthfully a saint. A genius. A Francis, Thomas Aquinas, Augustine, Paul, all rolled into one stubborn package. We're not going to let him down. We'll build that place and then we'll handpick the staff. Then . . . someday . . . we'll be in position to deal with these heretics!"

He spit the last word. Prial, draped in a pull-up chair, chewed the end of his dead cigar thoughtfully. Six hundred Catholic theologians had signed the statement or similar statements—if the press could be believed. It was a stupefying, open, intellectual dissent. There had never been anything like it—in terms of numbers or language. Not only that; cardinals, bishops, monsignors, priests the world over, were openly joining in. An ominous rumbling beneath the earth, which could not be ignored. All this considered, Prial did not think it wise to announce a ground-breaking for the theological center. This might be interpreted as their response to the statement. He told McInnerney this.

"It *could* be made to seem cry-babyish," Prial said. "You don't like what your theologians did, so you're picking up your marbles and going to find a new game . . . a new set of theologians."

"That's not it at all," McInnerney said. "We started the fund drive long before."

"I know. You know. A few others. But, nationwide, who knows? Up to now, nationally, it has been studiously ignored. If you throw it in the fire now, call attention to it, you're going to touch off a hue and cry. It'll be painted black. A reactionary move. The counterreformation. All that. We'll never hear the end of it."

McInnerney, chain-smoking, paced the space behind his desk.

"Is the money in the bank? IDA money?"

"Deposited Friday morning," Prial said.

"They can't cancel the check?"

"They *could*, I suppose. They won't. The Seymour Jones thing upset them hardly at all. Cold-blooded crew where money is concerned. No, I'd bet my life the money is safe."

They had not talked much about St. Luke's in the last week. What occurred there had been a shock to both men, something almost beyond understanding. Not so much the demands, the terms of the manifesto, which to McInnerney were patently absurd, not even worth discussing, but the way it had been presented. The calculated rudeness of interrupting a sermon, the shouting match across the communion rail in the presence of the Blessed Sacrament, the arrogance of the news media, the inescapable feeling of violence in the air. Prial had been assured by the police that nothing untoward would happen at the church. On the telephone Monday, to the police superintendent, a black, he spoke his mind. The superintendent dismissed it all airily, had even intimated Prial might get ahead of the game by tossing a bone to Jones. This suggestion—together with his reflection on the scene—had given Prial real pause. When the calls poured in all week asking how the Chancery would respond, Prial evaded—the matter was under study—but the more he thought about it, the more it seemed reasonable that some provision might be considered.

McInnerney permitted no such sentiment. The interruption had been an unforgivable insult, not only to him personally (or rather the office he held) but the Church, the Pope, God Himself. In his mind, when he allowed himself to think of the man, Charles Seymour Jones appeared as an implacable impediment to the theological center, an obstruction that must be pushed aside, destroyed.

He turned now to Prial and spoke forcefully:

"If you're certain the money is safe, we're going ahead with the ground-breaking. Nate, you're getting too sensitive to . . . No. Forget that. You're fine. I respect your views. I've heard them out. Now I'm making my decision, trying to think like Spellman would have thought. Not once in my life did I see him give way to minority pressure for something he truly believed. Did you?"

"No."

"All right then. Let's show that same stripe of courage for a change. I feel in my bones everything will turn out for the best. The Good Lord will watch over us. He wants this heresy stamped out as much—or more—than we do. Right?"

"I sure hope so. Because if He doesn't . . ."

"Set a date . . . not more than three weeks from now. Maybe Labor Day, when people are not working."

"Three weeks!"

"Not a day later," McInnerney said gravely. "Nate, I want you to invite every bishop in America to this ceremony—all two hundred and sixty-eight. I want this to be the most impressive turnout of the hierarchy we've ever had—bigger than Paul's visit to New York. This will show, more than anything else we can say or do, that the bishops are behind Paul, that they stand four-square for obedience, for loyalty, for the true Church. That no half-baked bunch of cry-babies can tell us what to do. A few of the liberals won't come. Don't expect Sheen and his bunch. But who cares? Nate, the battleground is right here. We have been chosen—like Helen Hanrahan prophesied—to plant the standard here, to stand firm for God and the Church. Let's do it right."

Prial was still not wholly convinced. He replied coolly:

"If you want that kind of turnout, I'll have to announce it tomorrow. I fear the press will certainly interpret this as a reaction to the theologians' statement."

"Let them interpret. God knows. Maybe in some inverse way, harsh publicity will help us. What did they use to say—any publicity's good publicity as long as they get the name right? The Francis Cardinal Spellman Theological Center. Let every left-wing journalist jump on us! Let them write! There is still a vast majority who believe as we believe. Maybe they'll be stirred up—and help."

"If we waited a little while," Prial said, thinking again of last Sunday, "people would forget St. Luke's. If you announce the groundbreaking right away, they might connect the two. That would be disastrous. Dynamite. What would you say to setting aside a little bit from the IDA money and announce—first—a new church for St. Luke's? We could probably swing it, kick it off, with a hundred thousand dollars."

"No," McInnerney said firmly. "That would seem like a concession to that madman Jones. If you appear to yield to his manifesto, can you imagine the floodgates you would open? We'd never hear the end of these absurd demands. No, absolutely not. In this archdiocese anyway, mob rule, street gangs are not going to dictate policy. Not a single penny for St. Luke's."

Prial stood up, stretched, re-lit his cigar. There was, he saw, no point in fighting McInnerney. The man was dead-set, absolutely determined, hell-bent. Damn the torpedoes! Full speed ahead! Feeling a duty, Prial made one last attempt.

"I was thinking the offer might look generous," he said. "It would take the sting out of Jones's argument. More importantly, I don't think anyone would be tempted to link St. Luke's with the theological center. See my point?"

"It's a good point, Nate, but I'll be damned if I'll give Seymour Jones a dime. Not a penny. In fact, I want you to start legal proceedings tomorrow to have him evicted from that gym. He's been making us look ridiculous long enough."

"Now that really will look bad," Prial said. "I don't think we ought to do that. Not now. Not with all we have going. You're just *asking* for trouble."

"I want him out," McInnerney said. "That was part of our agreement with IDA. Get an injunction or whatever we need."

"OK, boss."

McInnerney turned, smiling.

"Remember Truman? If you can't stand the heat, get out of the kitchen?"

"I can take it," Prial said. "I was just worrying about my boss."

"I can take it," McInnerney said, sitting down. "They think I'm a pushover. But we'll show them how to fight. They forget I was a back-alley Boston teen-ager, who scrapped for his life more than once. I know all the tricks, Nate. All of them. We've been too lenient too long. Too sensitive to the intellectuals, the columnists, the minorities, the spoiled priests, the so-called socially conscious nuns. That was John's fault—the Council. Every day that goes by, it becomes, in retrospect, a greater mistake. Ever since then, we've been carrying on as though we're politicians, like the Kennedys or somebody. The laity don't *vote* for us. *We* have the power. The power is absolute, derived from Christ, the Pope. For too long, now, we have been neglecting our own best people. Our majority. It's time the pendulum swung the other way."

He stood again, pacing energetically, talking on:

"Here's what we're going to do. First, get out the announcement, the invitations to the ground-breaking. That must take top priority in this See. Next, dispose of that St. Luke's mess, that Seymour Jones. Get him out of there. Then I want to answer the heretics in two ways. First, a series of pastoral letters. Then I want to meet—this week— privately, with every supervisor and person of authority in the archdiocese. Clergy and lay. No press statements. We'll direct all our energy to an internal educational program. For the pastoral letters, I want to adopt a tough tone. No compromise. Here, I have a text from the Book of Deuteronomy to help set that tone. Read this. Remember it?"

He passed a penciled script to Prial. The Vicar General read:

"Let there be no root among you bearing fruit that is poisonous and bitter. If after hearing these sanctions such a man should bless himself in his heart and say: 'I will follow the dictates of my own heart and still lack nothing; much water drives away thirst,' the Lord will not pardon him. The wrath and the jealousy of the Lord will blaze against such a man; every curse written in this book will fall on him, and the Lord will blot out his name from under heaven."

Prial silently cleared his throat, swallowed. It was, he knew, one of the harshest texts.

"All right," Prial said, laying the paper in his leather folder. "What else?"

"That's it for the moment. Oh yes. Helen Hanrahan has agreed to go on television to speak in our behalf—take arms against the theologians."

"What television?"

"Local shows. They're always begging her. She's never done it before. But she thinks this is important."

"I shouldn't have thought the TV people would want her views," Prial said. "They want dissent, don't they? Like Klein?"

"They'll take her anyway," McInnerney said. "She's tremendous box office. Whatever her views, she's good for business, like Bishop Sheen. She'll help their ratings. She's also going to write a series of columns supporting the encyclical and the Pope."

"Good. Well, if that's all, I better get cracking."

Prial gathered up his papers, the leather folder, and set a course for the door.

"Nate," McInnerney called to him. "Don't worry."

"I'm not worried," Prial said confidently, more confidently than he felt. He was now trying to remember the details of Helen Hanrahan's vision of March. Exactly what she had said about death and violence, fire and smoke, the crazy picture of the Pope sinking in his golden throne at sea. Trying to remember what she had said specifically about the Washington See. He swung open the heavy door and almost fell over Monsignor Ryan, who was standing, fist raised, ready to knock.

"I had a vision," Prial said to Ryan, joking, sweeping down on the corridor toward the elevator. Ryan, watching him proceed, did not immediately enter the Archbishop's office. McInnerney saw him at the door, and called:

"Come on in, Tom."

Monsignor Ryan was anxious. His freight was more bad news, a whole string of reports from Mrs. Munally over the last week, indicating disobedience, or worse, on the part of the All Saints' acting pastor, Father Daugherty. First, Halfway House reopened, apparently without authorization from anybody, and, according to Scafidi, the woman, ex-Sister Mary, living down there, unchaperoned. Next, Father Daugherty, locking his room, disappearing altogether for several nights—to Halfway House, as Scafidi maintained?—turning his duties over to that visiting Maryknoll priest, who helped himself to the collection plate. The account books a total shambles. The mortgage payment unsent. Mysterious, muffled telephone calls—from women, other unidentified people, speaking in some kind of code Mrs. Munally could not understand. All this Ryan had kept to himself, not certain he could rely entirely on the say-so of Scafidi and Mrs. Munally, not wanting to carry more bad news to his bishop, waiting for a serious, unequivocal act. It had come, that day, at all the Masses.

He entered the office hesitantly, refusing a chair.

"What's the matter, Tom? You're acting like an acolyte."

"I feel like one. Truly, I wish I were dead."

"Come on, out with it. What's up? You don't think you can upset me, do you?"

"Yes. I think I can. I just got word Father Daugherty gave out the theologians' statement at every Mass at All Saints'. Not only that, some reporters and photographers were there, interviewing."

McInnerney jumped to his feet. A red flush swept his neck, his cheeks, seemed to flood right into his blazing eyes.

"Get Prial back here, please," he said to Ryan.

Ryan, grateful for company, hurried to the corridor, called to Prial who was just entering the elevator. Prial returned immediately. At the door, Ryan repeated his story to the Vicar General.

"Oh, no!" Prial said, coming back into the office.

"We're going to deal with this promptly," McInnerney said. "Right now, in fact. Tom, I'm sending you back to All Saints'. You were right all along. I was selfish. Please order the car. We're going to pay Father Daugherty a little visit."

"A visit?" Ryan said, astonished.

"Yes. Come along, gentlemen. We're going to make an example of this rebel."

"How?" Ryan said, dreading the answer.

"I'm going to fire him," McInnerney said. "Let's hurry."

"Why not call him here?" Prial said.

"Because we are setting the example. Swift retaliation. In person. On the spot. Show them we're not afraid to appear on the battlefield. When the word gets around, maybe some others who were thinking of mutiny will think twice. Tom, how would you like your bishop to appear suddenly, angrily, in your room at the rectory?"

"I wouldn't like it at all."

"Well, men, let's get going."

The Chancery chauffeur, the one person in the Chancery carrying on the old Sunday afternoon routine, was startled from his nap by the Vicar General. He brought the car around promptly. The Archbishop,

Prial, Monsignor Ryan climbed into the rear seat, which was still stifling, in spite of the flow of the air-conditioner. Ryan had had no time to pack his personal effects. He would return for them tonight.

They rode out Massachusetts Avenue to Wisconsin, down through Georgetown, where barefooted hippies—many University students—strolled the streets in curious garb. McInnerney stared, thinking now of Daugherty's Halfway House, the drug addicts, the endless difficulties Daugherty symbolized. They crossed Key Bridge, swooped down on the George Washington Parkway, following the high bluffs of the Potomac. Across the river, McInnerney could see Georgetown University, once small, red-bricked, a bastion of sound theology. Now it was a-bustle with construction cranes, excavations, rising steel girders. Buried somewhere in that anthill was a theology department, heretics all, who were shaping the minds of those barefooted hippies, turning them into pot smokers, maniacs who would soon tear down the country, society, the university, the Church itself. Truly, the whole country had gone crazy.

Now it was cool. McInnerney leaned his head back on the seat, closed his eyes, sighed deeply, winding down, cooling off as befit a bishop, his unpleasant mission. At the left window, Ryan, monumentally uncomfortable, wishing he were a million miles elsewhere, blankly watched the trees zip by. At the right window, Prial, waiting for McInnerney to reopen his eyes, was forming a new case for caution.

The driver, still not fully awake, missed the exit for McLean. The confusion roused McInnerney, who opened his eyes, directed the driver to take the next exit and double back. When this had been settled, Prial spoke.

"I was just thinking," he began.

"I know what you were thinking," McInnerney said. "That if I fire him, the other young priests will rise up in protest, form a league with the theologians . . . et cetera."

"You might make him a martyr," Prial said. "His buddy, Klein, is lying in wait for this. He will certainly deify him."

"Exactly my thoughts," Monsignor Ryan said, clearing his throat.

"Both of you are getting soft in your old age," McInnerney said.

"Let's deal with one crisis at a time," Prial said. "We've got fifteen major crises all boiling at once."

"Which can all be reduced to one," McInnerney said. "A matter of obedience. I told you long ago that if our people persisted in acting like children, we must treat them like children."

"In that case," Prial said, "why not give Daugherty a slap on the wrist? If they are indeed children, they'll get the message."

"There may be much wisdom in that," McInnerney said. He had been thinking along the same lines.

"It wouldn't hurt to try," Ryan said.

Prial pressed: "As McNamara might say, don't use all your options. You can always escalate. But why wade in, dropping atomic bombs?"

"What do you gentlemen suggest?" McInnerney said.

"I'm not sure," Prial said.

"Why not restrict his duties," Ryan said. "Limit him to six o'clock Mass. That way, we can discipline him without losing his services. *Somebody* has to say the six o'clock. I can't say them all. I don't think he can do any harm at that time of morning."

"That's true," Prial said. "I like that."

"It won't work," McInnerney said softly. Then, after a moment's reflection, he added: "But I'm willing to give it a try."

The driver swung the limousine into the rectory parking lot, in line with the other three cars parked there: Daugherty's MG, Scafidi's battered Ford, the chromeless rectory Chevvy. The Archbishop had not been to All Saints' since the dedication two years past. Monsignor Ryan led the way around to the front door. They entered without knocking, stood for a moment in the foyer, listening. They could hear voices in the kitchen—Mrs. Munally's and Scafidi's, Ryan was sure. Daugherty was probably upstairs in his room. He turned to Prial and pointed to the stairs. Without hesitation, Prial went up, two at a time.

Ryan led the Archbishop to the den, where he arranged him a chair. Then he went to the kitchen. He found Mrs. Munally and Scafidi, seated at the table, drinking coffee.

"Monsignor Ryan!" Mrs. Munally sang out, joyously, scrambling to her feet. Scafidi too seemed overjoyed.

"The Archbishop's here," Ryan said, holding a forefinger to his lips. This news seemed to strike awe in the two servants. Then Mrs. Munally seemed momentarily panicked. Scafidi grunted, a sound that seemed to convey immense satisfaction.

"May we have some refreshments in the den?" Ryan said. "Tea and cookies or something?"

"Of course," Mrs. Munally said, scurrying about.

"I'm coming back to stay," Ryan said, pausing at the door.

"Thank God," Mrs. Munally said. Scafidi's intent dark eyes seemed to agree.

"I didn't have time to bring my things . . . my suitcase. I'll have to go back and get them."

"I'll go for you," Scafidi said, eagerly rising to his feet.

"No thanks, John," Ryan said. "I didn't have time to pack. I'll have to do it myself. Thanks just the same. I'll manage."

Mrs. Munally set the teapot on the stove, hurried to the dining room for the gleaming silver service, a housewarming gift to the rectory from an aunt and uncle of Daugherty's. Ryan said to her, almost in a whisper:

"Father Daugherty will probably be staying, too, Bridget. I don't know yet. It's a discipline problem. Anyway, I want you to be absolutely neutral for the time being."

"I understand," Mrs. Munally said, nodding somberly.

Scafidi heard none of this. It was not for lack of trying. He had edged his way back to the wall near the kitchen door. Seeing this renewed Ryan's concern about the man. He did not like him hanging around like this, did not want the Archbishop to see him. Ryan spoke quietly to him.

"We have some private matters to settle here, John. Why don't you go on home?"

"Good enough," Scafidi said gruffly, concealing his disappointment. Then, voice very low: "I told you. He's a devil!"

"I doubt that very seriously," Ryan said firmly. He did not like having this strange man hanging around the kitchen, openly hating Daugherty, carrying who-knew-what tales beyond the door. It was a serious matter which he would deal with later, without fail.

He returned to the den, followed by Mrs. Munally who brought the refreshments on the silver tray. The Archbishop was still sitting alone lost in thought. Ryan said:

"Your Excellency, you remember Mrs. Munally?"

"Of course," McInnerney said. "How are you?"

"Just fine, thank you," she said, setting down the tray, kneeling to kiss his ring. "I can't complain. We've missed Monsignor Ryan—I'll tell you that."

"I understand you have," McInnerney said. "Well, you can stop now. He's coming back. He's done a splendid job on the drive. We couldn't have done without him. All the parishioners should understand that."

"I'm sure they will," Mrs. Munally said, withdrawing.

"Good woman," Ryan said, sitting down in a lounge chair.

"Yes," McInnerney said, now very relaxed in his chair, in spite of the unpleasantness which lay ahead.

Father Daugherty descended the stairs behind Prial, engulfed by a sense of doom and disaster. Moments before, Prial had barged right into his room, unannounced, like an arresting officer with a warrant. Daugherty had been changing his clothes—from vestments to slacks and T-shirt, planning to leave that instant for a meeting with McDivitt and some other young, dissenting priests at Halfway House. In their special, amateurish code, McDivitt had called to say droves of new priests were anxious to "enlist" in the "crusade" against the Chancery.

The news that McInnerney was here, downstairs, waiting in the den, astonished Daugherty. He had prepared himself for retaliation, but not in this form, or so swiftly. The Enemy had infiltrated behind the lines, caught him (almost literally) with his pants down. To win a battle, he must seize, and maintain, the initiative, above all, anticipate every move of the enemy. He felt like a schoolboy. It must never happen again.

He went into the den, determined to do or say nothing that would reveal his hand. As with his last meeting with McInnerney and Prial, silence might prove to be golden. No intemperate outbursts. No ultimatums. No hand-to-hand combat. Let them do all the talking.

He nodded politely to his archbishop, but did not kneel to kiss the ring. To McInnerney, this was also an act of defiance. The second time the young priest had insulted the office. Also—he had not trimmed his sideburns. But, compared to the item on the agenda, these were small matters, better left unsaid for the present.

"Have a seat," McInnerney said coldly.

Daugherty sat on the ottoman, facing the Archbishop, the glare from the window behind him. Prial slumped into an easy chair. Ryan closed the door quietly and leaned against the wall, as though prepared to bolt the room.

"Young man," the Archbishop plunged right in. "I have been more than patient with you. When we last talked at the Chancery, I warned you that I would not tolerate disobedience in this archdiocese. I asked you to cut your ties with this man Klein—all the press. I pleaded with you to tend to your knitting, to the normal routine of this parish—the financial matters, which are not good, the salvation of souls—and above all, to abide by the guidelines established in *Sex in Marriage,* and my pastoral letter of last Sunday, in matters regarding artificial contraception. I specifically said no one in this archdiocese could preach or teach against the encyclical. Now—I've been informed—you distributed copies of the theologians' so-called statement, and called in the press to witness."

"Yes, sir," Daugherty said, almost eagerly.

"You concede this act of disobedience?" McInnerney said, a trifle astonished. "So casually?"

"I did not say I had been disobedient," Daugherty rejoined. "I have not been disobedient to my faith."

"But you've violated your vow of obedience to your Church, the Holy Father, and me."

"No, sir," Daugherty said. "I did not call in the reporters. They came of their own volition."

"They must have known in advance you would distribute the statement."

"I told no member of the press what I intended."

That was true. Klein had sent his journalistic team, Daugherty supposed, on hunch. True, literally, but in a broader sense, hairsplitting and deceptive. He had, after all, had Klein to dinner. He added:

"I had dinner with Klein earlier in the week."

"You what?"

"We had dinner."

"And you gave him this statement?"

"Yes, sir. He asked for it. I happened to have one. He could have called CU. They gave it to all the press."

McInnerney raised himself by the arms, then sank back in his chair, with a weary gesture to Prial.

"I don't understand," he said. "I'm baffled. He dines with Klein, gives him that statement, then says he has not been disobedient."

"To my faith," Daugherty said. "As for giving out the statement. It was in all the newspapers—the gist. My people wanted a copy of the full statement. I provided them copies, as a service. My people are quite intelligent, quite independent. They like to be totally informed and they form their own opinions. I, of course, also distributed your pamphlet, *Sex in Marriage,* and your pastoral letter as per your instructions. We furnished the congregation with both sides of the argument."

"Argument?" McInnerney said incredulously. "There is no—can be no—argument. The Pope has spoken. I have transmitted his teaching.

I'm not in a debate. This thing by these theologian crackpots . . . it means nothing. Nothing whatsoever."

"I'm afraid you *are* in a debate," Daugherty said, smiling. "If you don't believe me, ask my parishioners. Many of them believe exactly as the theologians. They oppose the encyclical, and therefore you. So, whether you like it or not—"

"If they believe this rubbish . . . this heretical nonsense . . . *you* have failed them. You have not taught. Not done your duty."

Daugherty smoldered silently, restraining the anger boiling inside his chest.

"I don't understand any of this," McInnerney went on, more quietly. "When *Casti Connubii* was published—you must have been a babe in arms then—I thought the matter was settled once and for all. Contraception was *absolutely* condemned. The language was unequivocal. Some theologians believed—and wrote—that *Casti Connubii* was infallible. Others wrote that the doctrine had been infallibly taught, all through the ages, whether the encyclical was infallible or not. No Catholic was at liberty to dissent from it. For thirty years *Casti Connubii* was considered so certain that no questions about its irreversibility ever arose. In 1964, Pope Paul said the norms of *Casti Connubii* were still binding. In November, 1965, he again advised the Council that *Casti Connubii* should be upheld. He said in October, 1966, that the traditional teaching is still valid and binding and that it was based on divine authority—not his own authority. And—God help us!—now the present encyclical apparently comes as a shock to you. What the Pope says doesn't convince you. But isn't it possible the trouble is with you? You think just because the Council opened up discussion, and there was intense discussion, including a commission, and because some theologians went over to the so-called new view, and the press promoted that view, and a handful of bishops, too, that this makes contraception right and legal? You think because the Council put new stress on freedom and the sharing of responsibility in the Church that we now have a democracy? The majority doesn't rule in matters of faith and morals. Christ didn't leave His kingdom on earth to a *'sensus fidelium'* —not to a bunch of debating theologians. He left it to a very ordinary group of men like you and me. With a fisherman named Peter at the head. The Pope speaks with 'the mandate of Christ.' Now that is something you—we all *have* to believe. The Pope's judgment is always final. No theologian can self-appoint himself to 'evaluate' a Pope's teachings. Not the theologians nor the psychologists nor the sociologists nor the mass media. I speak to you now, not as Father McInnerney, but as Bishop McInnerney. And I remind you of the words of St. Paul: 'Now I beseech you, bretheren, by the name of Our Lord Jesus Christ, that you all say the same thing; and that there be no dissensions among you, but that you be perfectly united in one mind, and in one judgment.' I am the Bishop of Washington, the successor of the Apostles sent by Christ. I have commissioned you to teach and preach Catholic doctrine, and to exercise your pastoral ministry both in confession and out of it, in strict accordance with the authentic teachings of the Catholic Church. To present this teaching, as you have done, merely as one alternative, is not in accordance with it. I cannot allow you to diverge from this teaching, because I can only authorize you to do what I am authorized to do myself. I have no power to authorize you to teach or preach or counsel anything other than the doctrine of *Humanae Vitae*. Now, after hearing this, do you still dissent from the teaching of the Holy Father and the True Church?"

Father Daugherty, having listened attentively to these familiar words, rose from his chair and pulled the venetian blind to shield the sun. Then he sat down again.

"Your Excellency," he said quietly. "The Council taught what all Catholics have always known, and believed, that the conscience is supreme. As the theologians say in their statement, emphatically, the encyclical is *not* an infallible teaching. The whole history of encyclicals is imperfect. Many of them—after theological debate—have been revised, because of changing views on doctrine, circumstance, politics, science. It is a common teaching of the Church—reaffirmed by the Council—that Catholics may dissent from authoritative, noninfallible teachings of the *magisterium* when there is sufficient reason. In this case, I happen to believe the theologians are correct. All things considered—and I give no weight to the opinion or the so-called bias of the press—there is certainly sufficient reason to dissent from this encyclical. But, even so, I have not preached against it."

Prial, leaning forward, elbows on his knees, spoke quietly.

"Your Excellency, the theological debate here seems to me irreconcilable. We could go on for hours—right into a debate on the whole matter of conscience. You have a busy schedule. Tom has to get going, back to the Chancery to pack. I'm up to my ears in work. . . . It seems to me that Father Daugherty has demonstrated disobedience—by word and deed. I don't think anybody would argue with that, do you, Tom?"

"No," Ryan said, shaking his head sadly, almost uncomprehendingly. "He admitted he had *dinner* with Klein."

"Am I also to be told with whom I can eat?" Daugherty said. "As well as how to cut my hair?"

"You were advised that Mr. Klein was intent on damaging this See, everything we have worked for . . ."

"He's just being an able reporter," Daugherty said curtly. "Really, sir. You can't deny there is a difference of opinion on the encyclical, can you?"

"But we don't wash our linen in public!" McInnerney shouted. "Can't you understand that?"

"Gentlemen," Prial cut in again.

McInnerney rushed on: "You are a spoiled child, Daugherty. There can be no dialogue with you. I shall therefore treat you as a child. I came here, determined to give you maximum punishment. The Vicar General and your pastor have urged restraint, a Christian approach. Very well. I give you that one last chance. You will consider yourself officially admonished. Your appointment as temporary pastor is revoked. Monsignor Ryan will return to this parish. With God's help, he will restore order and help you recover your faith. You will meanwhile, under pain of dismissal as a priest, refrain from further public utterances to any press media or other public body. You will be restricted to saying the six o'clock Mass. That is all. You have borne witness, Vicar General Prial?"

"I have," the Vicar General said, rising.

"Do you have anything to say?" McInnerney said, also rising.

"No, Your Excellency," Daugherty replied, standing. Inside, he was trembling with anger and fear and resentment and frustration. The blindness, the pettiness of this poor old man! It would destroy them all. He added: "I have nothing more to say at this time."

"Then, pray," McInnerney said. "Ask God to forgive you."

V

Father Daugherty lunged for the alarm clock, reaching it a microsecond before it shattered the stillness of the morning. That ability to beat the clock, which had not failed him since the seminary, was a psychic phenomenon that he could not understand. Every morning he lay back for a moment, giving his first thoughts to that deep mystery. The human brain was an infinity of riddles, like the universe.

He dragged himself from bed, stumbled in the dark to the bathroom, splashed cold water on his face. Beneath his feet, the rectory was silent, a tomb. Monsignor Ryan, a sound, late sleeper, safe in his room, where he had, over the last two days, gathered all the parish account books, ledgers, checkbooks, and his much-neglected donation envelope records. The two men had hardly exchanged two words since Sunday. On Monday and Tuesday, Daugherty had silently performed his single duty, the six o'clock Mass, serving Communion to the handful of worshippers—eight gnarled and sickly old women, three doddering, gaunt-faced men (retired senior citizens), and Scafidi, the surly, pious, daily communicant. Daugherty had delivered no sermon at these two Masses. They were short and sweet—not more than twenty minutes. The rest of the time—morning, afternoon, evening, he had spent at Halfway House with Mary, McDivitt, Klein, and the swelling group of young archdiocese priests who were enraged by the restriction placed on Daugherty, the announcement of the groundbreaking for the theological center, the injunction against Seymour Jones, the arrogance, stupidity, the sickness of the Chancery.

Daugherty dressed, lit a cigarette, sat on the bed reading his breviary, then glanced at his clock: five fifty. In a few minutes, less than ten, he would strike the first calculated blow of the counterattack. He would stand on the altar and publicly defy the Chancery. He would cross the line of obedience. He would preach against the encyclical and he would surely invite instant and drastic retribution. He would (as Klein had painted it) speak across the communion rail, to the congregation, the Chancery, the press, the Vatican, and to all the parishes, and Chanceries of the world. He would get things rolling. Here, in All Saints' on an August Wednesday, open battle would be joined.

The setting, the time, in a sense had been provided by Jean Favrot. On Monday afternoon, after the word about his restriction had spread through the parish in its mysterious way, Jean had telephoned Daugherty at Halfway House. She was incensed by the restriction, the attitude of the Chancery, by the harshness, the words of *Deuteronomy* in the latest pastoral letter. Both she and Bob had been appalled by the news of the ground-breaking—the Archbishop's insistence on that stupid project against all the advice of the fund captains. In fact, when he saw the announcement in the *Post,* Bob had sent off a letter of resignation to Monsignor Ryan.

Most of all, Jean had told Daugherty, she was upset by the fact that McInnerney (and Pope Paul) seemed utterly insensitive and blind to her own personal problems. Not just hers, but all the wives of the parish. They had had it up to here with this pay, pray, and obey routine. They weren't living in the Dark Ages anymore! And, by golly, they were going to let him know. She had been talking to the other wives. All were anxious to speak their minds. They had discussed a variety of ways: drafting a letter to McInnerney, getting up a petition, holding a press conference, even putting pickets around the Chancery, the way they had protested the I-95 thruway. Instead, she announced, they had settled on a silent, reverent show of force. On Wednesday, all the wives of the parish who could possibly make it would turn out for the six o'clock Mass. Daugherty's Mass. This news, this spontaneous display of compassion, love, faith, on the part of the laity—as the Council had encouraged—had moved Daugherty to tears.

The "silent protest," as it came to be called, seemed to offer the perfect "platform" for the counterattack's open defiance. They had all agreed McInnerney's insult to Daugherty could not go unanswered. For one thing, McInnerney had gone too far—put himself in a legally indefensible position. A priest was a priest forever. No bishop had a right to "restrict" his priest, to deny his mission of teaching the flock, of hearing confession, administering other sacraments. LeGuiese (by telephone) was emphatic on that point. By Tuesday morning, Daugherty, who had first urged caution, no spasm reactions, no half-cocked response, came around. The war was boiling, front page everywhere. If they were going to "humanize" the conflict, get things rolling, they would probably never have a better chance. For Daugherty, it represented his best opportunity to strike a blow for Jean Favrot—and then exit. Who could conceive of anything more dramatic, and newsworthy, than a church full of wives and mothers silently praying in protest? As Klein remarked, only half-jokingly, it was Heaven-sent.

Daugherty left his room at five to six. He descended the stairs on tiptoe. He went to the kitchen, very quietly gathered the handful of unleavened Host prepared, as always, by Mrs. Munally, left on the sideboard on a plate. He also took a loaf of bread from the sideboard. If there was a large turnout, he would need many more Hosts. Little pieces of bread would do.

He left by the front door, going into the dawn light, the cool morning air. There were already two dozen cars in the parking lot. Others were swinging in from the street. And beyond, near the church, Daugherty saw three big TV vans. That, he knew, had been Klein's doing. He walked toward the church, briskly now, feeling a vast responsibility, a surge of resolution, reminding himself, once again, that at each step of the way—no matter what the consequences—he must not give vent to the anger and hurt and frustration he felt inside. He must be considerate of his elders, and the great many—perhaps the majority as McInnerney claimed—of those for whom the Old Religion provided solace and peace, a sufficiency. They would never be able to enlist these. But they must not devastate them either.

By the time he reached the church steps, where Jean Favrot was standing with a clipboard, the parking lot was half full. It would be a tremendous, overflowing turnout. Daugherty, shifting the Hosts and bread to his left hand, shook hands with Jean, quietly thanking her.

"Thank *you*," she replied. She pointed to the parking lot. "We *all* thank you."

Daugherty nodded, holding back the emotion he felt welling up. He excused himself and hurried into the church.

Lying abed, Mrs. Munally was startled awake by the sound of the voices and cars in the parking lot. She leaned over and pulled back a corner of the shade, staring into the dimness, seeing the taillights of many cars. She roused herself, climbed out of bed into her slippers and robe. She hurried to the back door, unlocked it, stood on the back stoop. Then, coming out of the dimness, she recognized a figure, the unmistakable loping walk of John Scafidi. He was plunging, lunging, almost running, dragging his lame foot along.

"I was just coming to get you," he cackled out, when he saw Mrs. Munally.

"What's going on?"

"I don't know," Scafidi said. "Dozens . . . hundreds of people. TV vans over by the church."

"TV vans! Where?"

"Over there . . . behind the church. You can't see from here."

Scafidi pulled up on the stoop railing, panting.

"I'll get the Monsignor," Mrs. Munally said. "Go back and see if you can find out what's going on."

Mrs. Munally darted back into the rectory. She flew up the stairway, to Ryan's door, banged frantically, calling his name. He opened the door sleepily.

"I think you better come out," she said, with an air of desperation. "Something's going on. Dozens of cars in the lot. And TV vans."

"TV!" Ryan said, fighting to come awake. "What TV?"

"Out there."

"Where's Daugherty?" Ryan said, looking down the hall. "Is he in his room?"

"No. He's at the church."

Ryan frowned, stroking his chin.

"I'll be right down," he said, closing the door. Mrs. Munally hurried back downstairs to dress.

In the sacristy, Daugherty found six altar boys milling about, including young Bob and Joe Favrot. They were already dressed in black cassocks and white surplices.

"Well," Daugherty said cheerily. "Have we gone to the two-platoon system?"

"Everybody wanted to serve," Bob Favrot said sleepily, and without any conviction in his voice. The five other boys nodded sleepily.

"All right by me," Daugherty said, slipping on his cassock. He peeked through the door into the church. The pews were jammed, women were standing in the foyer, and along the side aisles. He closed his eyes and prayed—for inspiration. After a moment, he felt a firm hand on his arm. He opened his eyes. There, before him, stood Monsignor Ryan, looking sleepily grave.

"I'll take this Mass," Ryan said. "You go on back to the rectory."

"This is my Mass," Daugherty said in a low voice.

"You were *restricted* to this Mass," Ryan said, slipping on his cassock. "But you say Mass at my pleasure. If *I* want to say the six o'clock, then *I* say it."

"Do you think these people came to hear *you?*"

"I presume they came to celebrate Mass. To worship God. There is no cult of personality in the Catholic Church. There are no Billy Grahams. Now I suggest again that you return to the rectory. I'll speak to you after Mass."

He turned to the altar boys. "I'll just need two of you."

The altar boys huddled and whispered. The two Favrot boys and two others bowed out, removing their cassocks and surplices. They returned to the church. Daugherty saw them bend and whisper to their mother in one of the front pews. He saw, too, the look of anger that clouded her face.

Ryan took the handful of Hosts, left the sacristy for the altar, followed by the two altar boys. Daugherty watched from the sacristy door, uncertain now about his course of action. He would wait, see what developed. He could hear murmuring in the church. He looked through the door again toward the congregation. They were not happy. They were bending heads, whispering, also uncertain. At the far end, he saw Mrs. Munally and Scafidi, confiding.

Ryan said the Mass rapidly, not pausing for routine announcements. He read the Gospel for the day and returned to the altar to prepare Communion, as though it were any routine weekly six o'clock Mass. Now, suddenly, Daugherty heard a commotion at the rear of the church. A group of TV men, news reporters, and photographers were coming up the middle aisle. When Ryan turned to face the congregation, the TV lights went on, blinding him. He froze as though a grenade had exploded in his face.

The photographers fanned out along the communion rail. Ryan, fists tight, descended the steps from the altar, wide-eyed, enraged.

"Get out of here," he said, voice loud, firm, menacing, finger pointing toward the rear door.

The newsmen did not move. Photographers clicked pictures.

"I said out," Ryan repeated, in a louder voice. "You're in the presence of the Sacred Heart of Jesus. Out! Out this minute."

The congregation watched this confrontation, transfixed. Silent. The newsmen turned and walked slowly toward the rear of the church. The brilliant lights went off. Ryan stood at the altar rail, hands on hips, until all had left by the front door. Then he hiked up his cassock, climbed the steps to the altar, resumed the Mass. The congregation again bent in whispered conversation.

At the Offertory, two of the six o'clock regulars, the gaunt senior citizens, picked up the long-handled straw baskets and walked to front of the middle aisle. There, they genuflected and came back up the middle aisle where they extended the baskets. Jean Favrot leaned to the first woman in the pew.

"Pennies," she whispered.

The word spread instantly through the congregation. As the old men moved slowly back through the pews, nothing could be heard except the dull clunk of pennies falling into the collection plates. Those who had no pennies contributed nothing. No paper money, no silver fell into the baskets. On the altar, Ryan prepared the Communion, aided by the acolytes, who held the little cruets of wine and water. He served himself and the boys, then descended to the rail.

Not a single soul in the congregation stirred. For weeks afterward, there would be much talk of this "miracle" of communications—how after insulting the Monsignor with the pennies, the congregation had decided, almost as if divinely inspired, to boycott the Communion.

Ryan stood with his altar boys at the communion rail for a long while, waiting. At first merely astonished, he was soon angry, then fearful. He returned to the altar and finished the Mass, foregoing the litany and Prayers after Mass. He left the altar instantly for the sacristy.

The congregation did not move from its seats. The women sat impassively, staring at the rakish crucifix extending from the altar. In the sacristy, Ryan turned to Daugherty:

"I thought I told you to go to the rectory."

Daugherty did not reply. He stood, watching Ryan slip out of his vestments. The acolytes took off their ceremonial clothing and departed wordlessly. One of the old men came with the bag of coins. He set it on the table and whispered to Ryan.

"Pennies!" the Monsignor exclaimed, disbelieving.

The old man, too, departed without further word.

"*You* told them to do this," Ryan said, turning again to Daugherty. "This is scandalous. Sacrilegious. Wait until the Chancery hears. And the press. TV. In the House of God! You'll be sorry for this."

Jean Favrot appeared in the sacristy doorway, solemn, determined. She spoke directly to Ryan.

"We've come to see Father Daugherty. We won't leave until he's allowed to speak."

"Won't leave . . . ?" Ryan said incredulously.

His words trailed away in confusion. He did not know what to do.

Jean Favrot turned and went back to her pew.

"Maybe I better put in an appearance," Daugherty said to Ryan. "It's a lot of people . . . up early. At root, it's not me, but what I stand for."

"What *you* stand for?" Ryan said angrily.

"I am a priest," Daugherty said.

"You've got nerve, after this, calling yourself a priest. Why don't you get out of here? Go back to Halfway House, *go back to your woman,* your hippies. Leave us alone. Get out of the Church. This is not your religion. You're not a Catholic."

He stopped, face red, eyes blazing. Daugherty, stung, momentarily shattered, held his breath. What did he mean—*go back to your woman?* How much did he know? What did he tell McInnerney—if anything? He wished devoutly for time. Time to explain to Ryan, ask for forgiveness, to set things right before leaving. He had not meant to hurt Ryan, to evoke bitterness. Before he could say anything, Ryan spoke again.

"I'm sorry, Dan," he said. "I didn't mean that."

"I'm sorry too," Daugherty replied, eyes going to the floor. "I'm going out now. I have something to say. It won't take long."

"No," Ryan said. "I forbid you to speak in my church. Get out of the church. Get off the property and take your TV vans. If you don't . . . I'll call the police."

"I'm sorry," Daugherty repeated, gently squeezing Ryan's forearm, going through the sacristy door to the altar. He was afraid to speak now. Afraid that the retribution could expose Mary Murray, destroy them. He stopped, agonizing. He could not let the opportunity pass, could not let down Jean Favrot. It was too late. He went on. When he appeared at the foot of the altar, the congregation rose as one. Then the women applauded. At this, the newsmen returned, the brilliant TV lights came on. Daugherty smiled to the sea of faces, waved self-consciously, blinking eyes into the blinding light, then mounted the steps to the pulpit. He raised his arms. The congregation sat down. He tapped the mike, spoke:

"Thank you. Thank you, one and all."

The second thank-you was not heard. The mike had gone dead. In the sacristy, Ryan had turned off the PA system. He was now standing defiantly at the sacristy door, hands on hips. Daugherty tapped the mike again, realized at once what happened, descended the pulpit steps, swung through the gate at the communion rail, walked up the middle aisle until he was midway in the church. He spoke conversationally, informally. The photographers, swooped around him, kneeling, backing up, bending into unnatural positions.

"Thank you again," Daugherty said to the women in the pews. "No one, especially a priest, could possibly not be profoundly touched, profoundly moved by what has happened here today. I know, too, that the gathering was not for me personally, but out of respect for what I—and my fellow priests—stand for. I thank you in behalf of all my brothers in Christ. With your continued support, with your prayers, your faith and devotion, I know we shall prevail.

"I wish to say one thing in regard to Monsignor Ryan He is a good man, true and holy. He has devoted his life to God. Few of us could claim to have lived a better life. Remember him in your prayers. Don't think of him as an obstruction. He should not be hurt. We have hurt him here today, and for that I am truly sorry. Remember, we are first and foremost Christians, who live by the Golden Rule. We should prevail, but not at the expense of a good man like Monsignor Ryan."

He paused, not theatrically, but with genuine doubt. He might leave now, leave the work undone, the battle unjoined, the words unspoken. Leave—flee—with Mary to . . . to . . . to a tiny world of their own making, a very serene and secure place, comfortable, without controversy and scenes, flesh-crawling confrontations, a place of no hurt. His eyes fell on Jean Favrot, perched on the edge of her pew, attentive, expectant, very proud of what she had created here, no small piece of work for a Catholic mother of nine, who only a few weeks past had been obediently taking the parish census. He remembered the night at the hospital, his promise to her. He could not—again—ignore her. He turned back to the cameras, staring directly into the red light, the lens. He spoke with all the strength and conviction at his command:

"I want to speak briefly to you on the subject of Paul's encyclical, *Humanae Vitae,* and of our Archbishop's most recent pastoral letter. He states that if you do not obey Paul to the letter, the wrath and jealousy of the Lord will bring an evil curse on us all.

"By contrast, I call your attention to the thoughtful presentation of the theologians which was distributed here last Sunday. More than six hundred U.S. Catholic theologians have now signed the statement which holds, in simplest terms, that spouses may, in some circumstances, *follow their own consciences.* This dissenting position, I feel, is perfectly compatible with loyalty to Christ and the Church. We, as priests, must take into account not papal statements alone, not theological judgments alone, but also the practical day-to-day lives of those who are striving to live in the Grace of Christ. Therefore, we have chosen to speak out. I hope we can enter into dialogue with our Archbishop to explore, unemotionally and sensibly, the dimensions of this complex issue.

"In spite of the Archbishop's inclination to make it seem so, the encyclical is not an infallible document. Since it is not infallible, then it must be fallible and therefore subject to error, revisions, restatement, and independent judgment. As the distinguished Georgetown philosopher, Louis Dupre, a Catholic, has pointed out elsewhere, dissent is not in error but, rather, commonplace in the case of nonfallible utterances. It is my sincerest hope that by bringing this matter into the open, evoking a public dialogue, we shall succeed in persuading the Archbishop to this point of view, and ultimately the Vatican, and that from all this will issue a new policy that is reasonable, practical, and in tune with the world of today."

He paused a minute, looking into the attentive eyes.

"Quite apart from your own personal problems involved with raising many children in this day and age, which I know so well from the confessional and from my counseling, I would like to leave you with one last thought. There is today, ticking away, an ominous, fearful menace to the world, called by some the population bomb. At present birthrates, the population of the world doubles about every thirty-seven years. Think of that. Today three billion. In the year 2000, six billion. The scientists—including Catholic scientists—say there can be only one final doubling, that by the year 2000, we will run out of space, air, food, water to feed the world's population. The whole face of the globe will be swept by famine, epidemics, war—a desperate struggle for survival. Is this a world you want to leave your grandchildren? I think not. For this reason alone, we must convince Paul that he has made a serious error."

He paused again.

Many thoughts rushed into his mind. He might use this opportunity to catalogue all the faults of the modern Church. Yet he said nothing more. He concluded:

"Thank you. Thank you for coming."

Led by Jean Favrot, the women again rose in unison and applauded. Daugherty smiled, held up his two hands, making a "V" signal with his trembling fingers. The words were spoken, his duty done. Now he could flee.

Behind him, unseen, John Scafidi pushed his way through the throng of reporters in the middle aisle. He carried the wand of the Electrolux, low, on his crippled side. He came on feverishly, panting from the exertion, the anger. Close to Daugherty, he raised the wand, clutched it with two hands, and swung. The wand brushed and caught against a TV man with a portable shoulder-camera. Staggered by the blow, the camerman lost his balance, reeled sideways, falling against a pew. Still clinging to his wand, Scafidi raised it again.

"Look out!" a reporter called out. Another looked, reached, caught the wand in mid-air, twisting. Scafidi fought back, pulling furiously, shouting:

"The Devil! The Devil!"

No one understood his words, or that they were directed at Daugherty. The scuffling newsmen wrenched the wand away and held Scafidi's arms. The women in the pews looked on in wonderment and fear. Monsignor Ryan, who had been watching Daugherty from the altar, hurried forward to take Scafidi in custody, lead him away. Behind the altar, Ryan turned angrily on the trembling cripple:

"Go to the rectory. I will speak to you later."

"He's a devil!" Scafidi hissed.

"That may be," Ryan said. "But he's my problem, not yours."

"I'll *kill* him," Scafidi snarled.

"You will kill nobody," Ryan said. "Are you crazy? This is a house of God. A sanctified place. Now go to the rectory at once."

Scafidi loped off toward the sacristy door. Ryan followed with his eyes, aware now that Scafidi, like the parish books, was a serious problem that could no longer be put off. He was a pitiful case, but they must let him go. If he had struck Father Daugherty a hard blow . . . ! All of it on national television! In his church!

Daugherty, who thought the newsmen, not he, had been Scafidi's target, turned to the women in the pews, raised his arms again.

"Thank you again. Go home now. Be pleased. Let your hearts swell with joy that you have given one man strength and courage to do what he believes is right. Go home, fix breakfast. Love your husbands, your children. Go with God."

He turned and walked out the front door. The congregation stood and broke into low song: "We Shall Overcome," getting the words from cards Jean had provided.

Outside, the sky was bright in the east. Dawn had come. Daugherty, vastly moved by the diminishing sound of the protest song, threaded his way through the cars toward the rectory. He saw Scafidi's old car, the man at the wheel, speeding from the lot. Out of my life, forever, Daugherty thought. And none too soon.

He went directly to his room. He lit a cigarette, sat on the edge of the bed, read his breviary. Then he stood at the window, watching the cars leave, the clutches of women here and there, talking, gesticulating, the TV men packing their gear by the vans, the Tom Paines, Harriet Beecher Stowes and Victor Hugos of the age. He saw Monsignor Ryan and Mrs. Munally locking the church door, returning to the rectory. There would be no seven o'clock Mass. Daugherty pulled his suitcase from beneath the bed.

Sometime later, Monsignor Ryan knocked on Daugherty's door. Daugherty admitted him without comment. Ryan looked at the suitcase, the cardboard cartons in the middle of the floor.

"I spoke with the Archbishop," Ryan said, standing near the door.

"I assumed that," Daugherty said, bending, searching the empty drawers of his desk one last time.

"He'll be sending an official letter."

"That's not necessary," Daugherty said.

"I believe it is," Ryan said. "There are some other administrative matters . . ."

"We can do them by mail," Daugherty said.

"Yes," Ryan said. "That's a good idea."

"What was that nut Scafidi up to?" Daugherty said, thinking back on the confusion in the aisle.

"Oh, he was upset, that's all. I don't think he's all there."

"I've been saying that for months," Daugherty said.

"I'm going to give him notice."

"I saw him gunning out of the lot in that heap. He didn't look like he was ever coming back."

"I hope not," Ryan said. "Well . . . Dan . . . I wanted to thank you for what you said about me in the church. You didn't have to do that. I just wanted you to know, in spite of everything, that I'm sorry the way this turned out. You've certainly left me a mountain of work, a long road to travel. I don't understand you, but I believe you're sincere in what you're doing, so I forgive you for that. I will pray that you don't utterly destroy yourself. And . . . please remember me in your prayers."

"I shall."

They shook hands. Daugherty looked deep into his eyes. Was this a man who would stoop to personal scandal to win his case? It seemed unlikely. Yet . . .

"Good luck," Ryan said, turning, leaving the room.

"Good luck to you," Daugherty said, turning back to the room, feeling a sudden, terrible sense of loss, like a man cast loose at sea.

VI

Daugherty set his suitcase in the foyer of Halfway House. He stood, listening, holding the blue steel box with his valuable papers crooked in his arm. He heard Mary, inside someplace, talking, probably on the telephone. He picked up the suitcase, mounted the stairs sideways. There had been no room in the MG for the cardboard boxes. Later, he would return to the rectory for them.

"Dan?" Mary called from the lower hall. "Is that you?"

Daugherty left the suitcase and the blue box in the upstairs hall, descended the steps three at a time. She met him at the bottom landing, throwing her arms around his neck, kissing him feverishly.

"Tell me all about it," she said at last. "You want coffee?"

"Yes, please." They went to the kitchen.

"What happened?" she said, filling the tea kettle.

"It was . . . a . . . it was good and bad. The turnout was fantastic. Five or six hundred. I couldn't count. They were standing in the aisles . . ."

"Was there any press?"

"Everybody. Three TV vans, reporters, photographers, all over."

"How were you?"

"Let me finish. Ryan got the word and came over. *He* said the Mass."

"What did you . . . ?"

"I just waited."

He told her in considerable detail what had happened in the church, concluding with an account of Scafidi's insane attack on the press. He saved for the last what he considered most important, that which had preoccupied him all during the packing, the drive downtown.

"Among other things," he said, "Ryan intimated . . . I forget his exact words . . . something about us."

Mary set the coffee cups on the table with steady hand, concealing the stab of panic she felt. She sat down.

"Something like 'go to your woman,'" Dan added quietly.

Mary said nothing. She stirred the coffee with a stainless spoon, eyes fixed on the whirling vortex, thinking of the woman, Munally, the custodian, Scafidi.

"Do you think he told McInnerney?" she said.

"I have no idea. In any case, Mary, it's done. I gave them what they wanted. The press now has on record a young, defiant priest, shaking his fist at the Pope. I paid my debt to Jean Favrot. All the Jean Favrots. So now let's you and me get the hell out of here. Go find a quiet place and settle our lives—our problems—and get out of the limelight. We're simply too vulnerable to play around like this. Anyway, I don't like the publicity. It brings trouble. Always trouble."

Mary listened carefully, sympathetically. It was what she wanted. Yet she felt compelled, for his sake, not to jump.

"The people are rallying around you, Dan," she said. "They need a leader. You could be that, a marvelous martyr. I wouldn't want you to feel, later, that you missed out on something . . . that you had quit in the middle of the game. Beyond that, there's a practical matter. Where would we go?"

"We'll think of something," he said. "I just want to get out, get away . . . away from Klein. I don't really like Klein. I think he's sincere . . . at times . . . then I wonder. I mean, he's terribly ambitious, his paper has to show a profit. And I wish he weren't Jewish. Deep down, sometimes I wonder if the Jewish press might not be unconsciously trying to get revenge for all the decades and decades of stupid Catholic discrimination . . . not decades, by God. Centuries."

"Oh, I doubt that . . . really, Dan . . ."

"Anyway, to get back. Since I'm pulling out, they need a leader. All right. How about McDivitt? McDivitt is a *perfect* front man. He's forceful, a good speaker. He looks like the typical, small-town, All American boy, an astronaut type. Good image. And he has a way with the press. Let's talk to Klein privately about McDivitt."

"All right," Mary said. "But right now, speaking of Ryan, *we've* got a practical matter to discuss. We can't both live here unchaperoned, with all these people around. That would be asking for trouble."

"No," said Daugherty. "I guess you're right."

"Yesterday," Mary continued, "I went down the street and lined up a little furnished efficiency for me. If you'll help, I'll move my things down there. It's only half a block. I can still get over and cook for you."

She smiled.

"Good," Daugherty said vaguely, then added: "We'll attend to Mc-Divitt. Then we've *got* to take time out, real soon, and figure out what *we're* going to do. Right?"

"Right."

"I'm out now," Daugherty said, as if examining his personal status in a new light. "Fired. I don't have to mail that damned letter. They're sending *me* one. I wish I had sent it now. Resigned—before they drummed me out."

"*You* drummed yourself out," Mary said firmly. "Don't ever forget that, Dan. They didn't fire you. You provoked them into firing you. They had no choice. You did what you felt you had to do."

"True," he said. "That's true. Still . . ."

They heard a knock at the front door. Daugherty went out to the foyer. Through the screen, he saw Jean and Bob Favrot, and behind them, parked at the curb, the big white station wagon. He called back over his shoulder:

"Mary! The Favrots are here. Come on out."

He swung open the screen, shook hands.

"Come in. Come in."

"We went by the rectory looking for you," Jean said, coming into the house. "Mrs. Munally said you had left—for here. She said you had left some cartons, so we brought them for you."

"In the car," Bob added.

"Oh, you shouldn't have done that," Daugherty said.

"No trouble," Bob said.

Mary came from the kitchen. Daugherty introduced her to the Favrots as his "office manager, chief of staff, and cook." Jean wondered at this. The girl was so dark, beautiful . . . with perfect skin. Who was she? Where had she come from? What role did she play in his life? She seemed so very much at home here.

"I've heard a lot about you," Mary said to Jean. "Dan told me the whole thing this morning was . . . that you had an astonishing turn-out."

"He was fabulous," Jean said, wondering *what* Daugherty might have told this young girl—how much "a lot" truly meant. She beamed at Daugherty.

"I'll get the boxes," Bob said, going out the door. He, too, was curious about the girl.

"I'll help," Daugherty said.

They went to the wagon, unlocked the tailgate, and pulled at the boxes. Bob Favrot paused.

"I'm sorry the way it turned out," he said. "But, really, Dan, as I told Jean, it could have ended no other way. If I may . . . let an old politician put in his two cents worth. In all my years, I've never seen much good come of these direct confrontations and . . . pressure built up by leaking to the press. That's a myth. In power struggles, you must mediate, negotiate, compromise. Take and yield. As Lyndon used to say, reason together. Above all, you must avoid, like the plague, taking, or forcing the other guy into a corner . . . a position from which he can't retreat without losing complete face. Now both of you—both sides—are starting out in extreme positions. I don't know if all the damage has been done or not. But, if you like, I'll see what I can do in terms of some kind of mediation."

Daugherty listened attentively, leaning against the rear of the car.

"What did you have in mind?"

"I'm not sure. I thought I might call Mike Baracevi . . . head of the Washington lay association. Do you know him?"

"Not personally."

"I met him at an association meeting last spring. I . . . to be frank . . . I didn't think much of him. Sort of a loudmouth lightweight. But he does head up a legitimate institution. And, since the Council, as I understand it, laymen are supposed to do more in situations like this. I thought I might give him a call."

"I don't think McInnerney has much respect for the lay association," Daugherty said. "I heard he's refused to deal with them on a number of important matters . . . that he voted against the increased power for laity at the Council."

"Right now, the Chancery might just well be looking for a way to mediate. You never know. Nothing ventured, nothing gained."

"From what I know, I doubt we can mediate. Anyway, it certainly wouldn't do any harm. Has the association taken a position on the encyclical?"

"Not that I know of. I'd doubt they would—officially. It's a little too hot for them to touch. They're new, just feeling their way."

"I guess it is too hot."

"I'll see what I can do. By the way, Dan. I don't know how you're fixed financially. If I know Ryan—and I do—I doubt he gave you any severance pay. Here, take this to tide you over."

Bob Favrot took three $20 bills from his wallet. Daugherty accepted them gratefully. He didn't have a dime. He had not drawn his monthly salary at All Saints'. He had put aside nothing in a savings account. He had, in fact, given no thought to money—not since that one brief discussion with Mary the night she came back from Greenwich. He must think about getting a job. They could not get married with no job, no money. They could not live on handouts either.

"One more thing," Bob said. "I want to thank you for all you've done to help Jean. She seems to be coming on fine. She's got *me* going to that damned shrink, Dr. Cantor."

"How do you like him?" Daugherty asked.

"Very well-organized young man. Doesn't waste any time. Said I was a flabby, middle-aged slob."

"Really?" Daugherty laughed.

"Not in exactly those words. Almost. Anyway, he nailed me on the booze. Said I had a problem."

"What did you say?"

"I went on the wagon. And I'm taking tennis lessons!"

"Good for you!"

"I think they're ganging up on me. Maybe I ought to get my *own* shrink!"

"Maybe we could get a group rate," Daugherty chuckled.

They lifted the heavy cardboard boxes into the house, up the stairs. In the kitchen, Mary and Jean sat at the table sipping coffee.

"It's a damned outrage," Jean said, referring again to Daugherty's dismissal. "A slap in the face to all of us . . . one more act of arrogance."

"Yes," Mary said.

Jean looked at Mary over the rim of her cup. It was strange. The girl did not seem upset.

"After Mass," Jean pressed on, "we decided, right on the spot, to get up a signed petition to have Daugherty reinstated. Signed by every wife in the parish. Then deliver it by hand to the Chancery."

"I see . . ." Mary said, trying very hard to remain calm, to control the panic she felt. What was this curious thing between Jean and Dan? Why were both so hell-bent to help the other? Mary liked Jean, the openness, the strange, musical voice. But she did not like her energy, the do-gooding zeal. Dan could not be reinstated. Not after this morning. Especially not if Ryan had gossiped in the Chancery. Moreover, Mary did not want Dan reinstated. If he were, it would again leave their future monumentally uncertain. Yet she must not say or do anything to deflate Jean's enthusiasm. As Klein said, the housewives of the parish were invaluable allies. Every move they made, however futile, would help. A signed petition delivered to the Chancery by Jean Favrot, mother of nine, would be front-page, perhaps nationwide news.

"He's a wonderful person," Jean went on. "Everybody is furious. Nobody wants Ryan back . . . not now."

"He *is* a wonderful person," Mary agreed.

"That . . . that thing today took guts."

"Yes," Mary said. "He has plenty of courage."

"I was scared to death when that crazy man tried to hit him," Jean said.

"Tried to hit Dan?" Mary said, aghast. "Father Daugherty?"

"Yes."

"I thought he tried to hit a reporter," Mary said.

"Oh no. I saw it very clearly. He was after Father Daugherty."

Mary swallowed hard.

"Don't tell him," she said. "He thought he was after the press."

"He was definitely trying to hit Father Daugherty."

"We don't want violence."

"No. I agree. That would look very bad."

"It's bad in itself."

They heard a shout in the foyer, a booming voice:

"Dan? Dan? Are you here? Mary?"

It was McDivitt. Mary, happy for company, an excuse to break off from the inquisitive Jean Favrot, ran out to greet him. Daugherty came down the stairs, shouting hello. They all met in the foyer.

"I just quit," McDivitt pronounced with high excitement. "Turned in my collar."

"How? Why?" Mary gasped.

"A long story," McDivitt said, peeling off his black jacket, tossing it casually on the hall loveseat. He unsnapped his Roman collar, examined it as though it were a foreign object, flipped it atop his jacket, looking at it, and saying: "So long, buddy."

"Come have coffee," Mary said, pulling on McDivitt's muscular forearm. "Come on."

They went into the kitchen. Bob Favrot joined them. Daugherty made the introductions. McDivitt, holding his coffee cup, excitedly blurted his story between sips:

"Went to the mat with Prial. Tough customer. Told him, right out, that unless Dan were reinstated within the next hour, I'd resign in protest. Said he doubted McInnerney would consider it . . . Dan had betrayed a trust . . . all that guff. Seemed to be concerned mostly about the TV. All this time, the telephone going like mad . . . the press calling . . . Prial no-commenting every call. Did you hear that McFadden, Kelley, Dineen, Geary, McSorley . . . and even old Currie, he must be seventy-five . . . had issued statements supporting Dan? The whole archdiocese is rising up. Prial was really burning . . . not burning really. This is important. I think he was scared . . . running scared . . . like the two-minute gun had sounded and he was trailing fourteen to ten. In his time he was a great running back. Did you know that? Anyway, where was I? So we went right up to see McInnerney. Cool as ice. On the horn to some cardinal. Plotting, I guess. Then denouncing the press, *The New York Times*—have you seen their piece today?"

"What did he say about Dan?" Mary cut in.

"He's adamant. No reinstatement. Out of the question. Though—again—it seemed to me Prial might have been willing to talk. I had a feeling that if I could just get Prial backed into a corner alone, I might do some business. But, let's face it, the man is completely loyal."

"What happened?" Mary insisted.

"I asked him to reinstate Dan to a full-time priest, pointing out he had no legal right . . . that *he* had provoked Dan into the show this morning by restricting him . . . also pointing out all the women coming for the Mass . . . the deep and widespread sentiment. This meant nothing. He advised me to cool off, meditate, so I resigned."

The group fell silent.

"I hope," Daugherty said, "that you did it because of what you believe, and not out of some misguided indignation over me."

"Don't worry," McDivitt said with sincerity. "I'd already made up my mind. I think the Deuteronomy bit broke it for me. He's not going to threaten my people with an evil curse!"

"Good," Daugherty said. "I just hope we haven't all come down with some lunatic disease."

Bob Favrot listened intently to this inside, obviously exaggerated account of the Chancery's mood. He now spoke to McDivitt:

"You say you felt Prial might be malleable?"

"It *seemed* that way," McDivitt said.

"I see," Bob said, nodding his head, tucking that opinion away in his mind.

Jean Favrot had listened attentively, too. There was something hypnotic about McDivitt, the way he totally commanded their attention, filled the room with his sure, booming voice. A man of action! All on his own, going immediately to ask for the reinstatement! Perhaps her petition, coming on top of McDivitt's resignation, would now carry greater weight.

In the ensuing silence, they heard the front door bang, followed by a clatter of wood on wood in the foyer. Mary left the kitchen to investigate. She found Seymour Jones in the front hall, wearing a dashiki, weighted down with her Montessori apparatus, the red and blue number rods, struggling to keep any more from dropping.

"Seymour!" Mary exclaimed, rushing to help hold the apparatus.

"Hi, Sister," Jones said. "I brought your gear. The rest is in the car."

Mary helped set the apparatus on the floor. Then she followed Jones to his car, a green Mustang, double-parked in the street. Mary stood back, admiring the car.

"Where did you get this?" she said.

Jones opened the trunk.

"I bought it," Jones said. "After the thing at St. Luke's, the bread started pouring in from all over hell-and-gone. A trickle at first. Ten or twenty bucks. Then a torrent. Quarters, dollars, fives, a few twenties. The mailman started to bring it in big bags."

"Wow!" said Mary, clapping her hands.

"I felt the same way," Jones said. "I said, what the hell is this? I mean, I really hit a beautiful chord. I got to thinking, what am I going to do with all this money? So I went over to see a lawyer, friend of my landlord's. Very responsible. He says if I don't organize myself into a . . . an entity . . . it would be *taxable!* So, believe me, Mary, I got organized quick. Two days. Do you know that in the District of Columbia you can start up a religion, the whole works, without any special qualifications? Just hang out your shingle and everything you get is tax-free. Mary, you are looking at the new pastor of the Universal Church of Christ. This car here, tax-free, is registered in the name of the church, as will be all my future property and my income—all tax-exempt. I tell you, Mary, we must thank our forefathers who drew up the Constitution, guaranteeing freedom of religion. Do you realize I can marry people, bury people, hold baptisms, last rites? I can even ordain ministers in my religion. It's the sweetest little deal you've ever seen."

He lifted an armload of apparatus from the trunk. Mary stood, hands on hips, appalled by the swift change that had overcome this dedicated young man.

"Seymour Jones!" she said accusingly. "You can't possibly be serious. What do you mean, Universal Church of Christ? What kind of put-on is this? You can't throw away your faith and take up another because it's . . . it's tax-free!"

Jones lifted his foot to the bumper, rested the load on his knee. His dark eyes, the grave manner told Mary that he was very serious indeed.

"Sister Mary," he said. "Hear me for a second. Your religion was put on me like my name. I just took it up, automatically, without any real thought. Now, I study this thing all year long, and everywhere I turn, I wonder why I'm Catholic. You remember I told you about those slaves in Louisiana? The ones they hanged in the parish churchyards? What has it done for any of us? They wouldn't give you a place for your school, those poor little crippled kids. They closed me down—the best thing they had in the ghetto. Now, they've legally evicted me. They sold St. Luke's. There's no plan at all for a new church down there. The money's going to the suburbs. You know that. They shut down this place Father Daugherty had going. They crapped all over him. Why should I hang in there? You quit. Why not me?"

Mary reached into the trunk for a load.

"They fired Dan this morning," she said.

Jones closed the trunk with his free hand.

"Why?"

"He came out openly against the encyclical."

"Good for him," Jones said. "What is he going to do now?"

"We don't know yet. Get a job, I guess. Continue to fight from here."

"He won't have trouble getting work. Maybe you could start your own religion. Organize yourself into an entity."

They walked toward the stoop.

"How much money have you received altogether?" Mary said.

"About twelve thou', more or less. As of this morning."

"Oh, wow!"

"From every place you can imagine."

"What are *you* going to do?"

"I don't know. Now that I'm organized as an entity, I think maybe I'll tour around the country. Maybe go to the Democratic convention and maybe to Memphis and Atlanta to see Coretta King and the SCLC crowd. Jesse Jackson. I think this Abernathy is a loser. They may want fresh blood. Or, I may just tour around making confrontations, delivering manifestos. Keep my name in the papers."

"You certainly have made a good start with that."

"You folks ain't doing so bad yourself."

"What about the gym?" Mary said, going up the stoop.

"Oh, the hell with that. As my lawyer said, what do I need with a gym?"

"What about your boys . . . your kids?"

Seymour pried the screen door open with his foot.

"Right now I'm looking after Charles Seymour," he said, holding the door with his rump. "The Reverend Charles Seymour Jones."

Inside, they stacked the apparatus on the floor. Then they went to the kitchen, Mary making the introductions. Bob Favrot shook hands uneasily. He thought: So this is the famous Charles Seymour Jones! Nancy's black hero! Dashiki, Afro hairdo, the works. A troublemaker of the front rank, a real thorn in the side of the Chancery. If there was to be meaningful mediation, Jones could not be a participant. The trouble was, they were overly complicating things.

"The *Reverend* Charles Seymour," Jones said, smilingly when shaking hands with McDivitt.

"Reverend?" Daugherty said.

"I'll explain later," Mary said to him.

"Well," McDivitt said, "I'm the *ex*-Reverend."

Jones looked at Mary, shrugged his shoulders, as if to say: See? Everybody's doing it.

Jean Favrot shook hands with Jones, gushing.

"My daughter, Nancy, is still talking about you," she said. "When you played the guitar at All Saints'."

"Oh yes," Jones said, turning his face to Jean, remembering that Sunday, so long ago. .

"Seymour brought my Montessori apparatus around," Mary said to Daugherty. "He's been evicted from the gym."

"Are you physically out now?" Daugherty said.

"Out," Jones replied. "I hear you are too."

"Yes," Daugherty said.

"Stupid, stupid, stupid," Jones said, with a touch of anger. Then he shook hands good-bye. He had to leave. He was double-parked in the street, had much to do.

After he had gone, they heard more voices on the front stoop, then a loud banging on the screen.

"Grand Central Station," Mary said, going to the door again. There were half a dozen young priests there, some vaguely familiar. When she pushed the screen open, one spoke:

"I'm Father McFadden. This is Father Dineen, Geary, McSorley, and Kelley."

"Oh yes!" Mary said. "Please come in."

"Is Father Daugherty here?" McFadden said, leading the group into the house.

"Yes. Come on back. We're just having coffee."

They went into the kitchen. McDivitt boomed loud hellos and made introductions. Mary watched him admiringly. Yes, he was a leader. A commander. McDivitt proclaimed to the newcomers his hour-old resignation, relating a shorter version of the scene at the Chancery. The news seemed to please McFadden and the others. He said:

"We've come to try to work out some way to make a meaningful protest about Dan. We think it's high-handed and illegal. Reporters have been calling. We think, however, that what's called for is some form of organized response, perhaps a signed statement of some kind. Beyond that, we want to protest the encyclical. We don't want to be told how to think."

"Why don't we all go in the living room?" Mary said.

The group removed itself to the living room, taking chairs or sitting on the floor. They had no sooner settled themselves than there was yet another knock on the front door, footsteps in the foyer. It was Marvin Klein.

He was an intensely busy man these days, knee-deep in the Catholic war in Washington, riding in a semi-euphoria the story he had sniffed out, soundly tromping the competition, day after day. He now had a task force of seven reporters and photographers, led by George Emerson, working full-time on the revolt, determined to earn Emerson a Pulitzer Prize. Copyrighted *Tribune* exclusives were moving daily on the UPI wire. Klein had given himself almost completely to the story, lying awake nights, thinking of new angles, new ideas, new headlines. It did not hurt that he was "plugged in" with the dissidents, that he saw them daily, as unofficial adviser, comrade in arms.

He rushed into the living room, holding aloft the early afternoon edition of the paper, proudly displaying the huge headlines:

REBEL PRIEST FIGHTS CHANCERY
CATHOLIC HOUSEWIVES JOIN IN
PROTEST MASS

Beneath these, there was a photograph of Daugherty, standing in the pulpit, arms raised, outstretched toward the congregation.

Those in the living room gathered around Klein to read Emerson's account of the morning's events. There was, Daugherty noted with relief, only slight exaggeration.

"Golly," Mary said, reading. "Dan, that's a terrible picture."

Daugherty reexamined his likeness. It was smudged and blurred, but definitely him.

"You should sue," Mary added merrily.

Daugherty introduced Klein to the assembly. When he came to Jean Favrot, he added: "You remember my speaking of her?"

Klein looked at Daugherty, puzzled.

"She has nine kids," Daugherty explained.

"Oh yes," Klein remembered. "For all the Jean Favrots of the world."

Bob Favrot shook hands with Klein, wondering at his remark about his wife. He knew Klein, the *Tribune,* by reputation. On the Hill, the *Tribune* was looked upon as unofficial mouthpiece for the nonmilitant black element, a useful publication which no politician could afford to overlook in his reading. But why was Klein involved here? Why the easy informality?

"May I speak to you privately for a minute?" Daugherty said to Klein after the introductions.

"Sure."

They went into the dining room, into a corner near the rear window overlooking the small, littered back yard.

"Did you hear I was fired?" Daugherty said.

"No!" Klein said, eyes widening. "When?"

"This morning. After your boys left."

"Why didn't you call me?"

"I haven't exactly had time."

"For Christ's sake, how much time does a phone call take? I could have used that in the lead."

"No. No, don't do it. Look, we've got to take a minute and talk seriously. I've got a *real* problem."

"What is it?"

"This morning, back in the sacristy, when Ryan was blowing his top, he said something that led me to believe he may have told the Chancery about . . . about Mary and me."

Klein's face clouded.

"They wouldn't . . ."

"You don't know *what* they might do," Daugherty said. "They're going for broke. We'd be so far out on a limb . . ."

"I see what you mean. So what do we . . ."

"What we do is this. This morning, McDivitt resigned in protest."

"He *did?*"

"Yes. Now wait a minute. Slow down, damnit. This is important. What I think—Mary and I think—is that we ought to shift the spotlight to McDivitt. Make him the front man. He's very colorful, very forceful. He ought to be the public man, the spokesman for the dissidents. Not me."

"That's not going to be easy. In the public mind, you're already the—"

"*You're* the PR genius," Daugherty insisted. "You work it out. Otherwise, I'm afraid we stand to get that limb cut off. That could be disastrous for our team. Not only that, it would hurt Mary very much. I don't want to see her hurt. I struck my blow. Got things rolling. Now I want out."

"We don't want anybody hurt," Klein said thoughtfully, as though for the first time weighing the extent of the vulnerability.

"All right, then," Daugherty said. "Get your people on McDivitt. Start tomorrow with his resignation. Play it straight. Leave me completely out. He'd already made up his mind to get out anyway. We're eye to eye on that, are we not?"

"Yes. I see your point. I'll interview him and get a photographer over here later today."

"He'll give you some good quotes. He's very, very forceful."

"He seems so."

"Notre Dame man. All-American football player."

"Seriously?"

"Yes. Don't you remember? Joe McDivitt."

"Say," Klein said, glancing at his watch. "Look at the time. Let's catch the noon news."

They went into the living room. Daugherty knelt and fiddled with the knobs of the TV.

"I hope it works," he said doubtfully. "I think the tube is shot."

"Get it fixed," Klein said. "You guys need to monitor all the news broadcasts."

After some time the black and white picture popped into the screen, somewhat fuzzy, a commercial. Daugherty tuned out the loud hum. The crowd in the room gathered before the set, standing, staring silently. A stony-faced newscaster came on to read the noon news, leading with a story on All Saints'. He intoned:

"Violence erupted at All Saints' parish church in McLean, Virginia, today, during an early morning Mass called to protest the Chancery's support of Pope Paul's birth control ruling. An unidentified assailant, wielding a heavy pipe, charged into a group of newsmen covering the protest. He was subdued after a struggle that panicked the congregation, on hand to hear the acting pastor, the Reverend Daniel Daugherty, denounce the new ban against artificial contraception. Our cameras recorded the attack."

The fuzzy screen now showed the film, the interior of All Saints', Daugherty, first in the pulpit, then in the middle aisle. The camera panned across the faces in the congregation, then suddenly, as it was upended, the roof rafters, and then the floor, followed by a close-up of the newsmen, pushing, shoving. It concluded with a long shot of Monsignor Ryan leading Scafidi behind the communion rail.

The newscaster resumed with a less sensational recap of what had transpired that morning, displaying a brief clip from Daugherty's sermon. There had been no comment, the announcer said, from the Chancery. Later, he added, there would be an exclusive interview with the noted Catholic celebrity Helen Hanrahan, who would have some comments on the growing Catholic conflict in the Washington archdiocese. Marv Klein, a few of the young priests chuckled derisively. But they stayed tuned in, to see what she would say.

During the next commercial, Daugherty said to Klein:

"Damnit, what the hell is this? Why did they show the Scafidi thing? It was only a second or two. Nothing important. The congregation wasn't panicked."

"It certainly wasn't," Jean Favrot said. "They made the whole thing look like a campus riot. It was very, very dignified."

"The film was dramatic," Klein said. "It holds the audience."

"But it wasn't true," Daugherty said.

They kept watching, waiting for the Helen Hanrahan interview. After yet another commercial, she came on, sitting in a modern chair on an empty stage, opposite the interviewer. To Daugherty she looked much younger, much more glamorous than she had in person. The camera moved in close. For the first time, Daugherty noticed the hypnotic quality of her eyes. Even on this creaky TV, it came through, eerily, like Bishop Sheen. Daugherty nudged Mary in the ribs and whispered:

"*My* friend."

"She's a nut," Mary whispered back.

Helen Hanrahan spoke eloquently and convincingly in behalf of the Pope, Archbishop McInnerney, the Catholic Establishment, the encyclical. She implored all Catholics to lay down arms, to return to the fold, to join with her in a vast renewal of faith. Otherwise, she feared they might all provoke an Armageddon. As she spoke, the screen displayed a brief jerky clip of Helen at the Fatima shrine, for reasons not made clear. Concluding the interview, she reminded the Catholic audience that quite soon, Archbishop McInnerney would lead a groundbreaking ceremony for the "vital" new theological center at Catholic University, an open-air Mass to be celebrated by all the American princes of the Catholic Church. She exhorted all to attend as a demonstration of faith in the Pope and the Church and to send contributions to the Chancery. The camera dollied back for a long shot of the stage, then the screen dissolved into a deodorant commercial.

Daugherty snapped off the set. McDivitt, eyes still on the blank screen, spoke to no one in particular.

"That lady just gave me an idea."

"What?" Mary said.

"That ground-breaking," McDivitt said. "It's going to be a hell of a thing, isn't it? All the brass on hand?"

"So she says," Mary replied.

"Then why don't *we* use it?" McDivitt said, snapping his fingers. "Yes. The perfect scene."

"Scene for what?" Klein asked eagerly.

"A massive protest," McDivitt said, warming to his own idea. "Across the street, or wherever. In juxtaposition. An absolutely massive turnout of the dissidents—tens of thousands—not merely to protest the theological center, but to show all those cardinals we mean business. A fantastic show of force, like the 1963 antiwar march on the Mall. All of it on national television . . . , the coverage would be incredible. It could be the crowning thing."

"Right," Jean Favrot exclaimed, clapping her hands. "It's a perfect idea. Just perfect."

"I like it," Daugherty said firmly, delighted to see McDivitt assuming the leadership role.

They discussed McDivitt's idea for a full hour. Under his guidance, it grew in size, shape, grandeur, and force. Mary, Jean, Daugherty, the new priests, convinced themselves that the protest would be a decisive showdown, a real turning point, a grand goal toward which all the dissent might effectively be channeled. A peaceful, nonviolent, silent demonstration, a polarizing effort that could not fail to impress the whole world. It might even convince McInnerney, the Chancery, the Vatican.

Only one voice of caution was raised. It came from Bob Favrot, who, during the discussion, sat back, seeing the idea as an impediment to the mediation he had in mind through Baracevi and the lay association. When at last Bob felt compelled to speak—to say he thought a protest might decisively antagonize the Chancery—he was hooted down, most especially by his wife. This was, Klein informed him patronizingly, the era of "direct action." Bob winced inwardly at these words, but did not again speak up, lest he offend Jean, who was so obviously enamored of the new project.

Later, when Mary and Dan found a minute alone, Daugherty told of his conversation with Klein.

"He's going to shift the spotlight to McDivitt."

"Good," she said. "Now, what about us?"

"We should stay for the protest," Daugherty said. "Working behind the scenes. Absolutely no publicity. Meanwhile, we can work out our plans for the future. Then, after the protest . . . we'll take off."

"Beautiful," she said. "Beautiful."

VII

After her shampoo-set at David's, Jean Favrot swung by the Food Fair for her big weekly marketing. She locked the car, so that no mischievous boys might be tempted to ransack it, to harm the signed petition, which lay on the front seat in a bulky manila envelope. It contained seven hundred names, eighty-seven percent of the parish wives, a massive piece of work, the only copy. She had carried the project through with unflagging energy, in spite of Bob's carefully phrased doubts and the waning enthusiasm of those at Halfway House—now rechristened the Home for Spiritual Renewal—where Jean now worked, part-time. Daugherty would never be reinstated. They all knew it was a lost cause. But the signatures, Jean hoped, would say something beyond Daugherty. They were a ringing endorsement of his stand against the encyclical, a stinging rebuke to the Chancery.

Inside the store, she got a cart, took out her long list. She picked and chose methodically, checking prices (up and up) and net contents (down and down). Rounding the corner of Aisle Four, she came face to face with Bill Clark. He was wearing a charcoal-gray Dacron summer suit, white shirt, dark tie. His pipe was clenched between his teeth, bowl down. Jean stopped, stunned. She quickly turned her head away and swung the cart around, retracing her steps, mind reeling with hideous images—naked bodies, intertwined in a desperate embrace, the pills, the hospital. The nightmare she had forced from her mind; that belonged to an insane moment of her past.

She stopped again, caught in a traffic jam of carts, stock clerks with boxes on dollies, irritable women with hair in pincurls.

"Jean."

His voice cut into her feverish reverie. She turned, pretending surprise. She extricated her cart and pushed toward him cheerily. They drew aside, out of the stream of traffic, next to the meat counter. Jean's panic now turned to fear. She was unavoidably violating her word to Bob never to see Bill again. No one would believe it was an accident.

"How are you?" Bill said.

"Just fine. Fine. And you?"

She looked at his eyes, the clear, taut, well-tanned skin of his face, the even, clean teeth. Was it possible that she . . . No, it was not possible. This man in his business suit was an apparition, someone she did not know.

"Fine," he said. "Pretty busy these days. Doing my shopping on company time."

"How's the book?"

"Coming along. They got the computer on the line, finally, so the brass naturally wanted everything done yesterday. I get home pretty late now. But I've started Part Two and I'm plugging along."

"Did you find a typist?"

"Yes," Bill said, looking at the floor, as though the question pained him. "Young girl from the office."

Jean smiled, still looking directly into his eyes.

"She's very good," Bill added shyly.

"I'm sure," Jean said, raising her eyebrows. "Well . . . I better be running."

"Oh," Bill said. "I see by the papers your boy Daugherty is really stirring things up. Did you organize that pray-in?"

"Yes," Jean said. "I helped."

"I thought I recognized your fine Cajun hand," Bill said.

"We've got up a petition," she said. "I'm taking it down to the Chancery this afternoon. We hope to get him reinstated."

"Does he want to be?"

"Yes . . . I suppose so. I mean . . ."

"You better be sure. He might have a girl friend squirreled away."

"Bill Clark! That's nasty."

"A lot of them do these days. So I hear. More power to 'em. Anyway, it's good to see you busy, and looking so well."

"Thank you," she said, feeling the ends of her hair. Then quietly, and with meaning he could not fail to grasp: "The Devil finds work for idle hands, as my mother used to say."

"Yes," Bill replied, not failing to grasp. "That may have been *part* of it. Anyway, I have no regrets. By the way, how's your group? Did you know your friend Cantor put me in one? He's really quite good. Finishing up what I should have finished on the Coast. Putting me back together."

"That's good. Yes . . . I knew . . . he told me. I'm out of my group now. Bob and I are seeing him privately."

She remembered Margo, Mike, the whole nutty bunch. That, too, seemed part of another life, not her own.

"That's good," Bill said.

"We're trying very hard. Bob's on the wagon and he . . ."

She paused, wanting very much to say that Bob was treating her like a real person, that he valued her opinions and her ambitions, that he no longer flatly disapproved of the pill, that his disposition was immensely improved, that he was taking a greater—and more enlightened —interested in the children, that he was helping Daugherty in a small way, even though he disapproved of his methods, that she and Bob had *almost* torn away the constraints about sex. But she did not say any of this. Instead she said:

"He's taking tennis lessons."

"Terrific," Bill said.

"And he's lost fifteen pounds on the Doctor's Quick Weight-Loss Diet. The protein-and-water thing."

"Oh yes," Bill said.

"By the way," she said. "I still have your book . . . *Anna Karenina.* I meant to return it. I never did finish it. I'll get one of the boys to drop it by."

"Oh, don't bother. Keep it."

She did not press the point. The book had disappeared while she was in the hospital. If he wanted it back, she would have to buy a new copy. She had nothing more to say, about that, or anything else.

"Well, I've got to run," Jean said. "Million things . . ."

"Me too," Bill said. "Good luck at the Chancery."

"Thanks. Good luck on your book."

They pushed off in opposite ways. Jean went directly to the checkout counter with her few piddling items. The shopping could wait until later. She must get away as fast as possible, to avoid another awkward encounter in the aisles, to avoid being seen by someone else who might not understand and who might cause trouble for something that was done, finished, now a part of that inexplicable history people accumulate along the way.

Jean parked on a side street north of the Chancery. She shut off the motor, picked up the envelope containing the petition, and got out, smoothing the skirt of her dress, hoping she had picked the right one. *That* had been fifteen minutes of painful uncertainty, one voice telling her to wear a dark cotton suit with long sleeves, another telling her to wear the sleeveless Lilly. She had finally picked one somewhere between: an aqua cotton dress with short sleeves, to which she had added a brooch and matching pearl necklace. She did not want to appear either obsequious or defiant by her dress; merely neutral.

She approached the mansion, noting the young black pickets sitting on the grass in the shade. These, she knew, were leftovers from the St. Luke's thing, an issue that had been swiftly submerged by the tidal wave of the encyclical. Daugherty was right about that. Cathedrals, churches, were anachronisms, merely tempting places to hang still more myths, superstitions, childish customs, organizing places useful mainly for collecting money. But who was paying these pickets now? Seymour Jones, Mary had told her, had flipped off on another tack, gone with the wind.

She pushed the shiny brass doorbell. A white maid admitted her, leading Jean to a Queen Anne chair in the long marble foyer, beneath a photograph of Pope Paul with omniscient, stern eyes. She sat, primly crossing her legs, pulling down her skirt, adjusting the envelope in her lap, thinking of Bill Clark. It had been very unsettling, seeing him like that. Strange that he could have meant so much to her for a while, and now . . . Yes, she supposed Cantor was right. She *had* been using him. But, as Cantor also said, why not? There was no reason to feel guilt. The name of the game in this life was to take what you needed when you needed it. Everybody did.

A young priest approached her chair.

"Mrs. Favrot? I'm Father Lomangino. Archbishop McInnerney will see you now. May I show you the way?"

She rose, clutching the envelope, a trifle unsure, off to a clumsy start. She had not caught the priest's name. She followed him to the elevator. Going up, the priest spoke pleasantly about the searing heat, the dismal prospects for the Washington Senators, the crying need for a new manager. He led the way along the second corridor to McInnerney's office, knocked discreetly on the massive door.

Vicar General Prial opened the door. He was deferential, cordial, permitting no outward sign of the tension that was driving him and the Chancery to the point of exhaustion.

Jean Favrot's call for an appointment had touched off yet another testy scene with McInnerney. The Archbishop did not want to see her, did not want to accept delivery of the petition, calling the whole thing a "damned nuisance." Prial, after checking with Monsignor Ryan, insisted they see her. Jean Favrot had become, almost overnight, an important member of the opposition, a symbol around whom the protesting women were polarizing. She had surfaced in the newspapers, strident architect of that disastrous pray-in, the collection plate boycott, or rather, the giving of pennies. It had caught on, spread to the other suburban parishes, bringing on galloping financial peril for the whole archdiocese. Prial felt it was as important to "reach" the Jean Favrots of the archdiocese as it was the supervisors whom McInnerney was seeing privately, one by one, on a twelve-hour-day schedule, or the dissenting priests to whom McInnerney was now writing an anguished personal letter that had already grown to fifteen closely packed pages.

Now that she was here in the office, neither man gave any sign that she was unwelcome, or a problem, or that she bore more bad news. The Archbishop rose from his chair, smiling genially. He appeared to Jean almost saintly in his humbleness. He did not at all match her mental picture of him—formed by the pictures in the pamphlets and newspapers. For one thing, he was much smaller than she had imagined.

"Come in, come in," he said graciously. He came to her, ring finger extended. "Please sit down, Mrs. Favrot. Would you like some tea?"

"No, thank you," Jean said, genuflecting, kissing the ring, then sitting on the couch. "I really don't want to take up much of your time. I know you are a very busy man these days."

"For an old man," he said gently, "these are not easy times. What can I do for you? You have a petition, I understand."

"Yes, Your Excellency," Jean said.

She opened the manila envelope, withdrawing the petition. Then she spoke the words she had phrased in her mind on the drive downtown.

"I want to present you, in behalf of the women of All Saints' parish, a petition signed by seven hundred and thirty-six people—eighty-seven percent of the registration—requesting Father Daugherty be re-instated as our acting pastor, and be restored to his full authority as a priest."

She stopped there. The Archbishop weighed her words gravely. She passed over the bulky petition. McInnerney hefted it, leafed the first few pages, laid it on the coffee table, and replied slowly and gently.

"I'm afraid that's quite impossible."

"Well . . . why?"

"Because," McInnerney said, with an edge in his voice, "Daugherty violated a trust . . . violated his vows as a priest . . . preached heresy . . . and disobeyed authority. I gave him every possible chance. I counseled him. I prayed for him. He is an unstable person, not qualified to be a priest. All of you should know that."

"He does *not* preach heresy," Jean said, face flushing.

"You didn't come here to debate theology, I assume?" the Archbishop said.

"I'm not qualified to debate theology," Jean said, feeling a sudden surge of confidence that she must make clear what the petition implied. "Any more than you or the Pope is qualified to tell me what to do in my bedroom. Neither you nor the Pope seems to understand that an important part of a woman's dignity is her ability to control her procreation. Nor do you seem to understand how vital uncomplicated, unmechanical sex is to the meaning of love, and to family well-being."

McInnerney, surprised by Jean's force, was silent a moment, then said:

"My mother had ten children. She was a laundress, deserted by a drunken husband. You say that I, as an Ordinary, am not qualified, know nothing of the problems of married people! Mrs. Favrot, this is not true. You don't grow up, one of ten, in a household like that, without considerable insight into family problems. Then for years, after the seminary, I heard confessions. Let me tell you this. In those days— the old days—people were less hypocritical about sexual sins. There was much more honesty and humility about human weakness. Even though they repeatedly failed, repeatedly sinned, they didn't rise up and say the moral law had to be changed. They admitted that *their* lives had to be changed. They admitted they had to *try* harder. The weaker ones believed that no matter how many times they fell from Grace, a continuing honest effort was enough to satisfy the mercy of God. The whole problem today is that people, for some reason, believe regular sexual intercourse is absolutely necessary. We know that's not true. Many couples abstain because of illness, or separation—husbands in the Army or Navy—or for some other reason. I understand all about that . . . God created you, a woman, to have children through sexual intercourse, to perpetuate the human race, a massive responsibility. He did not create you primarily as a vehicle of unrestrained pleasure."

Jean interrupted with subdued anger:

"I have *nine* children."

"You should be very proud."

"I *am* proud of my children. But there was a time, not long ago, when I resented them. Father Daugherty taught me to know myself, and to understand many things. He saved me from . . . saved our whole family . . . from a disaster. Both Bob—my husband—and I feel that you are wrong about him. Not just him, the whole thing. So do the people who signed that petition."

"He is no longer *Father* Daugherty," Prial interjected.

"You have read . . . studied . . . *Humanae Vitae?*" the Archbishop asked.

"Yes."

"And my letters? The guideline pamphlet, *Sex in Marriage?*"

"Yes," Jean said. "But I have also read the statement signed by the six hundred Catholic theologians. I've read statements by Louis Dupre. Dr. Rock. The articles by Father O'Brien and Father Burtchaell at Notre Dame. I've read Hans Kung. Karl Rahner. Monsignor Gallagher. Bishop Robinson. Cardinal Koenig. The statements of the Dutch, Belgian, Canadian, and Mexican bishops. None of these people agrees with you. You, alone, seem determined to believe the encyclical was infallible."

"Some of the people you mention are Protestants!" Prial put in gently, like a lawyer who knew his Rules of Evidence.

"They are good people," Jean said, turning to him. "Theologians. Philosophers. Most of them are Catholic."

"But Mrs. Favrot, you are quoting a tiny handful of people. Do you realize there are twenty-seven hundred bishops in the world—most of whom support Paul to the death? Paul has said again and again, made it perfectly clear, that contraception is *immoral*. Can't you accept the continued teaching of the True Church?"

"I choose to follow my conscience."

"My dear," McInnerney said. "The obligation of a Catholic to accept the teaching of the Church on any grave moral problem can never, justifiably, be regarded as an offense against freedom of conscience. Rather, the free acceptance of that particular obligation is implicit in the free decision, already made and still continuing, to accept the claim of the Catholic Church to speak with the authority of Christ. Now, Mrs. Favrot, you cannot believe that I could regard a serious pronouncement of the Holy Father as a negotiable, arguable utterance? Surely you must know that, besides me, there are millions upon millions of Catholics the world over who accept his teaching, without dissent, on the contrary, embrace it with joy. Your mind, your emotions, have been stirred up by a lot of would-be fanatics who have distorted the aim of the Council, the so-called liberal policy, to exercise their own ego, with the aim, wittingly or unwittingly, of destroying the foundation and authority of the Church, and leaving the people of the Christian world confused, at sea, fearful, lost, forever denied the Kingdom of Heaven. If you foreswear authority, destroy the Church, let sexual freedom run rampant, you will tear marriages apart, destroy young lives. Religious traditions, truths, will pass away. There will be terror, savages in the streets, misery and hostility in the homes, hopelessness in the human heart. Man will have no clear picture of the afterlife, he will lose his reverence for God. If you take that away, what is left? My sole purpose in living, of exercising my office, is to prevent this . . . what could only be a catastrophe. I need your help. I need your husband's help. I need your children's help. You must work for me. Pray for me. Don't listen to Daugherty and his heretics. Listen to God."

McInnerney stopped, eyes filming with tears. Jean felt an immense wave of pity. His conviction was an awesome thing, like steel and granite all mixed together, immovable, unbendable, impenetrable. It was like family loyalty in the last century. She felt despair, as though she had let down God. This was all crazy. They couldn't win against this man. Yet . . . she must keep up her courage. She was a chosen representative of 736 wives and mothers.

"I listen to God," Jean said, her voice trembling. "I pray. I . . . I don't have your assurance . . . I . . . Your Excellency, you don't understand about sex. Do you know what the nuns taught me when I was a little girl? They taught me that sex was *evil*. Nasty. That men were animals. That I—as a good Catholic mother—must *submit* to the pain and the lust and the childbearing willfully . . . for *his* pleasure. They warned me not to wear a pearl necklace like this. The pearls would mirror my bosom! They told me never to leap a puddle, because the water might reflect my underpants! Think about that! After I got married, I came to *hate* sex. I hated my husband to touch me. It's only been very recently—after my eyes were opened—that it hasn't made me physically sick . . . I have a sixteen-year-old daughter, Nancy. She's not going to grow up with a sex hangup if I can help it. The chain has got to be broken. She's not going to have nine children, either. If we Catholics keep on having children, we'll bring on catastrophe. Disaster."

This plea left McInnerney and Prial speechless, uncomfortable. McInnerney opened his mouth to speak, but Jean rushed on:

"Because I believe that, from now on I'm going to follow my own conscience. You'll never, ever, convince me that an evil curse will fall on me because I did."

"Well," McInnerney said, groping.

"Another thing," Jean added. "You're not getting to Nancy. Never mind the sex thing. The only time she really turned on was when Father Daugherty had Seymour Jones play the guitar at Mass. That was the *one* time. And what did Father Daugherty get for that—for all his efforts with the kids?—another slap in the face. Seymour Jones, too."

"I'm sure Nancy is just going through a phase," McInnerney said, determined now to control the discussion. "It seems to be the thing these days. The newspapers and TV glorify these rebellious kids. You parents are far too submissive—brainwashed by the psychologists. Children lose their bearings without a firm parental hand. If you were tougher, more demanding . . ."

"You certainly aren't going to tell me how to discipline my children!" Jean interrupted, much offended.

"It's vital for them to develop a strong sense of values in the home,"
McInnerney said. "All of you depend too much on the schools to
give what they should be getting in the home. I think that's a very mistaken concept. Spare the rod . . ."

"We don't expect anything from your schools anymore," Jean said
angrily. "Not with fifty kids in a classroom, the shortage of teachers."

"We've done the best we possibly can," McInnerney said, smarting.
"To provide for your children's needs . . . But, I'll tell you this. If
this penny boycott continues just one more week, we're going to be
forced to close the system down. I'll sell it to the city."

Prial shifted uneasily in his chair.

"It's just something we have under study," he interjected.

"I don't think anybody would care," Jean said. "*We're* paying the
double cost—for the parochial system and the public system—and we
don't think it's worth it anymore. The nuns, the teachers in the parochial system, are too far out of touch, not qualified. They don't have
the higher degrees . . ."

"You pay a very small proportion of the upkeep for parochial
schools," McInnerney said. "Very small indeed. The tuition barely
covers the teachers' salaries."

"Then sell them," Jean said. "And plow the money into that *stupid*
theological center."

McInnerney was stunned.

"Mrs. Favrot. I'm . . . I'm really . . . I don't know what to say.
Surely, if ever the need for the theological center had been more clearly
demonstrated . . ."

"Not the kind *you* want to build," Jean said. "My husband—Bob—
even says it's wrong. You *had* him, but you lost him with that project.
I'll tell you that."

"The timing was unfortunate," Prial broke in again, vastly disturbed
by the scatter-shot course of the meeting, which had gone on long
enough. "Monsignor Ryan told me how your husband felt. But, as it
happened, we had no control on the timing."

"You said you want to help your daughter Nancy," McInnerney
said, taking a new tack. "That's why *we* want the center. It may come
too late to help you or me. But surely you can see that it will help
Nancy. All the children in all the years to come."

"No, Your Excellency," Jean said, exasperated. "*You* don't understand. It's *not* going to help her. It will antagonize her. She's . . . she's going to march against it. And so am I."

"That would be a terrible mistake," McInnerney said, sighing profoundly. "A tragedy."

"I guess that remains to be seen," Jean said, rising suddenly, satisfied now that she had said her piece, had discharged her responsibility to Daugherty, to Nancy, the housewives, herself. That she was up against a brick wall, to go on was pointless.

She genuflected, kissed the ring, and said good-bye. Returning to his desk, head bowed, shoulders bent, McInnerney asked Prial to please escort Mrs. Favrot to the front door.

Going down the elevator, the Vicar General clasped his hands behind his back, rested his chin on his chest thoughtfully. When the door opened on the first floor, he said:

"Mrs. Favrot. I wonder if you would mind, please, stopping off in my office?"

Surprised, Jean agreed amiably. He led the way, offering a chair. Jean, sitting down, remembered McDivitt's account of his morning in the Chancery, of Prial's equivocal position, of McDivitt's unfailing hope they might "get to" the man. It was certainly worth a try.

"I didn't want you to go away mad," Prial said, smiling, taking a seat behind the desk. "Or thinking that we're going to sell the parochial school system!"

"He was upset," Jean said. "I didn't really believe that. I . . . I was upset too. I'm sorry. This whole thing is . . . is very nerve-wracking."

"Indeed it is," Prial said. "Now, tell me about your daughter. About Nancy. We thought we had done a great deal to update . . . to get to the kids. Particularly the CYO thing, with the seminarians in informal clothes and all."

"That helped," Jean said, recalling how much Nancy had liked the open, casual attitude of the young seminarians who conducted these weekly sessions. "I think that was a good move. But they go from that approach to the conventional routine of the Mass, the formal Mass, and it's like two different worlds to them. Unrelated. You see what I mean? The spirit of the CYO is not carried over into the formal structure of the Church itself."

She went on discussing Nancy, the parochial school system, CYO, for fifteen minutes. Prial listened closely, making an occasional note on a yellow legal pad. Jean felt, like McDivitt, that Prial was at least *listening,* that as long as he did, there might be hope. When she had run out of points to make, unburdened herself of the whole school thing, Prial thanked her and rose, escorted her to the front door.

"I appreciate your coming very much," he said. "I'd . . . I'd like to keep this line of communications open, if I may. To me, this is a much more sensible way of dealing with our differences than name-calling in the press. I wish all of you would bear in mind that the press is just tickled pink about all this, that it's good for circulation and profit, that their motives, in spite of sanctimonious denials, are largely profit-oriented, and that, beyond that, they may have intense personal reasons for playing up our troubles. Remember, too, Mrs. Favrot, that when all's said and done, we *do* have a religion, Catholicism, imperfect as it may seem at this point. What we *do* have is better than none at all."

"Yes," Jean replied, extending a white-gloved hand, bidding good-bye, going to her car. She drove toward the Home for Spiritual Renewal, puzzling over his parting words.

VIII

Going out the front door of the Home for Spiritual Renewal, Dan Daugherty nearly collided with the mailman, who was standing in the darkness on the stoop, beaming a fountain-pen flashlight on the sign to the right of the door.

"Is there a Father Daugherty living here?" the mailman said.

"I'm Daugherty," he said.

"Will you sign here, please?"

The request, the delay annoyed Daugherty. There was a time, not too long past, when a Special Delivery letter would have been a special event. Now they arrived all day and night, with the flood of regular mail, the telegrams, the incessant long-distance phone calls. Every confused, dissatisfied, or wayward priest, nun, layman in the world, it seemed, sought—some desperately—spiritual advice. Thousands of others, sympathetic to the cause, merely wanted to contribute time or money. The press demanded interviews. Publishers pleaded for books. Television producers wanted "Specials." The beds in the Home for Spiritual Renewal were now all occupied by a strange assortment of itinerant priests, ex-priests, ex-seminarians, some bizarre in their habits, others pitiful, wretched wrecks, two obvious alcoholics. To open the mail and answer the telephone, there was now an "office" force of six women, volunteers working under Mary and Jean Favrot. Dan Daugherty, now "Mr. Inside," presided over all the chaos.

It was almost nine thirty. Daugherty, dizzy with fatigue, was two hours late for dinner at Mary's apartment. She had left at six, telling him to "hurry." But Daugherty could not get off the phone, the essential tool of the modern revolt. Over it poured, hour after hour, rumor, speculation, gossip, dark innuendo, and a few hard facts on the enemy, detailed accounts of what who was saying to whom. Many of these were provided by reporters, who were "trading" information between the two camps for new angles, new developments, "exclusives." McDivitt, who hated the telephone, complained they were becoming inflicted with "telephonitis," a dreaded, contagious disease that would ultimately destroy them. Daugherty agreed, yet felt it essential to screen most of the calls so that they would never again be caught unawares by the Chancery, as they had been on the morning of the pray-in.

The mailman offered a yellow postal form. Daugherty signed it, prefacing it with "Father," so that the bureaucratic form would jibe with the addressee on the letter. It was postmarked Bryn Mawr, Pennsylvania. It was addressed in his father's unmistakable hand, a precise, Palmer penmanship that had only recently begun to waver. Daugherty returned to the foyer to read it by the dim overhead light. It was the first word he had received since he telephoned his parents two weeks ago, on the eve of the pray-in. He had said nothing about the impending ceremony, merely that he had made his decision to leave. They had met this news with chilly silence.

The letter was brief, a single paragraph set in the center of the heavy, engraved stationery:

Son—
Your mother and I have been in shock since you telephoned, and since we saw your picture in the papers. We do not disapprove of your decision so much as the way you have gone about it. Can't you just leave quietly? Must you jar the faith of so many,

including your mother, who, as you know, has not been well? For generations we Daughertys have prided ourselves on staying out of the papers, except for births, weddings, and deaths. We've found, over the years, that public posturing brings only trouble —your friends become either resentful or contemptuous. You become a target for the hate of irriational people. None of our friends can understand your conduct, and frankly, neither can I. It is humiliation enough to bear without you going about shouting from the rooftops.

Sincerely,

Kevin P. Daugherty

Daugherty pressed his lips firmly, balled up the letter, jammed it in his trousers pocket. He went on the street, toward Mary's, sinking into despair. He had been half-expecting the letter for many days, dreading its arrival, knowing exactly what it would say. Many times he had been tempted to anticipate it, write them a long letter explaining all. But there had been no time. He was racing from crisis to crisis these days, like a company commander pinned down by withering machine-gun fire on a hostile beach. Even if there had been time, how would he explain? Compress into the pages of a letter or a long-distance phone call all the astonishing ins and outs of the last few weeks? It would take a book, and still (he knew) they would not understand. It would be futile—like debating with McInnerney.

He scuffed along the sidewalk, thinking about his father, stubborn, autocratic, pious, a businessman, pure Establishment, whose only contact with the public had been a brief, abortive effort in 1940 to help raise money for Wendell Willkie. After that he had withdrawn to his library, investments, his model sailboats, the *Wall Street Journal* and *Barron's*. A rich, self-centered recluse.

He swung into the foyer of Mary's building. It was dirty and smelled stale like most apartment buildings. He mounted the smooth stone steps to the second floor, going down the corridor to the rear. At her door—2D—he stopped, breathing deeply, seeking a hook for his plunging spirits, a note of cheer. The door was unlocked.

He walked in, calling her name. She peered from the pullman kitchen where she was working at the sink, fetching and pleasant, even with stringy hair. He walked to her, kissed her on the neck, smelling onions.

"You ought to keep that door locked," he said.

"I thought I locked it."

"Wide open. Again."

"The dumb thing is broken anyway."

"We've got to fix it. Otherwise, they're going to walk right in and cut your throat."

"I know," she said, rinsing the onions, cutting them into the raw hamburger. "Did you see that thing in the *Post* this morning? They got that senator right in his own elevator."

"I saw it. That and fifteen others. Nine tenths of the crime doesn't even get in the papers."

"I'm sure."

"Get it fixed."

"I shall. Tomorrow, without fail. Anyway—pray—why are we so owly tonight?"

She rinsed and dried her hands. They sat down in the living room, a small space, shabbily furnished.

"I'm sorry," Daugherty said. "Shall I fix a drink? I need one tonight, believe me."

"What happened?" she said. "When I left, you seemed in fine spirits."

"First I got a call from Klein. Wait a minute. Let me get the drinks."

He went back to the sink, poured two Scotches, a double for himself.

"What did he want?"

"Well, damnit, the moon, as usual. He was back on the St. Luke's deal. Wanted to know if we had anybody, anywhere, with an inside line to the Chancery account books. He's still trying to nail down the fact that St. Luke's money is paying for the theological center. Thinks that would be a great scandal for the protest."

"You know who put that idea in his head, don't you?"

"No. Who?"

"You. The afternoon . . . after . . . the afternoon he came by Halfway House all excited . . . and we told him about . . . us."

"I did? I don't remember that. God, I ought to be hanged. Anyway, then he wanted me to get one guy from every parish to get together figures on the fund drive, showing it was a failure, that the money raised could not possibly be paying for the theological center, that the archdiocese had a financial crisis with the penny boycott and all that."

"What did you do?"

"I blew my stack."

"I don't blame you."

Daugherty drained his drink quickly. He returned for a refill, this time a single.

"He never gives up," he said, plopping into the chair again.

"That's why he's good."

"I don't know when he sleeps."

"He told me he had insomnia."

"I feel sorry for his wife. Anyway, then, just as I was leaving, this arrived."

He reached in his pocket, withdrew the balled-up letter. He tossed it to Mary. She smoothed it out and read quickly, frowning, troubled.

"He didn't have to do that," she said, returning the letter.

"I was expecting it, actually. They don't understand. And I don't have time to stop and explain. Not that he would accept any explanation."

"Right," Mary said, forcing herself to be bright, cheery. "So, did you hear the good news today? Jean Favrot—God, what an indefatigable person she is—finally got a commitment from Senator Devereaux's office. He's definitely coming to the ground-breaking. On *our* side."

"I *heard* that," Daugherty said.

"Anyway," Mary said, still brightly. "Since he's committed, that means his people—all the kids—will work like demons to help us make it a success. It's a real coup, thanks to Jean."

"Fantastic woman," Daugherty said. "It took a lot of guts to go to the mat with McInnerney."

He returned to the kitchen for another drink.

"Don't get juiced. I have a good dinner. Hamburgers. Broccoli. Salad."

"I won't," Daugherty said. He returned to his chair, sat quietly, looking at the cheap straw rug, thinking. Then he said, "Maybe I *should* have left quietly."

"You did what you had to do at the time. Let's not play Cardinal Hindsight again."

"A certain madness sets in," he said, going on, now feeling the drinks. "The excitement of the thing. Your adrenaline builds up, fuzzes your judgment. It's thrilling as hell for a while, then . . . Frankly, I worry like hell about McDivitt and the others. I feel like I sucked them into this, that somehow I needed them to push me over the top. To face my uncertainty. To give my own going a certain universality."

Mary stared into her drink, silently. The letter had disturbed her immensely. It revived—again—her own misgivings about herself that perhaps she had pushed too much, helped to stampede him to a decision, a position she had been so intently trying to avoid. As Le-Guiese might have said, she must remain obstinately aloof during his painful divorce from the Church. Yet, for all her resolution, here she was, right in the middle of it.

"Dan, I hope you don't blame me."

"No. No. No. I don't blame anybody. It's nobody's fault but my own. Mary, now don't you go feeling guilty. Remember, *I* called you in Greenwich. I begged you to come back."

"I should have said no."

"Now who's playing Cardinal Hindsight?"

He got up, went to her chair, kissed her on the lips. That was good and peaceful and worth the pain and the hurt, the feeling of loss.

"Oh God!" Mary said suddenly, sitting up, perky and gushing. "I almost forgot! You remember when I was up in Greenwich, I sounded out some foundations? Well, I never had a chance to tell you, but I sent in a letter to the Ford people, one page, summarizing the work here, saying I would consider going ahead with it with proper financial support, et cetera. Well, today I got a letter from the director, the top man, saying they had a suggestion from somebody else—some unidentified educator—proposing a Montessori approach for the ghetto deprived in San Juan, Puerto Rico, and they were willing to commit fifty thousand dollars over two years if I were still interested in the grant and the location. Here, let me get the letter."

She went to the sideboard in the kitchen, rummaged through her purse. She came back excitedly, holding the letter.

"Hmmmmmmm," Daugherty said, scanning the letter. "Very nice."

"Isn't that nice?" she said. "Somebody cares, at least."

"A lot of people care," Daugherty said reprovingly. "Your work was outstanding. Everybody knows that."

"Do you suppose they read my thesis?"

"Probably. Or saw the reviews."

"Yes," she said, pondering this possibility. It had been favorably noticed in a few stuffy trade journals.

"Or they touched base with OEO or the Provincial, the people at CU, maybe LeGuiese. I'm sure they check around. They don't just shovel out this kind of cash without looking into it."

"I don't know. But—as I told you—they're plenty hard up for solid projects. Montessori has this cachet now . . . very *in* type of thing."

"Stop underrating yourself."

"All right. So they instantly recognized genius."

"Exactly. By the way, I got another offer today, too. Another book publisher. That makes . . . six . . . seven . . . now, eight. Some outfit I never heard of. Sort of glib, promoter type, pressing very hard."

"How hard?"

"Twenty-five thousand, but he wanted to keep *all* the paperback money, if there was a paperback deal. It's more advance, but the others only wanted *half* of the paperback. His big pitch was promotion. Said he would guarantee in the contract to spend not less than twenty-five thousand on promotion. That he had an inside track with Johnny Carson and Mike Wallace and Merv Griffin and he could get the book plugged on all the best shows."

"What did you say?"

"Same as I said to all the others. No."

Mary looked at her shoes, thinking. Their plan, of slipping away quietly after the protest, seemed now merely a dream. Dan no longer spoke of it. He had thrown himself into the work wholly and completely, seemed to thrive as a behind-the-scenes mastermind. He had made countless hundreds—perhaps thousands—of contacts all over the world with dissident elements of the Church. He was making vague plans, appointments, well into the fall . . . far beyond the protest day. Perhaps if he took money, withdrew to write a book, the dream would become reality.

"Perhaps you ought to think twice," she said. "Kavanaugh made a real killing with his book. Best seller. Longo . . . I hear his wife is doing a book too."

"Absolutely not," Daugherty said emphatically. "They don't want my theological views. They want a lot of personal stuff. All of them. How could I write the whole truth . . . without writing about us? I couldn't do a dishonest, slipshod book. Besides, if I put any personal stuff in, it would kill my parents."

"Probably," she said thoughtfully.

"I couldn't tell about the sex stuff in the seminary the way Longo did. Could you? I mean, Mary, could you really tell it like it was in the novitiate and convent?"

"Dan Daugherty! Are you implying we had a Peyton Place going behind those walls?"

"Homosexual Peyton Place. Don't forget, I've had plenty of nuns in my confessional. I *know!*"

"I never saw anything like that. *Never.*"

"What about that gal you used to write to all the time? The jock?"

"Dan Daugherty, you're getting juiced."

"Maybe I am. It feels good. Get me another drink, will you?"

He held his empty glass in the air. She got up and took it to the kitchen, thinking about the girl, remembering that she had not written since Greenwich, that probably she was hurt.

"That's all you're getting," she said, handing a weak drink to Daugherty, bending, kissing him. She sat on the floor at his feet, caressing his legs.

"You didn't mean that, did you?" she said, almost whispering.

"Mean what?"

"That crack about Fran. Being a Les."

"Hell no!"

"Do I satisfy you?"

"Of course! Now, Mary . . ."

"Dan . . . Dan, let's go away . . . *right now*. We don't really have to stay until the protest. Get out of this insane rat race. Away from all these fanatics. Look . . . I can take the grant from Ford. We could slip away to Puerto Rico . . . set up a school. Maybe you could talk one of these publishers into a serious theological book, essays or commentary, like Father Ong. Don't take so much money. Just a little . . . enough to live on. We don't need much. You could take your time . . . go up into your little writing room like Hemingway . . . write a little each day . . . and help me. It could be so wonderful, couldn't it?"

"Yes, it could," Daugherty said, returning to the kitchen, adding Scotch to his drink. He leaned against the sideboard, staring at the floor, picturing their tropical quarters, a small hacienda laced with bougainvillea, a Yucatan hammock slung on the upstairs gallery, langorous evenings, skin-diving along the reefs, his book (*A Search for God*) no imprimatur, touching off a sensation in the theological circles, raising hackles in the Chancery. Maybe she was right. He had done his part. McDivitt could carry on. Most of the heavy hauling had been done.

"How soon can we get out of here?" he said.

"Right now," Mary said. "I can run up to New York, see the Ford people. You come. Sign the book contract, then we'll go up to Greenwich. I want you to meet my family. Then we can leave for San Juan. No. First we'll ship my apparatus from here . . ."

"Wait. Wait. What do we use for money? I mean, to get started? Go to New York?"

"My five hundred dollars!"

"What five hundred dollars?"

"The five hundred my father gave me. Loaned me . . ."

Daugherty sat down heavily, enthusiasm ebbing.

"Or," Mary added hastily, "the money from *your* book contract. Then we could sell the cars. My VW must be worth a thousand. The MG . . ."

"Not worth the powder to blow it up."

"We'd have at least fifteen hundred to start."

"Of *your* money."

"*Our* money, Dan."

"I could sell my chalice," Daugherty said. "Those diamonds in it are real . . . Mother's present for my ordination. I guess they're legally mine. Worth a bundle."

"Then let's do it. Tomorrow."

"OK. Let's do it."

The telephone rang. Mary leaped to it, snatched it up eagerly. It was Joe McDivitt calling Daugherty. Mary gave him the phone, then went to the stove to start the hamburger. They would eat before Dan had another drink.

"Dan?" McDivitt boomed into the phone. "Did you get the latest word?"

"Word on what?"

Daugherty felt a sinking sensation in his chest. What now? Had they, in spite of total vigilance, been caught unawares again?

"You didn't catch Hanrahan on the ten o'clock news?"

"No," Daugherty replied guiltily. These days he usually never missed a news broadcast. "What did she say?"

"She announced—approvingly—that McInnernery had lowered the boom on everybody who signed the statement of conscience. All fifty-five priests."

"What did he do?"

"It's a massacre, Dan. I made some notes. Let's see, five fired outright. Fifteen restricted from certain sacraments. Twenty transferred to the boondocks—remote parishes. Fifteen censured, reprimanded, but left in place. It's crazy, Dan. Absolute madness."

Daugherty sat down wearily. Fifty-five priests spiritually slaughtered! It was madness. More madness. And now they were using Helen Hanrahan as a spokesman. Clever. If anyone could generate sympathy for the Chancery, she could.

"What happened to the mediations?" he said, voice dropping. "Did she mention them?"

"No. But the regular newscaster did. He said McInnerney refused to even see Baracevi, or anyone else from the lay association. He quoted Bishop Foster from Cleveland as saying he had made an attempt to mediate, offer his services, but no soap."

"I see."

"We can't take this lying down," McDivitt said threateningly.

"No," Daugherty replied. "They supported us, now we have to support them." He felt the deep guilt again—that the slaughter was his fault.

"She also appealed to everyone to boycott our ground-breaking protest, and support the Chancery."

"Did you call Klein?"

"Yeah. He was watching."

"OK, any more?" Daugherty said.

"Actually, Dan, this *might* be good news. I mean . . . the punishment is so severe, so arrogant, so illegal . . . it might backlash on them. It's *too* much."

"It'll backlash if we *make* it," Daugherty said angrily. "Did you give Klein a quote?"

"Not yet. He asked me to call him back."

"OK."

They hung up. Mary, standing over the stove, turned for an explanation. Daugherty, eyes filling with despair, repeated McDivitt's report, word for word. Then he poured another strong drink, a double.

"Fools!" Mary said.

"I didn't think Prial would let it happen," Daugherty said. "He's got better sense, a better feel for the PR. Poor bastards."

"I knew that Baracevi thing wouldn't work," Mary said. "No more than the Favrot petition."

The Scotch struck hard. Daugherty felt a sudden wave of anger boiling in his blood.

"We can't bug out of here now, Mary. Not just yet. We've got to put our backs into the protest. Help make it the most amazing spectacular in history . . . the history of the Church. Tens—hundreds—thousands of people. Now that he's slaughtered those innocent lambs, it's going to be easier. There are fifteen, eighteen parishes involved. They'll respond like All Saints'. They'll turn out. But we need organization, publicity—national publicity—money, contributions, headquarters, volunteer workers, telephones."

Mary served the dinner on plastic plates, listening as Daugherty railed on, the protest growing to immense dimensions in his mind. They sat in the living room, plates on their laps. She had to force his attention to the food. He talked as he ate, swilling Scotch, finally concluding:

"By God, Mary. This could be *it*. The more I think about it, the more I believe they've played right into our hands. We'll make McDivitt a real hero—another Billy Mitchell, an Admiral Rickover, a . . . a . . ."

She nodded her head, but she said:

"It *will* be important. But maybe not decisive. All these protests have a way of winding up with ambiguous third-act curtains. Don't build your hopes too high, Dan. Keep your perspective."

"I am. I am. The problem is . . . with women . . . you don't have imagination. Vision . . ."

"Think small and be surprised. And Dan, what happens if it comes to nothing? What then?"

"That's it," he said with finality, smashing a fist into his hand. "I know it'll do it."

"I mean, if it doesn't. If it's ambiguous?"

"It won't be."

"I know. And I said, what if it is?"

"All right," Daugherty said. "I see. I see. Put it this way: we'll go ahead with our plans. Let's set a date. No matter what, we leave one week after the protest. Seven days."

"You really mean it? Are you sure? Can you leave it?"

"I can't now. I owe that much to those guys. I'll put my back into this for them. An all-out smash. Senator Devereaux! Hell. We'll invite everybody under the sun. Hundreds of celebrities. Anybody who can walk!"

"Dan, you're impossible. One minute you want to steal quietly into the night. Next, you want to go out with a hundred-piece brass band. You're drinking too much."

"Not for *me,*" Daugherty said, jumping excitedly to his feet. "For them. For McDivitt. Then . . . I *promise.*"

Mary was still not sure. She saw the protest, and beyond it, still more. Protests. Television. Pray-ins. Worldwide crusades. A march against the Vatican.

"No," he said, coming toward her chair, knocking over the dregs of her drink. "This is it," he said. "I'll put it in writing."

"Never mind," she said, smiling, finishing her broccoli. "I think we've all had quite enough in writing for a while. We'll not sign any more documents or manifestos or petitions or statements of conscience."

"How about that little certificate we get from city hall?" Daugherty said, bending to kiss her, hand groping for the light.

"Dan . . . wait. My plate . . . look out!"

"You taste like Hollandaise sauce," he whispered, shutting off the light.

"You nut!" she said, clutching him tight, praying he would not crush her. Kissing, they transferred clumsily to the couch. Thoughts of his father's letter were now far from both their minds.

IX

Jean Favrot woke suddenly, as if prodded. She lay in the dark for a moment, listening. Yes! She could hear a faint trickle in the downspout, a steady drip-drip on the splash-block beneath the window in the side yard. She leaned over and peeped out the window. The sky was pitch-black. She squinted at the blurred, luminous hands of the clock. It was five after six, and, she was sure, drizzling. The weather report was, for once, accurate. It was going to be a miserable day. The mountain of prayer for clear skies had gone unheeded.

She sat up in bed, arching her back, hands pressing firmly on her hipbones. The sheet fell away, revealing her bare bosom, firm, almost youthful. She and Bob slept in the nude now—one of Cantor's ideas. The first two or three nights she had felt silly prancing about the bedroom naked, silly and self-conscious, like a schoolgirl indulging in a promiscuous fantasy. Bob had confessed, somewhat sheepishly, that he felt the same way. Like high school again. Slyly, almost guiltily, Jean had studied the amazing transformation of his physique. He had shed twenty-two pounds on the protein-and-water diet. The tennis had trimmed his tummy. He still had a small bicycle-size tire, but the big booze-pot had magically disappeared. His chest, long submerged under fat, had taken on the shape she remembered from years ago. His clothes hung on him like tents, but he looked ten years younger.

They had had sex once. The night after her period stopped and she began the next cycle on the pills, which she now kept in the open on the kitchen table with the vitamin bottles. (That had been another of Cantor's ideas: they were not to conceal the pill from Nancy.) The sex had been almost an adventure for both. It had been so long, neither could remember the last time. Bob had been shy. It may have been (he told her) the first time he had ever done it cold sober, with her or anybody else. He was gentle and considerate, anxious that she should come—so anxious that Jean herself became anxious, and, after that, for her it was hopeless; a frustrating situation that Cantor had predicted precisely. Once, during it, Jean had thought of Bill Clark, but she tore that image from her mind, determined to forget. Afterward, Bob had stunned Jean with a whispered confession: that for years he had been hungup because his penis was too big, that he did not want to hurt her. That was one reason he had slacked off the last few years. Jean assured him it had not hurt this time, that he should never be concerned about her coming; that she derived great pleasure just feeling him inside her. The way they talked these days!

She swung her legs out of bed, feeling the carpet with her toes, searching for her satin slippers. She stepped into her housecoat, zipped it up, went to the bathroom, rinsed her face with cold water. The shock brought her wide awake. She returned to the window, peeped out. Yes, it was definitely drizzling. Damn, damn, damn, she thought. The rain would curtail the turnout. McDivitt—ever optimistic—had said rain would help their side. That it would discourage the older people who planned to attend McInnerney's open-air Mass, but it would not discourage the younger people who would come to protest. Jean doubted this. She knew many mothers would not drag their children into the rain.

She padded down the hall to the front door. The *Washington Post* was propped inside the storm door, thick and dry. Jean glanced at the eight-column headline:

CATHOLIC CONFRONTATION AT CU

THOUSANDS TO GATHER IN PRAYER

Beneath the headline there were two photographs. On the left side, a group-shot of McInnerney, surrounded by the eight cardinals who had arrived in Washington yesterday to take part in the ground-breaking High Mass. There was another picture of the 200 bishops. On the right, there was a close-up of Joe McDivitt, ruggedly handsome, defiant. He was described in the caption as a "rebel priest" who would lead the ground-breaking protest in a ceremony on the CU campus opposite the ground-breaking site.

Inside, there were other stories, and a detailed map of the CU campus, showing the site, the parking areas, and other details. Jean studied the map carefully, thankful that the paper had got the details correct. It had been one of her jobs this last week to represent the dissidents at the interminable meetings with the police at the District Building, where all the details, rules, regulations for demonstration had been hammered out with the Chancery priest, Father Lomangino. She had never dreamed that "spontaneous demonstrations" were preceded by such an infinity of planning, or were so closely supervised by the police, who issued the permits.

She had time to read only one other item in the paper, her horoscope. Under Virgo, she found these words: "Go ahead with plans for today in spite of obstacles. Delay long-term social commitments until more important matters are resolved. Encourage rapport with those close to you." Jean thought of Annie Shields, next door. She had been lately—like a new person, friendly, open, sincerely seeking Jean's friendship. She had not asked a single question. The cozy little "political" talks with Bob had stopped. After the dust had settled, she'd drop over to Annie's for coffee and have a good, long chat.

Jean went to the kitchen, feeling an immense sense of pride. The show that day would be, to a very great extent, her own handiwork. The dissident priests were a kind of youthful, exuberant, swashbuckling crew, far more concerned with the overall impact of the event than the details for executing it. They were maddeningly casual and disorganized, leaving the grubby work to Jean and Mary and the volunteers. *They* had done the telephoning, the fund-raising, the coordination, the liaison with the police, the printing and distribution of credentials, and a thousand other little things, including the arrangements for the baking of the bread to be distributed at the mass-protest Communion. Jean could write a book about what it was like to be an insider—the comic, unbelievable, fantastic, frustrating, exhausting last two weeks. The work was done now, for better or for worse—finished last night in a midnight frenzy. There was nothing left to do except show up, pray that everything worked out, that the drizzle would stop. Then, tonight, go to bed early and sleep for two days!

The tea kettle whistled. She made two cups of instant coffee. Then she roused Nancy, who was sleeping soundly, innocently, like a little fairy princess, hair in rollers, then Bob, who rolled from the bed instantly, with an impressive erection. They both stared at it as though it were an extraterrestrial phenomenon.

"It's raining," Jean said, turning her eyes away.

"That's too bad," Bob said sleepily.

"Daugherty thinks it will be good for us," she said.

"It won't be good for either," Bob said. "It'll cut down the turnout by half. But . . . don't worry about it. There's not a damned thing you can do now."

"Except pray."

"The breaks . . ." Bob said, going to the bathroom.

Jean called Nancy a second time. Then she fixed breakfast. So she would be certain not to forget them, she put the envelope with the credentials—parking, admittance to the raised platform—just inside the front door on the floor. She penned a note and Scotch-taped it to the refrigerator door:

> EMMA! Please make sure the boys watch the
> demonstration on TV—beginning at
> 9:30.

Bob shaved, did five minutes of exercise in the bedroom, dressed, headed for the kitchen for coffee and poached eggs, his one-a-day vitamin. He felt very good, rested, like a new man. His breath came easier. He did not have gas.

For Jean's sake, he hoped the rain would stop. She had worked like a damned Trojan. That was all to the good. It had taken her mind off herself, channeled her energy. The protest wouldn't come to anything in the long run—the dissident priests were hopeless idealists pursuing the Holy Grail—but it was sure a hell of a lot better for Jean than reading Tolstoy.

John Joseph Scafidi knelt in the corner of his shabby bedroom, praying before the statue of the Blessed Virgin. She spoke to him clearly, gravely. The man Daugherty was a devil. He had come to earth on a flying saucer. He had contaminated All Saints', the other priests, the archdiocese. The authorities, to whom Scafidi had written, either did not understand or were covering up. It was, therefore, up to Scafidi to do God's work. Daugherty must be stopped now. He must not be allowed to make a mockery of the Archbishop's ground-breaking ceremony at CU. Scafidi nodded solemnly, crossed himself, rose.

He went into the living room. It was covered with news clips of the Catholic war in Washington. Someday, when he could take time from more urgent tasks, he would index and file these. Beneath a pile of clippings he found the package wrapped in brown butcher paper. It was the Smith and Wesson 38 Police Special, bought yesterday at the Sports Shoppe, with some of the money he had been saving for his trip to Lourdes.

The pistol was oily. He cleaned it with a rag. Then he took six cartridges from the box and inserted them, one by one, into the revolving cylinder. He went into the side yard, the drizzly gray morning. He fired all six shots at a tree. He had never fired a pistol before. It jerked his arm. His ears rang. Three of the six bullets thudded home, sending chips of bark flinging into the air. He returned to the shack, reloaded. Then he got in his car. He drove downtown toward the Home for Spiritual Renewal.

Mary Murray left her apartment wearing a plastic raincoat and hat over her sleeveless cotton dress. It was late—after seven. She had shut off the alarm, and then dozed again, a near-disaster. She was drugged with fatigue, could not think clearly. No sleep. Fifteen-hour days. Ten thousand details—half still undone. No wonder generals lost battles! There was never time to get things right. She had lived through it, borne along by a single sustaining thought: when the day was finished, she and Dan could slip away—forever.

The important things had been done. Dan had finished McDivitt's sermon. It was beautiful, eloquent, better than his Dostoyevsky sermon. He had also signed a contract with a publisher who did not insist on personal material. She had worked out the deal with the Ford Foundation. The Montessori apparatus had already been air-freighted to San Juan.

She hurried along the sidewalks toward the Home for Spiritual Renewal, avoiding the cracks and uneven concrete. On the stoop, she picked up the *Washington Post,* glanced at McDivitt's picture with great satisfaction. That part, at least, had gone well. Thanks to Klein's PR magic, Dan had melted from the public eye. McDivitt had almost effortlessly assumed the mantle. McDivitt was a marvelous Mr. Outside —cool, forthright, forceful—the darling of the media with whom he dealt all day long.

She went into the foyer. The lights were still burning in the living room, illuminating the debris, the paper, desks, overflowing ashtrays, paper cups. It looked like a political headquarters the morning after an election. She left the lights burning, hurried to the kitchen to make coffee. No sound came from the second floor.

When the coffee was done, she poured Dan a cup and carried it up the stairway. For some time now, they had observed an unwritten rule: no women above the first floor until after nine. But there was no time for college-dorm formalities. It was late—time for everyone to get moving. She tiptoed down the hall to his room.

The door was cracked open. She pushed against it quietly, entered the room. It was a shambles. Clothes lay strewn on the floor, the chair, the foot of the single bed. It smelled like a gym. Mary looked down at Dan, wondering how he could possibly rest in such a contorted position. He was breathing deeply—not snoring, but almost. She stood over him, holding the hot coffee to one side.

"Dan," she said softly, shaking his shoulder. "Dan."

He opened one eye, catlike. He groaned and rolled over.

"Dan!" she spoke louder and more insistently.

He turned on his back, pulled the wrinkled sheet over his stomach, smiled sleepily and mumbled:

"Am I dreaming or do I smell coffee?"

"Wake up, nut. Room service."

He propped himself up on elbows, reached for the coffee.

"Oh boy!" he said. "What time is it?"

"Quarter after seven. My alarm . . . I dozed. I'm sorry."

He sat back against the pillow and sipped the coffee. Mary watched him. In Puerto Rico, she would bring him coffee every morning.

"Where is the sermon?" she said. She wanted to glance at it again, one last time.

"On the bureau," he said. "I hope."

She found it beneath a pile of underwear, ties, and other articles. She moved the clothes from the chair and sat down. She scanned it quickly.

"It's just perfect," she said. "The best thing you've ever written."

He sipped his coffee, then said, "I'm glad. It's my swan song. How's the weather?"

"Lousy," she said, making a face. "Drizzle. They outprayed us."

"They're going to get wet too. Anyway, the TV will be there—I'm sure. Oh! Let me tell you. Ryan called here last night. I think he was very upset. He was worried about the money—the boycott—and the way Jean Favrot was stirring everybody up. He didn't understand what was happening to the world. It had got beyond him. Anyway, the main thing was, he said he wanted me to know again that he was sorry about what he said in the sacristy about the woman. That he had not said anything down at the Chancery. That as far as he was concerned, it was insane gossip from that madman Scafidi, and everybody ought to forget it."

"Thank God for that," Mary said.

"Yes," Daugherty said, sipping the coffee.

"What did you say?" she said.

"Just that I was truly sorry I hurt him," Dan went on. "That I had never intended to do that. That I had been guided by my conscience, which I had prayerfully consulted, and that I had done what it told me to do. He said I understood absolutely nothing about the theology of conscience, even though I had been raised a good Catholic."

"Well, you better get dressed," she said.

"Yes."

She walked to the door. Down the hall, she heard McDivitt whistling cheerily. Turning back at the door, she said softly:

"Dan. It'll be a great day—in spite of the rain."

She turned to descend the stairs. McDivitt came from his room in white jockey shorts, carrying his Dopp kit. When he saw Mary he feigned horrified shock and shouted:

"EEEEEEEEEEK! Woman on the second floor!"

Mary hurried down the stairs, shielding her eyes. She prepared a massive breakfast of eggs, bacon, toast, hotcakes, coffee, orange juice, cereal. The men came down, one by one, happy, casual, soldiers before battle. Some wore Roman collars, some, like Dan and McDivitt, business suits. They ate heartily. When they were done, Mary and Dan and McDivitt went out and squeezed into her VW. Mary drove, heading toward CU, windshield wiper slashing. McDivitt hummed to himself happily. Daugherty sat quietly, watching the wet streets slip by.

Archbishop McInnerney, eating breakfast alone in his bedroom, glanced at the newspaper headlines. Then he got up and stared through the great French windows into the hazy drizzle. It was a shame, he thought. The Mass would be performed beneath an awning, a tent with no sides. It would be stifling. The TV cameras would be hemmed in. The pomp and beauty of the High Mass, the pageantry of the ground-breaking itself, could not be captured. He prayed again that the skies would clear.

In a few hours, his promise to Spellman would be fulfilled. They would turn the damp earth with a golden spade. They would proclaim to the world that there, on that spot, a building would rise. From it would emanate words and ideas that would restore the equilibrium. Bringing people back to their senses. Bringing peace, harmony, under-standing and comfort to the fearful, the sick, the rebellious, the doubters. The True Church would go on another two thousand years, five thousand, twenty thousand, to the end of the world, spreading the Word as Christ had instructed them.

He picked up the *Washington Post,* stared at McDivitt's picture. Foolish boy. Blind. They were all blind! The McDivitts and Daughertys. The LeGuieses. The Kleins. The Favrots. The Seymour Joneses. Even his own Vicar General. They would understand, perhaps later. Under-stand that the True Faith was not a fad. That the Word was One, and Immutable, and Everlasting. That men, in passing, did not tamper with the Word.

He felt, now, a sudden pity for all those who had stood in his way, the blind ones. He wanted them to see again, to be reunited on this glorious, historical day. He knelt on the carpet and prayed aloud:

"Oh Lord, in Thy infinite wisdom and compassion, show us the way to peace and harmony, give us strength and courage to do Thy will, and bring us together in our devotion to Your hour of suffering, and bestow grace and light on those who gather today to pay homage to You and grant success to this small effort we make, that for all the days in the future, mankind shall know Thy true teaching, as You gave it to Peter, and thence to the Holy Father, and thence to Your bishops the world over."

Vicar General Prial pushed the door open quietly. He stood for a moment, looking down at McInnerney, head bowed in deep reverence. Then he knelt beside him, holding his Xeroxed copy of the day's agenda. It was turned to item 34:

8:43. *Archbishop leaves quarters for limo.*

The whole agenda contained 194 items. It would lead the official ground-breaking party, the hundreds of potentates of the Church, through a complicated day. It was a masterwork of precision and thought, the capstone of Prial's unflagging effort to make this occasion smooth and memorable.

Prayers finished, McInnerney rose. Prial helped him into his heavy vestments. McInnerney looked at the agenda. He was much impressed.

"A tremendous job, Nate," he said. He had said that in public the night before at the Chancery reception, then again during the toasts at the private dinner for the visitors.

"I wish I could have provided better weather."

"It doesn't matter. What matters is that we finally made it. In spite of him."

He pointed to the photograph of McDivitt.

"He'll be there, I'm afraid," Prial said.

"I pray for him."

They went to the elevator. Prial glanced at his wristwatch. They were already two minutes behind schedule. He had allowed five in his mind. On the ground floor, the door opened. The Chancery staff was lined up along the corridor, dressed and waiting. McInnerney adjusted his mitre, walked between the rows of smiling faces, returning the greetings, blessing them.

Near the door Helen Hanrahan, his special guest for the ceremony, was waiting. She wore a white linen suit, another of her incredible hats. She knelt and kissed his ring, feeling again the ominous vibrations. But she said nothing.

"God bless you, Helen," McInnerney said. "It's a bad day to get you out. Don't get your feet wet."

"I'll try," she said. "But I think it'll clear up."

"Is that official?" Prial joshed.

"Just a hope," Helen said. "I've already said all I'm going to say about this project."

McInnerney frowned, remembering her vision, her warning. With Prial escorting, holding the door, they moved out into the dampness. An awning stretched from the door to the limousine.

There were four motorcycle policemen parked in the drive. They were commanded by Pinky Dorn, Irish and Catholic, father of eight. Dorn had been the Chancery's special escort for twenty-five of his twenty-six years on the force. He was proud of that record, his job, his archbishop, his religion. Seeing McInnerney, he raised his gloved hand in respectful salute. McInnerney paused momentarily to ask after Dorn's family. They were all fine, Dorn replied. Two boys bound for the seminary, thanks to Prial's letters, at least one girl with a vocation —possibly two. This report pleased McInnerney.

"Your Excellency," Dorn said, "there are a lot of us pulling for you."

"With God's help," the Archbishop replied, "we cannot fail."

The Chancery party entered the limousine. Dorn and his motorcyclemen started their motors, turned on red lights, and pulled into the drizzle. They turned into Massachusetts Avenue, sirens going, Dorn waving traffic to halt.

Scafidi drove downtown via the George Washington Memorial Parkway. The Smith and Wesson lay on the front seat. Near Key Bridge, the traffic slowed, bumper to bumper, red taillights glowing in the misty gloom. Inching along, Scafidi noticed the engine heat-indicator climbing. It was the one instrument on the panel that worked.

He swung up the ramp to Roosevelt Bridge, eye on the needle, now leaning all the way over to "H." The radiator, he knew, would be boiling. Crossing the river, he looked down at the water. It was chocolate, swift, turbulent.

Leaving the E Street Expressway, Scafidi pulled into a gas station, left the engine running. Waving away the attendant, he climbed from the car, opened the hood. He batted at the radiator cap with his fingers. It came loose, rose on a tower of boiling steam, clattered to the concrete. Scafidi found a water bucket, poked the spout into the radiator.

"You ought to let that cool," the attendant said, looking over Scafidi's shoulder.

"I can't," Scafidi said. "I'm in a hurry."

"You might crack the block."

Scafidi shook his head. He emptied the bucket into the radiator, picked up the cap, screwed it in place, searing his fingers. Then he got into the car and drove away. The needle had fallen back to normal.

He drove north to New Hampshire, faster now, taking chances, speeding through yellow traffic lights. Off New Hampshire, he slowed, turned down a side street. He drew abreast of the Home for Spiritual Renewal. He shut off the engine and picked up the pistol. Leaving the car double-parked, he got out, closed the door, cut between two cars, and climbed the stoop, dragging his bad leg sideways.

He pushed open the screen, holding the pistol level. He walked into the foyer, eyes darting to the living room, hall, stairway. He could not hear a sound.

He walked to the kitchen. It was deserted. Dirty dishes, pots, pans lay everywhere. He loped back down the hall to the stairway. He called:

"Daugherty!"

No answer. He called again. Still no answer.

"They've gone," Scafidi said aloud. "Already gone!"

He returned to the car, raging at himself, the radiator. He climbed behind the wheel, turned the key. The engine turned slowly, as though the battery were low. The heat gauge was climbing again. The engine caught. Scafidi pumped the gas pedal feverishly, pulled in the gear, and shot off at high speed. Waiting for a red light at DuPont Circle, racing the engine, he took the map of CU from his wallet, laid it on the seat beside the pistol. The heat gauge was again on "H."

X

The land dedicated for the proposed theological center was a large, clear tract on Passion Drive, far removed from the bustling center of the CU campus. The nearest structure was the monumental Shrine of the Immaculate Conception, a quarter of a mile away, over the crest of a hill. The setting was almost pastoral. There was no sign of the nation's capital, the teeming ghettos, which lay beyond the CU campus.

The Chancery tent for the ceremony had been put up on the south edge of the tract, abutting Passion Drive. Spectators would stand in the open beyond the tent. The empty field opposite had been designated as the protest area. At the crest of the field, a half mile from the Chancery tent, the dissidents had erected an impressive wooden stand. It had a lectern, where McDivitt would speak, and behind it, rising steeply, seats for about two hundred people. The protest spectators would gather in the field around the stand. In between these spiritually opposing structures, in the middle of no-man's-land, cordoned off by police, stood the press stand. It was a squat wooden platform, eight feet off the ground, capped by a tentlike awning. It had TV camera positions facing both the Chancery tent and the dissidents' stand. It was equipped with folding chairs, temporary telephones, coffee urn, and other paraphernalia of the press.

Marvin Klein and Serena, who had come out of curiosity, reached the press platform by eight o'clock. It was crowded with TV technicians, soundmen, radio reporters, and personnel of the *Tribune*'s task force, led by the unruffled, soft-speaking George Emerson. The *Tribune* men were drinking coffee, testing telephones—speaking to Jim Cunningham on the city desk—or clattering away on their portable typewriters, held in their laps. They would be working against a tight deadline. By the time most of the spectators returned to their homes, the *Tribune* would be on their doorsteps with the story. There would be no leisurely return to the office. It would all be done from here, with Klein directing.

He had brought two fine pairs of binoculars—borrowed from the sports department. He now gave one pair to Serena. She maneuvered to get a view of the dissidents' stand, and then the Chancery tent. But there was little to see. There was nobody on the dissidents' stand except two or three technicians rigging the microphones. Klein sat down in a folding chair opposite Emerson. They discussed the deployment of the *Tribune* troops.

Klein was immensely proud of his men, the job they had done on the Catholic revolution. With Klein's inside connections, Emerson's skill and legwork, they had beaten the competition silly. They had broken so many angles of the story that the *Tribune* itself was now a major news source for the wire services and the local competition and for the august *New York Times,* which had now assigned three reporters to the story. Klein himself had become a minor celebrity in his own right. He had been interviewed on network TV news shows and featured in the *Time* press section.

Klein imagined that his work—his power—was having no small impact on the Vatican. He noted with pride that liberal Catholic prelates the world over were now rising up, fearlessly speaking out against the encyclical and Paul. Only recently, Cardinal Suenens of Belgium had denounced Paul for his "bureaucratic, static, juridical, centralizing tendency." Others were openly demanding popular election of bishops by laity and clergy, election of the Pope by a synod of bishops, a general downgrading of the Roman Curia and College of Cardinals. It was strong stuff. The stuff of real revolution. The stuff that usually preceded the downfall of insensitive absolute monarchies.

One thing was sure. *Tribune* editorial had heard no further complaint from the business side about its coverage of the Washington revolt. In fact, Klein had not even seen Kenneth Penn for six weeks. He had heard that Penn was in New York, closeted with the syndicate on some business problems. This news had made him vaguely uneasy. But he had been much too busy to follow up. The business-side shenanigans bored him anyway. Performance was what counted. He would stand—proudly—on his record.

At eight thirty the spectators began arriving. At first they were a small trickle, walking gingerly from the parking lot across the squishy grass, dividing at no-man's-land, going either to the Chancery tent or the dissidents' stand. They were white, orderly, solemn-faced. The trickle quickly grew to a flood, young and old, some carrying wilting placards, some wearing black armbands. Then the flood grew to a tidal wave, an awesome sea of umbrellas, gathering behind the tent and around the stand, which was now rapidly filling. The TV monitors displayed close-ups of the Chancery tent and the dissidents' stand.

Klein trained his binoculars on the dissidents' stand. In the front row, immediately behind the lectern, he saw the burly, blond-haired Joe McDivitt, talking, gesticulating excitedly to Daugherty. Behind them, several rows up in the ascending stands, Klein saw Mary and the Favrots. He noted these celebrities for Serena, who watched them with her binoculars.

"Is that Senator Devereaux?" she asked, eyes still glued to her glasses.

Klein examined the front row again. Senator Devereaux was standing, talking to McDivitt, who was also on his feet.

"Yes," Klein said. "He's going to read a poem."

Emerson sat down beside Klein.

"What's the crowd estimate so far?" Klein said, pointing toward the dissidents.

"I figure fifteen thousand," Emerson said. "But it's very hard with the rain, all the umbrellas. You can't tell how many may be under each umbrella."

"I know," Klein said, frowning. "I think more. What is the official? Is someone getting those placard texts?"

"Yes. We've got them. I talked to Morgan. He says twenty-five thousand but I think he's high. He hasn't set foot outside his cruiser."

Klein turned back to the crowd. He made a square with his thumb and forefinger. He roughly estimated the number of people he could see inside the square. Then he estimated how many squares would cover the crowd.

"I think about twenty thousand," Klein said.

"I don't know," Emerson said.

"Go tell Morgan to get off his seat and give us an official estimate," Klein said.

Emerson went down the steps in the rain to find Captain Morgan. Klein took out his notebook and jotted a few words on the page. Then he turned on his pocket transistor radio, tuned it to the all-news station. Above a background noise of a fake news ticker, he could hear the news announcer describing the scene.

"Here comes the motorcade!" a reporter shouted.

Klein and the others turned away from the dissidents' stand, swung binoculars toward the Chancery tent. They saw the long motorcade, twenty or twenty-five black Cadillac limousines, snaking up Passion Drive, escorted by two or three dozen motorcycle police. The TV cameras now went live.

Klein propped his binoculars on the rail of the platform. As the black cars drew abreast of the Chancery tent, he called off the names for Serena: "There's Cardinal Cooke. And Cushing. Reardon. Ritter. . . . McIntyre . . . Archbishop Lucey from San Antonio . . . Carroll from Miami . . . There—there's McInnerney getting out."

"Is that Helen Hanrahan?" Serena squealed excitedly.

"Yes," Klein said. "And the tall, dark guy. That's Prial. The Vicar General. You met him at Bennett's party."

"Yes," Serena said, eyes to the binoculars. "Isn't it funny. They all look just alike. The cardinals. Why are most of them so . . . so rotund?"

"I don't know," Klein said, puzzling this observation, which had not occurred to him before. "Soft living, I guess."

"All that Chancery food," Serena said. "The Pope ought to put them all on a diet. All except McInnerney."

She watched the potentates disappear beneath the huge tent, the limousines swing onto the grass, into the VIP parking area. Then she turned the glasses back toward the dissidents' stand.

"I think they're getting ready to start," Klein said. "Watch the TV monitors. You can see better."

"Look at all the people," Serena said, laying the binoculars aside, letting her eyes sweep in a 360-degree circle. They were pouring from the parking areas by the thousands.

Eight blocks from the boundary of the CU campus, Scafidi fell in behind the long line of cars inching toward the parking area. A half block later, the radiator boiled again. Steam smoked from the cracks in the hood. The engine coughed, died. Behind him, angry, impatient motorists honked their horns. Scafidi drained the battery dead trying to restart the engine.

A policeman appeared at his left window.

"Get this wreck off the street," he said.

"The battery's dead," Scafidi replied, then demonstrated with the ignition key.

"For Christ's sake," the policeman said. "We'll have to push it."

The pistol was still lying on the front seat. Scafidi covered it with his right hand, then swept it up and hid it beneath the seat.

"Get out and help," the policeman grunted. He was bent forward, shoving against the left window.

Scafidi climbed out. The policeman observed his limp. Then he said: "Sorry, pop. I'll get some help."

He turned, waved to the driver of the car immediately behind. The driver came forward, then two others. They pushed the wreck against the curb. Scafidi raised the hood. When the policeman returned to directing traffic, he opened the right door and got the pistol, shoving it in his belt, buttoning his jacket to conceal it. He set off toward the parking lot, hobbling along the sidewalk, heedless of pain, head bent against the rain.

Beneath the Chancery tent, Prial, clutching his agenda, presided as a kind of sergeant at arms. He guided the potentates to their seats, either at the altar or in the rows of folding wooden chairs. When they were settled in their proper places, he seated the distinguished guests, including Helen Hanrahan, show business celebrities, writers, the columnist Thomas Bennett, and others. By the time Richard Cushing, the senior cardinal, walked to the altar to begin the Mass, Prial had maneuvered the schedule so they were precisely on time. As Cushing genuflected at the altar, the red lights on the TV's at the rear of the tent glowed red. On signal from Prial, a monsignor switched off the huge, noisy fans.

Cushing, perspiring under the hot lights, rushed the Mass, intoning the chants in his deep Boston brogue. After the Gospel, Cardinal Cooke, representing the largest diocese, came to the lectern facing the cameras to speak briefly of the occasion and its meaning. He said it was a momentous day in the history of the Church, that it was a distinct honor to be present. He regretted that his benefactor, Cardinal Spellman, who had inspired them all to make the center a reality, was present only in spirit. He then read a message from Pope Paul, who called on all Catholics to support the center which would, in time, provide the wisdom and the Holy Spirit to seal the cracks in the Church and thereby insure its survival until the end of man. The center, the Pope said, should be named in honor of its spiritual founder, Cardinal Spellman. Neither man alluded to the protest gathering across the way.

After these messages, Cushing resumed the Mass. It was muggy, stifling beneath the tent. Prial gave a signal to restart the fans. Then he knelt beside McInnerney to receive Communion.

By the time Scafidi reached the parking lot, his clothes, hair, shoes, were soaked with rain and sweat. The muscles in his good leg ached; his heart pounded ominously inside its cage. He paused for a moment to catch his breath, to orient himself, to study the map.

A policeman wearing rain gear sauntered by, hard blue eyes observing Scafidi closely.

"Which way is the show?" Scafidi asked, between gasps.

"Over there," the policeman said. "Just follow the arrows and ropes."

Scafidi hobbled off. The grass underfoot was slippery. He walked with difficulty. His temples pounded. The policeman watched him, swinging his head from side to side, half in pity, half in disbelief. Crazy old man, out in weather like this.

Scafidi soon came to the rope barrier to no-man's-land. There were eight or ten police standing about, behind the ropes. Scafidi approached one.

"Where is the ceremony?" he said, still gasping.

The policeman looked at the old man with pity in his eyes.

"Which one?" he asked pleasantly. "The theological center or the protest?"

"The protest."

"That way," the policeman said, pointing. He watched Scafidi hobble off. He would have guessed an old cripple like that would go to the ground-breaking. It was amazing what the Church had come to these days.

On the dissidents' stand, the ceremonies were not so splendid or punctual. There was no pageantry, no sergeant at arms to prod. It was carried forward casually, almost amateurishly. McDivitt preferred to delay, hoping the crowd might swell to at least a quarter of the number they had expected. It began with a musical presentation. A rock group, five shaggy-haired boys with guitars, clustered around the lectern. The outdoor acoustics did little to enhance their music. It came across as a great blur of sound, like a huge electrical short-circuit. Among those in the stand, only Nancy Favrot seemed appreciative. She raised and lowered the Favrot umbrella in time with the mysterious rhythm.

After the rock group came Senator Devereaux. He laid his poem on the lectern, then stood tall and grave, heedless of the rain pelting his gray hair. He read his poem eloquently, with great feeling. It was brief, full of lofty sentiments about man and freedom. Those on the stand listened in respectful silence, straining to hear. When it was done, he turned, shook hands with McDivitt and Daugherty, the other priests and ex-priests, and hurried off to another appointment. Neither Mary nor Jean had heard the words. Yet they applauded vigorously.

The next event was the choral group of St. Timothy's, a suburban parish in Rockville, Maryland. Both the pastor and the assistant pastor of St. Timothy's had been banished to the boondocks. The church was presently unmanned by clergy. The choral group, led by a matronly woman, filed down the steep aisle to the lectern. They deployed around the mike and sang a deeply moving rendition of "We Shall Overcome." Many who could hear were reduced to tears.

Now Jim McDivitt came to the lectern. He raised both arms high over his head, making a V with his fingers. The immense crowd around the stand broke into cheers and applause. Umbrellas and placards pumped up and down like engine pistons. Smiling, projecting strength and confidence, McDivitt let the demonstration go on for several minutes. Then he turned to his sermon, the beautiful work of Daniel Daugherty.

McDivitt's podium style was forceful, almost spellbinding. He spoke softly, harshly, coldly, warmly, dividing mood and thought with dramatic pauses. Daugherty turned to smile satisfaction to Mary. She responded with a wink. Then Daugherty watched the black-and-white TV monitor beneath the lectern. It displayed McDivitt's face full-screen. The word was going over the airwaves to millions. It would be picked up, repeated, rebroadcast.

Bob Favrot listened to McDivitt thoughtfully. It was a good sermon, erudite, uplifting, not strident and shrill as he had expected. Jean was leaning forward, both fists doubled beneath her chin, nose beyond the protection of the umbrella, unconcerned by the dripping water. She was transported, involved . . . committed. Looking across the sea of people, Bob was proud of his wife. It was a decent, respectful show of force which, except for the bad luck of the rain, might have been spectacular. She had a true genius for organization and details, incredible energy. He must remember to compliment her tonight.

Scafidi was astonished, bewildered, and angered by the massive crowd that stood between him and the dissidents' stand, where he was sure to find Daugherty. It was a wall of human flesh, thrown up to keep him from the Devil.

He pushed and shoved rudely, gasping, dragging his lame foot, clutching his jacket at the waist so the pistol would not be jarred loose. He did not trouble to excuse himself. He lunged on, ducking the umbrellas, searching, like a football player, for space between people that would make his forward progress easier.

Those who had been knocked aside called after him angrily. But he was deaf to these insults. His eyes were fixed steadily on the stand, the figure speaking at the lectern. That should be Daugherty, exhorting, contaminating, blaspheming. . . .

Daugherty leaned forward, eyes shifting from McDivitt's back to the TV monitor to an elderly woman standing on the ground directly beneath the stand. The woman held an old-fashioned black umbrella. Her eyes did not move from McDivitt. Her face expressed neither approval nor disapproval. Why was she here, Daugherty wondered. What was going through her mind? Were we tearing away her foundation, as McInnerney claimed, or were we building her a new one?

His eye moved beyond her, in the direction of the parking lot. He became aware suddenly of a slight disturbance in the throng. A ripple. It was a man, flailing forward, leaving a wake of disturbed umbrellas and people. His path was ragged, a feverish zigzagging, more or less toward the stand. Daugherty watched for a moment, as though hypnotized. The man was certainly determined, certainly in a mad rush. He tore his eyes away, back to the TV monitor.

His eyes went back to the man involuntarily. Daugherty caught a brief glimpse of him, between two umbrellas. He came forward, relentlessly, almost urgently, lunging with a strange, contorted movement. Like a cripple.

A cripple!

Daugherty raised from his seat for a better view. Once, twice, he saw more than a glimpse. It was a thin old man, with gray hair, matted down by the rain. When he was very close, ten yards behind the old lady with the black umbrella, he stopped, raised his head, as if taking his bearings. There could be no mistake. It was Scafidi.

Daugherty, all senses shouting danger, turned to Mary. She had been watching him and then watching the man.

"Who is it?" she said, mouthing the words carefully.

Jean and Bob Favrot turned to look at Mary.

"Scafidi," Daugherty mouthed back.

Mary and Jean and Bob turned their eyes toward the crowd. Scafidi had disappeared. Then he resurfaced, just behind the old lady.

Daugherty rose to his feet, uncertain what he should do. He stood, frozen, watching Scafidi come toward the stand, rudely knocking aside the old lady. Now he was directly below, gasping insanely, glazed eyes sweeping from Daugherty to McDivitt.

In his haste to get at the pistol, Scafidi tore the button from his jacket. He could see Daugherty, looking down from the stand, terror in his eyes. It was the Devil. A terrified Devil!

Daugherty saw the unmistakable shape, the blue steel in Scafidi's trembling hand. He lunged for the railing, climbed to dive at the madman.

The pistol cracked once . . . twice. Bullets zinged skyward, over Daugherty's head, the stand.

Mary leaped to her feet, terrified, screaming. She ran blindly down the aisle toward Daugherty. McDivitt, astounded, paralyzed, stopped speaking. Daugherty vaulted the rail, fell through the air.

The pistol cracked a third time.

Daugherty felt a jar in his shoulder, like the kick of a horse. The kick half-turned him in mid-fall. Then he felt pain. He landed hard on his knees, at Scafidi's feet, gasping for breath. He wanted to roll and roll and roll as far as he could. To escape the next bullet and the next. But he could not move. He fell into unconsciousness, certain he was dead, the Act of Contrition on his lips.

Scafidi could not believe his good luck. He stared blankly at Daugherty—the slain Devil—lying immobile at his feet. He let his arms fall to his side. The pistol slipped from his fingers. It fell to the ground. He felt light-headed, drained, unsteady. He could hear a roaring in his ears, louder than the pistol. It was like a tornado closing over him, a great flapping of wings.

McDivitt had watched the unbelievable scene as though it were unfolding in slow-motion. Then, more by instinct than thought, McDivitt tore himself out of the paralysis, flung aside the pages of his sermon, vaulted the rail, aiming his hurtling body at the crazy old man. His knees struck Scafidi in the chest. The old man reeled back, as though hit by a freight car. McDivitt, bouncing off Scafidi, rolled on his side. He was on his feet instantly, hands clutching the old man's throat.

"You crazy son of a bitch!" McDivitt cried. Then, turning: "Get a doctor!"

On the press platform, Klein had been watching McDivitt, notebook poised, eyes switching from TV to binoculars, fingers jotting key words and phrases. He had seen Daugherty rise up, vault the rail. Then he heard the shots, like firecrackers going off. Klein watched the TV transfixed, the close-up of the confusion and pandemonium sweeping the dissidents' stand.

"What the hell?" a TV cameraman shouted.

"I don't know," another said.

Klein swept the stand through binoculars. He saw McDivitt flinging his sermon aside, plunging over the rail behind Daugherty. He saw Mary rushing to the rail, looking down, screaming hysterically. Klein felt a cold knot in his stomach. He knew before he heard the words.

"Somebody's been shot!" a reporter cried.

"Oh, my God!" Klein said.

"Who?" Serena gasped, standing beside her husband, eyes on the stand.

"We don't know," the reporter shouted.

Almost as one, Klein and the two dozen newsmen on the platform ran pell-mell down the ladder, raced across no-man's-land, ducked beneath the rope, and plunged into the crowd, toward the stand, the story.

The pistol shots, the sudden violent contortions of Daugherty and McDivitt, Mary's hysterical screams, touched off a frenzied panic in the dissidents' stand. In blind fear, the people rose from the grandstand seats, all intent on a single purpose: to get out before anyone shot *them*. They ran and stumbled forward down the aisles, toward the lectern, the steep steps leading to the ground. The stampede swept down on the Favrots and then Mary, who was caught and smashed against the rail. Jean Favrot, torn from Bob's grasp, fell headlong down the steps and came to rest face down in the mud. There she was crushed beneath a mass of thumping shoes, until Bob, holding Nancy by the waist, pulled her up by one arm.

Mary, crying in pain, fell to the floor of the stand, then rolled beneath the rail, falling to the ground alongside Daugherty. McDivitt stood overhead—shoving people aside—shouting to the hysterical mob:

"Give him air. Get back. Get a doctor."

Mary was certain Dan was dead. His body lay face down, a large bloodstain on his jacket shoulder. His legs lay twisted, grosteque. She crawled to him, turned his head, put her ear to his mouth. He was breathing! She raised his head and put it in her lap, sobbing.

"Don't move him!" McDivitt said to Mary, then to the mob, "Will you please stand back?"

Mary could hear screams everywhere. Women, irrational women, fighting away from the stand. She held Daugherty's head close to her breast and prayed, prayed that he would live, prayed that he would not be crippled.

"Is he hurt bad?" McDivitt said, looking down.

"I don't know," Mary replied, almost in a whisper, eyes dull with shock and pain.

Five policemen arrived almost at once. Three helped McDivitt hold back the mob, one stood over the unconscious form of Scafidi, pistol drawn. The fifth knelt beside Daugherty. He gently removed Daugherty's jacket, then ripped his shirt from the wound. He soaked up the blood with his handkerchief. Seeing the wound, the blood, Mary turned her eyes away.

"He's lucky," the policeman said. "It tore him up, but it could have been worse. Another few inches. . . ."

The panic from the stand now spread through the whole mass of spectators, like the shock waves of a cannon. The mob turned away from the source and ran like frightened horses toward no-man's-land. It collided with and then trampled Klein and the reporters racing toward the stand from the press platform. It overran the police in no-man's-land. It swarmed past the press platform, across the open, restricted area, toward Passion Drive, the Chancery tent, a wild, hysterical, screaming, blind stampede. Serena watched it tear by, horrified, desperately searching the faces for her husband.

Inside the Chancery tent, McInnerney heard a distant cry. The words were unintelligible, but the tone was unmistakable: alarm. Then came another. Then another. Then they heard a loud shout, nearby:

"Lookout, goddamnit. Here they come. Stop them!"

Now there were more close-by shouts. They came from the police lined along Passion Drive, guarding the Chancery tent. They were looking in disbelief at the onrushing mob.

"Form a line. Form a line."

Cushing stopped the Mass, turned, puzzled. The TV cameramen swung their cameras toward the street. The potentates and guests beneath the awning broke into excited babbling.

They heard the dull boom of a rifle, followed by screams mixed with defiant cries, now much closer. Prial ran to the street. What he saw, he would never forget.

The thundering mob had reached Passion Drive. They had not stopped. They had charged headlong, ignoring the warning cries of police, who believed the mob to be militant troublemakers, inflamed by the oratory on the dissidents' stand. They had formed a line, like nineteenth-century infantry. Behind them, those with rifles fired tear gas into the mob, touching off a new surge of panic and pandemonium. Now the police and the mob met, hand to hand, a brutal clash of fists, batons, a colossal misunderstanding. Prial looked on in horrified fascination.

He saw a young man with long blond hair collide with the police, flailing wildly. Two policemen instantly turned on him, grabbing his arms, throwing him to the ground. A third policeman rushed forward and struck the man on the back with his stick. Pinned to the ground, the man kicked and writhed and shouted.

Prial backed slowly toward the tent, heart pounding furiously. "Oh, my God!" he said aloud, when he found his voice. "I don't understand. It can't be happening. Who are these people? My God in Heaven!"

McInnerney joined the cluster of prelates at the entrance of the tent. They could see little in the clouds of tear gas. They could hear the shouting, the cries, the wailing and crying. Like Prial, McInnerney was confused, bewildered. He did not know what to do. He stood silently, listening, holding the gold-plated shovel.

"Get to your cars and get out of here," Pinky Dorn shouted. "On the double. Come on. Hurry!"

The chauffeurs, who were clustered at the curb, ran quickly to the cars. They started engines. The potentates, puffing, waddled from the tent to the parking area, climbed into the cars. Prial carried McInnerney and Helen Hanrahan along by an arm. They got in the car. It pulled from the lot to the street, guided by Pinky Dorn and his motorcycle riders. They drove straight ahead, into the dense white smoke, the battle.

A tear gas canister, fired in confusion, slammed against the right front windshield. The glass shattered. Helen Hanrahan buried her face in her hands and shuddered. Prial locked the doors.

Three wildly fleeing men rushed against Pinky Dorn, throwing him from his motorcycle. The machine careened off into the smoke, riderless, erratic. Dorn crawled from the path of the car. He scrambled to his feet, jogged alongside.

Prial lowered the right rear window and shouted to Dorn:

"Get inside!"

Dorn was bareheaded. Blood trickled down his forehead from a cut.

"Keep moving," he cried between grunts. "For God's sake, keep it moving. Get away from here. They've all gone crazy."

He clouted a man on the neck with his fist. The man reeled back, falling against the limousine. His right hand thrust through the window. It hung there, momentarily, bloodstained, dirty. McInnerney stared at it, transfixed, seeing the thin delicate fingers, the nails chewed down, the nicotine stains. Then it was gone. The smoke was gone, too. The battle.

"OK," Dorn huffed. "Open the door."

Prial opened the door quickly. Dorn climbed in.

"Step on it," he said to the chauffeur. Dorn knelt on the back seat between Prial and McInnerney, watching out the rear window, panting from the exertion.

"We're in the clear now," he gasped. "That was close. Tony, take this car directly to the Chancery."

"Are you hurt?" McInnerney asked.

Dorn took out his handkerchief, dabbed at the trickle of blood on his face.

"Nothing serious. Just a cut."

"We'll get something for it at the Chancery," McInnerney said, fingering his pectoral cross.

"I hope the others made it," Dorn said. "We should have evacuated much sooner. Much sooner. Those people are madmen. Turn on the radio."

Prial fiddled with the radio dial in his armrest. He turned to the all-news station. The newscaster was breathlessly describing the scene they had left behind: ". . . and police report the cause of the panic was an unknown assailant . . . who shot the dissident speaker, Father McDivitt, with a rifle . . . scores were injured or killed in the stampede . . . the hysterical mob which swept across Passion Drive into police lines guarding the Chancery tent . . . forcing the immediate evacuation of the Catholic hierarchy who were preparing to break ground . . . here is a late report from our All-News Reporter, Ron Black, at the dissidents' stand . . . Come in, Ron." The next voice was not so clear. It came through a background of static and voices. ". . . according to police on the scene it was not Father McDivitt but Father Daugherty . . . Daniel Daugherty . . . who was on the stand . . . shot once by a pistol . . . in serious condition . . . taken to Emergency Hospital . . . Scores more were injured in the panic . . . The identity of the assailant, who is still unconscious, is still unknown . . ."

The chauffeur drove fast toward the Chancery. In the back seat, McInnerney, Prial, Helen Hanrahan, and Dorn listened intently to the radio. Each new report brought the event closer to fact. It had all been a huge mistake. The mob had not attacked the Chancery tent. It was fleeing from the assassin. Scores had been injured, some seriously. None had been killed. At the hospital, Daugherty was recovering from a wound—exact nature unspecified—in the intensive-care room. The identity of the aged assailant who caused the panic and the unfortunate clash between police and spectators was still not known.

Helen Hanrahan was engulfed in despair. As the limousine approached the Chancery drive, she turned suddenly to McInnerney.

"It was just as I saw it."

"Yes," he said. He had been thinking that.

"It should never be built," she said. "Never. I was wrong to support it. I don't know what came over me. You've got to cancel it."

McInnerney said nothing. He nodded his head slowly, thoughtfully, remembering the hand in the window.

"This is only the beginning," Helen went on. "It will go on and on and on . . . until it is all as I said."

"Only the beginning?" Prial asked.

"Just the beginning," she replied, clasping her hands, sighing. Prial pursed his lips.

Dorn looked up.

"Beginning of what?" he said.

"Armageddon," she said, voice hollow.

"That I can believe," Dorn said. "Lady, I can certainly believe that. Yes. The whole country has gone ape."

"The whole *world*," Helen said, pressing her hands to her eyes.

XI

For all that day and the day following, Archbishop McInnerney remained secluded in his private quarters on the second floor of the Chancery. A somber mood enveloped the first floor, where Prial, recovering from the shock, set to work in his office typing out a broad program of reform which he believed the Chancery must offer to restore peace—and sanity—in the archdiocese. The measures he conceived, he believed, were sound and practical.

In his quarters, McInnerney was profoundly troubled, torn by indecision. He stood quietly for a long time, staring down into the garden or looking at the gray, overcast sky. He took out the personal letter he had been composing for the priests and reread its thirty-two closely packed pages. It was a good letter, half the story of his life, half a carefully reasoned explanation of why he could not teach something he could not believe, or that went against Rome. He read the *Tribune,* its front-page headline:

REBEL PRIEST SHOT AT PROTEST
SCORES INJURED IN WILD PANIC

The *Tribune* was given over almost entirely to the episode, eight or ten stories, photographs, eyewitness accounts. There was a beautiful, clear overview of the morning by George Emerson. McInnerney read it, marveling at the writer's ability to convey all the emotions of the time: the sudden fear, the panic, the senseless misunderstanding. How was he able to write it so quickly? The whole of page 4 was given over to a long story by Managing Editor Marvin Klein, recounting in detail the "history" of the conflict in the Washington archdiocese since March. It was headlined: THE TURBULENT YEAR. There were separate stories on the St. Luke's–IDA deal, the Reverend Charles Seymour Jones, the rebellion of the wives, the failing fund drive, Halfway House, Sister Mary's Montessori school, the penny boycott, the encyclical, John Carter, the theological center. There were brief profiles of Daugherty, McDivitt, McInnerney, Prial, Helen Hanrahan, and others. The assassin, John Joseph Scafidi, was described as a "loner" and a "drifter" and a "crazed religious fanatic." Beneath a headline, MOTHER OF NINE TRAMPLED ON STAND, there was an account of Jean Favrot's role in the "Catholic war."

The more McInnerney read and reflected, the more despairing he became. In the *Tribune*'s view, it was all his fault. Implied were these thoughts: he was too old, out of step with the times; he was a blind, stubborn reactionary and warmonger; he was an empire-builder, a brick-and-mortar bishop, pursuing fantasy. Beyond that, the institution McInnerney symbolized was archaic, bigoted, unwieldy, dishonest, lazy, timid, hypocritical, overaffluent. Its policies were turning away the bold, the resourceful, the young, the ingenious, the dedicated, and the brilliant. In a few years, it would crumble of its own dead weight. Yet . . .

McInnerney slipped quietly from his office, down the hall to the chapel. He locked the door. He knelt on the altar, head bowed, hands clasped on his chest. He prayed for a very long time, remembering Daugherty, Mrs. Favrot, Scafidi, all the injured, the hurt, the fearful. He prayed for McDivitt and Klein, for Dorn and Prial, for LeGuiese and Dupre, all those who had helped or fought him. Then he prayed that God would tell him, once again, what course he should follow. Then he returned to his quarters. In the evening, after drafting a personal note to Pope Paul, McInnerney sent for Prial. The Vicar General entered, humbly, quietly. He seemed haggard, tired.

"Sit down, Nate," McInnerney said.

"It's been a long day," Prial said, collapsing in a chair. "Well, I guess it's a real mess, isn't it? We should *never* have agreed to that protest. That was my fault . . . terrible judgment."

"No. I'm glad it happened. It cleared the air. Not the way I thought it might . . . but it did clear the air."

"What air?"

"My own, I guess. Nate, the error in judgment was mine. I should have listened to you and Helen. It was not time for a theological center. I was carried away . . . I let my own vanity intrude where it shouldn't. If God had wanted that theological center, He would not have permitted what happened. It's as simple as that. By the way, how is Daugherty coming?"

"The doctor said he's going to be all right," Prial said, lighting a cigar.

"How about Mrs. Favrot?"

"Not too good, I'm sorry to say. Ryan is keeping me posted."

"A tragedy," McInnerney said.

"Yes," Prial said.

"So now," Prial said, forcing cheer, "we pick up the pieces and move along. I've been noodling . . ."

He held aloft a piece of paper.

"What have you got?" McInnerney said.

"A policy paper," Prial said carefully. "A Chancery program."

"Go on," McInnerney said. "Give me the highlights."

"No sales pitch? Just the grit?"

"The grit."

"All right," Prial said. "Point one. We cancel the fund drive. Point two. We let the theological center die slowly. Just fail to mention it further. Point three. We take half the money from the St. Luke's deal and John Carter's land—with a little arm-twisting it becomes a donation to us—and build a church-school-recreation center for the blacks down there. Point four. We take over Halfway House and set up an agency for wayward kids. Point five. We reestablish the ghetto Montessori school—expand the program. Point six. We cease and desist on *Humanae Vitae*. Point seven. We abolish the financial council and open up our books to the public. Point eight. We reinstate most of the priests. Point nine . . ."

McInnerney raised his hand.

"That's good, Nate," he said, sighing. "Exactly as I thought."

Prial sat back, staring at the lighted end of his cigar.

"Read this," McInnerney said. "It concerns you."

He handed Prial his note to the Pope. It was a very brief, simple statement. It said that in light of what had happened in Washington this spring, McInnerney felt that someone with a more flexible outlook should take charge. McInnerney was, therefore, exercising the custom of naming his successor. He was recommending Ignatius Prial to be coadjutor of the archdiocese, with right of succession. He was sure His Holiness would concur. Prial sighed, returned the letter.

"Don't do that," he said. "Not today. Let some time go by."

"As always, good sound advice. No. I'm mailing it off tonight. You see . . . whether you do or not, I believe Helen's vision. My interpretation was wrong. I let my vanity intrude. Now I see very clearly. There is going to be, as she says, chaos. This is only the beginning. I can't handle the problem. I'm *part* of the problem. If I keep on fighting, I make it worse. What we need now are strong, flexible people like you to ride it out, find a reasonable course, mop up. I enjoin you to help *all* our sheep find refuge, as best you can, until the storm blows over. I'm going to stay around—your *eminence gris*—but you get the train running on time again. I pray that it will not be long."

"But . . ."

"No buts, Nate. I'm confident that you will do a good job. Now, get your program, get out of here. Get to work."

Prial rose, humble. Tears filmed his eyes. He came forward, took McInnerney's hand in his own. He knelt and kissed the ring. McInnerney laid his hand on Prial's head, turned his eyes to heaven.

"God, give this man strength and wisdom, humility and grace. Give him love and the Spirit of Life. Ease his way, that he may help others to find Your Kingdom, Your power, Your glory. In the name of the Father, the Son, and the Holy Ghost, World without End, Amen."

"Amen," Prial replied, head low. He rose, turned away toward the elevator—not looking back. By the time he reached his office, his eyes were dry, his mind churning with plans—moves he must make to restore tranquility in the archdiocese. He called a secretary to his office.

"See if you can get Father Joseph McDivitt on the telephone for me, please," he said. "Try him at Halfway House."

He would begin there, with a peace pipe. Bring McDivitt right into the Chancery on full-time duty. Then . . . he spread his program flat on the desk top, lit a cigar. . . .

Marvin Klein sat at his desk, reading copy, news ticker, the morning competition. The telephone jangled. It was Kenneth Penn.

"Could you come up," Penn said coolly. There was no trace of his usual charm.

"We're getting on deadline," Klein said. "Can it keep?"

"No. I want to see you right away."

There was a note of command in his tone.

"I assume it's important?"

"Very. For one thing, we—our board—are meeting this morning to . . . ah . . . discuss a new reorganization of management."

"A *what?*"

"I've just come down from New York. The syndicate board has voted me publisher and chief executive officer."

"Well," Klein said, momentarily confused. "Congratulations. I hope they gave you a nice, fat raise."

"They did," Penn said. "Can we meet now in the conference room?"

"All right," Klein said, hanging up, now feeling dread in his chest. While he had been performing, Penn had been maneuvering. There was no doubt in Klein's mind what lay ahead. He turned to his type-writer, pecked out a brief letter of resignation, put it in his rear pocket.

He stood, put on his jacket, aware that the usual hum in the city room had died. The men had stopped working. They were watching him silently. He smiled sheepishly. Then he peeled off his jacket. By God, he would not be pretentious. He would face the board—as usual—in his working uniform, shirt sleeves. He rode the elevator to the executive floor. He felt no fear.

The members of the board—Penn, the treasurer, secretary, two lawyers, a banker—were sitting gravely in their places around the long conference table. They avoided Klein's eyes, which were now defiant. Little boys, Klein thought, playing at games. He remained standing at the end of the table, determined, at any cost, not to lose his control, not to lash back, not to make the standard editorial speech.

"The board has duly met," Penn said. He sat uncomfortably at the head of the table, twirling a gavel in his palm. "It has concluded that your usefulness to this corporation has ended."

"Specifically why?" Klein demanded coldly. He did not want an answer to that question. He merely wished to make Penn's task more difficult.

"The editorial policy of this paper is reckless," Penn replied solemnly. "It has exceeded any standard of objectivity. It has inflamed when it should have encouraged peace, law, and order."

"It is the job of journalism to inflame," Klein said. "That was envisioned by the founding fathers. That is what is meant by freedom of the press."

He checked himself. Inadvertently, he had slipped into the speech he had been determined to avoid.

"Not when it hurts the Profit and Loss Statement," Penn said. "There is a fine line . . . I don't know where it is exactly. But the board feels you don't know either. It will take us many, many months . . . perhaps years to repair the damage you've done the P & L."

None of the other directors raised his eyes. They sat as though in pain.

Klein walked the length of the table. He gave his letter to Penn.

"That's my resignation," he said.

Penn seemed vastly relieved. The nasty business could be terminated. They could return to the important work, of selling, promoting, restoring lost profits.

"We've arranged some severance," Penn said. "A stake to carry you over."

Klein sneered, "Keep your money."

"Don't be foolish," Penn said.

"I said keep it. I didn't come to this paper for money. If I wanted money I would be in the business of making money. Like you."

He turned on his heel and hurried from the room, suppressing the rage tearing inside his chest. He rode the elevator down, walked to his desk. The reporters and editors remained fixed at their desks, eyes averted, hands busy. Klein put on his jacket, walked toward the door. A single reporter, George Emerson, came forward. He shook hands, walked with Klein to the elevator.

"You going to be OK?" Emerson said.

"Sure," Klein said.

"Don't let it break your spirit," Emerson said.

"It won't," Klein smiled.

"Editors get fired every day," Emerson smiled back. "It's an occupational hazard."

"So they say," Klein said. The elevator door opened.

"You were one hell of an editor," Emerson said.

The door closed. Klein rode to the first floor, bursting with pride. That was something to carry forward to the new enterprise. Yes, they would remember him as a great editor, fearless, uncompromising, honest. And he could always look in the mirror and not shrink. And maybe the legend would grow: that when the Catholic war broke beneath their very noses, by God, they were on top of it all the way. That wild ride, in fact, might even be a good subject for a novel.

Serena met him at the door. She was pale, wringing her hands. Seeing her, Klein felt a sudden, overpowering feeling of love. There was much work to be done here.

"You're looking at the best ex-editor in the business," he said, forcing cheer, going in, closing the door. He pulled Serena into his arms.

"I'm sorry for what I said last night," she said.

Klein said nothing.

"About Father Daugherty," Serena said. "It was not your fault. It would have happened anyway."

"Let's not talk about it now," Klein said. "What we need to talk about is the new life. We'll go away—get out of this damned town."

Then, suddenly, he felt despair. The scene at CU swept across his eyes again, Father Daugherty, Jean Favrot, and he felt the sinking sensation, the fear in his chest. Maybe they had all been right. Maybe he had overstepped. He felt very much alone. He held Serena tight.

As the visiting hour at Georgetown Hospital approached, Mary, sitting in a chair beside Daugherty's bed, woke him gently. He was propped on a mound of pillows, head turned to the side, eyes closed. Both legs, in heavy casts, were suspended aloft in traction. Daugherty opened his eyes and smiled wanly. His mind was fuzzy from the sedatives.

"Hello," he said to Mary, blinking his eyes.

"How do you feel?"

"I don't know. Groggy. Thirsty."

She got a fresh glass of water. He sipped through the bent glass straw.

"Are you sure you want visitors tonight?" she said.

"Yes. It's OK."

He remembered, then, the consultation with Dr. Love. Curious name. Good man. He had felt the sensation in his toes. He would be up and around in six weeks—on crutches. He was lucky. A superficial shoulder wound—two broken legs. As Love had said, it could have been his back. He set the glass on the bedside table.

"I had this thought," Daugherty said. "Or was it a dream? You remember my theory about the Irish and celibacy?"

"Which theory?"

"Do you suppose," he said, staring at his feet high in traction, "that we leaped on *Humanae Vitae* because, deep down, we were really fighting celibacy? I mean . . . the pill thing was a smokescreen—unconscious fantasy—for the fight we really wanted to fight, but didn't have the guts to fight?"

"You were fighting for Jean Favrot."

"I wonder," Daugherty said.

"Let's not talk about it. Can I get you anything?"

He smiled.

There was a rap at the door, soft, uncertain. Mary wiped her cheeks, smoothed the sheet, opened the door. It was Monsignor Ryan and Mrs. Munally. Monsignor Ryan carried a small vase of flowers.

"Good evening, good evening," he said cordially, going to the bed. "How are you, Dan? Jesus, Mary, and Joseph. Look at that cast!"

Daugherty extended his left hand. They shook hands solemnly.

"Oh," Daugherty said. "I don't believe you know Mary Murray. Mary, this is Monsignor Ryan. I believe you know Mrs. Munally?"

"How do you do?" Mary said, shaking hands with the Monsignor. She nodded to Mrs. Munally who looked away. Daugherty said to Mrs. Munally:

"She's my fiancée. We're getting married. Show her the ring, Mary."

If Mrs. Munally was shocked, she concealed it. Ryan did not. His face turned ashen. He bit his lip, said nothing, studied the pattern in the vinyl floor. Mary held her ring finger up, displaying the large diamond.

"The diamond from my chalice," Daugherty explained to Ryan.

"Oh, yes," Ryan replied, voice hollow.

"I don't need the chalice anymore," Daugherty said.

"No, of course not," Ryan replied.

He shuffled his feet uneasily.

"I saw the whole thing . . . live!" Mrs. Munally put in suddenly. "I saw you jump the rail and fall. It was ghastly . . . simply ghastly."

"Have you seen Scafidi?" Daugherty said to Ryan.

"No," Ryan replied. "They've got him in maximum security in the District Building. I took him some things . . . some food . . . cakes, things Bridget . . . Mrs. Munally . . . fixed . . . but they wouldn't let me see him."

"Some detectives have been out to question us," Mrs. Munally confided, voice low.

"Have they any idea why he did it?" Daugherty asked. "Any idea at all?"

"They think it's because we fired him," Ryan said. "Anyway, that's what one of the detectives told me. He's a . . . a paranoic . . . or whatever."

"Then why didn't he shoot *you?*" Daugherty said.

"I don't know," Ryan said uneasily. He had asked himself the same question too many times.

"*I* think it's because of Philadelphia," Mrs. Munally said, glancing at the door.

"Philadelphia!" Daugherty said.

"He came from there," Mrs. Munally said gravely. "You remember the coat? He wouldn't take the coat because it had that Philadelphia label."

"I knew some people disliked Philadelphia," Daugherty said, "but not enough to kill! For Pete's sake, Mrs. Munally, surely . . ."

"It goes deeper than that," the old lady whispered. "He was very poor. His mother was wronged by some rich people. You never know . . ."

"He was *very* religious," Ryan said, cutting off this line of speculation. "Very devout. It seems impossible he really wanted to kill."

"And how is Jean Favrot?" Daugherty said.

Mrs. Munally frowned.

"They don't know yet," Ryan said sadly. He set the vase of flowers on the bureau among the others. "Bob is pretty pessimistic."

"And the parish?" Daugherty said.

"Things are settling down," Ryan said. "Financially, we're shaping up. But it will take time. Much time. In the end . . ."

"Sure . . ." Daugherty said, thoughts wandering. He did not want to talk about Jean Favrot or the parish finances. That was part of the past. The old life.

"Will Scafidi be indicted?" Mary put in.

"I don't know," Ryan said. "I have an idea they're just going to commit him."

"He probably should have been committed long ago," Mrs. Munally said smugly.

"All of us," Ryan said, forcing a feeble smile. "Well, Bridget, we'd better go. We'll stop in again soon, Dan."

They left without saying good-bye to Mary. She felt the snub but said nothing.

Alone again, Daugherty called Mary to his side. She burst into tears, burrowed her face on his neck. He could feel the wetness of her eyes.

"Oh, Dan," she sobbed. "I'm so happy you're alive . . . I was *so* scared. God. I didn't believe you were breathing. I cried and cried and I held your head in my lap. I tried to be brave, but I couldn't. I'm a weak person, afraid. I was just thinking what a ghastly thing my life would be without you. I couldn't conceive of it."

He stroked her hair.

"Lucky," he said. "Just plain lucky."

"And all the people screaming and fighting and running . . . it was awful, Dan. We must never, ever again, get involved in anything like that. It was like St. Luke's . . . the feeling. I had it the minute I got up in the grandstand. I could *feel* it sweeping over me. Even before he fired. Then exploding . . . I can't take it. I *couldn't* live without you."

"You won't have to."

She raised her head, dried her tears.

"I'm sorry for being weepy. You might as well know. I get this way every month."

"That's all right," he said, not understanding.

"Oh," she said brightly. "I talked to Seymour today. He telephoned while you were sleeping."

"How is he?"

"Down. He went to Memphis. The King shrine. He was very disillusioned. He went to the room at the Lorraine. It's all very commercial. Charged him a dollar admission, then, inside, it was just a counter, like a bookstore. They are vultures, Seymour said, hustling in King's memory."

"Sick," Daugherty said. "The whole world, sick."

Mary nodded agreement.

"I'm sorry about Ryan," Daugherty said, suddenly shifting the subject. "I was determined not to shake his faith. But we have."

"I know."

"That is very bad," he said.

"Let's not talk about him."

"We have to."

"What do you mean?" she asked, with alarm.

"You know what I mean."

"You mean . . . we can't go to Puerto Rico?"

"That was a fantasy . . . now wasn't it?" Dan said.

"Yes." She turned her eyes away.

"We can't run away like this and leave the Ryans in charge," he went on. "It's our Church, too, you know."

"I know. You're right. It was a dream. We have to help. I shouldn't have shipped the apparatus. That was stupid. . . . Oh, Dan. I *did* want to go."

"You always said the action was here . . . and you *have* to be where the action is, don't you?"

"We both do," she said. Then sweeping her hand around the room, she added: "But no more of this!"

Daugherty laughed. "I'll say."

"Then what can we do?"

"Work quietly in the ghetto," he said eagerly. "The priest-house concept . . . bring religion to those people . . . hope, love—a living religion."

"And what about *me?*" she said.

"You come too—to help me. They won't try to stop us anymore. It's too big now . . . too far along. Too much has changed. In a little while, not many years, Rome will abandon celibacy . . . I'll be reinstated . . . we'll make out, as man-wife-priest. As Ryan always says, the Lord will provide."

Jean Favrot lay propped in bed on a mound of pillows. Her body ached from head to toe. Her right arm was twice its normal size. Her right ankle was sprained, bulbous. She was light-headed, dizzy, disoriented by the pain-killing drugs. Most of the time she drifted in a twilight, only dimly conscious of the people going in and out of the room, the noise of the children deep inside the house.

She was aware now of Bob sitting on the edge of the bed, holding her hand. She saw him through swollen, black eyes.

"How are you doing, honey?" he said.

"Fine."

"Can I get you anything?"

"Water, please."

"Coming right up."

He brought her a fresh glass of water in a clean glass. She leaned forward. He held the glass to her lips. She swallowed.

"Can't seem to get enough," she whispered.

"It's the Demerol," Bob said. "Makes you thirsty."

"I guess so."

She lay back, eyes on the ceiling.

"Do you feel well enough to see the children?" he asked. "They cooked up a little surprise."

She smiled feebly.

"Of course."

"They're still working on it. You don't remember, do you?"

"Remember what?"

"Never mind. It's a surprise."

She smiled feebly again. Bob could be so childish at times. All men were like that. Little boys, at heart. Remember? She could barely remember her name. Jean Louise Tibbideaux Favrot. Mother of nine. Trampled at protest. Such fame!

"How are you feeling now?" Bob said.

"Better," she whispered.

Thank God, Bob thought. He let himself think again of that horrifying moment on the stand, when the screaming hordes crashed down. The frantic plunge down the stairs. Finding Jean, pulling her back from the stairs, dragging her beneath the stand. Calming Nancy, who was hysterical. He shuddered. How lucky they had been! All of them.

Jean heard a curious noise in the hall, like singing. Bob rose and snapped off the bedroom light. Paul appeared at the doorway, carrying a birthday cake with candles. He was singing "Happy Birthday." He walked slowly, gingerly. Behind him came Bobbie and Joe and Nancy and Chris and Mike and Bill and Carol, holding Baby John in her arms. They came into the room, all singing, off-key and too slow, forming a circle at the foot of the bed.

Jean cried. She had not remembered.

Paul came near the head of the bed, holding the cake near her face. There were five candles, four in a row, then one above the row: forty one. The candlelight reflected in Paul's eyes. Jean had never seen anything so beautiful, so touching, so warm and kind.

"Blow them out!" Chris cried gleefully.

Jean propped herself up on her elbow. She took a deep breath and blew. The candles went out.

"Make a wish! Make a wish!" the children cried.

Jean lay back. She did not know what to wish for. There was nothing then, she wanted.

"What is it?" Bobbie asked. "What did you wish?"

"If she tells you, it won't come true, stupid!" Carol said, rocking the baby to and fro in her arms. "Will it, Dad?"

"No, daughter. It won't."

"I don't believe in it anyway," Bobbie said petulantly.

"Turn on the lights," Bob said.

The overhead light went on.

"Who has the plates and the knife?" Bob asked.

"I forgot," Nancy said. "I'll get them."

"You ought to do it in the kitchen," Jean whispered. "Don't cut it in here."

"All right," Nancy said, taking the cake from Paul.

"Get the presents," Bob said.

"Yeeeaaa!" the children shouted, stampeding down the hall. They returned instantly, shoving, crashing through the door.

"My goodness!" Jean said.

"Watch out," Bob said to the shoving children. "Don't bump your mother. Mike, get off the bed."

"I can't see. Joe got my place."

"You didn't say dibs," Joe growled threateningly.

"I did too!"

"You did not!"

"Boys!" Bob shouted sternly. "Pipe down. Knock it off."

"He got my place." Mike wailed, running from the room, crying.

Bob shrugged helplessly at Jean.

The children closed in, each vying for Jean to open his present first. Jean counted "Eenie, meenie, minie, moe," winding up on Bill's present. He shouted triumphantly. Jean untied the bow, unwrapped the box, setting the paper aside. It was a pepper mill.

"Oh, thank you, Bill," she said. "*Just* what I needed."

"I thought so," Bill said smugly. He flashed a smile of victory at his brothers and sisters.

Jean opened each of the packages carefully. They contained a ceramic ashtray, handmade in the Boys' Club art room by Mike; a package of balloons from Chris; a bottle of cologne from Nancy; a rubber alligator from Bobbie; a pair of zori from Paul; a package of Doral cigarettes from Carol; a wallet from Joe. When she was done, Jean gazed on the pile of trinkets as though it were Inca treasure.

Nancy returned with cake for Jean, a huge slice. Bob ordered the younger children to the kitchen for their cake and ice cream. Nancy ate with Bob and Jean, proudly enjoying this new privilege. It was Cantor's idea that she should be treated, on special occasions, as a grown-up.

"You know what I heard today?" Nancy said, gulping her cake.

"No," Jean said. "What did you hear?"

"Daugherty's getting married."

Jean looked at Nancy wide-eyed.

"You're kidding?" Bob said. "Who told you?"

"A little bird."

"Nancy Favrot!" Bob said. "You shouldn't spread gossip. *Who* is he supposed to be marrying?"

"Mary Murray. The ex-nun. Isn't that beautiful?"

"Who told you?" Jean said, setting her plate on the bedside table.

"Well . . . this new girl that moved in . . . you know . . . the Dorseys . . . just down the street? Well. She's a very close friend of this girl in Potomac named Sharon somebody. Sharon is a very close friend of Mary Murray's. So that's how we found out."

"I'll be damned," Bob said. "Are you sure?"

"Absolutely. Isn't it groovy? I mean . . . *our* priest is so famous!"

The telephone rang. Bob answered, then held the mouthpiece. He turned to Nancy:

"It's for you."

Nancy jumped up as though she had never before received a phone call.

"I'll get it in the den," she said, tearing from the room. She was back in an instant, instructing her father: "Be sure you hang up. And don't tell *any*body about Father Daugherty. It's supposed to be a secret."

When Nancy was on the extension, Bob hung up the phone, sat carefully on the edge of the bed.

"I'm not surprised at that, are you?" he said.

Jean shook her head. "They'll probably make a go of it."

"I think so."

Bob took a small gift from his pocket. Jean opened it slowly. It was a ring box, from Gault's. Inside, snug in its satin cushion, was an emerald guard ring.

"Oh, Bob!" she sobbed tearfully.

"You always said you wanted a guard ring."

She slipped it on her left finger, tight against her engagement ring. She held her hand up to the light.

"It's beautiful," she whispered. "Just beautiful."

He kissed her gently.

"What did you wish for?" he asked.

"I couldn't think of anything."

"Not anything?"

"I *have* everything."

Bob considered that. Then he said:

"I was wondering if you might like to go on a little vacation? We could have a little second honeymoon. I know that sounds corny but, . . ."

Jean was thrilled. It had been many years since Bob had asked her to go on a trip. It would be fun. Yet . . .

"Who would look after the children?" she said.

"Emma. And Annie. She said she'd be glad to help out. She really means it."

"That's very sweet. You're very sweet to me. But, Bob, I really don't want to go . . . will you be mad? I want to stay here for a while, right at home. I have to get the children ready for school. When I get on my feet, I want to get close to Nancy. I think I know how."

"But Cantor says you shouldn't get all wrapped up in the kids again," Bob said, frowning. "You've got to get around . . . do something."

Jean shook her head firmly.

"My children need me right now," she said. "I won't get too involved. I promise. But . . . Bob . . . did you see their faces tonight?"

"Yes."

"Aren't they the sweetest little kids in the whole world?"

"Yes."

"We don't need Cantor anymore," she said. "We've had a course correction. Can't we sail on from here by ourselves? Think of the money we could save!"

"But . . ."

She held her finger to his lips.

"OK, honey," he said. "You can sure be stubborn when you want to be. They always did say you have a mind of your own. I won't argue with that."

She smiled through swollen lips. She held her ring finger up again, admiring the guard, thanking him with her eyes. He bent again and kissed her.

"Happy birthday, sweets."

Tears streamed down her cheeks.

"Do you want to kiss the children good night?"

"Not tonight," she whispered. "Please? Will they understand?"

"Certainly. They're all lost in the tube, anyway."

"Good night, Bob. And . . . thanks for everything. Thanks for being tolerant of a nutty wife."

He stood looking down, loving her. Then he snapped off the light, pulled the door shut. Jean closed her eyes. She remembered the woman in Yucatan—her college roommate—and her letter, still unanswered. She had not found it between the lines, but she was certain now that it must be an arid, loveless life, full of tragedy and despair. That in all the world, there was nothing quite so important as Paul and Bobbie, Joe and Chris, Nancy and Carol, Mike and Bill and Baby John.

And Bob.

ABOUT THE AUTHOR

Clay Blair, Jr., emerged as a novelist of contemporary American power-wielders on the Washington scene with *The Board Room,* a story about the magazine publishing establishment. Before turning to fiction, Mr. Blair was for many years a Washington-based journalist for *Time, Life,* and *The Saturday Evening Post.* From 1961 to 1964, he served as assistant managing editor, managing editor, and editor-in-chief of *The Saturday Evening Post.* Among his nonfiction works are: *The Atomic Submarine and Admiral Rickover; Beyond Courage; Diving for Pleasure and Treasure;* and *The Strange Case of James Earl Ray.*

Mr. Blair currently resides in Key Biscayne, Florida, where he writes full-time and engages in his favorite outdoor pastimes—tennis, boating, and skindiving. He is now working on a new novel about the military establishment, with the Pentagon as the setting.